"UTMOST FISH!"

Hugh Wray McCann

SIMON AND SCHUSTER
NEW YORK

Dedicated to my Mother,

the sole surviving Officer of an army of eleven,

for service above and beyond the call of duty.

And to all men

who nobly bear their countries' arms.

Among Royal Navy motor-torpedo-boat
commanders of the First World War
the command "UTMOST FISH!" meant
launch all torpedoes simultaneously
at the target.

The First Lord of the Admiralty
adopted the term to indicate that
a matter had his approval and should
be expedited with all dispatch.

One of the characters in this story
went on to become one of the most
eminent figures of the twentieth century.

Other characters also actually lived
and breathed; still others lived and
breathed only in the author's imagination.

Several of the events occurring in the
story have been excerpted from recent
history. Such an event is Naval Africa
Expedition (1915–16), the official
Admiralty account of which will not
be available publicly until 1966.

The Luba nation embraces many tribes:
the Sanga, Lomotwa, Yeke, Bemba, Kunda,
Shila, Bwile, Tabwa, Zela and others.
The prefixes Ma-, Ba-, Bu-, and Ki-
are used before a tribal proper name
to designate the individual tribesman,
his tribe, the territory it inhabits,
and its language and customs respectively.

For example: A tribesman of the Sanga
is a *Ma*sanga. His tribe is the *Ba*sanga.
They live in the territory of *Bu*sanga,
and *Ki*sanga is their language and customs.

CHIEF CHARACTERS

NAVAL AFRICA EXPEDITION
(28 officers and men)

COMMANDER IAN H. G. FRAZER, Royal Navy, a Scotsman with a flinty sense of duty

SURGEON COMMANDER THOMAS CAVANAUGH, Royal Naval Volunteer Reserve, an amiable Irish doctor of tropical medicine

CAPTAIN OSWALD HUMPHREYS, Royal Engineers, an overbearing perfectionist

SERGEANT ANDREW SMITH, an old soldier

CHIEF PETTY OFFICER STOKES, an older sailor

PRIVATE PERKINS, a naïve young ex-coal miner

PRIVATE NANGLE, a disillusioned aristocrat

PRIVATE DEVLIN, a troublemaker

A FORTYISH CIVILIAN, CH, MP, First Lord of the Admiralty

ADMIRAL OF THE FLEET SIR JOHN FISHER, GCB,

GCVO, OM, First Sea Lord of the Admiralty

VICE-ADMIRAL SIR IAN H. G. FRAZER, GBE, KCB, Royal Navy (retd.)

MÖWE DETACHMENT
(200 officers and men)

LIEUTENANT COMMANDER ZIMMER, Imperial German Navy

LIEUTENANT ODEBRECHT, Imperial German Navy

LIEUTENANT ROSENTHAL, Imperial German Navy

If you can force your heart and nerve and sinew

To serve your turn long after they are gone,

And so hold on when there is nothing in you

Except the Will which says to them: "Hold on!"

If you can meet with Triumph and Disaster

And treat those two impostors just the same;

Yours is the Earth and everything that's in it,

And—which is more—you'll be a Man, my son!

RUDYARD KIPLING

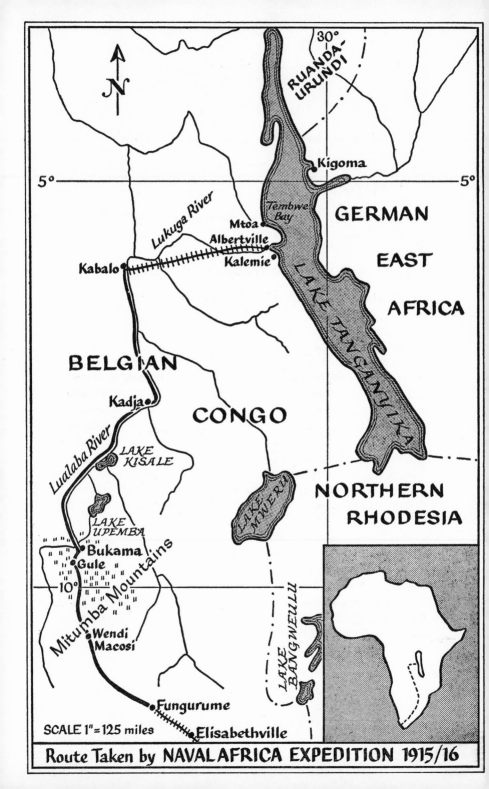

Route Taken by **NAVAL AFRICA EXPEDITION 1915/16**

I

A failure at nineteen and a half.

The thought furrowed the chaste brow of Sublieutenant Ian Frazer for the hundredth time; and for the hundredth time he laughed a shallow laugh. Less than four months ago he had ascended to the very pinnacle of his life—marching in the passing-out parade at Greenwich Naval College, with his sword swinging by his side and his young, blue eyes already on the rank, distinction and record of his grandfather in the service of the Royal Navy.

How magnificently the world had been his oyster. But if only he hadn't been so—no, he wouldn't think of it again. He'd promised himself that he wouldn't. His course was set. Nothing he could do would alter it.

The therapy was to think of something else. Anything else. Quickly, now. Fish and chips . . . Britannia rules the waves . . . God, no . . . From Land's End to John o' Groat's. Yes, that would do.

From Land's End to John o' Groat's . . . Miss Shields, the red-haired mistress at the village school in Ardrossan . . . good, keep going. . . . What was it she used to say? A Scotsman could go no farther north on Scottish soil than John o' Groat's and an English-man no farther south in England than Land's End. It had been his first lesson in geography, and he had learned it well. Miss Shields, of course, had been in error—especially the John o' Groat's part. He had always known it, but never until that moment had he felt so powerfully the urge to tell her so. He sat on a plank across two Diesel-oil drums in a wooden hut which was perched on top of the only hill on the island of Switha—a dozen miles *north* of John o' Groat's.

He peered through the cobwebby windows across the three-quarters of a mile of lead-colored sea to the island of Flotta. Yes, for him Miss Shields's myth had been exploded; yet the odds were that the infallible, indestructible Scottish schoolmadam was at that very moment perpetrating the same myth on a classroom of apple-cheeked Ardrossan Scots. Surely she must have mentioned the Orkney Islands somewhere, sometime. He couldn't remember when. It didn't really matter when. It wouldn't make things any easier....

It was six and a half years since he had stood with the other "warts" on the station platform at Dartmouth that rainy Sunday, waiting for the petty officer to herd them off to H.M.S. *Britannia,* the two permanently moored old wooden line-of-battle ships where they would live and learn for the next three years. It had all been so strange, but when they had dubbed his intakes the "Rodneys," the strangeness had begun to disappear. He had trembled at the gang-plank, then raised his hand in stiff salute and announced in the loudest, lowest voice at his command, "Cadet Frazer begs to report that he has come on board to join."

The seasons had taken forever to pass; the two landlocked years on *Britannia* had dawdled by. But that unbelievable day had finally worn around when he had become a "senior snotty," with all the privileges attending that august state.

For the next four and a half years Midshipman Frazer had de-veloped his sea legs on seagoing ships and an unflagging wonder at classroom precepts come to life. Sines and cosines had been trans-muted into latitudes and longitudes; calculus had assumed the di-mension of a workaday tool that told how much fuel oil for how many knots for a given engine efficiency; and discipline had begun to live and breathe as the embodiment incarnate of dependable, predictable action in times of stress.

In the June just past the naval zeal that had been fermenting within him for a lifetime had come to a head. He had sat upright with his peers in Nelson's Hall and listened raptly as Vice-Admiral Sir Ian Frazer, his grandfather, idol, namesake and guardian, on the eve of his premature medical retirement, pondered with them the full import of holding a commission in His Majesty's Royal Navy; what it had demanded from those who had gone forth from those very seats before them; what it would exact from them in the uncertain years to come; and how they would be repaid beyond full measure by recognizing their duty and performing it, for that was an insight given to few men in this world under God Almighty.

Suddenly he had become Sublieutenant Frazer. The Home Fleet's summer exercises . . . Scapa Flow . . . it could not come fast enough for him. His mettle had to be tested: his first posting—to H.M.S. *Waverly*, a brand-new auxiliary minesweeper. He was to be first lieutenant, or "Number One," to her skipper, a youthful lieutenant hardly three years his senior. She had been only a minesweeper . . . auxiliary, at that; but he loved all 231 feet of her, every one of her 537 tons. When her twin screws churned out 1,800 horsepower and her wake boiled away from her at 16 knots, he had stood on the bridge slightly intoxicated with this throbbing, metal extension of himself, relaying the skipper's commands to the engine room down the voice pipe.

No one had been able to reconstruct what actually happened. Had it been the light swell that summer day? Or the sudden fog that had billowed up out of nowhere? Or the confusion of the dozens of destroyers and motor torpedo launches screening the admiral's flagship from the mock submarine attack? Or had he, as they said he had, interpreted the skipper's "Hard aport" shouted against the wind as "Hard to starboard"?

If only the admiral's simulated attack had not called for the simulated sinking of his flagship; and if only the admiral had *simulated* the transferring of his pennant from his supposedly stricken flagship instead of actually climbing into his barge and steering across *Waverly's* bows toward the cruiser that was to be the new

15

flagship. If . . . if . . . if. . . . At any rate *Waverly's* bows had struck the admiral's barge a glancing blow—enough to toss the admiral, his naval staff and their heavy cylinders of rolled-up charts into the swirling 10-knot current of Pentland Firth.

It had been with profound trepidation that *Waverly's* "Number One" had supervised the ignominious pulling aboard on the end of common boathooks of said admiral and his naval staff—minus the exquisitely detailed battle plans and charts without which any further participation by Commander in Chief, Scapa Flow, in Home Fleet exercises had to be simulated.

Five weeks later a formal board of inquiry had disciplined *Waverly's* skipper, the young lieutenant, whereas Sublieutenant Frazer was absolved of any culpability and dismissed with a caution. However, barely a week following the good news came his transfer from sea duty to the Scapa Flow Shore Station—more specifically he had been elevated—to the one hill on the island of Switha as Movement Control Officer, Switha Sound.

As the winner of the Collingwood Prize for distinction in Tactics and Fortifications at the naval college, Ian did not for a moment question the wisdom of the Admiralty's establishing a checkpoint across the Sound. Granted there wasn't a bloody thing on either Switha or Flotta, but they did command the southern approaches to the Royal Navy's most powerful base in home waters—Scapa Flow. Scapa was the triangle of water bounded by the three islands of Pomona, Hoy and South Ronaldshay. Switha Sound was one of the three main entrances to Scapa. Naval engineers had floated a concrete boom across as an added precaution. A battery of naval artillery took advantage of Flotta's high hill to challenge unlawful entry. No, he had to hand it to the Admiralty boys. Their strategy was impeccable. His quarrel—for that is what it was—concerned their choice of senior naval officer for Switha—Sublieutenant Ian H. G. Frazer, Royal Navy. Why me? he had asked himself twenty times a day ever since he had arrived, and just as often the same answer had come back. Lately he had given up fretting about it.

The sound of someone crunching up the snow-covered path to the hut obtruded upon his latest reverie.

"Mornin', sir. Looks like we might not 'ave that snow they promised us last night after all," said a small, wiry figure in Navy duffel coat and hood, still puffing from the uphill climb in the biting cold.

"Morning, Stokes. . . . Ah, I see you've got my tea," greeted Frazer.

" 'S right, sir. Bit weak though, I'm afraid. Cook's weekend in Aberdeen, you know, an' I can't find things again."

Stokes pushed some papers to one side of the improvised desk on which Frazer was leaning and heavily set down the large, blackened billycan of tea.

"Watch it, Stokes. Want to spill tea over the entire Home Fleet, man?" Frazer said playfully.

"Sometimes I feels like spillin' more 'n tea over it, if you don't mind me saying so, sir."

"What, you too, Stokes? C'mon, now. Things aren't that bad, are they?" Frazer reached over to the windowsill in front of him and picked up a large mug, blowing into it several times and wiping the drinking edge on his sleeve. He extended the cup in Stokes's direction.

"Lemme slosh it around a bit, sir, first," offered Stokes. "You know, I'd like to know wot the hell Wiggins does with the tea every time he leaves."

"You and Wiggins never have got along very well since you both came up here, have you?" remarked Frazer.

Stokes began pouring the black steamy brew into Frazer's cup.

"When," muttered Frazer. Turning around on the stool, he reached up to a shelf loaded with books, charts, a field telephone and a miscellany of pencil stubs. Among the lot there was a tin can. With a skill born of practice he cradled the tin in his lap, uncapped it with one hand, dug in and came out with a handful of sugar lumps. Stokes extended his cup, and Frazer plopped two lumps into it. He saved one for himself before returning the tin to its place among the Admiralty charts.

"Don't have to worry 'bout me an' Wiggins none. 'E's not a bad bloke, really. Never tells a body where 'e puts anythin', that's all. . . . If you don't mind me saying so, sir, it's you I'm worried about."

"Me? Me, Stokes? What ever do you mean?" exclaimed the young Scotsman.

Leading Seaman Stokes shuffled on the dusty floor. He wondered whether he might not be overstepping the bounds of friendship with the youthful midshipman. But he was fifteen years older than the craggy-faced, good-natured Frazer—old enough to be his father, in fact. Protocol be damned, thought Stokes.

"Well, sir, forget about *Waverly*."

Frazer's face froze. The string of the casual bonhomie betweeen the two pulled taut. He looked into his tea for a long moment. For him it was difficult to think about *Waverly,* much less talk about her; it rankled on his palate. "I can't," he said finally. "And now, might I ask, what do you propose to do about it?"

"Nothing, sir. Not a thing. Seems to me just about everythin's been done already. But if you feel I oughtn't to mention it . . . then p'raps I should be gettin' back to the mess. Besides, I got a lot to do before—"

"No, dammit, Stokes. Stand your ground, man," snapped Frazer, a coarse edge on his voice.

It was Frazer's turn to shuffle. He felt rather foolish. Up here in the hut almost three months now, he had been conducting himself as if nothing had ever happened. As far as they were concerned, he had decided to remain just another chap with one stripe on his sleeve. He would just be one of the chaps, chat a little here and there, the odd Guinness or two, maybe a binge once in a while; enough to play the role, to make it look right, enough to keep them out of his life. But *he* could never forget it. Now with Stokes bringing up the matter again and the whole Swextha Island contingent knowing about it, he would again feel as if he was walking around with the front of his pants unbuttoned—everybody so bloody embarrassed, almost seeing what he had had for breakfast, but everyone too damnably correct to say a word. Stokes might as well have said, "Excuse me, sir, but I'm afraid your fly's open." And that was about how he felt. If he had been the blunt type, he would have thanked Stokes for the information and proceeded to button himself up in full view of all the onlookers, and let them think whatever

18

the hell they wanted to. But he was of the Frazers who had swept the Spanish down the drain in 1588; of a "long line of Frazers," his grandfather used to drum into him. "Don't go, Stokes." Almost as if he were standing outside himself he could hear his own voice, clipped and even.

"Been watchin' you, I 'ave, sir, these past months. I notices things."

"What sort of things, Stokes?"

"Little things, sir. Like the way you's always so proper like with everybody, even those who's tryin' to be friendly."

"Formal, Stokes, perhaps?"

"That's right, sir. If I didn't have a way of seein' into people, I'd say you was right out of King's Regulations, and I've been in the Navy long enough to know there ain't no such animal."

"Does this offend you, Stokes?"

"Well, no, sir. It don't offend me, but it's just—"

"If it doesn't, then why bring it up? Why bring it up at all?" said Frazer testily. He rose from the plank and stood squarely facing Stokes, little trace of the easygoing Frazer left. "We all make mistakes. You're old enough to know that, aren't you?" he snapped defensively.

"Of course we do. That's why I understand," replied Stokes quickly but gently. "There hasn't been the lad born that hasn't turned right when 'e should've turned left. The Navy's full of 'em. Take my boy 'Arry, now. When 'e was just a nipper—"

"You've told me about Harry. I know what you're trying to say, but, dammit all, Harry is a Stokes, not a Frazer. Can't you see the difference? Harry could have been anything he damn well pleased, but I had to be a Frazer."

The bitterness was coming out and Stokes was on the receiving end. "Sir," he began, "time I was gettin' back to the mess. We got a lot—"

"No, Stokes, I don't think you know what that means."

"Really, Mister Frazer, I've got two work parties ready to start on—"

"*Stokes*," he fairly roared. " *'Ten-shun!*"

19

Leading Seaman Stokes snapped to attention. His big delph mug smashed in little pieces on the floor and tea sprayed over the map table.

"Now listen, Stokes," the young officer said softly, his voice full of self-pity, "you damn well started this, and you're going to hear it out. . . . You're so right. I hate this Godforsaken island with a passion. Why? A bloody clerk. No more than a bloody clerk. Any damn fool can pick up his binoculars, read the name off a ship and enter it in a log. . . . Oh, but I mustn't forget. The job calls for very special qualifications: You must be able to read—and tell the time. I'm so bloody lucky, though. I spend six and a half years in His Majesty's bloody service. I can read and tell the time—so out of a thousand and one such clods in the world's greatest navy I'm the one who's nominated." The tirade had been almost in one breath, spasmodic, spontaneous; a bleeding off of the bile that had been corroding his insides ever since that gloomy day in Pentland Firth. He turned away from Stokes and stood looking out through the window again, his breathing becoming less audible, more regular.

The room reeked of their mutual embarrassment.

"Sorry, Stokes." Frazer seemed to concentrate on the scene outside the window.

Stokes's thin body relaxed from the rigidity of "attention." A warmth of understanding suffused the face that seconds before had been a window for hurt feelings. He walked awkwardly to Frazer's side and placed a hand on his shoulder. "Think nothin' of it, sir."

The window scene continued to hold Frazer's attention.

The fog that had blended the snow-covered ground and sky into a dirty-white drabness all morning had lifted. About half a mile from Switha a gray, trim-as-a-greyhound vessel knifed a rich white bow foam through the Sound on its way out into the North Sea.

Stokes reached for a brown leather case on the windowsill, opened it and handed a pair of binoculars to Frazer. Without taking his eyes off the ship, Frazer raised the binoculars to his eyes, focusing carefully. Both men watched in silence. The ship—a destroyer —cut her engines back to half speed, and from her bridge an Aldis lamp flashed a signal. Frazer's lips moved and he read: "Thanks—

for—repairs—rum—what—have—you—Request—permission—cross—boom—Thanks—again—*Ghurka*." He thrust the binoculars into Stokes's hand, grabbed the field telephone and cranked the handle. There was no reply. He cranked again. Still no answer. His eyes caught Stokes's for a second and he shrugged. The duty officer aboard the boom tug did not answer. Frazer knew that *Ghurka's* Aldis-lamp signal and the telephone call he was supposed to make to the tug duty officer, Sublieutenant Tattersall, were only formalities. They could run the whole blasted show without Sublieutenant Ian H. G. Frazer, RN, Officer in Command, Switha Island Movement Control, if they had to. He cranked again. The instrument's bell jangled nervously. The delay set him on edge. And there was good reason for it. From *Ghurka's* mast flew the pennant of a flotilla commander, usually a captain. So there would be a lot more brass than a lieutenant commander's to witness the impending blunder. "What's holding up that dolt on the tug?" he groaned. Through his binoculars and aided by a thin pencil of sunshine that had broken through the overcast he studied intently the two most senior officers on *Ghurka's* bridge. "Tattersall, you chump, move, dammit. Stokes, check the connections," snapped Frazer.

Stokes pulled the telephone from the shelf and hastily checked it. "Not the wires, I don't think, sir."

"Here, let me have a look," muttered Frazer, dropping his binoculars. He began unfastening the thumbscrews feverishly just as Stokes had done seconds before.

"Already tried that, sir," muttered Stokes.

Frazer felt slightly foolish at this action, and Stokes's comment irritated him. "That's right, you did, didn't you?"

H.M.S. *Ghurka* was less than 400 yards from the boom, but still the tug remained motionless as if derelict. Really is no point in getting rattled, thought Frazer. If I don't raise the tug, Tattersall will surely take it upon himself to open the gate. That's the main thing—to get the flotilla flagship out without any mishap. If they had to wait even a few minutes for the boom ship to go into action, the entire Home Fleet would hear about it.

Swit ha Sound was the "tradesmen's entrance" to Scapa, normally

21

used only by store ships. He could descend to no more demeaning station, he hoped. "Take a peek at the roof connections," said Frazer. "Maybe the snow's been too much for them."

Stokes was at the door in three strides and stepped into the bitter cold outside.

Frazer took the opportunity to explode quietly in a few choice phrases. This sort of thing was always happening to him—things over which he never seemed to have any control. Just a month ago he had ordered the men to discontinue the practice of a daily telephone-line check. Nothing ever happened.

Stokes clumped through the door puffing frosty air in front of him. "It's the roof, I'm afraid, sir," he announced glumly.

Frazer's face blanked. "Damn. Before we get one of the signals people up here—"

Stokes pointed toward the window. "Look, sir. Tattersall's come alive, looks like."

Their line of sight was from dead astern; thus the only clue to the tug's movement was a white bubble of foam around the rudder. The sight elated Frazer momentarily—until he saw that *Ghurka* had stopped completely. It took the tug a full five minutes to maneuver into position and another two to tow open the boom. H.M.S. *Ghurka* did not lose a moment. She surged forward on full power before the gate was fully opened, and her wake bucked Tattersall's tug around as though she were riding a swell in the open sea. Frazer followed her with his binoculars until she was well clear of the Sound. The sun was now seeping through the blanket of overcast. It glinted and sparkled from the choppy North Sea. *Ghurka* leaned into it, her smokestack billowing a thick, sure coal smoke. To the young naval officer there was everything about the sight that the landsman could not understand. It was a subtly proportioned alchemy of the body and the soul going all the way back to the early summer-morning hikes along the banks of the Clyde with his grandfather. The old man would ramble on and on about the sea; about how she was man's greatest friend but also his wildest enemy, and how you had to come to know her as a person before you could understand her.

It was a seduction destined to work powerfully on the little bairn

22

as he tagged along, half walking, half running, beside the great old man into his own manhood.

A week after *Ghurka* had taken her departure, a batch of Christmas post arrived. The mail put a festive spark into the existence of the two Royal Artillery batteries whose six-inch coastal pieces had to maintain their bleak vigilance of Switha Sound on Christmas Day while others reveled on the mainland. Too, Frazer and Switha's small naval complement—Stokes and the few ratings on Tattersall's tug—sought solace in post from home. Britain's being at war would have afforded them adequate reason for their enforced Christmas vigil; but they were all merely puppets jumping to the great Navy scare of 1893.

England, the great maritime power, could not much longer offer her Continental neighbors the standing and growing provocation of power, wealth and success. This was the reason for recent and disquieting German and French naval expansion, argued those in high places—with aggression against England as the inevitable consequence.

The modest wooden hut on top of Switha was indeed an improbable place for a copy of *Vanity Fair*, the social weekly. Stokes brought it up to Frazer together with the rest of the mail. The dependable, thoughtful Stokes also brought his blackened billycan of hot tea. The two supped and read in silence.

Frazer first read the letter with the Ardrossan postmark—counsel, strength and understanding from the old man. The two other letters were of little consequence. He flipped through *Vanity Fair*—his predecessor had been a subscriber—and stopped at the latest jingoist dissertation on the tense European situation: ". . . No nation has ever hated another more than France hates England since the days of the Peloponnesian War. They wish to revenge not only Trafalgar and Waterloo, but Cressy and Agincourt . . ." His thoughts went back to school days when so many of his colleagues talked of war, thought war, and hoped for war; of how war was the universal prayer of some so that they might win honor, glory and prize money. He also recalled the sober minority who had looked on the Royal Navy more as a world police force than as a warlike institution; had considered its job the safeguarding of law and order throughout the world—safeguarding civilization, putting out fires on shore, and acting as guide, philosopher and friend to the merchant ships of all nations.

Somewhere between these two poles his own personal philosophy vacillated aggravatingly.

"Almost forgot this, I did, sir," muttered Stokes, breaking into his thoughts, pulling a slim manila envelope from an inside pocket. It bore the stamp O.H.M.S. and was addressed in a penciled scrawl to Movement Control, Switha.

Frazer had been expecting it. It was from his local commanding officer on the main island; it ordered him to report on the following Monday to the Royal Artillery captain on the island. It seemed that there was need for an officer to oversee the procuring and distribution of supplies on the island. Even though the island was overrun with Army personnel, it still remained a Navy sphere of influence; therefore it was felt the victualing responsibility should be that of a Navy rather than an Army officer.

Frazer crushed the communication into a hard ball and tossed it into a corner with an oath escaping through his tightly compressed lips. I know what they're trying to do, he thought, but I'll be damned if they'll succeed; and he swore he would be the best bloody Officer in Command, Stores, they ever bloody well had.

2

The young Frazer may not have been the best naval victualer and quartermaster in the Royal Navy, but he was undeniably facile in his apportioning of cloth, serge, flannel, tobacco, salt meat, biscuits, rum, soap, flour and candles to those Switha Islanders who could lay a legitimate claim upon them. Yet, for one through whose veins coursed the spirit of a Nelson, the regimen weighed heavily tiresome and was appeased only by the respite of annual leave the following summer.

He spent but a few days of this with the old man in Ardrossan, for the religious fashion in which the unexpected turn in his naval career went unmentioned served only to highlight its importance. What might have been the usual rushed, summer reunion with scarcely time enough to exchange experiences now plodded along in platitude and awkward pause. So Frazer sought refuge in the anonymous garb of a civilian on holiday at an Irish seaside resort. . . .

With the passing of the years, Frazer advanced in rank and knowledge of how the Navy was victualed. Switha Island was duly left behind, and five years later he could—but he would not—take pride in the two gold stripes of a lieutenant RN, on his sleeve and a small desk in the nerve center of the entire naval service, the Admiralty. He was a small cog in the vast machinery of the victualing department. Through his hands passed the requisitions from the home victualing yards of Deptford, Gosport and Plymouth; and the depots abroad at Gibraltar, Malta, Halifax, Bermuda, Jamaica, Cape of Good Hope, Trincomalee, Hong Kong, Esquimalt and Sydney. Wondrous-sounding names that made him fret—often fume—with a longing that always capitulated to his flinty sense of duty and self-discipline.

The summer of 1898 in Ireland relieved like the removal of a tight boot. That year he chose Rosstrevor, a clustering of thatch-roofed, whitewashed cottages, modern bungalows, tired shopwindows filled with faded attempts at gay display—and predatory landladies.

At Dunnigan's Guest House the landlady fidgeted nervously with the straggly bun in her gray hair as she apologized profusely for the sad mix-up. It was beyond her "how in Heaven's name the two nice gentlemen could possibly have booked up the *same* upstairs front parlor for the *same* fortnight." She surveyed them imperiously as she decided what she would do. The long and the short of it, she said to herself, the tall, thin lad with the hawk face and the cow's lick, and the stocky, little one with the round face and the golliwog's mop. It being Whitsun, she told them, there wasn't another place in the village she'd recommend, them all being "packed to the rafters" with the exception of a place they called "Dirty Nellie's," and "one of the nice gentlemen surely to God wouldn't want to go down there, would they now?"

At the mention of Nellie's establishment Frazer recoiled visibly, but the little man blurted out, "Heads or tails, mister, eh?"

"Frazer," stiffly responded the Scotsman, very civilianlike in flannels and turtleneck pullover. "But I'm not sure, Mr.—"

"Tom Cavanaugh's the name, lad," said Cavanaugh, judging his companion in distress to be at least ten years his junior.

"I'm not so sure this is the way to go about it, Mr. Cavanaugh. I'm afraid I wrote Mrs. Dunnigan more than two months ago making arrangements."

Mrs. Dunnigan explored the pigeonholes in the ancient rolltop

26

desk and miraculously produced two envelopes. "Mr. Frazer's right," she reluctantly agreed, wringing her scoured-red, blue-veined hands.

Frazer inquired politely as to when Mr. Cavanaugh had written for his booking.

Mr. Cavanaugh couldn't seem to remember. What with his patients and one thing and another and five deliveries just the week before and a hell of a time getting a *locum tenens* and all that, he just couldn't recall, but he assured the man who was rapidly becoming his competitor that "it was in good time, though."

Mrs. Dunnigan exclaimed, "*Dr.* Cavanaugh, is it? Why didn't you say so, Doctor dear?" She poked deeply into the second envelope. "Here youse are. All down in black an' white." She peered at the postmark. "I can't make that out. Can you, Doctor?" She handed Cavanaugh the envelope.

The doctor's round, pleasant features slumped chinward. "Aye, I can that." He hitched up the waistband of his brown, plaid plus-fours and bent down to pick up his ancient suitcase.

"Oh dear," moaned Mrs. Dunnigan, massaging her bosomless chest in consternation. "Now, if that duffer of a Paddy of mine had his fat head screwed on, this would never have happened."

"I'll not hear a word of it, now, Mrs. Dunnigan," soothed the doctor, turning to go. "Nellie'll squeeze me in somewhere, that's to be sure." He nodded to Mrs. Dunnigan and Mr. Frazer with a broad smile. He pulled his peaked cap firmly on his head and nipped agilely down the stone steps to the street.

Frazer and the landlady watched him hail a passing jaunting car and saw him wave to them. They waved back halfheartedly.

"Well, then, Mr. Frazer," began Mrs. Dunnigan, recovering her professional composure, "won't you step this way an' I'll show you your room."

The three-story house looked as clean as the toe of a Chelsea pensioner's boot, thought Frazer. It smelled of linoleum and lavender. He made his way up the stairs behind her, noticing in passing her thick ankles, the design of square helixes on each side of the stair covering, the stark enamel whiteness of the toilet bowl through the open door at the top of the stairs, the dull sheen of rich brass in the stair rods, the grain of the worn banister, the stiff creases in a linen tablecloth on a dining room leaf-table set for tea.

"Here we are," gasped Mrs. Dunnigan after the rigors of the climb, opening the door to a large double room and walking in ahead of him.

The sun burst through two large dormer windows upon a floor of natural wood, charging the room with a sense of holiday. The wide writing desk, the ornately curved swivel chair in front of it, the two deep leather armchairs with their high backs by the fireplace, the colossal mahogany chest of drawers worthy of a ship's wardroom, the matching wardrobe, the four-poster brass bedstead, the marble-topped nightstands—one of them thoughtfully provided with a pipe rack, the other with a paraffin-wick lamp—and the glass-doored bookcase showing off the rows of conservative book spines and serious titles; these were the adjuncts of bachelorhood.

"Excellent," said Frazer, putting his black leather suitcase down beside a gleaming coal scuttle and breathing in the purity of "Mansion Polish."

"Bath's down the hall, Mr. Frazer," wheezed Mrs. Dunnigan, "and, of course, the usual." She pointed to the marble-topped washstand with its ornate jug and washbasin. She stood around for a moment crumpling her clean, floral, starched apron in her fists.

"Excellent," repeated Frazer, running his hand along the back of the armchair.

Mrs. Dunnigan appeared to tarry in embarrassment.

"Oh," shot Frazer, suddenly rummaging under his pullover for his wallet.

"Two pounds, ten and six," whispered Mrs. Dunnigan discreetly.

The money changed hands.

Mrs. Dunnigan edged backward toward the door, half bowing, grasping for small talk. "All bachelors here, Mr. Frazer, just as you said you'd like it in your letter. Used to have a wheen o' them factory hussies from Lancashire of a summer but"—she brandished her long bony index finger—"Dirty Nellie can have them. I run a respectable establishment." She pouted indignantly.

Frazer snatched his hand from the back of the chair and turned to face his new landlady. "I gather you don't think too highly of this Nellie's."

She embarked on a lengthy tirade against her competitor, her clientele, her prices and pastimes, "Not a fit place even for a black Protestant," she concluded.

"Yet you sent the other gentleman—what was his name? Dr. Cavanaugh?—there."

"God forgive me for it," she said piously, wringing her hands, "but as God's me judge, this is me last room an' there's devil else I could do."

The free flow of conversation grew sluggish and finally constipated. Mrs. Dunnigan went into reverse again. "Tea's at six sharp, Mr. Frazer." She closed the door and clumped down the stairs.

When she was halfway down the flight, Frazer's door opened. "Where is it, Mrs. Dunnigan?" he called down pleasantly over the banister.

"Down one flight, first room on the right," she responded.

"Not the dining room, Mrs. Dunnigan—Nellie's," he said.

Her face collapsed. "God forgive you," she said. She looked around furtively, stiffened and snapped, "I'll send the mister up . . . if you can wait that long," she added contemptuously.

Nellie's was as black as a street urchin's instep. Coming inside from the vapid lemon illumination of an overcast early June sun robbed Frazer temporarily of his sight. A soft warm hand grasped his and a softer voice breathed, "C'mon, luv, always room for one more." He groped around for his bearings and inadvertently prodded something soft, resilient and undeniably female. The edge of a chair hit the back of his knees. He gingerly explored its surface. It was empty. He would sit until his sight returned.

When it did, he found himself in a high-backed booth with a young woman. Another young woman with a male friend sat on the other side of the table between them. He stood up abruptly. "I'm awfully sorry," he mumbled. "Can't see a thing when you come in from outside, you know. I did rather stumble in on you. Do forgive me."

"What's the hurry, luv?" crooned the girl beside him, appraising him with approval.

29

"Really, I'm looking for a friend," he protested.

"Aren't we all, chum?" snickered the man.

"Beside, you've found one," said the other girl pleasantly. "Not bad either," she added, nudging her friend.

The two girls giggled.

The first girl said, "Would you believe it, ducks, but I said to Millie here I'd grab the next thing in pants that walked in here."

The other girl explained, "Pam's in the dumps 'cos her one and only left for Liverpool last week and she's in the dumps." The girl giggled. "Chaps are like buses, I always say. One drives out, another drives in."

"Is that right?" said her male friend, sulking.

"Too jolly right," retorted the girl. As she gestured positively, her arm hit her companion's glass of ale, spilling it over him.

The man jumped to his feet. "You spiteful little bitch!" he yelled, grabbing her murderously by the wrist.

"Do something, for God's sake," squealed the girl, pushing Frazer forward.

Frazer's nostrils filled with the man's bunched knuckles. Suddenly his world became a kaleidoscope of pain and color. When his head cleared, he heard a familiar brogue in his ear. "An' you talk about the quarrelin', brawlin' Irish." He looked up and saw the doctor, whose breath was redolent of a distillery.

"Actually I was looking for you, Doctor," he explained defensively.

"Aye," the doctor chuckled, "to be sure. But I was in my twenties once myself, don't forget." He looked professionally at Frazer's nose. "No harm done, but I've my doubts if Mrs. Dunnigan'll let you across her doorstep again when she hears o' this."

"I tell you I came down to look for you," insisted Frazer seriously.

"Well, I was over there all the time," argued the doctor, pointing toward the bar, a wide grin on his face, "but you seemed more interested in the local flora and fauna than this old spud."

Frazer fingered his nose tenderly. "I didn't see you."

The doctor laughed slyly. "Well, it's a good yarn. I believe you, of course; but thousands wouldn't. . . . What'd you want me for, might I ask?"

"Right now I'd like to know how long it'll take the swelling to go down. It could cost us our room."

"Our room?"

"That's why I came down. I want you to share it with me."

"Now, why would you do this for a complete stranger?"

"You're not a *complete* stranger. You're Tom Cavanaugh. Dr. Tom Cavanaugh, and right now *I* need a doctor. If you don't help me get this swelling down, we're both going to spend the night in Dirty Nellie's."

Cavanaugh stood back theatrically and stared at his new friend. "Sold to the man in the canvas socks," he announced. "We'll drink to that."

At half past eleven that night the two tiptoed skewly up the steps to Mrs. Dunnigan's and quietly entered the hallway. With the same care they traveled up the stairs toward Frazer's room. Mrs. Dunnigan stood vigil beside a black leather suitcase in the hallway. She shoved something in Frazer's direction. "Two pounds, ten and six," she snapped, "an' I'll thank you not to come back to Dunnigan's Friendly Guest House ever again." She escorted them down the stairs and across the threshold.

For the assiduous searcher there were other friendly guest homes in Rosstrevor. Frazer and Cavanaugh were assiduous searchers. They had to be that night. Their new digs could not match Mrs. Dunnigan's, but they did not care. They spent their days hiking in the purple Mourne Mountains that hugged the village to the water's edge, their evenings boating in Carlingford Lough and watching the wonder of the sun drop behind the hills of Omeath in a burst of silent splendor.

It was not until the end of the fourth day that they finally became "Tommy" and "Ian" to each other. This ushered in the first tentative exchange of confidences. Platitudes and pleasantries gave way to genuine discovery of each other—with Tommy leading the way.

Ian gradually learned of the life of a country doctor—from the gay days and nights full of study at Trinity, through the sweaty ordeal of the first real, live patient, to a small but busy practice in the aches, pains, grudges and gripes of fishers, farmers and stone-cutters, their wives and offspring. He discovered quickly that it was not enough to be able to counsel a midwife in a crisis, or to do the job himself, or to lance a carbuncle on a prim spinster's backside or bind a broken limb. The Irish general practitioner became the repository of his patients' joys and fears and privy to the unsolicited confessions of their shames and sadnesses. There was thrust upon him a new dimension which he feared he might have been unable to measure up to, had it not been for Elizabeth Cavanaugh.

She was the robust daughter of one of his patients, with an unswerving faith in the Almighty, the stamina of a Clydesdale and a relentless devotion to her husband. Always on the move, always on the go, Tommy recalled. That was why the paleness and loss of weight came as such a surprise; then the bloody sputum, followed by almost two and a half years of going back and forth between home and hospital. Then finally she died one night in her sleep. He arrived the next morning unknowing, a bunch of fresh spring violets in his hand. He had got off his motorbike on the way and picked them himself. The matron took them from him at the door and said she would put them in water. . . . When he saw her laid out, with her black hair framing her face, and her eyes closed as if in sleep and not a trace of the suffering that had lined her countenance, his mind went to the story of St. Theresa he had learned at his mother's knee. And he knew then there would never be another Elizabeth, so what was the point in ever looking?

"When did it happen?" asked Ian gently. They had parked their bicycles against a grassy hedge and rested by a tinkling brook in the shade of a willow.

"Three years, seven months and—let me see—two weeks ago," mused Tommy, looking at the brown moss-covered rocks at the bottom of the stream. He played his fingers in the cool stream. The soft Irish air hummed with the heady drone of a summer full of bees and butterflies. He looked up into the blue sky, here and there embroidered with puffs of cloud. He smiled. "God's in his Heaven, and all's right with the world."

"Not with you, it isn't," said Ian.

"You're right, lad," admitted Tommy, turning to face his companion. "Indeed you're right. But what's a man to do, I ask you? You hammer yourself silly with work to drown her voice from inside your head, but you can't pull a blind down on your dreams. You give her every stitch to St. Vincent de Paul's, so every time you put up a suit or take one down, the little drop o' scent she used doesn't catch you in the memory. You lock away all her little bits and pieces. You don't want them turnin' up every other day, remindin' you. You want to do all your penance in one lump—not string it out over a lifetime." He examined the elbow of his cardigan. "Aye, lad," he continued pensively, "three years, seven months, two weeks—and four days."

"You're not still marking off a calendar or something?" asked Ian.

Tommy looked sheepish. "To tell you the truth, I used to. I haven't, though, for a few months now; that is, not until this morning."

"Why this morning?" queried Ian.

Tommy twisted his arm so that a darn in the elbow of the cardigan was visible. "A neat little darner she was," he said, pointing to the intricately woven needlework. "See what I mean?" He shook his head. "When you least expect it, it starts all over again. And then it has to run its course." He cupped his hand and allowed it to fill with the brook water. "To run its course," he said, allowing the water to seep out between his fingers.

"Long time, three years," observed Ian.

" 'Tis that."

"Much too long, old man. 'S not normal."

"I've never pretended to be normal."

"What *have* you pretended to be, then?"

Tommy shot him a quizzical glance. "Do you really want to know?"

Ian nodded.

"Fond of my bloody work, if you must know," he declared without rancor. "Sick of my damned practice. Sick of prim white buttocks with carbuncles for the lancing thereof, sick of thrusting my hands into the bodies of fallow farm women and sorry for the little beggars they bring out, overcome by the halitosis of their whispered

33

confidences, loathing their imaginary ailments, and all the time telling myself I shouldn't be."

"Of course you shouldn't," commented Ian positively. "No doctor should, I don't believe."

"You don't believe," repeated Tommy. "You don't believe. . . . Don't try to soften it," he appealed gently. "I'm good meat for it. I'm a medical pretender, that's what. Out with it."

"All right, then, a medical pretender. A fraud, if you prefer," suggested Ian evenly.

Tommy looked away.

"But we're all part pretender, part fraud, Tommy. All of us."

"Nine-tenths?"

"As long as you're not ten-tenths."

"And maybe I am . . . what then?"

"Perhaps a temporary excuse . . . three years . . . but certainly no longer."

Tommy stared at him intently. "You just ups and says three years. Why?"

"Let's say three years, seven months and—what was it?—two weeks and four days."

"Why should you be so arbitrary? Perhaps you have *some* feeling for my predicament, but to come right out and—"

"Tommy," said Ian emphatically, "you want me to be. You want somebody, some impartial somebody, to be. You don't know me from a bar of soap, old man, but you want me to tell you to pull your ruddy finger out, get a grip on yourself again . . . and lay off the gin-and-bitters. We could have let it go at golf and a spot of rowing, but you're the one who opened his soul. I didn't."

Tommy rubbed his wet hands on the soft green grass. He spoke with clinical detachment. "Cut it off right now, right here, right at this moment, you say." He pondered.

"Right now," said Ian, nodding. "Like a light switch . . . maybe a sponge. You've been letting it dry without wringing it out first. Emotions are fine as long as you let them work for you—not against you. When they start doing that, you have to be the master of them, or you're lost. That's what my grandfather always said—and did."

"Your grandfather?"

Ian nodded. "My parents died when I was five. A boating accident. I don't even remember them. Family portraits and that sort of thing, but I don't remember them in here." He tapped his chest. "He's the greatest man I've ever known. The trouble with most of us, he used to say, is we haven't sorted ourselves out. We muck about with a fuzzy idea of ourselves and fuzzy ideas about why we're here. Almost like an admiral marshaling his reserves before a battle. Your job's to knock out the enemy. That's your goal. You fight to attain it. If you really are after the goal, you know you must fight; you accept that fact. Everything else is extraneous to your goal. Anything else will confuse the issue, cloud the goal, make its attainment all the longer, even prevent it altogether. Even emotions. If it means spilling a chap's bowels on the quarterdeck en route, you tell yourself this in advance, so that when it happens, you're not standing around trying to fit it all into your philosophy with the shot and shell flying. No, you've already thought it out beforehand. When the event takes place, something inside you just clicks into place."

Tommy looked at him intensely. "I'll say this much: You don't look like you talk."

"I should've thought I rather did," Ian said with a shrug.

"Have you ever seen a man's bowels?" snapped Tommy.

"I was speaking figuratively—"

"Well, I have. That puts me ahead of you," said Tommy directly.

"You're at least ten years ahead of me, Tommy," observed Ian.

"Thirty-five, I am."

"I stand corrected. Nine, then."

"A light switch . . . a sponge. Have *you* ever loved a woman— an' I don't mean for a day or a weekend—truly loved one with everything that's in you?"

Ian seemed to turn evasive. "We don't have to go into specifics. I have a principle of conduct that I regulate my life by—reason over emotion. That was how I was brought up. 'Control yourself, boy!' he'd shout. I can still hear him. Control yourself, boy. Be a man. . . . Well, I've been practicing at it since I was five. Don't misunderstand me. I'm not saying we should cross off emotions.

35

Far from it. It's just that when they enter into the human equation, we make them work to our advantage, or not at all."

Tommy sat back as if to digest what he had just heard, then asked, "Have you ever loved a woman with everything you've got?" Ian reddened. "I've never had to."

"Grandpa saw to that, too, eh?"

Ian stiffened angrily.

Tommy made light of it. "Ah, remember now, make your emotions work for you, not against you," he quipped.

That took some of the starch out of his pensive companion, but Tommy sensed the topic had gone far enough for the time being. He stood up, stretched luxuriously and suggested they could be back at the boardinghouse in time for tea if they pedaled at a fair clip.

On the way back they freewheeled around and down a country road that wandered aimlessly without much consideration as to destination. They gulped in the warm, moist air that rushed against their faces. Its stiff rustle protected the privacy of their thoughts.

The protocol of tea interrupted the exchange of confidences. It did not resume until the end of a lengthy chess game in the sitting room after nine that evening. Tommy had won, as he had for three successive nights. It was a chance remark that brought it on. "Play your men like you do your emotions, lad, an' see where it gets you."

"Back on that, are we?" commented Ian, filling his pipe.

His tone held a warning which Tommy sensed. He waved his hand nonchalantly as if to make light of it. "How about a turn around the harbor before we call it a night?"

The balm of darkness and the gentle lap of water against the harbor wall further freed their tongues.

"A hell of a man he must've been—your grandfather," observed Tommy apropos of nothing.

Ian sucked at his pipe. At each draw the glow lit up the bottom of his face. They leaned against a timber guardrail in the inky blackness and stared across the lough at the lights on the opposite shore. The water lapped lazily against the foundation timbers slick with a century of moss.

"Hell to live with from time to time," murmured Ian. He laughed softly. "I know he'd be hell to die with . . . probably never will die. One of those indestructible people who'll outlive us all. You know, like the Tower of London, perhaps. Can't imagine the country without it—or him. The sea's all he ever lived for."

"An' how does it agree with you?" asked Tommy.

"The sea? The Navy?"

"Aye."

Ian puffed strongly on his pipe. "I've never known anything else, really. It's always been the smell of salt air around our house. The place is full of pictures of ships. Everything he ever sailed in— or by—seems to be there. Sort of an Army-Navy club for all the old retired naval codgers around. You know what I mean—roast beef and Yorkshire pudding for the chaps every first Sunday or every second month; the 'thin red line' and all that sort of thing going on into the wee hours."

"At least you got your history the easy way—an' a lot of it first-hand," commented Tommy.

"True," replied Ian. "My English too. I had to have off by heart a new Kipling poem for each meeting. How they used to like that! They'd make a big fuss of clearing off the table and they'd sit around it with brandy and cigars. He'd pull me up on his knee, hit his brandy glass with a spoon and announce in a voice you'd only use in a Force Seven gale that the midshipman had been piped aboard and ship's company would come to attention." He laughed with a suggestion of nostalgia. "I was seven and, God, how I loved it." In the darkness he removed his pipe and began:

> If you can force your heart and nerve and sinew
> To serve your turn long after they are gone,
> And so hold on when there is nothing in you
> Except the Will which says to them: "Hold on!" . . .
> If you can meet with Triumph and Disaster
> And treat those two impostors just the same; . . .
> Yours is the Earth and everything that's in it,
> And—which is more—you'll be a Man, my son!

They both fell silent.

Ian broke the long silence. "That's the one he liked best of all."

"Heart . . . nerve . . . sinew," mused Tommy. "Kipling?"

"Uh-huh."

"Decidedly more poetic than Gray's *Anatomy*."

"Afraid I haven't got to him yet," said Ian seriously. "Is he any good?"

Tommy's puckish grin lay concealed in the dark. "Well," he said analytically, "I'd say Gray's plot's a mite obscure, but there's lots of characters—or parts of characters."

"Probably be too confusing for me, said Ian. "Straight, direct: that's Kipling. No searching for the hidden message. It hits you in the face."

"If you like being hit in the face," murmured Tommy.

"I like to know what's expected of me and what isn't. None of this subtlety for me. You plank down a map. You have to go from here to here. You chart a course—carefully, mind. And you hew to it. Same in anything you do."

"Your grandfather?" queried Tommy.

"Yes," answered Ian defensively. "Why?"

"Must be damn exciting—shooting off to all parts of the globe . . . a fighting arm of the world's mightiest naval power," ruminated Tommy. "Me? This time next week I'll be back in my surgery, and there'll be Paddy Menahan's walk five miles in from Brackney to be catheterized. Urinates seven times a week, he does . . . an' there's devil the bit wrong with the Faherty woman, an' if I didn't have the nerve to tell her so eighteen months ago, I can't very well do it now . . . an' there's—" He gestured hopelessly.

The silence creaked.

"I've no sympathy at all for you, doctor," said Ian finally.

"I'm not asking for sympathy." Tommy grunted.

"Sounds like it, old man."

"Merely an appraisal of my situation," said Tommy.

"After all," explained Ian, "you did know what you were getting yourself into. It's not as if it was sprung on you all of a sudden, is it?" He tapped the upturned bowl of his pipe in his hand. The cupped noise carried across the stillness of the deep lough waters.

"An appraisal, I'd gather, you've already made of your own situation," observed Tommy.

38

"Meaning?"

"Look, lad," began Tommy kindly. "You may sound like your grandfather; you may even think like him; I'll wager you even look quite a bit like him. But you're not *him*. I think I've been in the business long enough to tell when a man's content with himself and when he's not."

Ian reacted defensively. "What's being content got to do with it?"

Tommy pulled his cigarette from his mouth, slightly incredulous. "Everything, I thought. . . . Didn't grandfather?" His tone was gritty with a sudden sarcasm.

"I'll be charitable and assume your interest in my grandfather's observations exceeds your temporary offensiveness," said Ian evenly.

"I'd prefer you to be honest rather than charitable, old man. And quite frankly, *your* observations would be somewhat of a novelty."

Ian clicked the stem of his pipe on his firm, white teeth. "Somehow that irks you—my grandfather." He felt for the words. "Content wasn't—isn't—really the important thing with him. Duty was. Duty's the primary thing. The content part comes from doing your duty to the best of your ability."

Tommy harrumphed noisily. "Dreadfully simple . . . disgustingly simple."

"Not by a long shot," said Ian. "About as complex a thing as there is—to establish what's one's duty in life. Some of us spend that life trying to find out what the hell is our duty, then kick off before we've had a chance to do it."

"And supposin' you don't give a damn for your duty?" Tommy rasped. "Supposin' you just want a bit of fun out of life—the sort of fun you get from just kickin' around, tryin' this, then tryin' that. The sort of fun every young lad ought to have. The fun that's growin' up and findin' things out for yourself. Believe me, there's a sense of accomplishment there. Take it from one who knows. You've had your mind made up for you—long before you ever had a crack at makin' it up for yourself. Your grandfather's just usin' you to live out the rest of his life in uniform. No more, no less. . . . No, I put it to you. What if you don't give a damn for this duty you're saddled with? What then?"

"It's still your duty," insisted Ian, gesturing pointlessly in the darkness, "like it or not. That doesn't change. You can't change what you were put on earth for; but you can change yourself—your own attitude."

"I'd rather change my bloody job and let me be," gruffed Tommy. He turned to confront his friend. "*You* haven't done such a good job of attitude changin' that I can't see what's what. You haven't said one word about *your* work but what I've had to drag out of you. Aye, to be sure, I could almost draw you a picture of the old man, for you've been long and hard on *him*." His voice softened. "Ian, lad, when a man's fed up with his lot, he has to share it with his friends—that's myself here; when he's chokin' with the joy of the good life, he blabbers his head off, too. But you? I have to be suspicious. More than that: You're a nice lad, and—well—you're just so bloody neutral."

Ian grinned. "And you just abhor neutrality, eh?"

Tommy was not infected by the levity in his voice. "I abhor the selfishness of a willful old man," he grated.

"You abhor it," Ian observed evenly. "I accept." He stowed his pipe away in an inner pocket and suggested it was bedtime.

"But for the love of Mike, why?" expostulated Tommy as they mounted the front-door steps of the dark, brooding boardinghouse where they had received sanctuary.

Ian thrust his key hard into the lock. "Why? Why *not?* Why not content through duty? Show me a better way." He turned the key and pushed open the door, allowing Tommy to enter ahead of him. Tommy's silence encouraged him to go on. "Thought not . . . you know, if you *really* believed in whatever it is you do believe in, old chap, you'd abandon the backsides and carbuncles, wouldn't you?" He smiled wanly. "For mosquitoes and tsetse flies and such —things you can't lose much love over. *Tropical* medicine—not human, Tommy. That's your style, maybe. Off somewhere in the Dark Continent. But then, you're off to Bally-what's-it on Sunday night and me to Whitehall and—"

40

"And," interjected Tommy, "*your* course is set. But not mine. Not by a damn sight."

Ian could not suppress a smile as he ascended the stairs.

"Oh-ho, my bucko," challenged Tommy. "You think not? Don't be surprised if one of these days I ups and—"

"Backsides and carbuncles!" chaffed Ian.

"When I makes up me mind on somethin'—"

"Dropping your *g*'s again, Tommy," Ian reminded him from the first landing.

Tommy stood at the foot of the stairs and aimed his index finger at Ian admonishingly. "When I makes up me mind—"

"Backsides and carbuncles!" Ian called down.

Tommy hammered up the stairs two at a time. "May the Lord look sideways on you, you blackhearted *Sassenach*," he yelled.

"An' on both of youse!" shrilled the landlady, suddenly appearing wraithlike on the first landing armed with a paraffin-oil lamp. "It's half twelve an' what in God's name's all the ructions?"

Tommy was in no position to compose an adequate defense. The sudden rasp of her voice chilled his heart and froze the rhythm of his swiftly moving feet. He slipped one step from the landing and lost his balance. . . .

The leave they took of each other at the Rosstrevor railway station was the first of several in the two years that followed.

In the third year their friendship could be leavened only by letters: Tommy had gone to Africa.

3

Fifteen years after the boardinghouse door banged behind him, Frazer was a commander. All this time he had not seen the sea in a professional capacity, yet he was as close to the pulse of the Navy as one could possibly be without getting wet: He was temporary third-in-command of Personnel Section, Naval Branch, Department of Permanent Secretary, the Admiralty. Naval Branch was the funnel through which flowed all the paper work stemming from the edicts and decisions of their lordships of the Board of Admiralty in the officering and manning of the Fleet.

He knew Naval Branch about as thoroughly as he knew his three-room bachelor flat in Chelsea, for he had served most of his naval career under both roofs.

Progressing in knowledge and rank, Frazer had evolved to importance in enlisting boys and men into the Service; in seeing to the work and timetables of training ships; in authorizing promotions and discharges; in devising new badges and insignia; in administering the education, appointments, leaves, retirements, removals, restorations, claims, pensions, honors, distinctions, decorations, and medals of officers; and in managing the Corps of Royal Marines.

He was thus a man of broad administrative experience and solid reputation who had sinned against the Drake rankling underneath his breast, because of a resolute fluency with "in-pending-out" baskets, quarterly punishment forms, compassionate leaves, the apportioning of prize moneys, and that general compost of paper work which Naval Branch had to surmount in order that His Majesty's Navy might maintain its ceaseless vigil of the high seas.

As an assistant to the Assistant Director of Personnel he felt a prisoner of his perfectionism, and this rankled. He imagined himself rid of his neuter existence by some real challenge. Dammit, look at Tiny Wilson. A *Britannia* bunkmate, big Tiny was already FO2 (Flag Officer second-in-command) of the Third Destroyer Flotilla based at Valetta—the Mediterranean Fleet, no less. But few of his classmates called him Tiny any more. Even if a chap was a full year younger than you, the bonhomie of college days choked on the scrambled eggs of a vice-admiral's cap. Tiny's had been a promotion under fire; a deck-plate commission almost, Frazer glumly recalled. Alone he had tackled a shoal of E-boats off the Heligoland Bight five weeks after war started. Sure it was true: The senior service had been caught on that fourth of August with hardly enough young flag officers to swab a deck. Since then m'lords had been braiding the caps of hell-for-leather types like Tiny.

And there was that other devil, Hanratty. The bugger used to muddle around with toy engines when all the others would be swotting before finals. Now with even seamen taking to the skies and the formation of the Royal Naval Air Service, they had posted Hanratty to Dover. The last Frazer had heard of him, he was buzzing around in the blue over the Channel in charge of half a dozen eggboxes with wings, supposedly hunting U-boats. It was all very new; and so was Hanratty's appointment as full commander of the whole show.

Frazer, in his office on the second floor of Admiralty House, felt less acccomplished than an office boy in a blue suit. He had resigned himself to his own total eclipse by the Tinys and the Hanrattys and at least half a dozen other heavenly bodies that he did not wish to think about. And so it had taken him a whole winter to harden himself to the anonymity of his naval clerkship.

But spring brought with it the first timid rays of sun and suggestion. A Navy mobilizing for total war had ruptured its bulkheads.
The Royal Naval College had compromised on teeth and vision.
Its fresh-faced enrollment had overflowed into officer-cadet training units all over the land. Soon this beardless, graduated youth
would heed the pleading from the silent decks of the hastily ham-
mered-together frigates, minesweepers, corvettes, and destroyers
grinding down the slipways of the Lagan, the Mersey and the
Clyde.

But not soon enough, apparently. Frazer dipped into his "in"
basket one morning and withdrew from it his destiny.

FROM: First Lord   12th November, 1914
TO: Sea Lords, Secretary and Director of Personnel
     I have become increasingly disquieted by reports from Ad-
miral of the Fleet and Director of Naval Operations that the
supply and demand pictures for officer personnel for our latest ad-
ditions to Home Fleet are so seriously at odds. I propose, therefore, in principle, for your consideration that a plan be drawn up
by Director of Personnel whereby all administrative personnel
(officer) be whittled down to the bare minimum so that the able-
bodied, being desirous of executive seagoing duty, be allowed
that privilege.
     Hopefully this will help bridge the gap between our present
dire need and the accelerated Dartmouth and OCTU intakes
which will not be available for six to nine months.
     Pray let me have a note on this.
                                              W.S.C.

Frazer read with the bored attention usually lavished upon
routine memoranda. Halfway through he trembled. His heart and
eyes raced down to the signature—then back for a second reading.
He camped on every line. His agile mind fermented. . . .

By comparison the rest of the mail was just so much bumf. What
he could handle himself he slid over to the side of his desk of deal.
What was left he picked up and carried toward an impressive door
with ASSISTANT DIRECTOR OF PERSONNEL gold-leafed on it. He
knocked deferentially.

44

"C'min," came the grunted reply, and as Frazer entered, "Ah, Frazer. Morning."

"Good morning, sir." Frazer had emphasized "good."

"Not *that* good, Frazer, is it?" gruffed the solid fore-and-aft-rigged figure behind the huge mahogany desk: Rear Admiral Denby, Assistant Director of Personnel (ADP).

"*Six* from First Lord this morning." Frazer held up the sheaf of letters.

"Only *six?*" queried the ADP with mock dismay. "He must be sick or something. . . . Well, let's have 'em."

The ADP leafed through this morning's correspondence resulting from the latest Admiralty Board meeting, presided over as usual by the dominating personality of the First Lord of the Admiralty—a civilian. "Wants to remodel the Dartmouth selections boards. . . . Questions my rejection of that Navy entrant. . . . Wants a distinguishing sleeve insignia for OCTU. . . . Ah, here's something new." It was the memorandum which Frazer had read and reread. "I'll manage the rest of this," said the ADP, holding up the other five memoranda. "Look into this seagoing business, will you?"

"I have already, sir," said Frazer.

"Good man, good," said the ADP expansively. "That's what I like about you, Frazer. Always a jump ahead. That's how to move up in this place. Show 'em you can handle the responsibilities of the chap above you. That's how I did it. . . . Damned if I know what I'd do without you around here." He studied the "seagoing" memorandum closely. He rubbed his large, pale unweathered face with a dimpled hand. He held up the memorandum again and stared at a picture of *Dreadnought* at Scapa Flow hanging on the wall before him. "God, you know, for a minute you start wondering if you've been missing—" He laughed self-consciously. "Humbug, Frazer. We're too old for that sort of thing, of course." He drummed his fingers on the glass desktop. "What's it? They also serve who stay at home and . . . something or other. . . . Well, then. Get on with it. Can you let me have something in a week or so?"

Frazer nodded. He wondered if he really looked *that* old.

"Splendid. Send in my secretary, then."

So old Denby'd like me to "look into the seagoing business," thought Frazer. Give the chaps a crack at sea duty, eh?

He set about complying with the ADP's wishes. It always helped to use some concrete model around which the thing could be designed. This was miles better than fumbling about in the abstract. Deliberately and methodically Frazer used himself as the model.

In due course the ADP, and ultimately the Director of Personnel himself, approved what was subsequently designated Admiralty Instruction No. 1117. It went out to establishments from Scapa to Simonstown, from the Falkland Islands to Fiji, and to a greenbaize bulletin board on a second-floor hallway in Admiralty House.

Three months later it was December 1, 1914. A stack of applications for executive duty under the provisions of Admiralty Instruction No. 1117 lay on Frazer's desk. He glanced casually around the office. All heads were bowed in work. He slid open a desk drawer, withdrew three forms which he slid into the middle of the stack. He nonchalantly carried them into the ADP's office and stood aside with bored exterior and pounding heart while that august person fanned through them cursorily.

"Look all right to me," muttered Rear Admiral Denby. "How many's that to date?"

"Four hundred and sixteen applications, sir; three hundred and eleven approved, ninety-six rejected, and nine awaiting the medical director's ruling," responded Frazer promptly.

The rear admiral continued his perusal. He looked up at Frazer standing by his desk. "Be blamed, I will, if I'm able to understand these old duffers." He grunted. "Half of them are over forty-five and haven't been at sea since *Britannia* days. Most of 'em are doing a respectable job sailing a desk somewhere. But the buggers aren't satisfied." He continued looking at Frazer as if expecting some kind of explanation.

"Oh, I don't really know, sir, what the typical reason might be," volunteered Frazer. "I suspect, though, it's something to do with wanting to serve where they feel they can do the best job."

The rear admiral looked at him disparagingly. "Where they can do the best job?" he asked scathingly. "That's what you and I are here for, isn't it? *We* decide where they can do the best job; not *them*." He pointed to the stack of applications. "Know what this means? If the quack approves those nine, we have to come up with three hundred and twenty people to fill their jobs. After all, Frazer," he explained indignantly, brandishing one of the applications, "*this* is war, too."

Frazer said, "I suppose you have a point there, sir."

Rear Admiral Denby returned to his scrutiny of the applications. His breath came noisily. His pale jowls glowed pink with emotion that pumped to capacity the tangled skein of varicose blood vessels adorning the end of his large nose. "Like an old biddy her last time around—may as well give it a good go, it'll be her last." He harrumphed. Denby had been leafing through the applications in no particular order, but now he hunched purposefully over the top of the stack, thumbing through the A's.

Frazer tensed. The admiral never did more than spot-check. "Sir," he temporized, "perhaps there's more than meets the eye in this. . . . It may be a matter of conscience—"

"Eversham, by Gad!" expostulated Denby, jabbing at one of the applications. "What in blazes is *he* in here for? A third-rate person all the way. Knew him at Wick. And how the devil he ever wangled his way past the selection board in the first place I'll never know." He peered closely at the typewritten page. "Hm, a captain. Surprised he ever got up that far." He read on. "Dammit, this is a laugh. Says here he's been 'naval consultant to the Ministry of Supply.'" He raised his head and looked directly at Frazer. "Can you imagine old Froggy Eversham on the deck of *Warspite* in action, drawing on all his valuable experience at Supply to get him out of trouble?" He laughed sarcastically. "Old Froggy," he said again, shaking his head in disbelief, proceeding methodically to flip through the alphabet. He had reached the F's.

Frazer swallowed. "*Old*, sir?" he questioned disapprovingly, praying for something to distract Denby. "Captain Eversham's"— he glanced over the admiral's shoulder at Eversham's application— "almost forty-eight. Two years below the maximum age limit," he said matter-of-factly. He paused for a moment before adding, "I believe he's just a year younger than yourself, sir."

The admiral did not appear to have heard Frazer's dig. "Why

47

can't they be sensible people, Frazer?" he pleaded in overtones of definite annoyance. "Why can't they accept their lot in life—like myself, for instance? Or even you? We know our limitations, you and I. Solid naval citizens who've carved a niche for themselves; dependable people doing a first-class job; level-headed people not always wanting to dash off to glory somewhere. Can you imagine the two of us running off to sea at our age? What are you, Frazer? Forty-eight?"

"Forty-four, sir," said Frazer pointedly.

"Forty-four, forty-eight, fifty," he announced grandly with a sweep of his soft white hands, "it's all the same. We're all on the wrong side of forty for the outdoors." He shook his head again. "Froggy Eversham, by Gad. I'll never understand it. Almost as if *you'd* marched in here and told me *you* were running off somewhere. Absolutely ridiculous, I mean."

Frazer managed a smile. "What if I were to run off, sir?" he asked. He made it sound as if that contingency were as remote as the possibility of his giving birth.

The admiral roared heartily. "I say, that's jolly good." He laughed again. "That *is* jolly good, man." He pulled a large linen handkerchief from his left sleeve and wiped the tears of mirth from his eyes. "What would I do?" he asked, smiling after his amusement had subsided. "Purely academic, Frazer, academic. We both know when we're well off. You've been handling Commodore Buckley's job for the last year and a half. You have heard, haven't you? The medical people have finally written him off. It'll be a straight medical discharge, they tell me. You know what this means for you, of course. How does it feel to know you'll soon be out shopping for an extra spot of braid?" He stretched back in his swivel chair to enjoy his subordinate's reaction.

Frazer had not been privy to the department scuttlebutt. The news about Buckley, the permanent assistant to the Assistant Director, was fresh. "Sorry to hear it, sir."

Denby fixed him with a stare. "You odd or something? Sorry?" growled Denby.

"About the commodore, sir," Frazer added hastily.

"Oh, yes, of course. . . . And the promotion?"

48

Frazer's thin, ascetic features crinkled in an embarrassed smile. He had been a full commander for ten years—about four years longer than the average. Like many an officer in the peacetime Establishment he fretted intermittently over the dark possibility that he had been passed over for promotion to captain. The prospect of serving in his present rank and capacity until the optional retirement age of forty-five had always flooded his insides with a December kind of feeling. In peacetime at forty-five they suggested you retire; but at fifty they simply told you. At forty-four Frazer truly meant it when he replied, "Very pleased indeed, sir."

To the boy Frazer the indices of naval prestige had been honor, glory and medals; to the man they were the width and number of gold-braid rings on the sleeve. From a commander's brass and braid he could remove the dullness of the years; but in return, they gleamed little in his life.

Captain! . . . But the application!

"Tell you what," said Denby. "Have somebody clean his things out next door. The office is as good as yours. You can move in right away." The admiral's manner of speaking had taken on an inflection which indicated a new level of confidence now existed between them.

"But, sir," said Frazer, visibly distraught, "Commodore Buckley isn't even—"

The Assistant Director interrupted his protest with a pontifical gesture. "I'm putting the whole thing through this afternoon. Here," he declared officially, sliding the application forms to the side of his desk, "these are ready for the Director's signature."

Frazer bent to pick them up when Denby asked, "Have you any ideas on replacements, Frazer?"

Frazer replied, "I've had a search going ever since we posted 1117, sir. I'd say we've close to seventy-five or eighty probables to pick from at the moment, and more on the way."

The rear admiral leaned back again in his chair. He clicked his tongue and regarded the Scotsman with a stare of genuine admiration. "Dammit, Frazer, I rather like you, you know?"

"Thank you," said Frazer, flushing with embarrassment. "Will that be all, sir?"

"No, it isn't," announced Denby. "How about joining me at the Army-Navy for lunch?"

"Why," temporized Frazer, "I'm afraid that—well, I already have a—why, sir, I'd like to very much." It was his first deliberate lie in years.

The following day the applications, signed by the Director of Personnel, were back on Frazer's desk for action: matching them up with a backlog of personnel requests already in hand.

A week later a clerk arrived at his desk with a message stamped "Confidential." The Deputy Director of Naval Operations wished to see him. What the hell did *he* want? Frazer wondered.

4

At the head of a long, highly polished oak director's table stood a portly figure in vice-admiral's uniform. He was the naval secretary. "M'lords and gentlemen," he intoned ceremoniously.

He addressed some fifteen high-ranking naval officers and civilians sitting straight-backed around the table. Immediately they tipped their pipes over into glass ashtrays, mashed out their cigars and cigarettes, leaving nothing to mar the grand entrance of the First Lord of the Admiralty but a diaphanous blue cloud of smoke suspended above the heads of the assembly.

All in the bleakness of the high-ceilinged, pilastered, oak-paneled Admiralty Board Room rose as a stocky, sandy-haired, stoop-shouldered, fortyish civilian in a single-breasted blue suit appeared at the massive oak double doors and purposefully walked toward the head of the table. The click of his heels on the shiny mahogany floor muted as he reached the solid maroon carpeting. He was the Cabinet Minister charged by His Majesty's Government with the awesome duty of presiding over the naval affairs of the British Empire. As he reached the head of the table, he stood for an uncomfortably long time surveying the staring faces.

The naval secretary moved behind a thronelike oak armchair,

its elliptical-shaped seat trimmed in red leather. He slid it forward silently. The edge caught the back of the First Lord's knees.

"Oh," mumbled the First Lord, suddenly becoming aware of the chair. He sat down. As the others arranged themselves, his fingers explored the elliptically carved "bite" in his end of the table—a concession made to fat admirals, going back to the days of Nelson. Silence settled over the four Sea Lords, the Civil Lord, the parliamentary and financial secretary, their staffs and advisers. The Board of Admiralty was in session.

The naval secretary slid a thin, black folder across the table. The First Lord picked it up casually and flipped through the pages with a freckled hand, pausing every few pages to moisten his thumb on his nether lip.

"M'lords and gentlemen," began the secretary officially. "This special session is convened for the purpose of—"

The First Lord waved his hand. The formality could be dispensed with. He glanced down again at the open file. "Uh-huh," he said vigorously, "let's have at it, then."

The Director of Naval Operations (DNO) leaned on the table and pushed himself to his feet. "M'lord," he began, "we've been reviewing the possibilities for the last—"

"How's the leg?" interrupted the First Lord in round cordial tones.

"Much better, sir," said the elderly rear admiral with the wrinkled face.

"Fine, fine," declared the First Lord emphatically. "Glad to hear it. Now, what about this improbable matter?"

The eyes of all swiveled onto the DNO.

"For the benefit of the others," continued the DNO in a tired voice, "I'll recap the brief."

The First Lord looked up from lighting a huge cigar and nodded his assent. He noticed he was the only one smoking. "Smoke, by all means," he boomed with an expansive gesture.

The DNO continued. "Through his military attachés the King of the Belgians has been in continuous communication with our government over the situation on Lake Tanganyika." He unrolled

52

a large map of Africa onto the table and pointed to the lake. "Since hostilities broke out, Jerry's been making things quite difficult for the Belgians. Naturally he's interested in keeping the Belgians— and our own effort in German East Africa—off balance. The Belgians want our help. As long as Jerry has supremacy on the lake, he commands both its eastern and western shorelines. It's along the eastern shoreline that our Uganda and Rhodesian people are trying to join hands; and when they do, they hope to right-turn and hit von Lettow for six out of German East Africa and into the Indian Ocean." He managed a wan smile. "For months our military people down there've been nagging us about mopping up Jerry on the lake. Every time we move along that shoreline, Jerry craft shell the blazes out of us." He turned around and indicated the fiftyish man in the bemedaled uniform of a captain. "My deputy and his staff have cooked up something that perhaps we ought to look at."

The Deputy Director of Naval Operations (DDNO) rose nimbly to his feet. "We all must be living right," he shot breezily, laughing.

The Board of Admiralty sat stolidly unamused.

The DDNO seemed not to mind. "We had an incredibly good piece of luck a year ago," he continued unabashed. "A South African big-game hunter arrived in England to join up. He knows the area very well; used to hunt in it. We got in touch with him. He said we could put something over on the Hun by nipping a few small craft up the African toe and onto the lake."

The DDNO's somber audience, resplendent in medals, braid and raised eyebrows, sniffed suspiciously as though there was an unpleasant odor in the room.

"Some nipping," commented the First Lord, dryly taking the cigar from his mouth and extravagantly exhaling a cloud of blue smoke.

The DDNO continued with unabated zeal. "We looked into it. We think it can be done." For the next hour he sailed through the details of Naval Africa Expedition, expanding generously on the magnificent possibilities while broad-jumping the hazards. When he had finished, the Board responded with the enthusiasm of a Bil-

53

lingsgate fish merchant handed a Scottish five-pound note for a pair of kippers.

The First Sea Lord, the senior naval member of the Board, Admiral of the Fleet Lord John Fisher, shattered the silence: "You honestly believe this hunter fellow can see you through this—" *He* obviously did not believe it.

"Not the hunter, sir," answered the DDNO. "I'm afraid he's dead, sir."

All heads jerked as if tied to a puppeteer's string.

"Who, then?" demanded the Second Sea Lord, an admiral and Chief of Naval Personnel.

The DDNO turned about and walked to the huge oak double doors. He opened them and spoke to someone outside.

In walked Frazer.

Together they approached the table.

The Third Sea Lord, the Controller, a vice-admiral, adjusted his spectacles and growled, "Who's this officer?"

"M'lords and gentlemen," said the DDNO easily, "this is Commander Frazer, of the Director of Personnel's office."

Frazer swept off his hat and tucked it smartly under his upper arm; his heels clicked discreetly and his right hand rose with measured haste to his forehead in salute.

"He's found someone for the job," added the DDNO proudly.

"Where is he?" the Fourth Sea Lord, another vice-admiral, Chief of Transport and Supplies, wanted to know.

The DDNO took Frazer's elbow and whispered, "You can bring him in now."

Frazer whispered back, "He is in."

The DDNO looked around. He did not understand. His embarrassment was as if he had inadvertently introduced an old hoyden at a seminary tea.

"We're all waiting," declared the Civil Lord.

Frazer stood very correctly at attention and said, "I'm your commander, m'lords."

A slanted shaft of lemon winter sun filtering through the ceiling-high windows had suddenly broken through the blanket of cloudy

54

gloom outside. It caught the DDNO full in the face and melted his composure.

The long fragile ash from the First Lord's cigar noiselessly dashed itself to pieces on the table top. "What's going on?" he demanded.

The Director of Naval Operations glared at his deputy. "What's the meaning of this?" he snapped.

The DDNO's jaws moved with the regularity of a feeding fish, but no sound came.

The floridity of the First Lord's quadrangular face seemed to indicate that his polka-dot bow tie was too tight. He radiated a roseate glance at Frazer. "Frazer, is it?" he said.

"Yes, sir," responded Frazer calmly.

"You had better explain yourself," said the First Lord stiffly.

Frazer turned one-quarter left to face the First Lord. Not relaxing in his ramrod stiffness, he cleared his throat audibly. "M'lord," he began cautiously, "I am here because I am the best choice at the disposal of Personnel for the job at hand."

"You are, are you?" said the First Lord, affronted by the officer's apparent conceit. "Says who?"

The other members of the Board shifted in their chairs and exchanged glances which eloquently indicated that they shared the First Lord's sense of affront.

"M'lord," continued Frazer, "the requisition of the Director of Naval Operations called for an officer of the rank of either commander or captain—"

"With your permission, sir," interjected the Director of Naval Operations, nodding deferentially toward the First Lord, then addressing Frazer heatedly, "it also called for broad experience."

Frazer deflected the rear admiral's glare with equanimity. "In my twelve years in the Navy, sir, I have served in eight different areas —Scapa Flow, Promotions and Discharges, Education, Appointments, Leaves and Retirements, Claims and Pensions—"

The rear admiral interjected forcibly, "*Executive* experience, man, not administrative."

"With your permission, sir," said Frazer. He bent to unfasten the briefcase he had laid before him on the table. "I have here the requisition." He commenced reading from the relevant paragraph: "The officer finally selected should have a broad naval experience —"

"—commensurate with the undertaking," interrupted the rear admiral angrily.

Frazer looked up from the requisition with a puzzled expression. "I seem to have missed that part, sir," he said apologetically as he scrutinized the typewritten document before him.

Frazer's aplomb exasperated the rear admiral. "Dammit, not in so many words—"

The First Lord cut him off. "Who said *you* were the best choice, Frazer?"

Frazer turned again to confront the cherubic-faced Cabinet Minister. "Sir, by rank, experience and availability I was the department's first choice."

Admiral of the Fleet Fisher, the First Sea Lord, was getting tired of the niggling. He growled to the Second Sea Lord, Chief of Naval Personnel, "Who in blazes does the choosing up there?"

The Chief of Personnel muttered to the officer at his elbow, "You like to handle that one, Denby?"

Rear Admiral Denby, Assistant Director of Personnel, temporized by coughing and blowing into his large white handkerchief. "Technically, Sir John, *I* do," he said finally. He did not wish to elaborate.

"Well?" demanded the admiral of the fleet. "What do you mean, *technically?*"

Rear Admiral Denby shuffled about in his chair. He was paler than most of the Board had ever remembered him. "You see," he began tentatively, "departmentally we have had a system in effect at Personnel which I simply inherited from my predecessor. Works rather well most of the time. In fact, you all may remember—"

The Chief of Personnel turned tiredly to his loquacious subordinate. "Who, Denby, who?"

"My predecessor?" queried Denby blandly.

"No," snapped the Chief of Personnel. "Who selected this officer?"

56

"If you please, m'lord," interjected Frazer, "I did."

The Chief of Personnel looked up incredulously. "You?" he blurted out.

"Yes, sir," said Frazer.

The Chief of Personnel turned to Rear Admiral Denby. His face was flushed. "Denby," he pleaded. "What's happening here? Who approved this?"

Denby looked across at Frazer coldly. "I think I'm beginning to see daylight," he said with ominous softness. "Give me that!" He pointed to the requisition on the table before Frazer.

Frazer returned his gaze calmly and slid the papers across the desk.

Rear Admiral Denby accepted them without thanks and quickly flipped over to the last page. His stubby finger raced to the bottom right-hand corner of the page.

"Well?" demanded the Second Sea Lord. "Who approved it?"

"We both did, sir," said Denby flatly. He proferred his superior the requisition.

"Nonsense," gruffed the Chief of Personnel, snatching it from Denby's hands. "What the devil—" He jumped to his feet, taken aback at seeing his own unmistakable scrawl beneath the spindly longhand of Denby. "I don't remember," he began to protest, but he slowly thought the better of it. The rubber-stamp procedures rampant in his department might not bear exposure before so rare an echelon of authority.

The Cabinet Minister presiding at the head of the table had borne the interchange stoically, but his patience was thinning. "At the risk of postponing this interesting intradepartmental strife, could we proceed?"

The Chief of Personnel sat down huffily, trying to ignore the unfriendly look of the Director of Naval Operations.

"If he's here, he's here," announced the civilian. "Let's hear what he's got to say—if you've no objections, Sir John."

The old Admiral of the Fleet sat hunched over by the civilian's right hand. He stared at Frazer with a quizzical expression. He had seen the face before but could not recall where. His lips remained compressed. He shook his snow-white head.

"Carry on then, Frazer," said the Cabinet Minister. He raised his index finger admonishingly. "And do stand easy, will you?"

The tall, spare Scotsman's stiffness melted into respectful informality as he gripped the back of a chair and bent forward conversationally. He studied the highly polished toes of his shoes as if they might somehow hold the preamble he was about to formulate. "I'm in these chambers this morning by invitation—First Lord invited me." He acknowledged the disarmingly somnolent-looking civilian with a curt nod.

"I did, did I, now?" boomed the First Lord, examining a fresh cigar. "When?"

Frazer expanded on the genesis of Admiralty Instruction No. 1117. While he did, the First Lord intermittently quizzed in whispered conference the naval secretary by his side.

"All right, Frazer," the First Lord conceded grudgingly, igniting another cigar. "So?"

"Most of my career has been with the Secretariat, m'lord," Frazer continued confidently. "For over a dozen years I have sailed a desk in the service of His Majesty. How can I possibly aspire to a deck command? If you will permit me, I do have one forte—the ability of organization; and Naval Africa Expedition, as I've chosen to call it, seems to call out for its application."

"Instruction 1117," forcibly interjected the Chief of Personnel after being whispered to by the sullen-faced Denby, "I might point out, First Lord, is an example of Commander Frazer's forte in application." He made no attempt to hide his sarcasm.

"How so?" queried the First Lord. "Explain yourself, Frazer." As Frazer elaborated, the First Lord's grin widened behind his cigar's smoke screen. "Well, then. Let's get back to this African affair."

Frazer rolled on, exasperatingly impervious to the interruptions and diversions, stolidly refusing to alter the measured tread of his proposal. "I see the defeat of the enemy naval squadron on Lake Tanganyika as being two things—90 per cent organization, planning, logistics; and 10 per cent the element of surprise. I am an expert in the first element; as for the second, the element of surprise depends on luck—presuming the usual security measures are being enforced."

Admiral of the Fleet Fisher quietly brooded over the proceedings. Silence was abnormal for the ebullient seventy-three-year-old veteran of a score of major naval successes and as many major appointments. He growled, "You haven't done so badly in the luck department, Frazer; otherwise you wouldn't be here at all."

"Luck, Sir John?" teased the Cabinet Minister. "Or organization?"

For the first time that morning Frazer smiled. "I've had my share of luck, m'lords," he laughed gently, "with the exception of my first posting."

"Go on," prompted Admiral Fisher.

"No doubt, sir," explained Frazer, "you recall Fleet exercises off the Orkneys in the summer of '93—"

Subdued laughter rumbled in some quarter of the room.

"Never mind, Commander Frazer," said the Cabinet Minister, unsuccessfully masking a huge square grin; then he added mysteriously, "That was a bad summer for a number of us, I'm told."

The taciturn Admiral of the Fleet simmered under the askance glances of the Board. "There's a war to be won," he grumbled. "Can't we get down to cases, Frazer?"

"Of course, sir," said Frazer deferentially. "With your permission, sir," he said to the First Lord.

"Proceed!" said the First Lord, leisurely expelling a cone of heavy cigar smoke.

"As I said," said Frazer resuming, "I have been an organizer for almost the entire twenty-two years of my service. Obviously the idea of approving a member of the Secretariat for the task of removing the German naval squadron from Lake Tanganyika is, to say the least, novel to m'lords. But if you please, the task is 90 per cent organizational and only 10 per cent executive, as you will readily see from my definition of the problem." He withdrew from his briefcase a sheaf of typewritten documents and passed them to the principal Board members. "You will readily see, m'lords, the basis for my contention . . . and the soundness of my proposals.

And as to my selection of myself for the post: I simply had more attractive qualifications for this assignment than any other prospect. I would have been imprudent if I had disqualified myself merely because it was I who was doing the selecting." He paused while they perused the documents.

Frazer's presentation had been quietly confident, carefully respectful; but the five lords, their staffs and attendants seemed to hold the entire matter in contempt of the Admiralty, almost as some mild sacrilege. By the ominous inertia of their stony silence they seemed to indicate that they would never soften from the tradition that a man may not question the wisdom of where he is called upon to serve, only that he may not be serving to the limit of his capacity to serve.

"What's all this?" demanded Admiral of the Fleet Fisher, stabbing the sheaf of documents with his forefinger.

"Naval Africa Expedition, m'lord," replied Frazer, "accomplished on paper to the point where the necessary boats ride at anchor on prepared slipways at the Belgian harbor of Albertville—some forty miles athwart Kigoma, the main German base on Lake Tanganyika. From that point on the affair would appear to be a tactical one—a matter we may leave in the hands of the boat commanders."

"Cocky fellow, what?" whispered the Third Sea Lord through his hand to the Fourth Sea Lord.

" 'Athwart,' " chuckled the Fourth Sea Lord guardedly. "I'll wager he had to look it up in *Falconer's*." His reference was to the British bible on nautical matters.

"If m'lords will turn to page three of the brief," continued Frazer, "I should like to expand on this in organizational terms."

"He rather likes that word 'organization,' doesn't he?" observed the Civil Lord, nudging in the ribs the parliamentary and financial secretary.

For half an hour Frazer continued with his exposition.

The venerable body which dictated the broad general uses of British naval power around the entire world was not accustomed to considering the opinions of a mere commander. Had the tall, austere figure before them worn the weatherbeaten countenance that goes with years on the bridge, or had his smart but silent uniform only clinked a little with at least one row of medals, or had he brought with him the flush of even his first investiture at Buckingham Palace—had only one, but preferably all, of these recommendations been his to display, the lords of Admiralty House might possibly have looked upon him with more relish. But neither Commander Ian H. G. Frazer nor his uniform had any of these to favor him. Despite the undeniable logic and soundness of his approach to Naval Africa Expedition, it was regarded by the Board as a bald impertinence that one destitute of the trappings of line-officer prestige should so presume upon them. The braided, beribboned Board was of the Establishment; the individual before them had come up "aft through the hawsehole." In the rigidly structured, cloistered, ofttimes narrow and unjust protocol of the Navy, Frazer just would not do.

"Frazer," said Admiral of the Fleet Fisher, "you have, or seem to have, done a fair job of presenting your case—on paper. But what experience do you have in the intricacies of command? There's that intangible ingredient known as leadership. You may have the men, the material, the plan, even the element of surprise; but without the magic spark of leadership it can all come to naught."

Frazer returned his gaze with sincerity, "I cannot deny, sir, that I lack experience in the area you refer to. But I submit that three-quarters of the success of any undertaking lies in preparation." He rummaged around in the leather briefcase again and withdrew a yellowed newspaper clipping. "You, sir, in fact, made approximately that statement to the press on the occasion of the first Bar to your D.S.O.," Frazer reminded him unemotionally. "It was during the Egyptian war, 1882. As captain of H.M.S. *Inflexible* you bombarded Alexandria and led a naval brigade ashore, thereby considerably shortening the campaign. Quoting from the *Morning Post* of that date, you were reported to have said, 'Initiative be damned. The crew and I planned it all out ten days in advance. Every man jack of us simply did the job we'd trained for.' " Frazer looked up to confront the old admiral.

He concentrated heavily on his fingers saying nothing.

The Third Sea Lord piped up: "If preparation is three-quarters, what's the remaining quarter?"

"Analysis of the men's talents, m'lord," Frazer declared evenly, "then the utilization of those talents in the place where they will do the most good."

"Book talk, Commander, a lot of book talk," snorted the Third Sea Lord.

Frazer shrugged deferentially. "Indeed it is, m'lord—naval textbook talk—from a naval textbook entitled *The Gunnery Manual of the Fleet*. It was used extensively during my years at the Royal Naval College. The author is now the First Sea Lord of the Admiralty."

The Third Sea Lord wilted.

Admiral of the Fleet Fisher exploded from his solemnity with a laugh at the vice-admiral's embarrassment. "No offense taken, Willie," he mumbled, shaking his head and stoking his pipe. "I'd forgotten about the bally thing m'self."

"Nowhere do I see any provision for fuel," observed the Fourth Sea Lord, the vice-admiral and Chief of Supplies and Transport.

"There are two chief reasons for this, m'lord," explained Frazer. "One is that we have been unable yet to select the type of vessel we intend to use. We have, of course, several in mind. It would be imprudent to embark on a search for vessels until the scheme had been approved by m'lordships. Secondly, whatever the amount of fuel we need, it may not be necessary for *us* to bring it along at all. We simply acquaint the Belgian government of our intentions and allow them the privilege of supplying all the fuel and supplies while we are at Albertville. In return, we promise to restore them as masters of the lake."

"Any reason why we can't manage that?" inquired the First Lord, contentedly drawing on his cigar.

The Civil Lord frowned. "You never know with these Continentals, but there's no harm in trying."

The First Lord's eyes scanned the faces of the men around the table; then he motioned with cigar in hand. "That'll be all, Commander Frazer."

Frazer came to attention and saluted smartly. He retrieved his briefcase, turned about and left the room. Wait till I tell Tommy, he thought.

No sooner had the massive oak doors closed than the Chief of Personnel exclaimed, "Absolutely absurd. Quite out of the question."

The First Lord scribbled something on a pad. "Why do you feel that way?"

"Why?" he asked haughtily. "Drake himself couldn't pull it off. Don't forget, he's been with the Secretariat all his life. Besides, I'm damned if I like the way he's done this right under my nose—qualifying himself under that new regulation and all that."

The First Lord held up three sheets of paper and remarked, "Under your nose? This is your signature, is it not, accepting him for general line duty? Come, now. You signed it a month ago. Surely you should have spoken up then."

"Dammit, that was the week I had the blasted measles," he gruffed.

"Recalling that we lost a cruiser and two destroyers along the Heligoland Bight that week," teased the First Lord, "could it possibly have been German measles?"

The entire company laughed.

In his manner the usually volatile Admiral of the Fleet could sometimes combine the gravity of an undertaker with the judicial demeanor of a High Court judge. He sat forward in his chair and tapped the tips of his fingers together. "I have no quarrel over the propriety of Commander Frazer's transfer from the Secretariat to general duties. But can we afford to lose an officer of such proven administrative ability to such an improbable—possibly disastrous —venture? I dare say there are a score of men eminently able and willing, I might add, to undertake a proceeding of this dimension."

"Sir John, that there are such able men I have no doubt," conceded the First Lord. "That there are such willing men—well, show them to me."

"But, sir," contested the recently deflated Third Sea Lord, the Controller," "he talks glibly about vessels. What vessels, I would ask? What armament? What tonnage? What sort of weapons? And may I point out, gentlemen, to the variables of size of unit and weight of weapons, there must be added a third: the size and power of the enemy. Where is his intelligence estimate?"

The Naval Secretary interjected deferentially, "If you'll permit me, Admiral." He flipped through several pages and ran his thumb heavily down the gutter of Frazer's brief and commenced reading.

"Enemy vessels include *Kingani* and *Pangani,* sister ships, each 53 tons, 55 feet, 7 knots, 37-millimeter Hotchkiss pom-pom mounted in bow, range 2,600 yards . . . *Hedwig von Wissman,* light, passenger vessel, 70 feet, too weak to carry anything heavier than pom-pom, 37-millimeter Hotchkiss pom-pom for'd, range 2,600 yards, 1½-inch gun aft, 360-degree traverse . . . *Graf von Gotson,* 1,500 tons, 200 feet, 8 knots, armored troopship, capacity 900, 37-millimeter Hotchkiss pom-pom, one 22-pounder, two 4.1-inch guns salvaged from *Königsberg*—"

"The *Königsberg!*" thundered the First Sea Lord. "By God, how'd they manage that?"

The German battle cruiser *Königsberg* had been at sea in the Indian Ocean. She vanished the day war was declared. For weeks she ravaged British merchant shipping. Finally the Navy hounded her up a German East African river where she ran aground. Nine months later her crew blew her up.

The civilian finally broke the silence. "Read on."

". . . *Graf von Gotson* is greatly superior to anything we could mount in terms of range and weight of metal. . . . Belgian support is limited to *Alexandre Delcommune,* unarmed lake steamer, 90 tons . . . also unarmed motorboats *Netta, Tenton, Vedette, Dix Tonnes.* Belgians planning to build 1,500-ton lake steamer to rival *Gotson* . . . so far have got no further than the name, *Baron Dhanis.* They are approximately 1,300 miles by caravan train from their supply base on the Atlantic Ocean. The main enemy base is Kigoma, 800 miles by rail from his main supply base at Dar es Salaam. We cannot hope to match him ton for ton or gun for gun. Our superiority can be in the element of surprise. It will be our only superiority. . . . That's it, sir," concluded the naval secretary.

At that moment the doors of the chamber parted and a youthful lieutenant entered. He handed a naval signal to the First Lord, saluted briskly and left.

The First Lord perused it for several seconds. "Just been handed the latest report from Operations," he said gravely. "The German First Cruiser Squadron slipped through our North Sea patrols in the small hours of the morning." He looked up from the paper, his dimpled face pale and drawn, his blue eyes dim. "They're shelling our coast. The towns of Hartlepool, Whitby and Scarborough. Civilian casualties are feared to be high."

"Then why waste time with trivia?" protested the aged Admiral of the Fleet. "This thing's absurd." He rose. "Let's get to the War Room immediately."

The others gathered up the papers before them.

"Pray, gentlemen, your opinions on this quickly," said the First Lord, firmly laying aside the signal, looking at the First Sea Lord.

The Admiral of the Fleet shook his head.

"And you, sir," asked the First Lord of each of the four Sea Lords.

Two were against—the First and Second, the seniors; two were for—the Third and Fourth, the juniors. A negative ruling was inevitable.

In the long still silence of the Board Room there was no noise but the occasional creaking of a chair. The thin winter air outside carried the clangor of Big Ben to the ears of those assembled. It was noon. That same institution had regulated the proceedings at this table for centuries, had almost seemed to set the tenor of the assemblies in the past. That morning the bell in the clock tower of the Houses of Parliament rang dull and bleak. From the Board Room walls William IV and Nelson, fresh from his Nile victory, looked down understandingly.

"M'lords," began the First Lord somberly, "I can see that some of us have no stomach for this undertaking. Others find some merit in it. I need not remind you of the fortune which has befallen us in the many spheres wherein His Majesty's forces—not merely the Royal Navy—are presently committed. We may not detract from the success of the enemy. The future is heavy with foreboding. The British public quietly broods. Impressions are unfavorable to the Admiralty. We cannot bring home to the outside world the vastness of the seas or the intense exertions which the Navy is making in so

65

many areas. After more than four months of war and several serious losses we have nothing to show on the other side. Nor may we answer convincingly the question 'What is the Navy doing?' A prime function of defense has been imposed upon us. Thus the danger arises of our being driven into a defensive naval strategy and habit of mind. I am under the obligation of rupturing this defensive obsession—by searching for every conceivable chance of counter-offensive. Naval Africa Expedition represents such a chance." He began to assemble the documents on the table before him. "It would be a venture which, in both the slim chance of success and the singular effort demanded of its members, hinging solely on the element of surprise—for who in his right mind would try it?—would be in the magnificent traditions of the naval service." He looked directly at the senior naval member of the Board. "Utmost Fish, Sir John. Have Plans Division assist this singular officer in launching the enterprise at the earliest possible moment. Time is not on his side: the African rains care nothing for him or us." He walked to the wooden-paneled desk of Lord Nelson near the fireplace. It was 5 feet 4 inches tall, Nelson's height, and since his day the minimum height for enlistment in the Royal Navy. On it he signed his authorization of the expedition.

The following day the head of Plans Division, Department of Naval Operations, was handed a memorandum from the Deputy Chief of Naval Staff, setting forth Naval Africa Expedition. A hand-written note attached to the official memorandum read: "Frazer personally will select the members of the expedition. However, since he is clearly not equipped to manage anything but the most rudimentary naval matters, some competent military engineer must be recruited. Frazer will, for the benefit of the naval service, be in nominal command of the operation. (This is not part of the official record.)"

The note was unsigned, but the head recognized the handwriting. It was as good as an official order.

5

It was July, 1915. The African winter was waning, but to the Europeans in the Belgian Congo village of Fungurume it was summer. Mercilessly the orange orb glared on their pale necks.

A double set of rusty railway tracks snaked through a cluster of straw kraals. Here the rail traveler up the African boot got out and walked.

A huge locomotive shunted half a dozen goods wagons into position. The lazy air quickened with the chatter of men, the drone of machines and the stentorian bellowing of orders. Occasionally the locomotive blasted off steam, stampeding the gaping natives back to their kraals.

The fair-skinned men in the topees, khaki uniforms and puttees worked at a moderate pace that never seemed to slacken. The stacks of crates and piles of equipment pyramided as the day wore on. Sweat streamed down faces. It mixed with a brown gauze of dust that clung close to the ground. A slight breeze would have done it, but no breeze stirred. A few shed their topees and were roundly cursed by a squarely built, red-faced man with three stripes on his shirt-sleeve. He did not mind the sleeves up, he warned them, but "anybody caught without his topper'll have his arse kicked."

The big sergeant had worn a path from the railway siding to a copse a quarter of a mile away. There a single tent gleamed stiff and white in the sun. Approaching it for the umpteenth time that day, the sergeant almost bumped into Commander Frazer, in bush jacket and shorts.

"Sir," said the sergeant, "stores and gear'll be dumped within the hour—then brew-up for tea."

"Very good," murmured Frazer.

The two stood outside the tent, looking toward the siding.

"Manage the tractors tonight too, Sergeant?"

"Think the chaps are just about all in for today, sir. I was hoping we might get our heads together on it tonight. Lot of weight in one of those things."

"You're right. They've been slogging all day. But we must make every use of daylight." Frazer's tone held a quiet urgency.

"Of course, sir." Smith removed his topee and mopped his face and neck with a damp handkerchief. "Is it always muggy as this, sir?"

Frazer bit on the stem of his pipe. "How long have we been in Africa, Smith?" he asked matter-of-factly. Frazer raised his left hand, running his thumb over the other four fingers, counting aloud: "—twelve, thirteen, fourteen, fifteen. Fifteen days today, isn't it?"

"Fifteen, twenty-five, a hundred and five," groaned Smith. "Swear I'll never get used to it."

"Don't worry, Sergeant. They told me the first seven years are the worst."

A babble of anxious voices from the direction of the siding brought the exchange to an end. The laboring soldiers had circled around a figure on the ground.

"Better have a look-see, Sergeant," suggested Frazer.

"All right, all right, what's it this time?" Smith demanded as he strode toward the group.

The men shuffled to one side as Smith entered the circle. One

68

man was lying on his face at full length on the ground. His topee had rolled to one side, exposing his pink neck.

Smith squatted by the unconscious man, grabbed a handful of tunic and pulled him over on his back. He thumbed back the unconscious soldier's eyelids and peered in. He checked the pulse. He looked up. "Peterson, down by the tent gear and water bags, the stretcher. On the double! Four of you stay here," he ordered. "The rest of you back on the job."

Peterson raced back with the stretcher.

"A hand, you men," snapped Smith, placing his hands expertly under the shoulders of the body. The others helped with the feet. The four lifted the stretcher and walked off.

The four young soldiers had never carried a stretcher before. The unconscious man's arms flopped out on each side like a rag doll's. Smith folded them in. He pulled out a sodden handkerchief and daubed away the moisture on the man's forehead. He looked back and saw that the man's topee lay in the dust. He jerked his thumb to a soldier tagging alongside. "His topper," he shot. "Walk in step, you baskets," he shouted to the stretcher-bearers.

One of them said in a singsong Welsh accent, "Sergeant, do you think it's going to be like this all the way?"

"Passing out like bloomin' females, you mean?" said Smith, sniffing contemptuously.

"Well, yes, Sergeant."

"My first time out here, myself. Don't ask me. Living high, wide and handsome on an ocean liner for the last three weeks, eating your fill and sleeping your lives away, that's what ails you all. Can't expect laboring not to get you down . . . and not in this ruddy sun, either."

One of the four bearers spat an oath.

Smith pretended he had not heard. It was part of a sergeant's job to know when to take a man on and when not to. The CO could make big speeches about policy and tactics and such like, but sergeants got the things done. It was a sergeant's job to translate, to interpret.

Smith had led companies in Flanders, almost 100 per cent regulars. They were the professionals a sergeant liked to work with. No trouble at all. You knew how much they could take, so you knew just how much you could demand. Sure, they moaned—moaned just as much as the conscripts he had on hand for this job—but in regulars it was a healthy sign. The time to worry was when they took slogging through the mud, slush and corruption with the neutrality of a donkey flat on its arse being lambasted to its feet with a two-by-four.

Hardly a year had passed by since he had run into that same bloodless neutrality. The mud, slush and corruption had been at Neuve Chapelle and Loos where his company had flung itself against the cruel barbs of the German frontline trenches. The "Old Contemptibles" had wandered aimlessly back in the direction of their own trenches, shoeless in the slushy mire of a French winter, blind with insensibility, bristling with that neutrality, that negation of the human spirit, that incubates in the warm, spilled blood of close friends. Yes, it was a healthy sign. Private Devlin's monosyllabic curse was good luck.

The aid station was the first in a row of five bungalow tents that flanked the headquarters tent. As they approached they were met by the short, slight figure of Cavanaugh. His shirt-sleeves were rolled up. The stretcher quartet halted by the tent entrance. The doctor casually eased back the eyelids of the man on the stretcher. He chatted lightly, his serious fingers gently exploring the inside of the limp wrist. "Been baking in the sun?"

"I think so, sir," said Smith.

"You think what?" Cavanaugh inquired.

"I think he's been baking in the sun, sir," repeated the sergeant.

"Hmm. I don't believe you're done yet," said Cavanaugh to the youth, now showing signs of life. "Maybe we ought to put you out for another fifteen minutes—Perkins, is it? All right, inside with him."

They maneuvered the stretcher into the tent and lifted Perkins onto a wooden cot.

"And now I'm afraid I'll have to shoo you all outside. Can't expect me to drive out any evil spirits while you fellows clutter up the exit."

70

The tent cleared but for the sick man, the doctor and the sergeant. Cavanaugh put an arm around Perkins and helped him into a sitting position. He handed him two salt tablets. "Sergeant," he said, nodding toward the medicine cabinet, "fetch me a tin of water, please. You know," he said, accepting the enamel mug and handing it to Perkins, "I just had an idea."

"What's that, sir?" asked Sergeant Smith.

"You military people are generally so conservative. I've hit on something for getting us over that 6,000-foot plateau everyone's so concerned about."

"Something the commander's already working on, by any chance?" Smith asked conversationally.

"No," said the doctor mysteriously, easing Perkins back into the supine, wringing out a wet compress and applying it to the youth's forehead. "No, this is definitely something quite new. Actually the only reason I mention it is that perhaps you can help me iron out some of the wrinkles before we turn it over to Commander Frazer."

"I'll be glad to do all I can, sir," Smith promised fervently.

"Young Perkins, believe it or not, gave me the idea not two minutes ago. . . . Smith, if we were to feed the chaps yeast and then set them out there to bake, they'd be self-rising, wouldn't they?" He advanced the proposition with clinical gravity.

"Somehow I don't think the commander'll buy it, sir," said Smith seriously. "I see one big flaw in it already."

"You do? What's that?"

"Well, for one thing, yeast might get the men up, but what about all the gear? The engines? The boats?"

Cavanaugh's face fell in mock disappointment. He affected a tone of hurt. "I did say, you remember, there were a few wrinkles to be ironed out. I haven't really thought the thing through at this point, but I'm not going to dismiss it just because of a few silly traction engines and motorboats. Tell you what. Give me a few days to develop it, all right? Then we'll see the old man."

"A few days it is, sir. And now if you'll excuse me, sir, I've a few sentries to post."

"Righto, Smith," said the doctor, grinning.

Smith walked out of the aid tent and into the early evening smiling. He headed for the other side of the Fungurume camp. When Smith walked into the NCO's tent, Chief Petty Officer Stokes was reclining on a cot in his underwear. "Got the right idea there, Charlie," said Smith, pulling off his shirt and falling onto his cot. "Just what the doctor ordered." He spent some time yawning and stretching.

" 'Ey, mate," said Stokes, "don't get too comfortable over there. 'Ow about postin' a few chaps around so the wogs don't run off with all our gear?"

"Got another forty minutes yet," sighed Smith, lying back and clasping his hands behind his head, his eyes closed.

The two lay in silence.

"Andy," said Stokes.

"Mm."

"Don't you think this is all a little bloody silly?"

Smith's eyes opened. "What? Having to mount guard so these black fellows don't steal us blind?"

"Not that," grunted Stokes. "This 'ole bloody expedition like."

"Off on that again, are you?"

"Just thinkin' out loud."

"Well, don't think too loud, Charlie. They'll hear you on the far side. Don't think they'd like it."

"I'd like to bet there's a lot o' them thinkin' the same thing, if the truth be known."

Smith stretched again. "Bit funny coming from you, Charlie. You being Navy—and a volunteer too."

"S'pose you're right, mate."

"Why'd you volunteer, anyway?"

"Sometimes I really wonder myself. I'm too bloomin' old for this adventure rot. Hard to say, really. S'pose it was 'cos 'e asked me. 'E 'as a way of askin'. . . . You'll find out, Andy."

"Sergeant Smith, captain'd like to see you," announced an orderly, poking his head through the tent flap.

"All right, all right. I'll be right there, tell him." Smith made no move to rise after the orderly had left. The tone of his reply had been one of annoyance. His was more than the annoyance that comes from having a nap interrupted. He unlaced his fingers, pulled his knees up jackknife style and pivoted around on his rear end so that his raised booted feet were over the side of the cot. He stamped them noisily on the hard ground. "Wonder what Hump wants," he muttered, reaching for his shirt.

Smith dressed in slow silence. He picked up his topee, breathed on the brass cap badge and rubbed it briskly on his sleeve.

"Think you was goin' down to the Old Frog and Toe, you would," said Stokes.

"Not tonight, Charlie," grunted Smith as he gave himself a final check in the shaving mirror hanging from the tent pole. "Maybe tomorrow night. . . . Where're you hiding your boot brush, Chief?" he said, frowning at his boots.

" 'Ere, mate. Catch." Stokes tossed him a brush.

Smith spat expertly a couple of times on the toes of his boots and buffed them into the black brilliance that lay hidden beneath a thin film of dust. This was about as much a concession to Humphreys as he intended to make. "Don't wait up for me," he shot over his shoulder as he stepped through the tent flap.

The headquarters tent was empty when Smith arrived. He removed his topee and smoothed down the little hair he had, wondering how long he would have to wait. He stood by Humphreys' desk for a few minutes, then started pacing back and forth, his topee in his left hand, his right free for the salute. In the five minutes that followed he had time to see how Humphreys had got himself a typewriter, a big desk blotter, an inkstand, an ivory horn full of freshly pointed pencils and an "in-pending-out" basket. Flush with the top right-hand edge of the desk blotter lay a stack of War Office Quarterly Punishments forms. Frazer's table was a model of simplicity: a large Admiralty chart of southern Africa and a three-eight Webley. Smith was getting impatient. He walked outside, thinking that perhaps it might be best to wait out there. As he did so, he spotted the huge figure of Captain Humphreys striding toward him. Smith saluted as the captain drew within a few paces. Humphreys touched his swagger stick to the brim of his topee and ducked through the tent opening in one movement. Smith followed him in.

73

Humphreys sat down at his card table, adjusted his blotter a fraction of an inch and looked up at the sergeant.

"You wanted to see me, sir?" asked Smith.

"Smith, when are you going to learn to remember regulations? You know a sergeant is supposed to be an example to his men, don't you?" grated Humphreys.

Smith was visibly stunned. "I'm not quite sure I know what you mean, sir."

"If there's anything I detest in a subordinate, it's evasiveness. Of course you do! What's the regulation on wearing headpieces?"

"Oh, you mean I wasn't wearing my—"

"You damn well know what I mean."

"Well, sir, I'd been waiting in here for you and I just stepped out to—"

"The matter's closed, Smith. Do you understand?"

"Yes, sir."

Humphreys had been staring at a point above Smith's nose and directly between his eyes. It was an old trick. Psychologically it made the adversary feel inferior and ill at ease. For the longest time he fiddled with his toothbrush mustache, saying nothing. He took great pains to extract a gold cigarette case from his shirt pocket, select precisely the cigarette he wanted, light it and inhale luxuriously. Finally he pursed his lips, allowed the smoke to stream out of his nostrils, rested his elbows on the table top and flicked the imaginary ash from his cigarette into an ashtray. "And now, Smith."

Smith stood silently at attention. He had run into types like Humphreys before. You never knew just how to handle them. You had to experiment to find the most effective defense.

"Smith, not only do you seem to be flaunting King's Regulations regarding the wearing of the uniform in tropical climates, but you apparently have taken it upon yourself to ignore company orders of the day. And, Smith!"

"Yes, sir?"

"Don't tell me you don't know what I'm talking about."

"I'm afraid I don't, sir."

"You're not really *afraid*, Smith, are you? Not really *afraid*, eh?"

74

"No."

"No what, Smith?"

"No, sir, I'm not afraid."

"Pity."

Humphreys pulled several papers off the top of his correspondence basket and thumbed through them. "Ever seen this, Sergeant?" Smith looked down from "eyes ahead" and rotated the piece of paper so that he could read it from his side of the table. It was a carbon copy of an original headed: Naval Africa Expedition. Underneath were the words: Order of the Day, and the date: 2 July, 1915. What followed was a roster of names. He recognized it quickly. He himself had made up the penciled draft from which it had been typed. "Yes, sir," he said, "I'm familiar with it."

"Read me this," ordered Humphreys, indicating a particular passage with the tip of his swagger stick.

Smith read aloud, "The following other ranks will parade by the flagpole at 1700 hours for Parade of the Guard: Henry, Nicholson, McConnell—"

"That's all, Smith," interrupted Humphreys, looking at his wristwatch. "It's twenty-seven minutes past five now. In case the arithmetic may tax your faculties too severely, I'd remind you that this should have taken place twenty-seven minutes ago."

The captain resumed fiddling with his mustache, allowing enough time for the reprimand to sink in. His red, windburned face wore a look of suppressed exultation. "What do you have to say for yourself, Smith?"

"Nothing, sir."

"You disappoint me, Smith." It was true. He wanted to get Smith going. It was more fun that way. "Is there an excuse for this?" He knew there was no way in which Smith could worm out of this neglect of duty.

"Sir, I have an explanation," said Smith evenly.

"You may give me your *excuse* verbally now, Smith, but have an original and one carbon of it on my desk by tomorrow morning," declared Humphreys officially.

"Begging the captain's pardon, but it's an *explanation*—not an excuse."

75

"Don't quibble with me!" Humphreys thundered, rapping the camp table with his swagger stick. There was something in the sergeant's tone he did not like. "Now, then, Smith."

"Well, sir. It's quite simple, really. We crossed back over the thirty-degrees-east-of-Greenwich line—oh, I'd say about first light yesterday morning. It must be that you forgot to set your watch back an hour. . . . Will that be all, sir?"

Humphreys' face flooded with hot, angry blood. The pressure puffed the blood vessels on the side of his neck and temples to the diameter of heavy cord. So engorged were his eyeballs that he found it difficult to see. A trapdoor had sprung open and he was plummeting down into a red sea of humiliation. There he remained, wallowing in a thick curd of viciousness and resentment toward the man who stood so poised and self-assured in front of him.

The hate was still spewing to his extremities when sentry was posted and the Union Jack lowered and removed for the night.

76

6

"Gentlemen, you all know why we're here. Some of you've been in on things from the very beginning; some of you haven't. Just to be sure we all know as much—or as little—as possible about what's up ahead, I'm going to take the liberty of a brief recap. For security reasons we've had to circulate some conflicting stories."

There were a few audible groans in the headquarters tent. Some of Frazer's audience of seven officers turned to one another with eloquent shrugs. Others perked up with the fresh enthusiasm of men who have just been told the post has come in.

He sat on the edge of a camp table. He crossed one leg over the other and laced his fingers over one knee. "The Hun's on Lake Tanganyika in strength," he said. "It's our job to sweep him off it. It doesn't sound much, but there are a few points which could prove troublesome. You've all heard that the Navy has no craft up there at all—otherwise you can be sure we wouldn't be going to all this bother hauling *Mimi* and *Toutou* along. What you may *not* know is that the Belgian marine people don't have any either."

"Cripes," groaned Sublieutenant Bannister, *Toutou*'s boyish-looking commander.

The others remained silent. Bannister had articulated their feelings succinctly.

"Does that mean, sir," continued Bannister, "that—"

"Bannister," urged Frazer gently, "would you mind holding the questions till I finish?" He began to light his pipe.

"Now, where was I?" said Frazer. "Ah, yes. When we get *Mimi* and *Toutou* on the water—and in case any of you have any doubts, that's precisely what we intend to do—the Allies will have the sum total of two warships on Lake Tanganyika. Small ones admittedly, but warships nevertheless." His pipe was drawing miserably. He excused himself momentarily while he probed inquisitively in the bowl with a pencil point.

Mimi's commander, Sublieutenant Dodkins, whispered to Bannister by his side, "I wish he'd bloody well get on with it."

"All in good time," Bannister whispered back. "We've got all the time in the world."

"You've been grossly misinformed, Bannister," observed Frazer pointedly.

Bannister's fair-skinned face reddened.

"Time's not on our side at all," continued Frazer. "I mean the rains. Once it starts, it pours for weeks on end. Solid sheets of it. Dr. Cavanaugh's been in Katanga before. He'll tell you all about it. Little streams even become swollen torrents. Everything's swept away in one mad rush." He took the pipe from his mouth. The stem described little arcs in the air. "When it's all over, there isn't even a semblance of a road or track left." He paused again, taking long powerful pulls on his pipe, experimenting with the draw by blocking and unblocking the bowl with a matchbox. He unfolded a map on the table and motioned with his pipe. "Can you all fill in around here?"

The seven circled the camp table.

"Here's the lake." He pointed to a long sausage of blue on the chart. "And here *we* are." He made a heavy cross southwest of the lake with a stubby pencil. He placed his thumb on the cross and stretched his hand so that his index finger reached a black dot midway up the west coast of the lake. "That's Albertville, our destination." He held up his hand, thumb and forefinger about four inches apart. "This, gentlemen, is 500 miles, give or take a few. The first 150 of that will be Capt. Humphreys' responsibility— virgin terrain all the way. He's going to hack a road through it to Sankisia. The Belgians have a railhead there. At Sankisia we rail the gear the twenty-odd miles to our next objective—the Lualaba River."

The officers peered intently at the map as Frazer's pipestem moved northward along the railway from Sankisia until it intersected an east-west tributary of the Lualaba at Bukama. "From Bukama the Lualaba flows northward and parallel to the lake. The lake's a hundred miles or so off to our right. Naturally we'll take maximum advantage of the river. It'll float us to Kabalo. The Belgians have rail facilities laid on there. From Kabalo it's a train ride to Albertville. That's the broad picture. . . . Any questions?"

Frazer puffed casually on his pipe and surveyed his audience. "C'mon, Bannister, I couldn't keep you quiet a moment ago."

"Well, sir, how strong is Jerry on the lake exactly?"

"We can't know *exactly* at this point. We have to assume about half a dozen gunboats and assorted craft."

"And armament, sir?"

The commander did not answer directly. It was his pipe again. He concentrated on the bowl. "Again we can't say exactly, but we must assume they can at least match our three-pounders. In all likelihood they're mounting sixes—possibly even twelves."

"I see, sir," replied Bannister, pretending that he did. He was not so junior an officer that he could not see the full implications of the commander's statement. Our two three-pounders against their sixes —or maybe twelves? Could be like fighting off a rifleman with a slingshot, he thought.

"Question, sir," announced a freckle-faced boy with one pip of an army second lieutenant on his shoulder straps. He was Humphreys' engineering aide.

"Yes, Martin."

"What's our strength in 'other ranks'?"

"Naval plus army?"

"The lot, sir." Martin nodded.

"Naval?" began Frazer, running down a list of names on a clipboard he held. ". . . five, six, seven. Seven naval; thirteen Army," he announced as if there might be some who would doubt him. "Twenty in all, Martin—plus ourselves makes twenty-eight in all."

"Then, sir," Martin began with the cautiousness of a solicitor before the bar and with the deference to authority such an occasion would demand, "can twenty men really hack through 150 miles of bush before the rains, never mind reach Albertville? I mean, sir, is it realistic? Is it?"

"Oswald," said Frazer, "I think that's your bailiwick."

The spindly stool which had been enduring the large engineering officer's weight squeaked with relief as Humphreys rose. He bypassed Frazer to direct his remarks to the young second lieutenant. "May I remind you, Martin, that I'm the engineering officer here, and if Commander Frazer's grand plan calls for us to 'hack' through the bush, then that is what we shall do." He looked around to observe the reaction.

No one seemed anxious to challenge Humphreys' authority or his ill-concealed belligerence, except the red-haired Martin.

"But twenty men, sir," pleaded Martin. "Can twenty men handle it? And the rains can't be more than a few weeks off."

Humphreys resented the other's persistence. His jaw muscles tensed and untensed noticeably. His whole demeanor was that of a quiet, disciplined martyrdom. "Didn't they teach you to count at Sandhurst, Martin?" he snapped.

"I'm afraid I don't quite follow you, sir," said Martin blankly.

"They certainly seem to have overdone the officer-and-gentleman code in your case," announced Humphreys heavily. "*Twenty* men, you say? Martin, on this one *everybody* lends a hand. I'm counting on twenty-seven of us at least. I'm hoping *you'll* be sporting enough to lend us a hand."

Bannister's guffaw detonated Dodkins. Instantly the whole tent exploded with laughter. Martin joined in cautiously.

"All right, all right, as you were," called Frazer finally. "This is a staff meeting, not a circus. . . . Now, where was I?"

Since the meeting had begun Cavanaugh had been observing from his precarious position on a shaky footlocker in the rear. "Ian," he prompted, "you just about had us on the lake."

"Yes, I had. Thanks, Tommy. Well, to get on with it. When we do get to Albertville and look across the lake, we may even be able to see Jerry. It's Jerry country on the other side—all the way to the Indian Ocean. They like to call it German East Africa." He returned to the map. "Think of it as perhaps a bar of soap you're holding." He held up a clenched fist. "The fingers represent our troops in Kenya; the heel of my hand, the colonials from Northern Rhodesia. Squeeze—and out pops the soap. No need to tell you who that's supposed to be—and right into the Indian Ocean with it! Our military people have tried this maneuver in the past, joining hands along the eastern shore of the lake, but a certain Lieutenant Commander Zimmer sees to it that his ships' guns cut our lads to shreds each time we try it. Attend to Herr Zimmer. Those are our orders. Any questions? If not, that's it for this morning."

The officers spilled out of the tent into the hot dry noon air.

"Tommy, do you have a moment?" called Frazer.

Cavanaugh paused by the tent flag. "Moments have I, yes; but days perhaps, just one. It be the moments, though, that count whene'er we're alone," he announced grandly with a theatrical gesture.

"Keats?" Frazer inquired.

"Cavanaugh," declared the doctor.

"So that's what you're doing when you're supposed to be counting the aspirin, eh?"

"Aspirin of the soul, if you wish. You wouldn't rob me of the pleasure of making my aspirin as palatable as I know how, surely?"

"*You* prescribe aspirin as you see fit, old man. *My* job is to get this lot on the lake. Actually that's what I wanted to talk to you about."

"Aspirin?"

"Aspirin, plus. Plus quinine, morphia, the whole bag of tricks. How well are we stocked? Can we handle whatever comes up?"

"It's East African cattle country, the stamping ground of the tsetse. God knows some of them are big enough to stamp. When they do start—well, you know as well as I do there's not a bloody pill made that'll rouse a man with sleeping sickness."

"Yes, I know. Keep mum on that sort of thing, Tommy. The less they know about it, the less they'll worry about it."

The doctor stood by the captain's table, hands thrust deep into the pockets of his bush jacket. "Damned poor preventive medicine," he said pleasantly.

Frazer smiled understandingly and laid a hand on his shoulder. "Time enough for all that when we reach the lake, old man."

"Come, come, Ian," chided Cavanaugh playfully, "if I don't start right in with it, you might have enough chaps around to hold a wake—and not a man jack more."

"Aren't you a trifle morbid this morning? Wakes, no less. Where's that eternal Celtic optimism?"

Cavanaugh wagged his index finger in the manner of a parent admonishing his child. "Oh, it's there, all right, but there's been something added to the prescription ever since I chatted with those tropical lads in Jo'burg."

"Such as?" queried Frazer.

"Tincture of realism," replied Cavanaugh, flipping through the pages of a small, black notebook that he had taken from his shirt pocket. "Morphia—no worries," he read. "Quinine—enough to float a battleship. Barbiturates—enough so that none of us will lose any sleep over—"

"All right, Tommy, out with it." Frazer rose from his seat on the camp table, crossed to his slightly built friend and folded his arms across his chest. "No need for you and me to fence."

"Agreed," said Cavanaugh. "We've been friends too long for that." He resumed paging through his book again. Slowly he looked up, his brows wrinkled inquisitively. "What's the most important thing in the world to you right at this time?"

"Getting to the bloody lake, of course," responded Frazer instantly.

"You may as well know. They tell me we couldn't have timed it better if we'd tried. The anopheles and the tsetse've been procreating their ugly heads off this year. Malaria and encephalitis, Ian. A

82

whacking great packet of it we'll be walking right into." He re-turned to scrutinizing the notebook. "The bastards seem to thrive on you—especially when you're tired and hungry, if you follow me."

Frazer examined the bowl of his pipe in thoughtful silence. Finally he asked, "How's your patient?"

"Perkins?" shot Cavanaugh. He snapped his fingers. "Bad case of heatstroke and he bashed his elbow on the way down. Glad you reminded me. I've a dressing of his to change." He smiled and ducked through the tent flap.

7

On the fourth day up from Fungurume Smith screamed. . . .

Ahead of Naval Africa Expedition the Kundelungu Mountains squatted. They might have gone around—but would not. There was no time. The sky could vomit its waters tomorrow.

Humphreys was carving a route straight up the contused hypotenuse of waist-high brush and random tree life stunted by the parched soil and bedrock bald in patches or ruptured into cairns of shrapnel.

Too often these grew huge and stopped forward movement, veering Humphreys aside from his obsession with directness. Repeatedly they jacknifed to halt the line of march, the steam tractors and the trailers they towed. The tirelessly imaginative Humphreys quickly conjured the solution: He disconnected trailer from tractor, drove tractor ahead a distance, hooked one end of a steel cable to the trailer, the other end to the steel flywheel of the tractor. Once the flywheel rotated, the cable wrapped around it and reeled forward the unwilling trailer.

For the sixth time that day they were "cabling." Humphreys and Frazer stood on a huge carbuncle of rock and surveyed the scene below.

"Cable away!" roared Humphreys with the wind.

The slow chug of the steam engine raced to a fast pulse. The cable tautened. Seven tons of boat and trailer balked. The engine chugged. The men clumped around to watch. Several laid a hand to the steering dolly to steer the trailer around the elbow bend.

Lieutenant Martin stood halfway between tractor and trailer close to the cable. Alternately he looked back over his shoulder to check the revolution of the flywheel, then forward to direct the steering. Five yards in front of the trailer the lumpy terrain fissured off at right angles to the line of march—the narrow, dried-up bed of one of a hundred streams which live furiously during the rains but die with their passing. Abruptly, the dolly wheels wedged fast in the fissure. The trailer's forward movement jerked to a halt—but the flywheel of solid steel still turned.

"All hands to the trailer!" bellowed Humphreys from his vantage point.

Down below, Smith and the men grunted and strained to execute the command. Without warning the steel shaft of the steering dolly kicked ninety degrees to the left. The knot of cursing soldiers exploded as if a grenade had gone off in their midst.

Martin sensed danger. "Stop the engine! Stop the engine!" The wind blew his frantic order back rudely into his smooth, frightened face.

Smith pulled himself to his feet, winded. He looked up and gulped.

Martin pistoned across the twenty yards to the tractor.

Smith tingled with exquisite horror. Before his eyes the first fine hairs of braided cable sprang apart.

It was then that Smith screamed. "For Christ's sake, duck, sir!"

It was too late. The cable twanged apart. All heads jerked up. All saw the cable curl back like an angler's line and entwine itself around Martin's body. Instantly the tractor engine surged upward to a runaway hammering that exploded in oblivion.

Frazer and Humphreys scrambled from their rocky knoll and hopscotched to the scene.

Humphreys dashed toward the tractor. Under an angry white cloud of hissing steam the steel beast tried to hide its scattered entrails. He surveyed the mess. "Incompetent bunch of swine," he rapped. "Set the whole damn thing back weeks." He grabbed a handrail and pulled himself powerfully up onto what had been the operating platform. The plates had buckled under the tremendous impact of the explosion. The heavy flywheel had ensnarled itself in tangled skeins of steel cable and had ripped itself off the crankshaft. The big Parsons boiler resembled a used toothpaste tube.

The engineering officer climbed down from the useless hulk of machinery. His massive frame vibrated with anger. His vitals were corroding with the knowledge of what this would do to his meticulously laid timetable. With long, purposeful strides he propelled himself toward the trailer where Frazer knelt by Martin's side.

"You're going to be all right, Martin," soothed Frazer.

The others stood around in a circle, gaping at the grotesque figure of the sandy-haired, freckled young subaltern as he lay on his back with phlegmy, bright-colored blood bubbling in his nostrils.

Cavanaugh hastily examined the raw furrowed flesh generously leaking blood into his shredded khaki shirt. "How's that stretcher coming?"

"Here it is, sir," said Smith as two anxious-looking soldiers broke through the circle and opened a stretcher by the injured man.

Cavanaugh, Smith and the two medical aides carefully moved Martin onto it. He screamed when his momentarily unsupported back sagged, but bit down hard in denial of the pain that burned through his hairless chest.

"Back to the clearing with him," said Cavanaugh.

The stretcher-bearers hobbled across the lumpy ground with their slight burden.

Smith, grim-faced, motioned the pale, curious soldiers back to work.

Cavanaugh and Frazer watched them depart without really seeing them. Frazer suddenly ejaculated, "Good God! The man in the tractor!"

Both turned around to see Humphreys advancing.

"The other chap, Oswald. Is he all right?" called Cavanaugh anxiously.

86

Humphreys hove to ominously. "Of all the dirty rotten stupidity," he grated. "The bastard ought to be court-martialed! Christ, I'd like to get my hands on him!"

"What shape's Peterson in?" shouted Frazer.

Humphreys snapped. "Any idea just how much this'll set us back?"

Frazer stared at his Number One with utter disbelief. "Stretcher!" he roared out, whipping around and jogtrotting the fifty yards to where the mass of ruptured metal still smoked in the vertical noonday sun.

Cavanaugh and Smith followed. The trio searched the area in the vicinity of the tractor. They found nothing. They moved off the cleared trail and into the thickly interwoven brush.

"Here, sir, what's this?" called Smith.

At a point thirty feet from the edge of the clearing the knee-high grass was beaten down as if some huge snake had slithered off into hiding. They followed the trail for another few yards. There they found what they sought. Crumpled in a heap lay the almost naked body of a man. It was the tractor driver. The front part of his body glowed lobster-pink where the superheated steam had scalded away the layers of skin now adhering in filmy cobwebs to his inert form. In places the blood ran freely where the cruel brush spines had raked his cooked flesh. In a convulsion of scalding agony he had ripped off his clothes, and now the balm of unconsciousness suffused his terror.

"This isn't Peterson," said Cavanaugh. He pulled back the man's eyelids, taking great pains to avoid disturbing the panes of freshly grafted skin blistering the man's face. "He's out. Your blade, Smith."

Smith handed the doctor the flat-bladed panga that hung from the belt of every man in the expedition.

Gingerly gripping what clothes remained on the unconscious figure, Cavanaugh dexterously scalpeled away the last shreds of bodily covering. "Stretcher."

Two bearers moved forward.

"Steady as she goes," cautioned Cavanaugh. "He needs every square inch of skin he's got left."

87

"Wasn't Peterson supposed to be our tractor man?" demanded Frazer, grimly puzzled, as they headed for the aid tent. "I don't understand it. The poor devil's face is such a mess I don't know who he is. Smith?"

Smith, walking at the foot of the stretcher, grimaced uncomfortably, unanxious to take the questioning gaze of Frazer by his side. "It's *Porter,* sir."

"Porter?" snapped the commander. "What was he doing on the tractor? Did Captain Humphreys know about this? . . . Porter? Our explosives man, wasn't he? What'd he know about handling a tractor"

"Well, sir, if you don't really mind my saying so, there's nothing to it—just one lever you push in when you want to go slow and out when you want to speed up. Didn't seem no reason why Porter couldn't handle it, seeing as Peterson's such a wizard with a line and that stream we crossed yesterday's full of trout; and I thought the men'd like a change from bully 'n' biscuits."

"A commendable thought, Sergeant," Frazer conceded stiffly, "but look where it's got us."

He took off his topee and wiped the sweat from his brow. "Tommy," he asked softly, "how does he look?"

"Know better when I've had a chance to look him over. But at a guess I'd say first-degree burns over two-thirds of his body."

"Pretty bad, eh?"

Cavanaugh nodded emphatically.

They walked the rest of the way to the medical tent wordlessly.

Inside, Lieutenant Martin lay on a stretcher. All the color had drained from his usually pink, cherubic face, giving him the pallor of the dead. As Porter was set down beside him, Martin's eyes flashed fear and revulsion at the hideous sight of his stripped, scalded body.

Cavanaugh summoned his two medical orderlies. "Look, you two. Got to work fast. Get all Porter's clothes off. Fast as you can, scrub up and smear tannic all over him. It's his only chance. I've got to try something on Martin."

"How is he, sir?" whispered one of the orderlies.

88

"Bad, I'm afraid," confided Cavanaugh. "Looks like internal bleeding. Anyhow, get to it."

The aides scurried off.

Frazer had been standing off to the side, thinking it best to stay out of the way. Now he approached Cavanaugh hesitantly, a worried questioning look furrowing his brow. "Tommy?"

"Bad, old boy, I'm afraid," said the doctor, reading his look. He had already peeled off his sweat-sodden khaki shirt and was carefully scrubbing his hands in an enamel basin.

"Both?" asked Frazer.

Cavanaugh nodded. He dried off his hands and moved briskly to a metal cabinet. He snapped back the doors and ran his fingers along a row of bottles, stopping at a blue-colored, transparent liquid labeled "methylated spirits."

Frazer moved over behind him as he uncorked the bottle and poured some of the fluid over his hands. He held them up and allowed the liquid to course down over his wrists.

"Going to operate?" said Frazer.

"It's his only chance. Could be one of half a dozen things—ruptured spleen, stomach, lungs, who knows what? And I've got to find it before he loses too much blood. . . . Orderly!"

The two orderlies were busy on Porter. At the doctor's call, one rose quickly and hurried to Cavanaugh's side.

"Clean up fast as you can and ready the surgery kit," he ordered him briskly.

"Very good, sir," said the orderly, moving over to the metal basin.

Cavanaugh rummaged through the medicine-cabinet drawer and came up with a fresh white gown. He was busy getting into it when he looked up and again read Frazer's face. "Nothing else I can do. I know what you're thinking: What chance has Martin with a quack who's spent his life peeking at squiggly things through a microscope? That's what I'm wondering myself. . . . Now, why don't you be a good chap and take care of your boats? I'll keep you posted." His tone was final.

Frazer nodded and left the tent.

89

Outside, Humphreys stalked up and down the trail haranguing thirteen soldiers and sailors drawn up at attention in two lines. He would pace for several minutes, composing his comments, then grind them out bluntly. "You all know what this means, don't you? Theoretically twice as long to get to the lake. Don't you believe it." He paced again, rolled his sleeves farther up his arms, doffed his topee and wiped out the sweatband. "No, not twice as long—just twice as hard. Isn't that right, Sergeant Smith?"

Smith stiffened.

Humphreys pointed his swagger stick at the sergeant and rapped out his rhetorical question a second time. "That is right, Sergeant Smith? We will all work twice as hard, will we not? And we will not deviate one minute from the timetable?"

"If you say so, sir," conceded Smith with enough reluctance in his tone to indicate to the men his real feelings.

"Good," grunted Humphreys sarcastically. "That's what we need: the uncompromised loyalty and enthusiasm of all ranks." He resumed his pacing. As he walked he slapped his swagger stick noisily against the side of his leather leggings. "Smith," he demanded, stiffly coming to a halt, "how far have we come today?"

The sergeant pulled a thick notebook from his pocket and thumbed through the pages. "Sir, I estimate about four and a half miles."

"You *estimate?*" thundered Humphreys. "Don't you *know?*"

"I estimate, sir. I don't know."

"And why don't you? That was one of your responsibilities."

"One of the men was handling that, sir."

"Who?"

"Lance Corporal Porter, sir."

Humphreys unfixed his stare from Smith and ran it up and down the ranks. "Porter!" he called in the grand manner of the parade ground. "Lance Corporal Porter!"

"Porter's in the aid tent, Captain Humphreys," said Smith.

"Get him out here on the double, Sergeant," snapped Humphreys.

"Sir, Porter was on the tractor when it blew up," said Smith evenly.

Humphreys paced again. He stopped and glared up and down the ranks. "Peterson!" he shouted.

There was no answer.

"*Peterson!*" he shouted again.

"Captain Humphreys," said Smith, eyes forward.

"Smith?" snapped Humphreys.

"Peterson's part of a work party I sent back to the lake we passed yesterday."

"What in blazes is he doing at the lake—swimming? *He* was supposed to be operating the tractor, wasn't he?"

"That's right, sir," replied Smith.

"And why wasn't he?"

Smith seemed to weigh his words. "Sir, Peterson's a wizard with the line. The men've been overdoing the bully 'n' biscuits for the last ten days. I decided a little trout wouldn't hurt 'em. So I—"

"So you took it upon yourself to endanger the entire expedition by sending Peterson out fishing while some nincompoop blows up half our equipment!"

Smith held his tongue.

"How many others out there with him?" inquired Humphreys with sarcasm.

"None," came Smith's abrupt reply.

"What, Smith?" demanded Humphreys, poised to exploit an opening.

"None, *sir*."

"Much better, Sergeant. So while the rest of us down here work, break our backs, Peterson's off on holiday angling, eh?"

From among the two lines of men came the wisecrack: "A nice kettle of fish."

"*Ten*-SHUN," roared Humphreys, his substantial girth expanding dangerously.

The soldiers and sailors snapped to smartly.

"So we think it's funny, do we?" he said, his eyes narrowing. "Well, we'll see." He resumed his pacing, hands joined behind his back, swagger stick jammed into his right oxter. "In a few minutes you'll fall out for lunch. Eat hearty. Enjoy it. In future, you'll lunch on the move. Understood?" He paused to observe the effect.

91

The men stood stiffly mute and sweated in the burnished glare.

Humphreys resumed his pacing. "Four and a half miles, Sergeant? Before you climb into your bags tonight, you'll have put another four to that. Is that also understood? Smith! Unhook the other tractor. Push that pile of scrap iron out of the way somewhere. Hook both trailers to the other tractor. You've been clearing the trail twelve feet wide on the turns. Make it fifteen now. And it'll be five minutes off each hour from now on, not ten. Forget about quitting with the sun. Believe me, we're all in for a little night work. One more thing. Recall your angler, Smith. You're going to be damn glad of just bully before this is over."

The men commented collectively with an extravagant demonstration of impassivity.

Sitting on a large rock outside the aid tent puffing on his pipe, Frazer had witnessed the scene. The engineering captain's manner, his whole approach, ran against the grain of all he stood for; yet Humphreys was his "Number One," by plan and protocol the one to implement the plan hammered out initially back at Admiralty House and subsequently by himself during the long voyage from England. He bit down on the stem of his pipe as Humphreys laid into the men. The tirade mounted. He decided that some sort of subtle intervention was long overdue. He rose and tapped the bowl of his pipe against the heel of his boot. He made sure to create the maximum of noise as he crunched his way across the fine rubble of the dry riverbed.

Humphreys ignored his approach. ". . . and that ought to hold you people for the present—as long as your noncommissioned officers don't come up with any other ideas about making this into a Girl Guides picnic. . . . All right, Smith. Fall out the men."

"As you were, Smith," Frazer called out conversationally.

Humphreys acknowledged his presence with a curt nod of his close-cropped head.

"Men," said Frazer, "stand easy."

They relaxed audibly.

"I think there's something they ought to know, Captain Humphreys." He turned to the men. "You're all probably wondering about Lieutenant Martin and Lance Corporal Porter. Afraid they're both in rather bad shape, but Dr. Cavanaugh's in there with them right now. He's doing all he possibly can. If there are any further developments, I'll be sure to keep you informed. Well, that's about all I can say for now. . . . Smith. Carry on."

The sergeant took two paces forward, snappily clicked his heels and saluted. Both officers saluted in return, Frazer with the palm-down casual salute of the Navy, Humphreys with the palm-forward stiff gesture of the Army.

Smith about-faced and yelled in his best Aldershot manner, "Ten-*shun!*"

Fourteen pairs of heels kicked up a cloud of hot dust as they clicked to attention.

"*Fall . . . out!*"

Frazer and Humphreys turned around and walked toward the aid tent.

The men broke ranks. It was lunchtime. They filtered off in twos and threes in the direction of a clump of scrawny mountain trees. They slumped down into the trees' welcome shade while a tall corporal handed out cans of bully beef and loose biscuits. "He certainly turned out to be a nice one, didn't he?" the corporal grunted to nobody in particular.

"If you ask me, he's a bit of a bastard," concurred the Welshman. He held up the four dried-up crackers that the corporal had tossed him. "I'd like to bet you him 'n' Frazer's not eatin' bully and—"

"How the hell do you know, Taffy?" challenged the North-Countryman in his slow, soft-spoken way. He meant no malice.

"Well, man, just look at him—the way he's always done up to the nines. Have you ever seen him with a hair out of place or without a shine on his boots? Why, he thinks he's God's gift to the Army. And the rest of us all's roughin' it. I mean, who does he think he is?"

"I'll tell you, I don't know," volunteered the North-Countryman. "Remember how he kept to himself on the ship? I mean, he didn't hobnob with any of the other officers. Queer sort."

A few feet away from the rest Private Nangle, a public-school product, stared at the chunk of bully beef in the bottom of his mess tin. He finally raised his eyes. "I say, would any of you chaps like a spot of *pâté de foie gras?* You can have mine, you know." He proferred the tangy-smelling bully beef in the direction of the others.

The morsel was roundly refused.

"Nangle," said the Welshman, "save it for dessert. . . . Hey, maybe the nipper here'd like it." He looked over the heads of his comrades toward the base of a distant tree where the red-haired Perkins ate quietly by himself. "Hi, lad!" called the Welshman, beckoning.

The youngster rose nimbly and made his way over to join the older soldiers.

"Seconds?" the Welshman asked him, pointing to Nangle's mess can.

"No, sir, not for me," he demurred politely.

"Dammit, that's a good one," roared the North-Countryman. "Look, laddie, we're goin' to have to find a bigger topper for him if you keep up that 'sir' business."

They all laughed—except the boy.

"What's ailin' you, lad?" asked the North-Countryman.

"C'mon," urged the Welshman. "You're not goin' to let that big sod of a captain get you down, now are you?"

The apple-cheeked, freckle-faced youth squatted on the ground. "Well," he began cautiously, pushing a thatch of hair out of his blue eyes, "I don't like the sounds of him." He paused to scoop up the last piece of bully beef with a biscuit. "And I'm wondering about Porter and Lieutenant Martin."

There was little sound but the occasional rattling of mess gear. The men shifted uncomfortably.

Finally the Welshman spoke. "Look, Ginger. You'll have to excuse us. We're a crude lot, but that's what the Army does for you."

"That's not it at all," interrupted Nangle pontifically. "Each one of us is bloody glad it wasn't him. If it didn't happen to us, then it just didn't happen."

"Nangle," said the North-Countryman conversationally, "you're an awful pain in the arse. Nobody's interested in your scientific hogwash."

Nangle rose to his feet and headed off into the bush.

"Think I'll have one too," muttered the North-Countryman rising.

"If you ask me," said the Welshman reassuringly, "his bark's worse than his bite. He'll bear watching, that's for certain. But, now, you take a sergeant like old Smith. He was at Wipers. I'm thinkin' he's sized up your man good. He'll give him just *so* much rope."

The youngster eyed him uncertainly. "Captain Humphreys'd make two of the sergeant," he announced with awe.

The only other shady spot on the brush-covered slope was occupied by six men. They did not speak the soldiers' language though they dressed about the same. They were volunteers from the famed Dover Patrol who would sail the gunboats once they reached Lake Tanganyika. Technical experts though they were, they had not been spared the stomach-knotting, back-rending agony of carving a trail through tangled undergrowth so tall and dense as to obscure the sunlight; but their chief job was to fuss over *Mimi* and *Toutou*. A sharp branch could puncture a thin hull. They had no patches. Only an elaborate naval workshop could coax the kinks out of a bent propeller shaft.

From Fungurume northward Chief Petty Officer Stokes had swaddled the boats in heavyweight tarpaulins. Cinched down tightly to the long, flatbed trailers, they should be safe enough, he thought. Nevertheless, each night when the remainder of the expedition battened down for the night, he stood over the sailors as they stripped off the tarpaulins to explore shaft and hull for signs of damage.

Mimi and *Toutou* had been the result of a hard-fought compromise between Frazer and the skeptical and reluctant Director of Naval Operations. Stokes could remember the first time he had seen them—at Thornycroft's big yards up at Teddington. They had been specially built to the specifications of the Greek government for seaplane service. When Frazer saw them that sunny May morning, he shouted exultantly to Stokes, "This is more like it!" They weighed four and a half tons. That was about what a steam tractor and fourteen men could handle comfortably through the jungle, they had reasoned. Their eight-foot beams presented no problem, but their forty feet of length conformed reluctantly to the dozens of corkscrew and hairpin bends that had led up from Fungurume. And now that they had spent so much sweat and blasphemy in forcing the brutes up the slope, not even exuberant Bannister and Dodkins could scare up much enthusiasm for the blessedness of their 2½-foot draft and 18-knot fleetness.

"Quiet bird, ain't he?" said Leading Seaman Crann.

"Who?" asked Stokes.

"That Frazer," said Crann.

Stokes rubbed his shin thoughtfully. "Never says much 'less what 'e's got somethin' to say."

Crann pushed back his topee and uncrossed his legs. "If you ask me, he shoulda said plenty a half an hour ago." He winked at the other sailors. "You all heard big Fish Eyes pee on your better half, Chief. Why didn't he tear him off a strip?"

Stokes said, "Don't you bother your arse none 'bout the commander. An' Sergeant Smith, 'e was wet-nursin' brass 'ats like the big fellow in the Boer War. So . . . eat your bloody B 'n' B."

"C'mon, Chief," insisted Crann. "You and him was at Scapa, eh? What makes him tick?"

" 'Ow long you been in?" growled Stokes.

"The day after we took Jerry on."

"Used to be a grocer's clerk, didn't you? Customer's always right, eh? They must've told you that. Same 'ere: Officer's always right when 'e's in front of 'is men—even if 'e's all wrong. Do you twig?"

"That go for NCOs too, Chief?" laughed Crann.

"Backbone o' the bloody Navy, mate," rumbled Stokes, "an' don't you forget it. . . . You might even be one yourself one day."

"If I ain't careful," quipped Crann.

8

The Lord ruleth me: and I shall want nothing. He hath set me in a place of pasture.

He hath brought me up on the water of refreshment: he hath converted my soul.

He hath led me on the paths of justice for his own name's sake.

For though I shall walk in the midst of the shadow of death, I will fear no evil: for thou art with me.

Thy rod and thy staff: they have comforted me.

Frazer read from Cavanaugh's dog-eared Douay Bible. David's magnificent psalm of reassurance came over starkly simple, less embellished than Protestant custom. But it did the job. Martin and Porter minded not. They lay mute and coldly uncomplaining in heavy canvas shrouds, poised at the edge of two crudely dug holes. There were no two ranks of impeccably clad military figures standing shoulder to shoulder, rifles at the ready. With the sun still unwilling to venture over the rim of the world, the camp of the Britons on the slope toward the Maniku Plateau was a chill and neuter place. The men come to witness the departure clumped around Frazer as he read, their shoulders braced roundly against the cold. The steam of frosted breath clouded the morning air. The coughed liquid crack of stubborn phlegm assailed the ceremony.

Thou hast prepared a table before me against them that afflict me.
Thou hast anointed my head with oil: and my chalice which inebriateth me, how goodly is it!
And thy mercy will follow me all the days of my life:
And that I may dwell in the house of the Lord unto length of days.

Frazer looked up, closed the Bible and handed it absent-mindedly to Cavanaugh. "All right, Sergeant Smith," he said mechanically.

As Smith's work party consigned the two to the bowels of the earth, Frazer wondered about the little he knew of them and how their mothers might take it. They who had writhed in the labor of bringing them into "this vale of tears"—one of Tommy's expressions—had they ever dreamed that flesh of their flesh might lie stiff under foreign soil half a world and half a life from their tiny cribs? It was the final, irrevocable relinquishing of the apron strings. . . . Now they were in. Shovels clanged on juts of rock. The soil rose. He would soon commend Martin and Porter to the neatly ruled columns of the official log.

Fancifully there drifted back into his mind a boyhood fascination with the dirgeful saga of another war:

Not a drum was heard, not a funeral note,
As his corse to the ramparts we hurried;
Not a soldier discharged his farewell shot
O'er the grave where our hero we buried . . .

Tongues of flame leaped into the predawn air from a half-dozen campfires. The heat and light helped to evaporate the depression; so did the stimulating aroma of bacon frying on that ubiquitous adjunct of all British military operations—the Primus stove. The men circled around the fires cross-legged eating. Fifty yards away the tents of the officers and NCOs glowed yellow from the hurricane lanterns inside.

The shadows cast on the side of the headquarters tent belonged to Frazer, Humphreys and Cavanaugh. During the meal the movements of the shadows were those of men deep in discussion. The large shadow on one side of the table moved its head vigorously and gesticulated with raised hand. The shadow of the orderly appeared briefly to clear away the enamel dishes. Immediately they were replaced with the shadow of a large map over which the three pored for some time.

By the time the sun had risen, the men had already dedicated themselves to the job at hand. The day would progress as had every other day: As soon as they had cleared a quarter of a mile or so of brush, the tractors would tow the boats forward. And so they would clear and tow all day. Meanwhile another work party would move through the campsite, striking tents and march-ordering the gear for the next night's encampment.

Shortly after dawn Frazer pushed aside the log. He sat at the camp table studying the map. Cavanaugh entered, wearing peaked naval officer's cap, collar and tie, tunic, jodhpurs, leggings and field boots. His oval face was in mourning.

Frazer shared his mood. "I still think someone else ought to go, Tommy," he said quietly.

"Look, we're not going through that again," said the doctor tiredly. "We've lost a tractor, two good men." For a moment he was silent. "I don't give a rap what he says. Even if we worked the chaps twenty-four hours a day, we still couldn't make up for the loss. I'm the only one who's been in these parts before, the only one who knows their lingo."

"Yes, but what happens if we need you here? There's nobody here who—"

"Hogwash, Ian. Even *you* could've done better than I did last night," chided the slight little man.

"Oh, what bloody stuff and nonsense," said Frazer in exasperation. "You know damn well neither of them had a chance. Said so yourself when we brought 'em in. You did your best."

"Oh, to be sure," replied Cavanaugh sarcastically. "A fine job I did of protecting myself even before I laid a hand on them. A physician should conduct himself as though he were in a kind of court: A man's healable until proven not so, not a lost cause before you've even given him a hearing. I'm going, and that's that."

Frazer regarded him sternly, then waved his hand in surrender. "All right, Tommy."

The doctor pulled thoughtfully on his chin. "The Sanga at Wendi Macosi are our best bet. They were a lot better organized than the other Baluba. I don't imagine things have changed much in eleven years. Besides, I like to think I had something to do with saving a little tyke by the name of Matubele—his mother didn't pull through, though." The wiry little man's face untensed as his thoughts wandered back over the years. "Called me *Engai,* they did, after it was all over."

"What's that?" asked Frazer.

"God Almighty, believe it or not."

"You're our man, then, Tommy," conceded Frazer reluctantly. "When should we expect you?"

"Give me about four days to get up to Wendi, a day or two there, then two more to get back again. As long as you don't blow up another engine, you should be well up the slope—maybe even on the top—next time we meet. A lot less brush. The going'll be a damn sight easier. About eight days, then, and I'll see you."

"Fetch us back another tractor," quipped Frazer.

"Two of 'em, if you like," said the doctor expansively.

"Who're you taking?" asked Frazer, becoming serious again.

"Crann," said Cavanaugh. "You won't be needing him till we reach the lake. He's good with the compass, they say."

"The best. That's why I picked him," said Frazer. "Who else?"

"Perkins."

"Perkins? Why Perkins?" queried Frazer. "He's just a skinny wee lad. Isn't he the one that can't take the heat so well?"

"He's got a pair of shoulders. It's all I need," said Cavanaugh offhandedly.

Frazer's brow furrowed thoughtfully. "I'd pick one of the brawnier chaps if it were me," he said, "but I suppose you know what you're doing."

100

"I'll make for Wendi Macosi," announced Cavanaugh, "by the easiest foot track, then."

"Fine, Tommy," said Frazer. He folded the map, then looked up. "But what happens if we need you here?"

"You never give up, Ian. Listen, I'm leavin' you both my first-aid lads. They know where all the pills are—and what they're for. Dammit, man, you can't *all* come down with foot-and-mouth in eight days. Even if you do, I'm quite sure—"

At that moment the lemon rays of the winter sun cast the large figure of Captain Humphreys on the tent flap. He stood silently taking in the unusual sight of the doctor dressed in full field gear. "So you're going?" he said.

"I am, that," replied Cavanaugh evenly.

"You're wasting not only your own time, Dr. Cavanaugh, but quite possibly the time of the entire expedition, because—"

"And I've told you, Oswald, that you're wasting your time trying to talk me out of it."

"*I* can not only reach the level," Humphreys bored on, ignoring the doctor's interruptions, "in *six* days—"

"But can the men?" interrupted Cavanaugh.

"—but also make up for the time lost to date by simply moving at night along the level—"

"And when would the men sleep, Captain?"

—"so that the time *I* make up, *you* lose because we have to beat the bushes looking for you, Dr. Cavanaugh."

Cavanaugh flushed angrily. He surveyed his adversary for a moment. "In that contingency you won't have to do much beating. There's not that much bush on the level. Don't forget, I've been here before. At least that's worth something."

"Dr. Cavanaugh, because of the recent adjustment in the strength of our unit, I would be the last person to detract from your *uncanny* skills in the medical arts, but—"

"Why," muttered Cavanaugh, moving toward the huge engineering officer menacingly, "you horrible big bastard. Mother of God, but I'd like to—"

"*Gentlemen!*" roared Frazer.

The little Irishman pulled up short on his way across to Humphreys, whose massive bulk seemed to dominate the discussion like a Gibraltar.

"Oswald," said Frazer quietly, "I believe you have matters outside to attend to."

Humphreys did not budge. "Commander Frazer, it doesn't really matter if Dr. Cavanaugh goes or stays. If he *goes,* he'll need me to beat the bushes for him. If he *stays,* he'll need *me* to help him sit down and hold the hand of every malingerer who pulls a muscle. That's time we don't have. We can't afford that time—either way."

Frazer could feel his Scottish blood simmer. "May I remind you, Oswald, that I'm in command here."

Humphreys would not quit. "This sort of interference by a medical officer—it's against King's Regulations. This is a purely military matter. His specialty's in lower forms of life. I repeat what I said early this morning. I believe—"

"Captain Humphreys!" exploded Frazer. "The rank of military captain is several grades in authority *below* that of naval commander!"

Humphreys saluted, pivoted smartly and left.

Cavanaugh collapsed onto a stool.

Frazer rummaged in a crate of personal gear and produced a bottle of Old Bushmills. "Tommy," he said softly, "here." He poured into two dirty mugs. "A drop of the 'crater,' " he said, mimicking the Irishman's rolling *r*'s.

The doctor sat trembling, staring into the golden potion. With a sudden, impulsive motion he downed the rich, fiery liquid in two gulps. He licked his lips and extended the mug in the commander's direction.

Frazer refilled it.

With two gulps the doctor dispatched the second cup. "If I'd kept my gub shut," he said miserably, "we'd both be behind desks where we belong." He hooked up the two-thirds-full bottle of Bushmills and stuffed it into his pack.

Outside, Leading Seaman Crann and the baby-faced Private Perkins waited. They came to attention and saluted as Frazer and Cavanaugh emerged.

"As you were," said Frazer. "Think you can navigate Dr. Cavanaugh as far as Wendi Macosi, Crann?"

Crann shifted uncomfortably on his feet. "Compass and a heading's all I need, sir."

Frazer replied, "Fine," and asked Perkins, "Sure you really want to go along, Perkins?"

The boy straightened up and looked squarely at the commander. "Sir, I volunteered."

"Good," said Frazer, turning to Cavanaugh. "You seem to be in good hands, Doctor."

It was the usual light remark that Frazer naturally made, a remark that just as often triggered Cavanaugh into some equally light banter. But this time the face of the Irishman had petrified into a mask of indifference. "We're off, then," he muttered, hefting his pack and stumping off.

Crann and Perkins dutifully followed a few paces behind.

Frazer watched them until the knee-high savanna grass had swallowed them up.

He returned to the headquarters tent. In the full light of dawn he thoughtfully studied the flame of the hurricane lantern. He raised the globe and blew it out. His gaze roamed aimlessly around the tent. When his eyes alighted on the two empty mugs, his brow acquired an extra furrow.

With Tommy gone, Ian slept full the solitary nights. There was no little philosopher cross-legged on the opposite cot, putting the day in perspective. Messing wallowed along as a purely functional activity with a full belly as its sole objective. He would sit at the head of the bare table valiantly scraping for small talk. The others abandoned him to it.

Humphreys would eat in Puritan silence and with impeccable table manners, excuse himself and retire. The noncommital deference of the junior officer rankled in Ian.

They were trying to tell him something, he told himself, but he dismissed it—at first. There had been the long weeks of preparation in England where his indefatigable mastery of detail had pulled the

103

loose threads of proposal and counterproposal into a solid fabric of attack. Aboard the liner there had been long days of discussion of specific problems: Would the Diesel oil of the Belgians at Albertville be too crude for *Mimi* and *Toutou's* thoroughbred engines? Before leaving England the plan had been to pick up *another* trailer for hauling fresh water all the way from Fungurume. Could not the boats' fuel tanks be temporarily adapted for carrying water? This would mean alterations in the tanks—and of the route so as to bring them through many local watering holes. This he had done.

The Belgian maps were not up-to-date. Frazer had spent two days in Pretoria running down an old Afrikaner who had hunted big game in the area and knew it intimately. Together they had revised the maps.

Aboard the liner they had experimented with loading into the two boats' thin hulls all the impedimenta of a twenty-eight-man expedition. The most scientific method—that was what he had been after. They would leave behind what they could not jam in. They had to boil down Naval Africa Expedition to the most mobile unit possible. Thus he had rejected the earlier plan for recruiting natives. Natives could work harder, longer and exist on less than they could. But security—natives gossiped by bush telegraph. If the senior German officer at Kigoma, Lieutenant Commander Zimmer, were to hear their tubs thump. . . . Besides, Tommy had said that natives were not keen on traveling far from their own villages. He would have to pay off and hire a new crew every fifty miles. Food could come out of tins, but the old Afrikaner had promised tons of fresh meat on the hoof en route, so he had scratched half of the tinned stuff.

Would all his nice textbook plans work? *He* was in command; he would see that they did. And it was anticipation nurtured as were once his first faint stirrings of pubescence.

But there was Humphreys.

9

Despite his fifty years the wiry little doctor moved nimbly ahead of Crann and Perkins. His legs bowed thin and frail under the thick woolen socks protecting them against the coarse brush. They had a strength and persistence that did not come from the sinew and muscle of which they were composed.

Crann and Perkins tramped along behind him. They had not talked for a long time. The doctor's mood had made them sulky. So had the altitude; so had their rifles and the bulky canvas bags straining heavily on broad leather straps over their shoulders.

"If he don't slow down, he's going to fall down," said Crann.

The thin, eighteen-year-old Perkins struggled along by his side. "That'll make two of us, then," he panted.

Crann was worried. "He'll not last long this way, Ginger. We'll have to knock some sense into his head, lad."

The pace did not slacken until noon, when they collapsed onto the ground in the shade of a sprawling sausage tree. They lay on their backs for five minutes of silence.

The sound of ripping tin opened Crann's eyes. The doctor was attacking a tin of bully beef. His small hands were trembling.

"I'll get it, sir," offered Crann.

The doctor pulled back. "Open your own, Crann," he said brusquely. "Just have time to eat and run. Not very polite, is it?"

Perkins and Crann supped in silence.

A sausage tree is a tortured knot of wood. It is several trees growing out of one seed, trunks intertwined, branches extending horizontally so far out that they become too heavy to sustain their own weight and curve backward to the earth from which they sprang so hopefully. En route the branches sprout a thick mushroom canopy of foliage. It was an orphan on the bleak African heath, and its gnarled, pustuled limbs welcomed the alien life basking in its shadow.

Crann could feel the welcome as he lay on his back again after the bully, biscuits and water, squinting at the long, engorged pods suspended from the limbs by lengths of viny stalk.

No sooner had Cavanaugh bolted down his food and announced that they would have only five more minutes than his stomach renounced the pressure of the morning and violently contracted. The neat little man emitted a bovine grunt and churned out a rank gruel between the calves of his outstretched legs.

Crann hastily offered him his canteen.

Cavanaugh waved it away. "That's yours," he insisted, wiping the gall from his lips with the back of his hand. He groped around on his webbing for his water bottle.

Crann helped him unhook it.

The doctor meticulously swilled out his mouth. Again he wiped his lips with the back of his hand. "We'll be off again, lads," he announced, rising to his feet. He put his hand to his ashen face and swayed slightly.

Crann and Perkins exchanged glances.

"I'd like to check on our position, sir," said Crann offhandedly. "We've been weaving around a good bit."

"Do we have to?" queried Cavanaugh with a trace of annoyance.

Crann nodded. "Just to be on the safe side, sir."

"How long's it take?"

"Oh, five minutes, sir."

"Hurry it along, then, Crann."

Crann motioned to Perkins to unfold the map case. On the pretext of getting a better sighting on a distant rugged promontory Crann walked out of the doctor's earshot, Perkins following him. He placed the map on the ground and went through the motions of taking a bearing.

"We're not lost, are we?" asked Perkins anxiously.

Crann flipped back the lid of the compass. "Not a chance, chum," he whispered, hooking his thumb in the carrying ring and extending the compass at arm's length. "But, we got to slow him down somehow." He closed one eye and lined up the vertical reticle with a notch in the rolling hills fifty miles away that marked the edge of the plateau. He took a notebook from his shirt pocket and penciled in several notations. "We'll just take our own good time about this, mate." He laid the map on the ground and the compass on the map, rotating the map so that the grid lines ran north-south. On the map he located the notch—the valley they would pass through on their approach to the plateau. He made several deft strokes on the map with pencil and miniature parallel bars, then circled an intersection. "We're not lost. We're right here." He put the point of his pencil on the spot. "What's he up to?" he muttered, still concentrating on the map.

"Looking right at us," whispered Perkins, "probably wondering what's keeping us."

Crann took a long time to fold the map and put away the compass. "He's had another five minutes, for all the good it'll do him. We've made close to twenty miles so far. Damn good. Maybe he'll wear down a bit by the afternoon. He'll have to."

The two returned to the sausage tree where Cavanaugh impatiently awaited them. They picked up their canvas bags and moved off.

Crann strode ahead in the van. Perkins dangled in the rear. Cavanaugh fretted along in the middle, forever jabbing Crann in the backside with the stout staff which the stocky seaman had cut for him.

"Three days to get there!" the doctor repeated endlessly.

Finally Crann said, "Three days, sir, and you're trying to go it in two." He mopped the sweat from his brow with an extravagant gesture.

"For God's sake, man," puffed the doctor, "if I can do it, so can you. Now, hold your tongue and put an inch to your step."

"Beg your pardon, sir," Perkins piped up, "it's you he's worried about, not himself." They were the first words Perkins had uttered in an hour.

Cavanaugh shook his head. "The next thing you'll be doing is stoppin' off to feed me some hot milk. Now, quit your chatter."

Crann was worried. Cavanaugh was the only one who could speak the natives' language. If he should fold, the whole thing would be a lost cause. He was a tough little bugger all right, but not as tough as he thought—and obstinate as hell. Why? Crann had stood outside the headquarters tent that morning long enough to know why. The little man would flatten himself to prove Humphreys wrong. Crann did not doubt the size of the little fiftyish Irishman's heart, only about the way it had to be pounding to do three miles an hour *up* the slope. With his mop of hair and moonface he reminded Crann of a friar out of Sherwood Forest. Even under the steep-domed topee the expression lost none of its monkishness. But now, after six solid hours of climbing, it was as if the rigor of monastic subsistence had astringed the visage of the novice.

It was close to six. Two hours of daylight remained. The sun was waning. The slope lay soaked in shadow. The breeze of the Katanga highlands blew chill on their moist brows. They unrolled their shirtsleeves and turned up their collars against the capricious temperature.

At the crest of the slope the bedrock of the continent had broken through the verdure. Slates of fractured shale, cairns of volcanic rubble and massive single boulders ornamented an east-west fault line a half mile wide. Perkins and Crann halted to take stock of the situation, but Cavanaugh waded into the river of jagged granite, hopping from one boulder to another.

"C'mon," grunted Crann. "We'd better stick close to him. He's liable to come a cropper on his eyebrows."

They scrambled after him.

When Cavanaugh's short legs could not span the distance between one boulder and the next one, he used the long staff to pole himself across the extra inches.

Squatting together on one of the boulders, Crann and Perkins swapped embarrassed grins as they observed their leader's performance.

"About time we quit greetin' over him, lad, eh?" asked Crann, his dusty features wrinkling into a grin.

"Aye," assented Perkins admiringly. "Like an old goat he is."

"He made a couple of sheep out of the two of us," said Crann, rolling crumbs of dust from the corners of his eyes but studying the doctor fifty yards ahead. Slowly his expression changed from admiration to puzzlement . . . and from puzzlement to concern.

Perkins' face was a question mark.

The doctor had halted, it seemed. His head was not bobbing up and down as it had been.

Crann and Perkins rose tentatively from their haunches—then lunged forward on the double.

The doctor was "doing the splits" between two boulders.

Only the staff kept him from dashing himself to ribbons on the shattered granite ten feet below. His right knee quivered like a fiddler's elbow. He struggled to pole-vault himself forward, but his wobbling legs were spread beyond the point of no return. The day's exertion now exacted its toll—a cry of help came from the proud little man. His strength was ebbing fast. Even though he was not an ounce over eight stone, his weight was enough to cause the sweat of his clutched hands to grease the staff, pulling his aching legs farther apart. The bulky green canvas bag bore on his body like a millstone.

Crann inched to the edge of the first boulder. "Lay hold of me," he commanded, extending his left hand to Perkins. He stuck out his right to the doctor. "Grab it, sir," he shouted.

To do this the doctor had to match the full weight of his body plus the twenty-pound bag with one hand. "I can't," he gasped. "I can't."

"C'mon, sir, try it, sir. You gotta try it," urged Crann.

"Can't make it, Crann," he groaned.

"Try, dammit," roared Crann.

Cavanaugh's scrawny arm shot out like the tongue of a chameleon. Crann snatched at it and missed.

Cavanaugh sagged two inches before regaining his two-handed grip.

"We'll go below," snapped Crann. "Hold on half a moment longer, sir." Crann and Perkins scrambled down the side of the huge boulder and picked their way gingerly across the sharp, flinty volcanic debris until they were directly below the doctor.

"We'll have to catch him, lad," said Crann. He called to the doctor. "All right, sir. Any time you're ready. Just let her go."

There was not much breath left in the doctor, but he managed to gasp, "This is all so bloody ridiculous."

"Save your wind, sir. C'mon, now. Let her go, sir," pleaded Crann as he and Perkins braced themselves, arms outstretched. He realized that if the doctor failed to jump while he still had some control over how his body would fall, he would collapse and fall any old whichway, possibly injuring the three of them.

The obstinate little physician hung on despite the fact that his body was yielding like clay under the modeler's thumb. "Got myself . . . into this . . . get myself out," he panted.

Down below Crann swore and shook his head at Perkins. "How do we get him to jump?" he pleaded. He looked up again at the doctor. "Jump, sir. Jump!"

Cavanaugh's painracked face appeared between his arms: "Out of the way. Going to jump. Out . . . of . . . the . . . way!"

"No, sir!" Crann screamed. "Don't jump by yourself! You'll smash up on the rocks, sir! We'll catch you, sir! Just let her go! We'll get you!"

"Out . . . of . . . the . . . way," came back the doctor's halting reply.

Crann and Perkins looked at each other helplessly.

"Jesus Christ," muttered Crann.

Perkins pondered. "Maybe if we . . ."

"What?" shouted Crann, fuming at his own helplessness.

Perkins looked up at the doctor, who was sinking fast. "Dr. Cavanaugh, sir. How are we going to explain this to Commander Frazer, sir?"

"You young devil!" wheezed Cavanaugh with breathless fierceness. "Look out! I'm on my way!" Down he plummeted with arms and legs skewed out at all angles.

Crann and Perkins had been face to face when the doctor thudded down upon their clasped hands. The force hammered Perkins' head into Crann's face.

Perkins' fingers explored the impression made by Crann's dentures in his skull.

Crann daubed at his mouth and nose with a dirty khaki handkerchief.

The doctor lay on his back catching his breath. He pushed himself up on his elbows and looked at Crann.

Crann stared at him moodily.

Cavanaugh began to laugh.

Crann gaped at him.

Cavanaugh's laughter grew.

Perkins looked at Crann and snickered. Soon the doctor and the youth were howling uncontrollably.

Crann's expression was that of a cow looking over a gate.

"Your face looks like," began Cavanaugh, but his words surrendered to a convulsion of laughter. All he could do was point at Crann's face and howl. "Your face looks"—he tried again—"looks . . . like . . . you . . ." He had subsided. "Crann, old man," he finally managed, "your face looks as if it had a severe case of hemorrhoids."

Perkins exploded again. Tears were running down his cheeks.

Crann's expression of bland ignorance was now leavened with the dawning of understanding. He looked at his blood-soaked handkerchief. His face looked as if it had been brushed with blood. He touched his nose, embarrassed. He tossed his canvas bag aside, slipped out of his knapsack and unbuckled the flap. He withdrew a shaving mirror and cautiously brought it toward his face. Soon he was grinning.

They all laughed together.

After Crann had cleaned up, he said to the doctor, "Well, sir, I don't know that I'd go along entirely with your diagnosis."

"No, Crann?" asked Cavanaugh, affecting disappointment.

"No, sir," declared Crann flatly. "Not hemorrhoids, sir. Piles, maybe. Only officers have hemorrhoids, sir."

And their laughter detonated again and was lost on the ears of the denizens of the high veldt.

The Baluba are a happy and a hardy people. Most of the Baluba nation's tribes are renowned for their good nature and courage in the face of adversity. Yet the group of Basanga tribesmen that ringed the fire in three large circles—the oldest on the inside circle, the youngest on the outside—did not chant as they were wont to do. All the way around knots of them engaged in furtive chatter. The one called Matubele spoke quietly but urgently in the guttural tribal tongue, Kisanga. Those around listened with respect, for even though he was the youngest son of Emphema, he wore the thin scars of a prince on his cheeks and forehead. Against the campfire's glow the ebony blackness of Matubele's finely featured face glistened. The Kisanga tongue may have been guttural, but Matubele used it as smoothly as any of the elders, almost as smoothly as old Emphema himself. His glibness was a fitting complement to the high cheekbones and delicate nose on which rested his regal mien. Old Emphema had chosen well to select Matubele over his other seven sons. Indeed there had been grumbling when the old chief had named him over his oldest son, who had been the choice of the elders because it was natural for the *oldest* male to have conferred upon him those duties that a father could no longer discharge.

Sickness had hit the entire Baluba nation hard, as it had all the cattle keepers. Many young men and women had shriveled and died. Those who had not died walked around with a great weakness in them. Where once working with cattle had been an honor which every uncircumcized Baluba boy anticipated with joy, it was now a burdensome responsibility. Faced with this unholy blight on his people, Matubele had made a shocking suggestion—that the women be allowed to take on some of the men's work. He had made the suggestion first to his father, as the ways of the Baluba called for. He had been castigated severely. Had he not heard that it was forbidden for women even to come close to cows? Did he not know that a woman's hand on an animal meant a curse? But it had given Emphema another idea for conserving the strength of his Basanga warriors: Let the *women* make the yearly pilgrimage to the great water of Bangweulu for salt instead of the men. Let the males remain behind to tend to the herds.

And so it was that the women had set out on the long, dangerous journey. They would not be back until the sun had gone down behind the hills thirteen times. But Emphema and his sons, the elders and the whole village saw the sun in the hills fourteen times and the women had not come. On the seventeenth day, three wives had come staggering up the hill toward the village exhausted. Theirs was a tale of woe, of attack by an unfriendly tribe which had robbed them of their salt. Those who had not been raped and had their throats cut had been forced to flee into the swamp, where few had escaped the devil who opened his huge mouth and sucked them into the world below.

Henceforth there would be no safaris by the women, Emphema had decreed. Yet the god of the cattle, who had wrought this upon them, would have to be appeased. The slain women had been delivered up to him as had the animals who had fallen with the sickness and the people with the bulging necks. But how appease him? Emphema summoned Mafuta, the wizard, who held in his head the names of all the gods and could speak with them, to explain why the cow god should use his people so.

He spent two days with the contents of his sacred bag—the dried eyes of a jackal, the hair from a stillborn goat, the leaves of a sausage tree and the testes of a monkey. These he ground into a paste in a hollowed-out elephant's tusk. When the compost had dried, he sprinkled the powder on the ground outside the entrance to his hut. By the hour he squatted at the entrance contemplating. Occasionally he thrust his long, bony fingers into the tusk and withdrew a pinch of the contents which he would blow toward the point on the horizon where the sun was born each morning. But most of his day was spent twig in hand tracing mysterious patterns in the sand about his doorstep.

At the end of the second day Mafuta presented himself at Emphema's kraal, announcing that he had been successful in divining the will of the spirits. They were annoyed—as he had predicted they would be annoyed—because the girl child born before the last new moon, the one with the withered leg, had not been drowned as he had directed. The deformed one, explained Mafuta, had been sent as a test to see if the Baluba nation still abided by the will of the spirits, and out of all the Baluba, the Basanga had been honored. Did not Emphema remember how the vote of the elders had been evenly divided, and when they had asked for his vote, he had voted *against* the drowning? There was no doubt now in Mafuta's mind what course must be followed. The girl child must be plucked from the paps that gave her suck, placed in a basket woven with vines and weighted with stone and pushed off the bank into the gurgling eye of the river where the water swirled fastest and deepest. If the cow god was to be appeased, declared Mafuta, this course must be followed.

Mafuta's wisdom could not be questioned a second time. Chief Emphema accepted the verdict impassively and instructed a servant to summon the elders and the princes. Soon six old men and seven young boys sat on the cowhide rugs in a half circle around him. As the sooty particles from the single fish-oil lamp flitted around them, speckling an old face here, a young one there, Emphema grunted through the formality of undoing his earlier decision on the deformed infant.

The following morning the mother stood mute as Emphema and two of the elders told her of the decision. For a long moment she looked into the round face, then pulled her breast from the small one's greedy mouth. With downcast misted eyes she unquestioningly delivered her own flesh according to the ways of the Baluba.

As the child wriggled in Emphema's arms, two stick-legged youths who had been wandering in the bush raced into the village and up to his side. After bowing in deference to the chief, they exploded in a chatter of excitement over what they had seen: three men with heads and skin the color of the sole of a Masanga's foot.

The old man's eyes narrowed. He handed the child back to its mother and pointed toward her hut. He turned to the two elders, the senior members of the council. The village must be warned, he told them. The whitefaces must not be welcomed, nor must they be turned away. They might be as the white-faced traders in years gone by who had given them, in return for their cow hides, honey-colored waters that had bred devils in the bodies of those who had drunk of them. But they might also be as the black-robed men calling themselves "father."

Emphema croaked an order. A servant appeared. Emphema croaked again. The servant scurried into a nearby hut, then emerged followed by a short man dwarfed by the massive hollowed-out log he embraced. It was covered with animal skins at both ends. He laid the drum on its side and began pounding the head with the heel of his hand.

The dull, sonorous rumble of his tattoo drew the villagers wide-eyed from their banana-leaf-thatched conical-roofed huts out into the light of day. Emphema told them gravely of the coming of the whitefaces and how they must conduct themselves. In the ways of the tribe they would allow the newcomers to take the first step, be it for good or evil. Again he croaked an order, and his people dispersed to await the arrival of the strangers.

At the time when the sun was one handsbreadth from the purple hills, three whitefaces broke through the heavy clumps of bush ringing the village. They were led by a small one. He approached with arm extended, palm facing down. "I have no rock to harm you," announced the stranger.

Emphema stuck out his bony arm and replied, "Nor do I have rock to harm you. Why do you walk in the land of the Sanga?"

The small man looked up into Emphema's face. "We are in need of help, and the generous hearts of the Sanga are known afar."

"Where do you come from?" demanded Emphema suspiciously.

"We come from a place of four days' journey, *mzee,* where there are many more of us who need your help."

Emphema started at the sound of "*mzee,*" the term of respect for the aged, coming from the lips of the whiteface. His eyes narrowed. The traders had honored him as *mzee* when they had convinced him that the golden potion would be more than worthy exchange for their cowhides. His tired old body stiffened. His inquisitive eyes shifted from the round, bearded face of the small one to the green bag hanging from his shoulder. For him the bag bulged with mystery. "You have called me *mzee*," he said solemnly, "but others have come in the past who have called me *mzee* to my face, knowing it is the sound of running water to an old man's ears. But they have felt otherwise in their hearts."

Kongolo and Mukulu, the senior elders, nodded vigorously and whispered to each other. Slowly the women and children ventured from their kraals and edged toward the spot outside Chief Emphema's compound where he was interrogating the newcomers.

"Who is he, and who is he?" Emphema demanded, pointing at the boy and the man, "and why does this one have his hair painted the color of a cow's skin?" He pointed at the boy again. "Is there a *thau* upon him? He must not lay his hand upon us. We are thrice cursed already."

The small man turned to his two companions and said something in the tongue of the whitefaces, causing them all to laugh.

"Is it good to make fun of one, then ask that one to help you?" reproached Emphema.

"*Mzee*," said the small one quickly, "we do not make fun of you. His hair is not painted. It has been as the color of cow skin ever since his birth waters gushed."

Emphema appraised the boy. "He is your wizard?"

"No, *mzee*. Many whitefaces have hair the color of the skin of the cow."

"I have not seen them," croaked Emphema.

"Nor have we," concurred Kongolo and Mukulu in unison.

The small one took the strange youth by the arm and brought him toward Emphema and the six elders. "Feel him, *mzee*. He is as I am and you are."

Emphema, Kongolo, Mukulu and the other elders recoiled from bodily contact with the boy. They jabbered nervously.

"*Mzee*," declared the small whiteface, "of all the Luba nation, we have come to the Sanga for help, for even ten days' journey from here they know of the kindness and wisdom of Emphema. I myself have known of it. Will you help us?"

"How do you know of us?" queried Emphema.

116

The small whiteface removed the anthill from his head and smoothed his old hair. He stepped forward until his head was the width of two hands from the old chief's face. "*Mzee*," he announced, "you are a bloody *pambavu*."

The whiteface had called Emphema an idiot.

Emphema's eyelids blinked rapidly over eyes filmy with cataracts. Kongolo and Mukulu stiffened in insult.

The villagers murmured and brought their spears to the ready.

Slowly Emphema extended his clawlike hands to touch the shoulders of his insulter.

The whiteface stood his ground as Emphema's knobby fingers explored his face and head. "Where's that little *mtoto*, Matubele?" he demanded belligerently.

The chief's scrotum of a face wrinkled in a toothless smile. "Kafana!" he cried. "Kafana!"

" 'Kafana' is close," chortled the small whiteface, nudging his two companions proudly.

Emphema's grizzled face shone with delight. "It is Kafana!" he croaked again. "Kongolo! Mukulu! Kafana has come again to help us in our need. Nzambi, the Great God, has not forsaken us. Matubele! Come forward, my son."

The young prince stepped forward, and his father presented him with trembling hands. "My son, you have heard it said how there was a curse upon you when the birth waters flowed, and how a whiteface wizard worked the wonder of your first shout." He pointed toward the small whiteface. "This is Kafana. It was he who did it."

Kafana stretched out his arms in welcome. "So *this* is the little *mtoto*," he exclaimed, gazing upon Matubele with disbelief.

"Father," demanded Matubele sternly, "is this the one who sent my mother to join her ancestors before I ever had the chance to know her face?"

Emphema's face darkened. "You have the wicked tongue of your uncle," he lamented. "Go, open your heart to him who made it first beat in you!"

Kongolo, Matubele's uncle, sulked.

Mafuta, the wizard, charged, "How could the potions of the white wizard have wrought their magic had not first I banished the curse?"

The old chief raised his hand. "Silence! Kafana and his friends will think the Sanga have lost their manners. . . . Enough. The elders and my sons will join us inside."

They sat in the chief's soot-laden hut and talked of many things: of how Kafana had come to their village years ago when Emphema had taken his last wife; of how Kafana had dwelt among them and learned their language, eaten their food and spent hours in the tall grass and by the riverbanks searching for creeping and flying things; of his magic tube that made the tsetse the size of the turtle; and of his black bag of *grigris,* any one of which could cast the evil *mipajis* out of the bodies of those cursed with sickness.

Emphema recalled how his "little" wife had lain in the birth chair, her belly glistening large and round like that of the snake that has pulled itself over the body of the squealing pig. But the child would not come. Somehow his wife had offended the spirits of her ancestors, and she had been cursed. The other wives, he continued, stood around pouring root juices down her throat and thrusting the rendered fat of the elephant into the pursed hole in her body. And when she screamed, the midwives snatched their hands from rubbing the faintly stirring life within her and clamped them across her mouth. On the fourth day Kafana returned from the bush to find her with less breath than it takes to extinguish the flame on a dampened reed—and the heaving life in her belly stilled. And Kafana ordered the pots of water to boil and Emphema's wife taken from the birth chair and placed on the floor; and as Emphema, his wives, sons and elders stood mutely by, Kafana passed his hand over her, and the silent mound of her body split like the ripe pod of the sausage tree; and he raced through the night to the bend in the river where the cool waters flowed deepest. There he walked, and the dumb one in his arms went beneath the waters and came out again with a tongue that never ceased wagging.

Kafana talked of the Basanga of generations gone by, when they had lived in the great rain forest to the south, enjoying great tribal

118

pride, the finest of warriors, a larder overflowing with *posho* meal and forests thronging with impalas.

Emphema sought his visitors' sympathy for the flood, pestilence and tribal war which had reduced the Basanga to the point where their greatness now existed only in song and dance. But, he added hastily, with the return of Kafana, it must mean that Nzambi had been moved to lift the curse of illness and starvation—and perhaps even the girl child with the withered leg could be allowed to grow fat at her mother's breast.

"No!" screeched Mafuta, the wizard, rattling his necklace of teeth. "The whitefaces must not interfere." He held up his goatskin bag of charms, warning them that he, Mafuta, and he alone, was the intermediary between the Basanga and the spirits of their ancestors, and that he had consulted them and knew what must be done: the girl child must die—for so the elders had decided at their second council.

In his elation at beholding Kafana again and enraptured with the tales of a past gloried in, old Emphema had inadvertently compromised the special deference due Mafuta. Mafuta was the most powerful man in the village. Other Sanga villages might have one who made charms and sick remedies, and another for communing with the gods and spirits of departed villagers, but in Wendi Macosi Mafuta did both. When Kafana asked the whereabouts of the girl child and suggested that he might wish to see her, Emphema caught the darkness in Mafuta's face and the scowls of the senior elders, Kongolo and Mukulu, and trapped his restless tongue between his gums. Among the six wise and aged *mfumus,* only Kongolo and Mukulu wore the bright red feather, the *nduda,* in the hair. It meant that they had once killed a man in fair contest.

All the while the seven princes sat cross-legged and silent. Matubele could no longer hold his thoughts. He sought his father's permission to speak. "Why do you come here? What is it you wish of us?" he demanded of Kafana.

Kafana explained.

"And why do the English journey to the Great Water?" Emphema croaked.

Again Kafana explained.

Emphema frowned. "The Basanga have no quarrel with those you call German. Is it right that we should become part of this Great Battle you speak of by helping you, Kafana?"

The elders murmured their approval of their chief's concern.

Every Masanga, Kafana pointed out, knew of Kimungu Banze and his wife, Mouya Buya, the Bakalanga commoners from whom sprang the great Baluba nation. And every Masanga knew of the son to these two, Kongolo Mukulu, cruel and merciless man who became king and buried his mother alive because she laughed at him, who married his own sister to protect his throne, and who later became so jealous of his own son that he threatened to kill him, too. Had not the Baluba risen up against this unjust man and taken his head? It was just that they had done so, Kafana told them; they had done it in just anger, and among good men there was always a place for just anger. So it was, too, he continued, with the English and Belgians on whom the Germans had forced war.

"I do not like the Belgians," shouted Matubele, "because they say it is wrong to wear the *nduda*. They say my uncle was wrong to have taken a life to earn the right to wear it."

Kongolo inhaled proudly as all eyes rolled to the bright red feather in his hair.

Mukula, the other *nduda* wearer, spoke up fiercely. "If helping this whiteface helps the Belgians, I shall forbid it."

The four other elders nodded their concurrence.

Emphema looked dismally at Kafana, then turned his attention to the princes. "My sons?"

They huddled in whispered conference, then the oldest spoke. "We honor you, our father, our uncle and the wise *mfumus*—but those who call themselves the Belgian White Fathers are good to the Sanga. They bind our wounds and sores and tell of a god who loves all—"

"A god who says we must not seek the *nduda!*" shouted Kongolo. "Have the Sanga turned into a tribe of old women?"

In the tense silence which followed, the flame of the bikele-fish-oil lamp flickered. In the thick smoke the eyes of the three whitefaces welled with tears. Emphema squinted around at the faces of

120

the assembly, then came to rest on Kafana's. "You have heard what has been said, Kafana. Do you wish to speak more?"

Kafana coughed and rubbed the soot particles from his eyes. "Only this, *mzee,*" he said gravely. "Ask any little *mtoto* who was it who did greatest harm to the Baluba nation, and he will say its second king, Kongolo Mukulu." Kafana looked across to the two elders with the *ndudas* in their hair. "Is it wise, therefore, to hold to the counsel of the two *mfumus* who share his name between them?"

The eyes of Kongolo and Mukulu flashed hate.

Matubele jumped up and shouted, "You have insulted my uncle —you," he added contemptuously, "who killed my mother!"

"Enough!" squealed the wizened old chief, imperiously clawing at the stifling, smoke-laden air. "I am a spent old man, but I am still chief! This *chauri* is at an end!"

When Kongolo and Mukulu left Emphema's compound that night, they did not hasten to cleave to the warmth of their wives who awaited them; instead they stole through the darkness to the hut of Mafuta, the wizard, and spent much time there.

10

The ping and clang of flat steel blades rang through the morning. The expeditioners gnawed away at the stubborn, finely woven brush, tangled plaits of mountain vine and coarse, thorny bramble smothering the long incline to the plateau top. At five thousand feet a lungful of air did not go far. Fatigue sped to a man's vitals. Where once a tough stringy individual like Private Devlin could swing his panga all morning long without strain, the pace now wrung beads of sweat onto his brow and sent his heart's thunder to his eardrums.

Devlin's body revolted against a ball of pain in the center of his back. This nagged his furry throat to profanity. The ball of pain grew in diameter. Its radius reached down for his loins and up for his scapulae, fingering into his right arm and wrist. "Frig," he ejaculated, the expletive opening the seal of his parched lips.

They all cursed when they came upon the dead octopus of a tree stump smack in the line of march, its lifeless tentacles still clutched deep in the dried-up riverbed they had been following. Rather than drag the gear up three feet and out of the riverbed to bypass the huge, gnarled baobab stumps, they carved or blasted them out. All work would cease as the demolition corporal drilled his holes and thrust

122

home his cylindrical charges. Seldom did he have time to tamp to his professional satisfaction. Every second wasted was a lost gold nugget to Humphreys, who never seemed to be more than half a dozen long strides from anywhere. He had harassed the corporal into elimination of the most stubborn root in under five minutes. These were minutes celebrated by the men on their backs where the shade was closest, the grass softest, until the thin air swallowed up the dull crack and the acrid smoke. That would be the signal. "Up and at it," Smith would bellow, and again the blades would swish and hum.

Snakes were always a welcome diversion. Men squealed as boys as they rushed in for the kill, afterward punting the severed lengths of reptile around, indifferent to the crimson life sauce congealing on their heavy boots. The excitement over, they bowed again to their nagging responsibility.

The restless movement of the panga's serrated haft had built the surface of Devlin's hand up into corrugations of horny, polished skin. The sweat coursed, lubricating his aching fist, twirling his panga uncontrollably. Devlin's calluses sloughed away. The soft pink underskin winced with the coarse panga haft. Devlin swore.

Six feet from him Nangle worked away like a machine. It annoyed Devlin that the son of a wealthy aristocrat could do laboring work without buckling under the strain. "C'mon, your Lordship," he shouted with false joviality, "get your bloody back into it." He grinned as if he were enjoying it.

Nangle ran his hand over his wet face. "You'll fold before I do."

Devlin laughed falsely. "Hear that, you blighters? His Lordship's gonna show us all up. . . . Gawd, but I'd like a big long drink of water."

"Why not a big stout while you're at it?" grunted the soldier beside him.

"Frig you, mate," retorted Devlin. "I'm after water, that's what I'm after."

"You know bloody well what's with the water," said the Welshman. "Now, man, why don't you shut your face and get on with it?"

They relapsed into the privacy of their own thoughts.

123

As the line of men advanced they came upon another stump. It was closer to Devlin than to Nangle. They both worked their way around it.

"Eh, Marmaduke," shouted Devlin, "you forgot something."

Nangle looked back and appraised the stump. "That's yours," he muttered.

Devlin straightened up with a scowl. "I like that," he shouted, appealing to the men on each side. "His old man owns a factory. He's always going on about how the British workman's shirking his responsibilities and such. The stump's yours. You're not the gaffer back at the factory now. C'mon, Marmaduke, be a good boy, now."

Nangle was short; a little flabby as becomes the aristocracy, but there was thirteen stone of him. He unbent and turned to Devlin ominously. "Call me that just once more and it'll be the last time." It was the first time that Aloysius James Nangle, scion of the landed gentry, had spoken in such tones.

The line of march left the stump behind.

Fifteen minutes later Humphreys stalked through the area with Sergeant Smith in tow. "What's this?" he demanded, pointing an accusing finger at the stump.

"I don't quite know, sir," temporized Smith, trying to size up the situation.

Humphreys scowled. "Left *this* for dynamiting?" He walked over to the stump and surveyed it briefly. "Could pull it out myself," he snapped. He pointed to the line of men ahead. "Find out who's responsible and bring him here, Smith."

Smith walked purposefully forward to the array of bobbing backsides. "All right," he announced grimly. "Who's the slacker?"

The work continued as if the men had not heard him.

"Which of you silly baskets left that bloody stump behind?" he grated.

Devlin straightened up and turned around to face the sergeant. "Sarge," he began.

Instantly there was a noticeable slackening in the tempo of the work as the rest of the men sought to hear what Devlin would say.

"I'm cuttin' along here," Devlin continued, "and Nangle's by my side, and . . ." His voice trailed off as he looked around at his companions.

They had stopped working and their ominous glances stabbed him.

"Well, Devlin," demanded Smith, "out with it."

Devlin shifted uncomfortably.

"You know you're holding up the work," snapped Smith.

Devlin's large Adam's apple bobbed up and down like a cork on the tide. "Sarge," he began again, "There's an awful drouth on us all. Can't you wangle us some water?"

Smith shook his head disgustedly. "You know as well as I do what Captain Humphreys said." He walked around in front of the row of men and sighted down on the stump behind them. "You and Nangle," he said finally, "come with me." He walked quickly down to where Humphreys waited, impatiently tapping his leggings with his swagger stick.

"These them?" queried Humphreys as they approached, pointing with his swagger stick.

Smith nodded.

Humphreys turned to Devlin and Nangle. "You two are shirking your duty," he declared officially. "Know the penalty for that in time of war? What do you have to say?"

Nangle spoke for the first time. "It seemed to be a job for demolition, sir."

"Dynamite?" asked Humphreys scornfully. "I could rip it out with one hand behind my back. We can't throw away valuable dynamite just because you two are too damn lazy to swing a pick and shovel. Smith!"

"Yes, sir."

"Have them *dig* it out," he commanded.

"Very good, sir," said Smith. He turned to Devlin and Nangle. "All right, on the double over to the equipment pile. Picks and shovels."

"No picks or shovels," snapped Humphreys. "Pangas'll do them fine." He had the habit of some officers of completely ignoring the presence of the "other ranks" when addressing their NCOs.

The highborn Nangle gritted his teeth too late to clamp down on

125

the remark that escaped his lips. "I'd be interested in seeing Captain Humphreys uproot a stump with a panga and—"

"*Nangle!*" roared Smith. "You don't speak unless you're spoken to!"

Humphreys' brow bulged. The lower mandible tensed and untensed but he held on to his composure. He impaled Nangle with a baleful glare. "Is there anything else Private Nangle would like to see?" he asked almost politely.

"There is, sir," replied Nangle evenly in flagrantly Harrovian diction.

"And that would be?"

"I'd like to see the captain do it with one hand behind his back."

Smith blanched as if kneed in the loins. His nether lip sagged and incomprehension glazed his eyes.

Humphreys glared at Nangle, searching his face. "And you, Devlin?" he suddenly inquired.

"Me, sir?" questioned Devlin with a stupid look on his face.

"Yes, *you,*" said Humphreys. "What would *you* like to see?"

Devlin said nothing.

"You, Smith?"

The abrupt question took Smith completely off guard. He swallowed uncomfortably.

As Humphreys surveyed the three, his widely spaced features wore the expression of one insulted. His face was almost square, made more so by the thick neck of the weight lifter he could have passed for. Head and neck never varied in width—a thick solid column of bone, muscle and sinew planted solidly in his immense frame. There was almost no nose, a mere button of flesh appended to the blankness of his widely spaced features. It was hard to resolve all the features into one impression. If Humphreys wore an expression, it was one of boredom. Perhaps the eyes were the most striking—the gray, colorless eyes of a fish; unblinking for the most part, glaring impassively, never betraying the soul of the man behind them. The solidity of his trunk threatened to split the seams of his service shirt, especially when he rolled up his sleeves. Then the several layers of fabric strained severely under the demands of his expanding, uncompromising biceps. "Well, Smith? I asked you a question," he shot.

The middle-aged Regular Army veteran of Flanders aborted the embryo of fear that threatened to choke his windpipe, detached the panga from his own belt and proffered it to the captain. "You may use mine, sir," he said quietly.

Humphreys' eyes stood out like organ stops. He scabbarded the swagger stick in his right legging, unbuckled his Sam Browne, tossed it to one side, unbuttoned his shirt-sleeves and fastidiously rolled them up above his elbows. Several times he rubbed his hands vigorously together before accepting Smith's panga.

Smith, Devlin and Nangle followed him to the tree stump.

For half a minute Humphreys circled it, scrutinizing the grain of the wood and the direction of the roots. Suddenly he called to Smith, "Remove your belt!"

Smith reacted as if he had heard improperly.

"Your belt!" snapped the captain.

Smith hurriedly unfastened his belt and held it loosely.

Humphreys did an about-turn. "Now tie my left hand behind me."

Devlin, who had stood awkwardly by all this time, opened his mouth as if to say something, but he caught Smith's warning glance and gulped down his advice.

Smith slipped the tongue of his belt through one buckle slot, forming a loop which he slipped over Humphreys' left hand and pulled tight. He slid the tongue through a belt loop on the back of the captain's Bedford-cord jodhpurs, then back again through the other buckle slot. He tugged twice, choking the leather firmly up against the buckle and thumbing the prong hard into the unpierced belt surface.

Humphreys pulled several times to make sure the belt would hold. Without another word he raised the panga in his right hand and brought it down savagely on the ground about the stump. The bright steel blade flashed silver arcs in the air as it sliced into the soil about the exposed roots. After a score of evenly spaced slashes he turned to attack the second root. Each stroke seemed to be as

127

heavy and as accurate as the one before it. By the time he descended upon the third root, Smith, Devlin and Nangle could see the large Australia-shaped patches of dampness about his armpits. The sweat trickled down his brow. As the shock of the impacts traveled up his arm, into his barrel chest, up the solid column of his neck and into his skull, the droplets shot off to become steam in the furnace of the forenoon. The trio stood transfixed as the massive engineering officer's tree trunk of an arm rose and fell with the inexorable regularity of a steam hammer. As he began the assault upon the fifth root, the islands of sweat on his belly and back touched shorelines. The once-stiff khaki drill shirt sagged limply over the sodden waistband of his jodhpurs. And on he hacked, his enormous girth expanding and contracting like the respiration of a dying whale. His bright-red face glistened. Phlegm rattled in his throat. But his iron will refused to concede to the desperate pleadings of his chastised body. Convulsively he coughed out a bulb of mucus. His head quivered with the spasm, knocking his topee flying. The sun's predatory rays smote the bone of his balding scalp almost audibly. They scrambled his brain. Only pride impelled him to the sixth and final root. Its reflex action generated the current for his flailing arm as it drove the dulling blade deep into the gritty African topsoil. Now that he had carved the soil from around the visible roots, he still had to sever them at the point where they burrowed into the ground. The round, symmetrical sound of metal biting into dead wood sustained him for the final ordeal. All roots were severed. He flung aside the panga and bent down to grasp one of the roots.

Bludgeoned into awe and admiration for the man and unable to restrain themselves, Smith, Devlin and Nangle involuntarily jumped forward to lend a hand.

From somewhere Humphreys summoned the strength to wave them back.

Abruptly they halted.

Humphreys again laid hold of the root and pulled. It did not budge.

In spirit the three transfixed witnesses laid hold and pulled with him. The root seemed to clutch deeper.

Through eyelashes slick with sweat Humphreys gazed dizzily at the defiant stump. A quarter-inch root still held. He kicked drunkenly at it with his heavy field boot. It snapped. He grabbed the free end with his hand and began dragging off the heavy stump. Four yards from the spot Humphreys' body tried to rebel. But the man would stomach no mutiny within himself. He commanded his heels to dig in. He threatened his spastic right hand if it should shame him by relinquishing its grip. He bullied his flesh to endure. Pain was more palatable than failure.

Humphreys staggered back to camp, his topee dangling by the chin strap from one hand, his sopping shirt clinging to his heaving, spent frame. His gait wobbled. His feet dragged. His brain was addled. But the swagger stick jutted out from his right armpit with a new superiority, a new arrogance. He knew that his name would be on the lips of every man that night.

Long after the twilightless African winter night had hugged the land they still dwelt on Humphreys. By the fitful light of campfires they huddled cross-legged; they talked little, thought much. But soon the rigors of the day drove them to their tents. The flickering fires alone were left to frighten away curious animals. Three sentries patrolled the campsite; not very vigilantly, for this was the back of beyond and who would be about to bother them?

One by one the oil lamps inside the tents snuffed out. Grotesque and misshapen shadow demons conceived in the dying campfires danced eerily about. From countless miles off the singular sound of two hyenas wailing in harmony pierced the attenuated night air. Someone coughed. The wooden floors of the tents squeaked as the weighty bodies of men heavy with fatigue changed position in their sleeping bags.

Devlin was wide awake. Long after his tentmates had gone to sleep the ex-soap-factory hand's brain pulsed with color pictures of Humphreys in action. In the darkness he smoked a Woodbine, holding it in his hand after the fashion of the English workingman —with the tips of two fingers and the thumb, the glowing end pointing toward the palm. It was true: he hated the big bastard as heartily as everyone else; but, he thought, was that reason for almost murdering him? And indeed that's what they'd almost done. They'd forced him into a corner. Now, if only he'd turned around and ordered *them* to do the same thing, he told himself, he'd have felt a damn sight better. Sure, it might've killed them too, almost; but they'd have felt as if they'd paid for their little lark with the stump. Like when he'd gone off on a tear during primary at Aldershot and sat out seven days in the glasshouse for it. That way it was over and done with once and for all. This way it hung around your neck. . . . S'posing he'd keeled over with his heart! Then what? Who'd have taken over? Not the Navy gaffer. It didn't seem like he could beat his way out of a paper bag.

The pain from the day's raw effort had settled in the marrow of his bones. It nagged with the resolute insistence of a burn. He could not sleep. He unbuttoned his sleeping bag and slipped out of it. He fumbled in the dark as he dressed, taking pains not to waken the others.

Outside a heavy mist clung to the ground. It was an hour after midnight. Even so, Africa had not yet surrendered to the great hungry atmosphere above all the heat it had garnered from the day.

Devlin did not bother to button up his heavy khaki tunic. With his hands dug as deeply in his pockets as he was in thought, he shuffled around the edge of the camp. As he picked his way over the loose rocks and between the clumps of mountain growth his mind wandered back to Port Sunlight. What a ruddy name—Port Sunlight, he said to himself. Who ever heard of it? But there wasn't a man jack of them hadn't heard of Lever Brothers. Everybody used soap; at least they were supposed to. He'd have too, if he'd had water to spare. Cleanest man in the street coming home from work of an evening he was. Nellie used to like that, she did. All of her other gentlemen friends smelled of motorcars, she used to say; but he, Albert, was different. Not that she didn't like motorcars, but the others used to bring 'em home under their fingernails, so she said. He wondered where Nellie might be tonight. He waved his hand around and the mist swirled in eddies about him. Suddenly he noticed for the first time that there was no smell of dust. There was always dust—in your eyes, nose, throat. Even in your food. Even in your water.

Water! God, if that isn't the wrong word to say, and me with my mind on Nellie. She'll be out with some chap who smells like motorcars, if I know my Nellie. . . . Humpy's being a bastard about the water. . . . Well, Nellie likes to play the field, but I know where her heart lies. . . . A half a bleedin' cup at ten, another half at four. . . . Nellie and me has plans for after. . . . I bet *he's* getting more than one bloody cup a day. . . . When I get back to Blighty, it's Nellie and me down the aisle. . . . The dirty rotten sod, if that ain't a big story—saving water for the tractor 'cos it's one machine doing the work of two . . . men before friggin' machines, if you ask me.

A sharp point of pain pierced his left buttock. Instinctively his hand shot to his backside, and he yelped as his knuckles rapped against the blunt side of a bayonet.

"Dr. Livingstone, I presume." It was one of the sentries. He playfully jabbed at Devlin with the bayonet fixed to the end of his Lee-Enfield. "You're out late, chum."

Devlin wheeled around in surprise. In the dark he couldn't quite make out the features of the sentry. "Bloody joker," he shouted. "Almost got me in the arse, you did."

"If you're not careful," warned the sentry nervously, "you'll have Tarzan himself out of bed."

Devlin was not mollified. "What the hell you doing on? You're supposed to a medical orderly." He rubbed his bum tenderly.

"Tell *him* that, will you?" said the sentry. "Smith says no such thing as special duty no more."

"And to think we volunteered for this lot," growled Devlin. "And there's the water . . . I've had my friggin' fill, boy."

"Aye, so you've had your fill. And what are you goin' to do about it? French leave?" The sentry laughed quietly.

"I shoulda gone with the doc," muttered Devlin.

"Why didn't you? He asked for volunteers."

"Think the old bugger'll ever find his way back again?"

"Why do you call him that?"

"What? An old bugger? 'Cos that's what he is. That's what they all are—buggers."

"Hold on, now. What did he ever do to you?"

"Damn little he's ever done *for* me—or for Porter."

131

"We lost Martin too, you know."

"Huh, another friggin' officer. He did nothing for neither of 'em."

The sentry hefted the rifle in his hands. "Nothin' that'd mean anythin' to you, Devlin," he said softly.

Devlin stared at him challengingly. "Like what?"

The sentry appeared embarrassed. "He helped Martin say an act of contrition."

Devlin grinned. "You a fish-on-Fridays?"

The sentry nodded defensively.

"Martin, too?"

"Aye."

"Fancy that now, the three of you."

"Four of us. Perkins too."

"A perishing little gang of you, eh? . . . What'd he do for old Porter?"

"He sat up with him all night."

"Fat lot of good that did him. Then what?"

"Then he got stuck into a bottle of Bushmills. Got real blotto."

Devlin's eyes lit up with interest. "I told you they was all buggers. A tot of rum a day, eh? A good old Navy custom. What about the Poor Bloody Infantry? . . . C'mon, where'd he hide it?"

The sentry bristled. "He didn't hide it," he said indignantly. "It's sitting in there on the shelf of—" Suddenly he broke off. "Look, you'd better be getting back to where you belong. If Fish Eyes knew you were out here, it'd be your head in your hand—mine too."

"You're right. Indeed you're right," assented Devlin, becoming suspiciously agreeable. He turned around and picked his way back to the tents, quickly disappearing in the fog.

132

I I

About the same time that Devlin twitched around fitfully in his insomnia he had a companion in his misery seven tents away. Sergeant Smith had also sought some consolation in tobacco—a Player's Navy Cut this time, a butt that he had extinguished more than an hour ago and placed carefully on the upturned ammo box by his cot. As he drew on it the cherry-red tip glowed brightly and bathed the inside of the tent in a muted, dull-red glow. He knew from the studied lightness of the breathing that Stokes, the chief petty officer, wasn't asleep either. "You asleep, Charlie?" he whispered.

"Aye."

"Sorry, chum."

Outside the creatures of the high veldt barked and cried as if unhappy that they, too, could not sleep.

"Got a light?" asked Stokes.

Smith leaned across, offering his cigarette butt to his companion. Stokes accepted it and held it to the end of a fresh cigarette. "Ta," he said, returning the butt to Smith.

The two smoked in silence.

"Whatever got into you, Andy?" asked Stokes.

133

"Blowed if I know, really." Smith sifted his thoughts. "I don't like the bastard, for one thing."

"Show me the perisher that does. Do you s'pose 'e 'ad an old lady like the rest of us?"

"If you ask me, I think he was drilled for."

"So 'elp me, he might. 'E's hard as nails." Stokes lapsed into the comfortable silence of the dark tent. "But I'm surprised you let 'im get your goat like that, Andy. S'not like you. You been at this soldierin' business long nuff so's not to let the likes of 'im get you down."

"It's all bloody fine for you to talk. You don't work under him like I do."

"C'mon, mate. I been in the Navy twenty-three years. I've run into me fill of Humphreys before. You know how to 'andle 'is likes? You stand up there in front of 'im and take it all like you was a duck in the rain, then you turn around and do it your own way. After all it's *wot* gets done, not *'ow*." Stokes paused to pull heavily on his cigarette. "Why *did* you 'and 'im your chopper, Andy?"

"Weren't you around after the tractor went up? Dammit, don't you see how he didn't give a frig about Porter and Martin? Sure, I've been soldiering the biggest part of my life, but I've yet to run into a bigger all-around bastard."

Stokes applied the butt to a fresh cigarette and sucked. "Andy," he said quietly, "I've seen that D.S.M. in the bottom o' your shavin' tin. Also know 'ow you got it, an' I know there's three platoons pushin' up poppies who didn't get medals . . . an' so I think I know why you volunteered for this lot. . . . But I knows you're a long'eaded enough fellow not to let it get in the way of a job to be done 'ere. . . . 'E's a slave driver, but there's not a damn thing he asks he won't turn 'is own 'and to, if 'e 'as to. I don't 'ave to tell you. . . . You know, it's a lucky bugger you are 'e didn't 'ave *you* dig up a stump somewhere."

"Wish to hell he had," muttered Smith. "But he's a fly one: he knows I wish he had, so he won't ever. He's worked it so I'm to feel I owe him something for as long as we're here. A fly bugger!"

"Aye, 'e's fly," admitted the petty officer grudgingly, "but fly or

134

not, man, you can't take it away from 'im—'e's gettin' us there, ain't 'e? An' that's wot we're all 'ere for, ain't it?"

"Right," agreed Smith, "but if he's splitting the men into—" He stopped abruptly. "Charlie," he whispered cautiously, "you hear something?"

In the darkness the petty officer cocked an ear. "Ah, you're 'earin' one o' them jungle love matches. . . . Wot's this about splittin'?"

"Didn't you hear 'em talking tonight: Humphreys this, Humphreys that, Humphreys the other thing? If your precious Frazer doesn't wake up, he's going to find that bloomin' swagger stick up his arse."

Stokes said, "You said they all 'ated 'im?"

For the first time since the conversation had begun, Smith was stuck for a ready answer. Finally he said, "Perhaps I should say they all envy him."

"Wot you really mean, Andy, is *you* envy 'im," said Stokes quietly. "Is that it?"

Smith's reply came clogged with reluctance. "If I do, I'm not the only one."

"You're thinkin' of the commander, maybe," suggested Stokes. Smith didn't reply.

"Nark it, Andy. Don't you know there's more ways 'n one to skin a cat?"

"I know all about that," argued Smith, "but *he* may turn out to be the cat . . . Charlie, there's something going on out there." The sergeant peeled off his sleeping bag and pulled on some clothes. In the peat-bog blackness of the inside of the tent his hand went instinctively to the Webley stuck in his boot.

What Smith had heard sounded like the low, plaintive keening of an animal in pain. It had stopped now, and as he stood outside the tent with the mist eddying about his waist, he strapped the weapon to his body and cocked his hand to his ear. There it was again—a rising and falling sound of some living creature. It seemed to come from the far side of the encampment, over by the boats. But it stopped again, and he wasn't sure of the direction. He stopped dead-still, listening. In the waning heat of the earth the

135

primal smell of his own body's labors wafted up into his nostrils. Like the others he had not bathed in weeks; the voracious appetites of the tractors had had to be sated first. The cry came again —from the direction of the tractors. Could be, he thought, as he stole across the camp, something's wandered in attracted by the fires and got tangled up in the spokes of the trailer wheels. If that was all, he did not want to wake up the whole camp. He could take care of it himself. He made a mental note to tear a strip off the sentries—and the corporal of the guard. It was their job to be on their toes to everything. God, he thought. Supposing Jerry's somehow got wind of the whole picnic. They've caught us with our bloody skivvies round our ankles! . . . Couldn't be, he assured himself. Nevertheless he slipped the Webley out of his holster.

The two trailers stood one behind the other a hundred yards away from the edge of the campsite in the dried-up riverbed. The sound seemed to be coming from the far side of them—perhaps in the brush. A gentle breeze blew from the north. If it's an animal, Smith told himself, I'd best come up into the wind. He circled around the trailers.

Fifteen yards from the stern of *Toutou* his ankle buckled under him. He stuck his arms out wildly to protect himself as he fell. His body slapped down heavily on a patch of hard, sunbaked clay. The Webley struck a rock. It went off like a cannon. In the eternity of silence born of the report Smith could not believe the new sound that now assailed his ears. "Christ, it can't be," he gasped. And then again came the strange sound—a human voice in song:

> 'Ma rambler, 'ma gambler, 'ma long way from home,
> 'N' if you don't like me just lemme 'lone.
> 'L'eat when 'm hungry n'drink when 'm dry,
> 'F moonshine don't kill me, ah live till ah die . . .

Devlin sat under the trailer. He was dressed warmly in his birthday suit. A rapidly weakening jet of liquid from *Toutou*'s fuel tank played on his head and coursed down his body.

As the incredulous Smith approached Devlin, he suddenly be-

136

came aware that his boots were sinking in what should have been hard-baked mud. The awful truth hit him sudden as a club. He growled an obscenity. "In the name of Christ, what'd you think you're doing, you crazy bugger?"

"Good ole Sarge," cooed Devlin, drunkenly beckoning with a bottle. "C'mon have a bath, man. C'mon, water's fine."

Smith closed his eyes and gritted his teeth. Imprinted in color on his retina blazed a huge sign reading: FOUR HUNDRED GALLONS OF WATER DOWN THE DRAIN! A current of anger raced to his hands and he bent down to grab Devlin. In all his years of soldiering Smith had never tried to grab a naked man. He quickly discovered the paucity of convenient handles on the nude body. He straightened up, enraged with the frustration. He snatched the bottle from Devlin. "Old Bushmills," he snapped, in disbelief. Suddenly he pitched the bottle far into the brush and pivoted quickly to turn off the spigot. He remembered the shot. The guards would be upon them in a moment. God, so might Humphreys. No, after that stump, he'll be sleeping like the dead. Yet the thought stung him into decision. He grabbed Devlin by one foot and pulled him from under *Toutou.*

"Best bloody sergeant 'n th'ole Army," Devlin droned drunkenly as he slid on muddy buttocks across the gravelly riverbed. "Aw!" he shrieked, as the layer of mud wore thin. "M'arse, Sarge, m' bleeding' arse, Sarge!" he screamed. "'M losin' m'arse, Sarge!"

Smith released his hold. "That's the best part of you gone," he said angrily.

Devlin, sprawled out on the ground, forgot his pain and broke spontaneously into song again.

> 'Ma rambler, 'ma gambler, 'ma long way from home,
> 'N' if you don't like me just leave me alone . . .

"Captain Humphreys isn't going to like you when he finds out how naughty you've been," observed Smith evenly. "On your feet, damn you."

Devlin coaxed his long, lean, fish-belly-white body out of the

137

supine. He dripped as much of maudlin sentiment as he did of the expedition's water supply. He tried to embrace Smith. "Best NCO a fella ever had," he said.

His thatch of wet hair stuck in Smith's face. He helped himself to a handful of the sergeant's shirttail and briskly commenced to dry off his chest and armpits.

Smith swore and pulled his shirttail from Devlin's hand.

Devlin looked hurt. "Not cross with me, Sarge, are you?" He broke into tears. "Just lil thirsty, 's'all."

Smith grabbed him by the arm and began to lead him back to his tent. "How the hell do you think the others feel? Don't you think they might be a little thirsty too?" Smith knew it was impossible to reason with a drunk. He merely talked to keep the choking rage from closing up his throat. "Where'd you get the Bushmills?"

"Nangle's rude to me, Sarge, too," Devlin went on sobbing. "Sed I smelt."

"For Christ's sake we all smell," Smith snapped.

"Sez I stink like a Turkish wrestler's jockstrap," cried Devlin.

Smith prayed that the guards had been swinging the lead and had not heard the shot. He led Devlin the long way back to his tent—along the edge of the campsite.

All the while Devlin chattered on incessantly in his stupor. He clung to the sleeve of Smith's tunic and seemed not to mind the chill that had just begun to set in. "Ah, don't stink," he whined in the sergeant's ear. "Ask ma popsie, Nell. She sez 'm cleanest chap sh'ever went out with."

Smith stepped quietly. They had circled around close to the officers' tents. He held his breath in case Devlin should stub his toe and do what the pistol shot apparently had failed to do.

"You're all right, Sergeant. You're not a bugger like the rest of 'em," droned Devlin. He seemed to be sobering up a little. He cocked his head and gave Smith what he hoped was a friendly smile. The best he could manage was a drunken leer. "Y'aren't gonna turn me in, are ya, Sarge?"

"If you don't quit your blabbering and shut up, I damn well will."

The click of a hobnailed boot on mountain rock froze Smith in his tracks. The naked Devlin strolled on unhearing. Smith grabbed him by the neck and flung a hand to his mouth. He dropped agilely to his haunches in the broad-leafed grass and pulled Devlin down with him. Devlin squirmed. His eyes rolled in fear. "One peep out of you," whispered Smith, "and I'll wring your bloody neck."

Two men were searching within the camp perimeter.

One of them said, "All I know is I heard it, but I can't say where it came from."

Smith recognized the voice of one of the sentries.

"Sure it was a shot?" asked the other.

He recognized the other voice as that of the demolition corporal.

"Could've been a rock crackin'," said the corporal. "Happens all the time when it cools off."

The sentry and the corporal continued to poke around in the brush a few yards from Smith and Devlin.

Smith reflected on the ridiculousness of his being discovered . . . my God, Devlin bare-arsed too! But he, Smith, was a senior NCO. He could nip the whole thing in the bud by stepping out in the open, confiding in the two guards and getting them on his side. If not, they would stumble upon the wet ground, Devlin's clothes— and the Webley. They would head straight for his own tent; and not finding him, they would rouse Humphreys. He had just decided to reveal himself when the shivering Devlin erupted with a violent sneeze.

"In here!" shouted the corporal. He darted forward and beamed his flashlight on the senior NCO and the nude private squatting together in the tall grass. "Well, I never!" exclaimed the corporal. "What have we here?"

Smith rose. He blustered officiously to mask his embarrassment. He knew the men would make his life hell if it got around. "What the hell does it look like?" he snapped. "You should have been here hours ago. Sleeping on the job, eh?"

The corporal's face crinkled in a puckish grin. "Looks like we got here a bit too soon."

The sentry snickered.

"Get your bloody minds above your navels and this stupid clod back to bed," growled Smith, "and get back here on the double!"

139

"Right, Sarge," said the sentry, reaching for Devlin.

All the song had been drained out of the nudist. As the sentry looked at him and snickered again, gone was the noisy, ebullient nuisance of two hours ago. In his place stood the forlorn figure of a shivering half-drunk with a bleeding backside and a hank of pubic hair adorning his maleness like an overgrown sporran. But suddenly the sentry's mirth stuck in his craw. How had Devlin come by his high spirits? he wondered. He slung the Lee-Enfield over his shoulder and guided his mute, unhappy charge back to his tent. The sentry was suddenly as glum as Devlin. He remembered telling Devlin about the doctor's bottle. If Devlin had pinched it, he and Devlin could both be in a real mess.

Smith told the corporal what had happened. "Humphreys better not find out about this," he warned him. "Who else's on tonight?"

The corporal rattled off five names.

"Good," snapped the sergeant, "they'll all keep their mouths shut. Get any one of them and the chap with Devlin over to the trailer. Find that damn pistol and Devlin's duds and get 'em back to him. There's water all over the place. What time's it?"

The corporal squinted at the luminous dial of his wristwatch. "Five past two."

"Won't hardly dry up in four hours. Have 'em bale out the water holes. Slosh it around. Fill up the holes. Get rid of it somehow. And tell them not a bloody word to anyone. Understood? And if anybody asks about a shot, give 'em that lot about the rock. All right?"

The corporal stood his ground.

"Well," snapped Smith, "what are you waiting for?"

"What happens when they turn the cock on *Toutou* and nothing comes out but fresh air?"

"You get them two over to the trailers. I'll think of something."

The corporal left without comment. Ten minutes later he rejoined Smith by the trailers, the two sentries in tow. He put them to work.

"Sarge," mused the corporal, "why cover up for the bleeder? I think he's got it coming. He really narks me, he does."

"What good would it do?" asked Smith. "I don't need him either,

140

but if the cat gets out of the bag, Humphreys'll surely dream up something nasty for him—not that it mightn't do him a lot of good, but it'd give the screw another turn for the lot of us."

An hour later the two sentries had dispersed the telltale pools of water and recovered Devlin's clothes and Smith's pistol.

"You're all cleaned up here," Smith told the sentries. "Now back to the bags with you, and you don't know a thing and haven't heard a thing."

The two soldiers left the sergeant and the corporal standing in the misty darkness brooding over the next phase of the job.

"First let's check the water levels," said Smith softly. They untied the tarpaulins, climbed into the boats and unscrewed the caps.

In the process Smith juggled his thoughts. When he had discovered Devlin, the water had been just dribbling from the spigot onto his head; therefore *Toutou's* tank had to be close to empty. Yet he remembered it had been full the previous night. A *full* tank and an *empty* tank have one thing in common: they don't slosh around on the trail and make all that noise. He thought: If *Toutou's* tank stays as is, Humphreys'll hear it's not full like it's supposed to be. So we'll have to let out all *Toutou's* water. But what do we do with it? Can't just waste it. Be a bloody crime in this heat. . . . He remembered that since stopping back at the last water hole, they had been filling the tractor boiler with water from *Mimi's* tank. So *Mimi* ought to be half used up now. That's it! Pour the little drop that's left in *Toutou* into *Mimi*. It won't be near enough to fill *Mimi* completely; so the sloshing'll still come from *Mimi* like before. And *Toutou?* She'll be bone-dry. Not a sound from her—just what you'd expect from a full tank.

He told his scheme to the corporal, and they boarded *Toutou*.

As he played his flashlight beam on *Toutou's* wet dipstick, Smith frowned.

"Well?" demanded the corporal.

"Maybe he wasn't out here as long as I thought," mused Smith, scratching his cheek. "With all 'em pools around, it bloody well looked like it." He passed the stick and the flashlight to the corporal.

The corporal examined the stick. "Half a tank?"

141

Smith nodded without enthusiasm, for half a tank meant a lot more water to transfer to *Mimi* than Smith had surmised. *Mimi* could take it all—if she was half or less. "Have a go at *Mimi*."

The corporal took the flashlight and disappeared over the side. He reappeared some minutes later, shaking his head. "Don't know as it's gonna work, Sarge. 'Bout three-quarters full."

"Damn!" Smith's fingernails dug at his scalp for inspiration. "Can't help it. Just have to dump the overflow somewhere."

"Sarge!" cried the corporal excitedly. "I hope you know what you're doing. What if we run dry 'fore we get to the next hole?"

"That's the chance we have to take. C'mon."

"We don't *have* to, Sarge. The bleeder ain't worth it."

Smith stared at him ominously. "You coming or aren't you?"

"Oh, Lord. All that lovely drinking," moaned the corporal regretfully.

Using the jerricans strapped to the trailers, they worked more than an hour to transfer the water. Smith found that with *Mimi* as full as he dared make her so as to allow space for "slosh," and with the jerricans full, about twenty gallons still weighed guiltily in *Toutou*'s belly. They could dump it in the brush; but because Humphreys already had them on a short water ration, Smith could not bring himself to do it. "Nip back to the mess tent," he told the corporal. "Get something that'll hold water."

The corporal took off. Later he returned with a large two-handled galvanized pail over three feet high. "We'd better get a bloody move on," he warned glumly.

Smith looked at the dustbin approvingly. "That's the ticket. What's the hurry?" he asked casually. A smile of relief from the tension of the past few hours lit his features. "It won't be light for another two hours."

"Forget it," snapped the corporal. "I almost tripped over you know who."

The smile on Smith's face went out like a snuffed candle. "Where?" he gulped.

"There was a light on in his tent when I went back. As sure as hell he's snooping."

Smith's mind worked rapidly. "Quick! The pail!"

They slid the pail under *Toutou*'s keel and turned the spigot. They jumped with shock. The strong jet of water struck the bottom of the empty pail deafeningly like a colossal udder-squirt on the bare bottom of an empty milking pail. Both of them dived to shut off the spigot.

"Whatta we do now?" groaned the corporal. "If he didn't hear that, he must—"

"Shut up," snapped Smith. Suddenly he tore off his tunic and his shirt. He tied the sleeve of the shirt to the spigot, allowing it to hang so that the other sleeve touched the bottom of the pail. He turned the spigot. The water seeped down the sleeve quietly.

A watched pot never boils. The level could not rise fast enough for the two tense soldiers. Smith rammed the spigot lever over hard to the limit. They entertained visions of the big engineering officer tramping in on the top of them. . . . After an eternity the level had climbed to the two-thirds mark. But they had endured one anxiety only to take on another. Would there be *too much* water? Now the level seemed to surge upward malevolently. The spigot stream's power and volume defied their most urgent supplications, profane or prayerful. With the water level three inches from the top and still rising, the corporal gripped the sides of the pail. His knuckles glowed white in the dark. "The frigger ain't worth it," he grated.

"S'going over the top," groaned Smith. "Quick! The jerricans!" He jabbed a finger toward the bush. "Empty 'em in the grass. Get 'em back here on the double."

The corporal darted from under the trailer and stood up to claw frantically at the straps securing the six jerricans so recently filled. If the water overflowed onto the ground, there would be no time to mop it up before Humphreys stumbled onto the scene. But they could not turn off the spigot unless *all* the water had been drained from *Toutou*. If any remained, there would be that telltale sound as soon as they started moving forward, and Humphreys would be on to them. With a full jerrican in each hand tugging at his shoulders, he stepped heavily across the dried-up riverbed. Several times he tripped and almost lost his balance in his precipitous haste. Once he stumbled and his right knee thudded against a sharp rock. The intense pain churned his insides, and the bitter bile of his

143

bully-beef supper gurged upward into his mouth. A few yards from the edge of the riverbed he set down the jerricans and sprang upon the screw caps. He longed to snatch for a fast drink. It was going down the drain anyway. But fear clutched at his stomach, spoiling his magnificent thirst. The two jerricans surrendered their contents to the greedy mountain growth.

When he rejoined Smith, he was greeted with the curt order: "Forget it. Stow the cans."

"Now what?" groaned the corporal. The spigot was dead. He swore. The water level stood calm and silent an inch from the rim. Disconsolately he restrapped the jerricans.

"Gimme a hand here," said Smith. He pressed the lid on the pail.

"C'mon," he said, grabbing a handle.

The corporal took the other handle.

They lifted—and the deadweight almost capsized in their unsteady grips. The handles were too close to the center of gravity for stability. Their hearts thundered. They lifted again. They stumbled through the brush. Through the steel handles, the 300-pound weight wore deep into their hands and racked their shoulder sockets. The sharp bottom rim smashed against their ankles. Three hundred yards from the trailers, their stale breath heaving, the two soldiers rested limp on their backsides.

The corporal hugged his knees. Smith coughed deeply, then spat with a satisfying whole sound. "Hope Devlin appreciates this lot," he gasped.

"Like to stick his bloody head in it, I would," retorted the corporal.

In three minutes their breathing had returned to normal.

"You got the tarp on *Mimi*, didn't you?" asked Smith.

"I thought *you* got it!"

It was Smith's turn to swear.

The corporal coaxed his reluctant body to his feet, grumbling.

"Never mind," muttered the sergeant. "I'll get it." He pulled himself to his feet and picked his way silently back to the riverbed. In the dark a smile crept over his plain, fleshy features. He even managed a dry laugh, for suddenly the to-do had fallen into its

144

ridiculous perspective. He imagined himself in some comfortable sergeant's mess after the war gaffing about it with the other NCOs; maybe at Aldershot or Tidworth swapping yarns. He could hear himself tell how they'd almost lost the war 'cos a drunk soap-factory worker from Liverpool had taken a bath when he shouldn't have. Like many a situation a fellow finds himself in during wartime, it wasn't very funny at the time it was happening; but he knew it could be a whacking great yarn one day. They'd pound the tables, roll in their chairs. But right at the moment there wasn't a hell of a lot funny about it. They'd been on the go for sixteen days. After losing one tractor Humphreys had been slogging twice as hard to make up for the loss. The one tractor had been double-timing it too. When you double-timed one of them, you maybe triple-timed your water consumption, so the tractor had to come first with the water. And for twelve days they'd all been existing on one mug three times a day.

Noon was always the worst. Cook always tried to put something on for breakfast and again at tea time; but noon was a hothouse and lunch a hunk of dry bully that stuck in the gullet—unless you could suck up enough spit to grease it down. Crackers for dessert made you wonder if one day they'd ever come up with a way for a chap to reuse his own sweat. Why stop at sweat? As you unbuttoned and squatted in the high grass and panted to unburden yourself of a week of bully, the pool between your boots frothed away down into only God knew where. Keep it to yourself, otherwise Humpy's liable to pass the pot around. It'd make a nice touch for the mess of a Saturday night when it was all behind them. But not the sort of yarn he could spin the wife—if she ever did get fed up with running around and came back to him one day; and maybe only a real laugh once he got out of his head the sound of all the schoolboy volunteers he'd ordered over the top dying and screaming for their mums.

It took Smith three minutes to batten down *Mimi*. He made a final check of the area. All water mopped up. All tracks covered.

He left to rejoin his friend in conspiracy. "Any sign of you know who?" he inquired.

"Not a bloomin' soul 'cept the sentries," whispered the corporal.

"Good. Let's have another go."

As they bent forward to pick up the pail a distant voice barked, "Who goes there!"

They froze. They recognized the voice of a sentry. But who was he challenging? The only challenges like that occurred in army manuals.

To the challenge came the bellowed answer, "Captain Humphreys!"

The conspirators simultaneously swallowed nervously.

A Lee-Enfield boomed like the slam of a door in an empty cathedral.

"We're sunk," wailed the corporal.

"Who in blazes are you shooting at, you imbecile?" thundered Humphreys from somewhere.

The corporal whispered tremulously, "I'm getting to frig outa here." He slithered off into the dark among the tall brush.

Smith moved noiselessly after him and grabbed him by the wrist. "Stand your ground," he grated.

The lanky corporal crouched like a whipped cur. "He finds us with this lot and we're sunk. Stealing water, he'll say. Then what? Bastard could shoot us."

"Shut up. He hasn't caught us yet."

The coarse sounds of Humphreys browbeating the sentry carried across the clearing. On the receiving end was the sentry who had escorted the nude Devlin back to his tent. Humphreys ranted on, "You clumsy idiot. Why did you open fire on me? You fathead! Answer me!"

The sentry stuttered his reply. "Well, sir. I didn't . . . I didn't rightly know it was you, sir."

"What? You didn't know it was I? What the blazes do you mean? Didn't you hear me identify myself?"

The sentry was too cowed to answer.

"Well?" demanded Humphreys.

"Yes, sir."

"Then why in the name of Christ did you discharge your bloody weapon at me?"

"Well, sir," began the scared sentry with difficulty, "usually if

146

it's one of the chaps, and I say 'Who goes there?' he'll say 'the Kaiser.' "

The massive engineering captain seemed on the verge of apoplexy. "Corporal of the guard!" he roared.

Smith nudged his trembling companion. "Go see what he wants."

The corporal balked.

"Get going!" commanded the sergeant. "Get right out there. Make believe you've been on rounds."

The unhappy NCO marshaled his reserves of fortitude and prepared to step out into the open. He buttoned up the neck of his tunic and tilted his topee forward to the proper angle. "Frig Devlin," he muttered earnestly. He crawled out of the bush and stepped into the approaching dawn. As he did so, he switched on his electric torch. Its brilliant piercing cone of light dispelled some of his apprehension and invested his presence with some authority. He played the beam around as if looking for something. When it fell upon the bulk of the engineering captain and the ashen-faced sentry by his side, he shouted solicitously, "Corporal of the guard here, sir! Did you call, Captain Humphreys?"

"Where've you been?" demanded Humphreys. "And cut the blasted torch."

The corporal's cone of illuminated comfort clicked out and the corner of his mouth twitched.

"Where've you been? You hear a shot?"

"Shot, sir?" declared the NCO innocently. "Must've been one of those silly rocks again, I said to myself."

"Rocks?" queried Humphreys.

"You know, sir," explained the corporal readily, "you get one with a bit of a crack in it, and a bit of rain gets down in there and 'fore you know it it freezes and your rock pops."

"You dull bugger," Humphreys observed. "It hasn't rained here in months. What sort of instructions do you give the sentries when you post 'em?" He jerked his thumb in the sentry's face. "This incompetent swine almost killed me."

The corporal looked disappointed. "I told you to look sharp," he upbraided the sentry. He turned to the captain. "An unfortunate

147

accident, sir. He missed you. Won't happen again, sir, I assure you."

Humphreys snickered adenoidally. "Your assurances are as good as this nincompoop's aim. Put him away somewhere." He looked around, his eyes ferretlike. "Where's Smith?"

The corporal swallowed nervously. "Smith, sir?" he temporized.

"Smith! Sergeant Smith! *Sergeant Smith!*" bellowed Humphreys. "Ever heard of him?"

"Oh, you mean Smith, sir," said the corporal. "Sleeping, sir. Said we wasn't to disturb him till morning." Instantly he realized he had put his size twelves in it.

"Who does he think he is?" asked Humphreys. "Get him out of his bloody bed."

The corporal stammered, "Sir, I don't think he's in his tent, sir."

"How do you know?" Humphreys demanded.

The corporal felt his knees go weak. "I sort of . . . ran into him in the bush, sir."

"Doesn't Smith read standing orders? Nobody but sentries and corporals of the guard outside the perimeter after dark. How long ago?"

The corporal hesitated.

"How long ago?" persisted Humphreys.

"A couple of hours, sir. He's probably back in his tent by now, though. He just went out to have a—well, you know, sir."

"Two hours?" demanded Humphreys incredulously. "Lost himself, probably. All right. Organize a search party right away and find the ass."

Smith observed the trio in the gathering light. He had to think fast. It would be daylight in another half hour. Even if he managed to sneak back to his tent and later explain away his absence somehow, a search party would discover the pail. Humphreys would soon put two and two together, and his mathematics was impeccable. While maintaining his lonely vigil, Smith had been kneading a small stone. It gave him an idea. He scooped up a handful, stood up and fired them high into the air.

"Over there!" Humphreys shouted hoarsely. He grabbed the

sentry's rifle and tore toward the place where the stones were crashing into the brush.

The sentry ran after him.

The corporal sensed what was up. He lagged behind.

Smith saw Humphreys and the sentry disappear into the brush. He called softly to the corporal. "Quick, for God's sake."

The corporal nipped back to Smith's side. He looked fearfully at the pail. "Let's dump this friggin' lot," he pleaded.

"Not on your bloody life, chum. C'mon."

Through tangled brush, rock and crumbled shale their burden lay upon them each step of their unlit way. Their shins bled. Tears rolled freely down the corporal's cheeks. "Jesus, my hands! My hands!" he moaned.

Smith's lips were drawn tightly over his clenched teeth. Agony gashed crow's-feet around his eyes. "Another fifty feet," he groaned, grimacing.

"Not the mess tent," groaned the corporal. "Aid tent."

Inside the aid tent the two medical orderlies snored deeply, oblivious to the cruelly labored breathing and quiet sobbing as the two NCOs exerted their last dram of strength to manhandle their nemesis back into the tent.

Their sobs would have turned to tears had they only known that the pail was a medical refuse bin—the bottom of which still contained the debris from the doctor's surgical efforts on Martin and Porter.

12

Cavanaugh started. Crann was roughly shaking his shoulder. He could hear feet shuffle outside the hut. He rubbed his eyes and saw it was morning. "What's up?" he said hoarsely.

"Dunno, sir," replied Crann anxiously. "Looks like a parade or something."

Perkins called from outside the hut. "They're coming this way, sir."

"The Webley, sir?" Crann inquired anxiously.

"In the pack," grunted Cavanaugh.

Crann called outside to Perkins. "Nip back to that clump of rocks where we hid the rifles! Fast, mind you!"

"Wait," commanded the doctor.

"Wait?" snapped Crann incredulously. "Might as well have a peashooter as one Webley against that lot, sir." He clawed at the straps of the doctor's pack and explored inside for the pistol. He withdrew it, broke it down to inspect the chamber and stuck it in the doctor's hand.

Cavanaugh declined. "You take it. I can look out for myself. Hide it. And the bags. Don't let them out of your sight. Do you hear?"

Crann jammed the pistol into the waistband of his pants and pulled his shirttail out over the butt.

Cavanaugh called Perkins inside. "You two stay here. I'll call you if I need you." He got down on his hands and knees and crawled out through the small opening and stood upright in the early morning.

A long column of Basanga wound slowly but deliberately in the direction of the hut of the Britons. Emphema, his sons, the elders, and Mafuta, the wizard, walked regally in the van. As Emphema approached within speaking distance, Cavanaugh greeted him in traditional fashion. The old man returned his greeting warmly. The other Basanga ignored him. Emphema led the column around the hut and toward another hut some seventy-five yards away.

Emphema halted in front of the distant hut. A man and a woman with a baby in her arms emerged. Mafuta advanced with a wicker basket. The woman placed the child in it.

"My God, no," whispered Cavanaugh.

The column turned around and followed Emphema toward the bend in the river where the waters flowed stillest and deepest.

Cavanaugh ducked inside and told Crann and Perkins what was happening.

"Crikey," sighed Crann with obvious relief, "I thought we were on today's menu or something."

Cavanaugh frowned. "Do you understand, man? They're going to drown a helpless baby."

"Yes, sir. But they must've drowned dozens of 'em before we ever got here. I mean, what's the point of making a big fuss about it now? We're lucky it's not us in the basket."

Cavanaugh paced up and down inside the hut. "You understand what's happening?" he asked Perkins, as if desperate to find someone as appalled as he.

"It's awful, sir, really," said the youth, shaking his head. "What ever for?"

"No time to explain now," shot the doctor. "Grab the bags. We're going, too."

Crann balked. "Are you sure it's wise to get mixed up in something that doesn't concern us, sir? We've a duty, sir," he reminded him tactfully.

"Good God. What do you think *this* is?" he snapped.

Crann and Perkins shouldered the bags and followed the doctor out of the hut.

All the villagers of Wendi Macosi were gathered on a high promontory jutting out into the slowly flowing, meandering, rush-choked river. There was no sound save the stiff breeze whistling through the reeds and the undulating wail of the infant, whose parents stood behind Mafuta the wizard.

The three Britons stood a cautious distance from the ceremony. Cavanaugh explained what was taking place.

The long, thin Mafuta, his hair oiled and braided, tufted bangles on his wrists and ankles, and draped heavily around the loins with tiers of grass cloth, busied himself importantly with the Kisanga liturgy. He stood before the infant's mother and announced why this had come to pass. The villagers stood mute and respectful.

The mother listened but she did not seem to hear. Her tearless eyes looked out upon the river. They crossed to the shallow side, where she had often eked out the stringy, stunted products of her husband's untidy patch of garden by fishing. Here she had hidden her long baskets among the tall reeds and chased the crabs, bikele and mudfish into them, and patted the slime of the lazy river's bed up into high circular dikes, emptied out the entrapped water with a calabash ladle and scooped up the stranded, wiggling life into her cheap, faded apron of Manchester cotton.

Among the slim Baluba agriculturalists, her husband stood out. He had been born into a fishing tribe of Baluba, but somehow had become one of the Beilande, who wandered through Kisale and Kibara trading grass cloth for zebra skins and salt. The man's thin, underdeveloped legs were characteristic of the Baluba who fished, but they supported a torso having an abnormal development of the chest, shoulders and arms which made him an oddity. True to the Baluba belief, which sees in any unusual natural object the dwelling place of a spirit, he had long been regarded with great respect.

But now, Mafuta told the villagers, it was at last clear the kind of

152

spirit that lived in the man's body—an *evil* spirit. The withered leg of his child was testimony. At last, he continued, it was clear to him why Engai had fouled them with the curse of miserable crops, fishless streams, dying cattle, the sleeping sickness and the great swelling of the necks of his people. This was a great morning, said Mafuta, because forthwith they would be uncursed.

Cavanaugh, Crann and Perkins edged closer to see Mafuta place the babe in the vine basket. Several of the villagers handed him small rocks. These he accepted and placed around the child's body. Finally he tied a vine rope to the basket handle. Mafuta moved to the edge of the promontory. The silent villagers crowded up behind him. Mafuta lowered the basket.

"*Panzi!*" shouted Cavanaugh. The doctor scrambled up the side of the rise and elbowed his way through the tightly packed throng.

Crann and Perkins stood nervously below.

Mafuta held on to the rope. The life-bearing basket swung above the water like a pendulum, ticking off the last few minutes. The wizard's expression of priestly resignation suddenly screwed up into narrow-eyed hate.

The villagers murmured loudly.

Down below, Crann groped inside his shirt for the hard butt of the Webley. "Crazy idiot," he muttered.

Perkins stammered nervously, "Maybe I ought to get the rifles."

"Maybe," grunted Crann, his eyes fixed rigidly on the scene atop the hill. "Give'm a moment yet. Can't tell what he's up to. S'liable to get us all killed, he is."

Cavanaugh had broken through the circle of angry villagers and walked toward the native dignitaries, his right hand raised in greeting. "I have no rock to harm you," he announced solemnly.

Emphema returned his greeting, but Mafuta said, "It is not the rock you use to harm the Basanga, but your tongue, little man. You are not welcome here. This is a sacred place which your presence will defile."

Emphema glared at Mafuta, but risked no reprimand of his wizard. Mafuta would not easily forget anyone who might diminish his standing before the assembled village.

"Did I defile it, Mafuta, the night I walked from these very waters with Matubele in my arms and there was life in him that you and your bag of tricks couldn't put in him?" asked Cavanaugh.

"And you," countered Mafuta, "let a demon fly out of his mother's belly and it has returned to curse us." He began lowering the rope.

Cavanaugh rushed forward and grabbed the basket from Mafuta. "God's curse on you, you bloody heathen!" he shouted in English.

Mafuta shouted. A hundred black hands seized the doctor. Mafuta moved to the river's edge again and lowered the basket.

As if sensing danger, the infant began wailing.

In desperation Cavanaugh shouted to old Emphema, "Oh, *mzee!* This must not happen!"

Emphema glued his eyes to the oscillating basket.

"*Mzee!*" persisted the doctor. "There are other ways to lift the *thau* upon your people than death! You yourself were not for the drowning, *mzee!*"

Emphema shouted a command. The doctor was released. A scowling Mafuta once again had to haul up the basket.

"Kafana says there are other ways," declared Emphema seriously, "and we—"

"There are no other ways but what the spirits have whispered to Mafuta!" shrieked Mafuta. He poked a derisive finger at the doctor. "This little one has no voice with our ancestors. He has no power like Mafuta." He glowered at Emphema. "Foolish old man," he spat, "what do *you* know of the things of Mafuta?"

The senior elders, Kongolo and Mukulu, gravely whispered their counsel in the old chief's ear, shaking their heads.

"But Kafana," protested Emphema, "has a power—perhaps a power like that the night he plucked Matubele from his mother."

Mafuta walked deliberately across to the doctor and stood in front of him. Mafuta prodded him with a horny forefinger. "They have gathered here to witness the words of the spirits put into deeds. They will not leave this hill until it is done." He smiled evilly. "If you have a power, whiteface, lead them down this hill and back to their huts. This will be a power for all the village to see."

154

Cavanaugh surveyed the stolid faces of the villagers. He found no solace in the carved-ebony sameness.

Emphema could read the disciplined hopelessness in the doctor's eyes. In the land of emotion, all men speak the same tongue. The old headman croaked, "*Kufa tutakufa wote.* As for dying, we shall all die."

"*Ndio,* yes," agreed Cavanaugh. "But," he asked Emphema, "why, then, shouldn't all the villagers with the large knots in their necks drown themselves in the river *kesho u subuhi,* tomorrow morning? Or, better still, *upezi,* at once?"

"Kafana! *Simameni!* Stop!" screeched Emphema, his temper rising. "*Unataka nini?* What do you want?" The old chief had looked into the faces of his people and knew too well what was in their hearts. "*Kusema ni kuzuri, na kutokusema ni kuzuri.* To speak is good, and not to speak is good," he gasped resignedly. He nodded to Mafuta to continue.

"Wait!" shouted Cavanaugh. "I will lead them from this place," he announced solemnly.

Mafuta pulled back, his face contorted. "Ha," he squealed, "this little whiteface puffs like the pigeon and crows like the cock. Do you hear? He will lead you from this holy hill."

The thin-boned villagers packed more tightly together.

"I will lead them," repeated the doctor, "but I command a price."

"The pigeon now commands," said Mafuta scathingly. "What will you command? I do not fear your command." He spat. "Lead them from this hill and you shall have your price."

"The child returned to its mother," demanded Cavanaugh. "No more, no less."

Mafuta peered darkly at the doctor. He closed the few paces between them and studied the short little man intently. He looked inside his shirt and up his sleeves. To have made such a demand, the whiteface must have a powerful charm. His horny fingers fixed on the wooden identification discs around Cavanaugh's neck. Mafuta cried exultantly. He studied the discs minutely, then tossed them aside, contemptuously. "It is agreed, pigeon."

Cavanaugh looked around unsurely. He thrust a hand into his

pocket. All eyes were on his bulging pocket. Suddenly he whipped out his hand.

The villagers pulled back, whining.

Cavanaugh held a grimy khaki handkerchief. He ceremoniously wiped his forehead.

The villagers acted as if expecting him to breathe fire.

"Crann! Perkins!" he yelled.

His two companions, marooned on the outside of the stockade of black humanity, now elbowed their way inward, their rifles at the high port.

"Give me those!" snapped the doctor in annoyance.

"But, sir," groaned Crann pleadingly, "if the worst comes to the—"

"Hand them over—smartly," snapped Cavanaugh again.

Crann and Perkins surrendered their weapons sullenly.

"The Webley, too, Crann."

Crann swore roundly as he turned over the pistol.

The doctor laid the three weapons on the ground beside the basket containing the fretful infant.

"Unload 'em," he commanded Crann.

Crann squatted on his haunches and emptied the magazines of all three. "Well, it was bloody nice while it lasted," he commented to no one in particular.

The villagers fretted, suspicious.

"All right," said Cavanaugh conversationally, "now the bags."

"Have you gone mad, sir?" blurted Crann.

"We'll start with yours, Perkins," continued Cavanaugh, unheeding.

Perkins balked. His fingers tightened on the leather strap of his canvas bag.

Crann's voice was charged with urgency. "My God, sir. You're tipping your hand. They're our aces in the hole!"

"I'll be damned if I'm going to lecture you on military obedience," said Cavanaugh primly. "Hold by them, then. I'll use mine. They'll get so damned mad they'll pull your fool heads off to get at them." He turned to face Emphema, Mafuta, the elders and the

156

princes. His dainty hand felt for the press fastener on his canvas bag. It clicked. He raised the flap.

Some threescore eyes followed his arm as it rose, hesitated—then disappeared. The doctor's mute audience held their hands up in front of their faces as if to protect against the whiteface's evil.

The fetish Cavanaugh pulled dramatically from the bag was alien to the Basanga. It was a yellow box more than a hand long, two fingers thick, with red stripes from a red eye like the rays of the waning sun. He held it high. He caught a fingernail under a shiny metal piece that hinged back and forth like the wing of a bird.

The young prince, Matubele, gazed transfixed. He disliked the man who had robbed him of his mother, but hostility surrendered to curiosity. The boy jumped forward. He fingered the mysterious metal piece.

"Here," offered Cavanaugh. He hinged back the metal piece and tipped the box forward. A white powder poured out into the heart of the boy's hand in a conical heap. He looked up into the doctor's face, puzzled.

Cavanaugh licked his finger and stuck it into the powder. He removed his finger, stuck it in his mouth and grinned broadly.

Wide-eyed, Matubele did likewise. He smacked his lips once, twice, thrice. He squealed. "It is the powder from the lake!" he shrieked. "It is the powder from the lake!" He danced around the doctor, wildly licking his hand clean. He stopped before him, his empty, cupped hands begging for more.

No sooner had Cavanaugh refilled Matubele's hand than his seven brothers threw their princely reserve to the winds and wrangled for the doctor's favor. Gleefully he poured each a handful, then stood back to observe the reaction. They milled around in epileptic intensity, cramming the precious mineral in their mouths, licking their trembling hands clean, chasing after every spilled crystal.

Mafuta snarled a vile oath.

Cavanaugh looked him squarely in his smoldering eyes and deliberately tossed a box high into the air above the tightly packed villagers.

Long before it had completed its parabolic arc, five hundred

157

fingers grasping from a hundred scrawny outstretched arms clawed for possession. Horny heels hammered on the hard earth as the monstrous cordwood of thin, black bodies moved abruptly from the edge of the promontory. The weaker, shorter ones fell under and their fear was trampled out of them in anguished moans unheard in the noise.

Vainly Mafuta squealed his warnings and spat his curses.

The doctor scrambled down the hill toward the village, tossing out boxes of salt in his wake as though laying a paper chase. Each time he lobbed one, the tangled, screaming knot of Basanga behind shot forward like the losing end of a tug-of-war team.

Crann and Perkins trotted by his side.

"Nice work, sir," said Crann nervously, "but do save enough to bribe the buggers into giving us the hand we need."

"Not a chance," panted Cavanaugh. "They know each of us arrived with a bag. They'll tear us to pieces if we don't hand it *all* over to them. Even then they may still tear us to pieces."

"Make a run for it then, sir?" asked Perkins, his voice faltering.

Cavanaugh shook his head. "They'd have us in two shakes, lad, they would."

"What then, sir?" beseeched Crann.

The doctor stopped dead in his tracks. He grabbed his two subordinates by their shirtfronts. "We finish what we started. Do you hear me? Chuck out all the salt you've got. There's no other way. Remember, we've got to keep our heads."

Crann laughed nervously. "We may not have an awful lot to say about that."

"Oh, shut up, man, and get along with it," blustered Cavanaugh.

Suddenly Crann unshouldered his bag and slung it over Perkins' shoulder.

"Where in blazes do you think you're going?" challenged the doctor.

"The weapons, sir," pleaded Crann. "I can nip back in all the fuss and they won't be any the wiser."

"Out of the question, Crann," declared the doctor. "You don't understand what's up. I surrendered the weapons for the effect. These blighters've been after salt for months now. That's one of the

158

things they were supposed to be drowning the little tyke for—so as their ancestors would send 'em a pinch o' salt—and a lot of other things besides. We're spirits, man. Maybe even gods. Gods don't need guns. . . . C'mon, now. Keep walking and chucking."

"For God's sake, man," shouted Crann, "don't you have a grain of sense in your head? The weapons's our only chance. We started out with sixty one-pound boxes between us. There's fifty of them wogs if there's a one. What the bloody hell happens when we run out of the friggin' stuff and that pack of ravin' lunatics is on our heels? What do we say? 'We're out o' bubble and squeak, ladies and gentlemen. How about some fish-and-chips'?"

Cavanaugh grimaced. "For the love of God, man, while you're gabblin' here, they're gainin' on us. The more of this stuff we chuck out for them, the longer it's going to take them to get to our hut. And the longer we have to think up something. Move on, now."

Crann stopped flat-footed in his tracks. He announced woodenly, "I'm not budging another inch till you tell me what you're going to do when they start pilin' into our hut and us without a stick to defend ourselves."

"What *I* am going to say to them, Crann. *Me?* I am not going to breathe a word. Perkins here'll do all the talking."

Crann stared incredulously. "Perkins, sir?" He was sure he had not heard correctly.

Perkins stood with mouth ajar. "Me, sir?" he gulped.

Cavanaugh nodded.

159

13

The scrape of Nangle's heavy boots on the bare ground woke Frazer. He rose on one elbow. A book slid off his blanket. "What is it, Nangle?"

Nangle bent to retrieve the book, picking it up and casually glancing at the title.

"Give me that," said Frazer curtly, pulling the book from the soldier's hand. "Well, what is it?" He glanced at his watch. It was 7:15 A.M.

"I was looking for Captain Humphreys, sir," Nangle said woodenly. "We've run into trouble. A gorge, maybe forty feet wide, at least fifteen deep. But I didn't mean to bother *you*, sir. Sergeant Smith sent me after Captain Humphreys."

Frazer sensed the sarcasm. "Oh, he did, did he?" he said acidly. "And you didn't want to bother me, eh?" He tossed the blanket aside petulantly.

Nangle replied confidently, "My orders were to rouse Captain Humphreys, sir."

Frazer sat on the side of his camp bed and poked his thin, hairy legs into his pants. "You already said that. Now tell me about it, Nangle."

160

"It's a gorge, sir. Not like the others, though. Runs for as far as the eye can see east and west. Sergeant Smith doesn't think we can afford the time to go around it."

"How far up?"

"About a mile, sir. The recce party discovered it about an hour ago."

Frazer stood up and pulled his shirt over his head. "Wasn't it on the map?"

"Not that I know of, sir."

Frazer seemed to be in no hurry, spending much time tucking the shirt into the waistband of his shorts. He sat down again and concerned himself with the business of putting on socks and field boots.

Nangle stood awkwardly by.

Frazer looked up from tying his laces. "Go back and tell Sergeant Smith I'll be out to have a look-see shortly."

Nangle looked him squarely in the eye. "*You* will be out shortly, sir?"

"Yes, Nangle, *me*," retorted Frazer.

When Nangle left, Frazer picked up his topee and examined the sweatband minutely. Should he or shouldn't he waken Humphreys? He had kept Humphreys and the naval engineering lieutenant, Magarity, company while they worked until three that morning on a faulty steam connection on the tractor. No, he reasoned. Humphreys needed his rest.

Using a mirror strung from the ridgepole of his bungalow tent, he lathered his face generously, massaging it heavily into the coarse gray-black stubble. He studied the face. The Frazer nose jutted out beyond the froth; part of the aristocratic mien that had helped Frazers before him to high naval distinction.

If only the eyebrows had grown thick and horizontal, the total impression would have been one of geometrical symmetry and strength. As it was, they petered out into thin crescents of disciplined hair, diluting the promise manifested by the clean, sloping lines of the nose; a lack of promise which the rectangular strip of mustache underlined rather than concealed. A high, rounded forehead threatened the face with a certain feminine sensitivity; this was effectively forestalled by the severe regulation naval haircut,

161

but even more so by flinty blue eyes deeply mounted above the high promontories of his cheekbones. From these the jawline dropped cleanly down and—at the last moment—across to file off the plane of his chin.

The job was done. He stood in his underwear. His flitting eyes stilled on the open footlocker. He withdrew a glistening brown pair of leather leggings and a pair of Army officer's jodhpurs of the very finest Bedford cord—nonregulation items, to be sure, for a naval person in most parts of the world, but not in the informal remoteness of Katanga, far from the protocol of the Establishment. . . .

✿

The men stood gaping into the huge crevasse in the earth and shaking their heads doubtfully. In the shrill of conversation and the chugging of the tractor at low pulse, Frazer's approach went unnoticed.

He walked up behind Sergeant Smith. "Well, apart from this, we don't have a thing to keep us busy this morning, Sergeant," he quipped.

Smith wheeled around. "Oh, he grunted in surprise. "Morning, sir. I'd say we had our work cut out for us, all right."

Frazer edged closer and peered into the crevasse.

Smith covertly studied the commander's nonregulation regalia. He looked up suddenly and caught one of the sailors furtively shielding his mouth and snickering to his comrades. Smith fixed them with a threatening glare.

"Bit of a monster, Smith, isn't it?" commented Frazer.

"And how, sir," concurred Smith.

"Move some chaps out along each side, Sergeant. See if we can't go around it."

"Not a chance, sir. Already have. The bleedin' thing goes on for miles."

After a moment's silence, the two of them suddenly spoke at the same time.

"Sorry, sir."

"My fault, Smith. Go on. What was it?"

Smith looked uncertain. "Well, sir, the captain's sure to have an idea." He knew he should not have said it, but it was too late.

"Thanks, Smith. I didn't know you had that kind of confidence in me."

Fifty yards away Sublieutenants Dodkins and Bannister walked toward Frazer.

"Do you see what I see?" said Bannister incredulously.

"Well, I'll be blowed!" shot Dodkins.

Once by Frazer's side, they saluted and cordially said, "Good morning, sir."

"You people have any ideas?" queried Frazer.

Dodkins and Bannister seemed to have lost their spontaneity.

Dodkins volunteered, "Why not throw a few timbers across, sir, the way we managed the others?"

Frazer's eyes roamed the terrain: matted coarse, short grass; waist-high clumps of cactus; islands of tropical heather; giant, candle-shaped tropical cardinal flowers and towering, top-heavy ragworts like blazing golden torches. "Fine, Dodkins," said Frazer, "if we had the timber. But I don't see a thing out there more than twenty-five feet long. Do you?"

They shielded their eyes and looked out.

Lieutenant Leeds, the gunnery officer, walked toward them. "Morning, sir," he said, saluting—frowning.

"Morning, Mr. Leeds," said Frazer. "How would you handle it?"

Leeds said, "I took a tramp off to the east, sir. About a mile, maybe. Same width, I'd say, but not more than fifteen feet deep. We could maybe dig out the edges. Make it a 45-degree-slope approach—and exit."

Frazer said, "Pretty steep—45 degrees."

Leeds shrugged. His eyes discreetly scanned Frazer's attire.

"What sort of digging gear do we have, Sergeant?" asked Frazer.

"Picks and shovels, sir, and crowbars."

"And dynamite," mused Frazer. He moved to the edge of the crevasse again and looked down. "Leeds," he called. "What are we waiting for? Let's see your place."

Ten feet of clay had not been crust enough to curb the mighty upward buckling pressures of aeons ago.

Frazer gazed down and remembered that on the Admiralty chart the Maniku Plateau was colored blue, which meant that it had been born over five hundred million years ago. Five hundred million years! His own colossal insignificance stuck in his craw, and that of Naval Africa Expedition, and that of the Great War. Inflated in his leggings and breeches, he suddenly recoiled from himself as he would after stepping on a ripe caterpillar making its moist, peristaltic way up a smooth rock. But Leeds's voice intruded upon his introspection.

"Here, sir," he called. He pointed down into the crevasse.

The floor was fifteen feet from where they stood, but the sides dropped off sheer, trapping debris piled up by thousands of rainy seasons.

Frazer examined the obstacle and turned to Leeds. "You'd like to carve into the sides. Make the U into a V having a whacking great angle at the bottom, eh?" He fashioned his hands into the shapes of the letters.

"More of a shallow crescent shape, I'd say, sir," Leeds observed meticulously.

"What do you think, Sergeant?" asked Frazer.

The sergeant spoke without hesitation. "Not a chance, sir. Might be fine through that clay, but the rest's all solid rock. Dynamite'd take us days, it would, sir. Use up most of it."

"Leeds?" queried Frazer.

"He's right, sir. It would mean a mountain of work, but I don't see what choice we have."

"And you two?" Frazer asked of Dodkins and Bannister.

"Personally, sir," declared Dodkins positively, "I wouldn't make a move without Captain Humphreys."

Bannister dug him in the side. The expressions of Leeds and Smith registered their disapproval of the youth's brashness, but the harm had been done.

"I see," said Frazer stiffly. "It's reassuring to know I have the confidence of my officers."

164

Bannister stepped forward, hand raised in explanation. "What Lieutenant Dodkins means, sir, is that—"

Frazer cut him off. "I know what he means," he said acidly. "Sergeant!"

Smith stepped forward. "Yes, sir."

"I want things moving right away," he declared officiously. "Bring up all hands. Get them cracking on cutting down every tree around here. When they—"

"But, sir," protested Smith. "It's fifteen feet across there. There's not a stick around here that long."

"I don't intend to *span* it, Sergeant," declared Frazer. "We'll chuck every log we get our hands on *into* the hole. *Fill* it up. That's the idea. Fill it to the brim till it's level with both sides. Understood?"

"Well, sir. Yes, sir," responded Smith. He lacked his commanding officer's enthusiasm for the plan. "But I don't believe we've enough around here to fill the bill."

"Then we move back the way we came. Down the slope to the heavier stuff. We'll build it up in dumps as we cut it. Then tractor it up here."

Lieutenant Leeds frowned. He asked conversationally, "How much time do you think that'll cost us, sir?"

"I have no idea," snapped Frazer irritatedly. "But less time than your proposal. And the longer we stand around like spare parts, the more time it's going to cost us. Smith! I want all hands on this. Do you hear? Cooks, orderlies, the lot. You can count on all the officers, too."

Smith pulled his notebook from his shirt pocket and thumbed through it. "Devlin, too, sir?"

Frazer frowned. "Devlin? Of course Devlin. Why the devil not, man?"

Smith ran a stubby finger across the page. "He's laid up, sir."

"Laid up?" questioned Frazer. "With what?"

"Eh," began Smith, "piles, sir. The bleeding kind, I believe," he volunteered clinically.

Frazer shrugged. "We'll have the M.O. take a look-see the moment he gets back . . . but all the rest, mind you," he added sternly.

"Of course, sir," said Smith. "Right away, sir." He made to leave.

"One other thing, Sergeant. Water—for the tractor?"

Smith reopened his notebook and ran his eyes down several entries. He seemed to be inordinately long at it.

"Well?" said Frazer abruptly, producing his own notebook. "I'm not entirely up to date. I make it"—he flipped over a few pages—"*Toutou* full; *Mimi* less than half a tank to go. Right?"

Smith produced a stub of a pencil, wet the lead in his mouth and computed in slow earnest.

"Look, Sergeant, this is no time for an expedition audit. *Toutou* full! *Mimi* about a half! Right?" Frazer expostulated.

"Certainly no more than that, sir," announced Smith lightly, snapping shut the notebook.

"Good," grunted Frazer. "Get on with it, then."

Humphreys stirred and stretched. The breeze of the highlands changed, and the excited pulse of the steam tractor impacted upon his awareness.

"Rodgers," he bellowed, balancing on one foot, struggling to get into his jodhpurs.

The orderly called, "Coming, sir," from somewhere and appeared at the tent flap. "You called, sir," he observed redundantly. He read the unshaven look of impending catastrophe on Humphreys' face.

"What's going on here? Why wasn't I wakened?" snarled Humphreys.

Rodgers looked quickly at his feet, taking an instant to compose himself. "Commander's orders, sir. You was all in, sir, he said, an' I wasn't to bother you till you came around on your own."

Humphreys shuffled outside in his bare feet. Only three tents remained—his, the mess tent and the aid tent. All the others were piled up in neat stacks ready for moving forward. He flushed beet-red with anger. . . . When his normal coloring returned, it was to a face shrewd and calculating. He turned around to Rodgers.

166

"Breakfast, sir?" asked Rodgers apologetically. "Cook and I was hanging on like."

Humphreys regarded him absent-mindedly.

"We've got to rid up, sir, you know," continued Rodgers.

"I know what you have to do, Rodgers," temporized Humphreys. "I know very well. Yes, I'll breakfast—whatever's going. I'll be dressed in fifteen minutes." He turned and went into the tent.

The tractor chugged into the clearing filled with busy men. Frazer stood on the deck plate. The curved steel canopy forced him to stoop slightly; there was a hard, predatory look about him. The engine raced and idled spasmodically as he inexpertly turned the machine around and backed it up in front of a pile of logs. He finally halted the tractor, climbed down off the deck plate and joined the group of officers and NCOs.

Nearby Nangle and Devlin panted at each end of a long, cross-cut saw as they worked through the solid girth of a stunted baobab tree. In their unskillful hands the gleaming steel blade shrieked its protest in short, sharp ringing whines.

"Frig it," said Devlin, wiping his forehead. He coughed.

"Get on with it," snapped Nangle.

"Wait a moment," said Devlin. "Look here, will you?" He had just caught sight of Frazer.

"A Frazer in Humphreys' clothing," observed Nangle, nonplussed.

"What's *he* up to?" exclaimed Devlin.

Nangle stared for several moments, then pulled his gaze away. "Let's get on with it. He's probably going to a masquerade ball somewhere."

"The bastard didn't invite me," said Devlin.

"Oh, shut up, you clod, and get on with it," shot Nangle.

"All right, all right, your lordship," said Devlin.

Nangle let go of the saw handle and came around to Devlin, his knuckles bunched, teeth clenched.

"I'm sorry, chum. Honest," stammered Devlin, alarmed.

Nangle stood over him menacingly. "Next time, you maggot," he said thickly. "Next time."

Frazer's hawkeye caught sight of Devlin and Nangle. He jabbed a finger in their direction. "Smith! Stokes! I'll have no slacking."

Smith shouted, "You two! Nangle, Devlin! Get on with it!"

Frazer's eyes searched the terrain. They alighted on the log piles. "Not enough," he snapped.

Magarity said, "There's more to the southwest, sir. About five or six miles. Stokes and I had a look."

"Not *fast* enough, I meant. They aren't putting their backs into it, Magarity. Are they, Stokes?" He noticed Stokes staring at him. "Well, Stokes?" challenged Frazer.

Stokes hesitated. "Eh, sir, fast enough? Two or three stacks an hour, sir," he asserted.

"We must do better," Frazer said curtly.

Magarity spoke up. "I thought we were doing quite well, sir, actually. Seven loads dumped in this morning so far."

"The level isn't rising fast enough up there," declared Frazer in a voice that would stomach no argument. "We haven't made more than a dent in it."

"If I might make a suggestion, sir," said Lieutenant Leeds, the gunnery officer, "we've four piles just sitting around waiting. If you were to open up the throttle on the monster, we might be able to move the stuff up as soon as it's cut."

Smith bit down on his lower lip.

"Very good, Leeds," assented Frazer. "If you think they can keep up with it, hop to it, then!"

The officers and NCOs hurried off.

"Sergeant Smith!" called Frazer.

Smith turned around. "Yes, sir?"

"Smith, I'm going to need a hand with the water." He indicated the tractor. "Bone-dry, she is."

"I'll get a couple of men and—"

"Nonsense, man, I can handle it myself—with a little help. Trailer's over by the mess tent?"

"Yes, Commander Frazer. *Mimi*—we're still drawing from

Mimi, sir. You'll want a man, then." He turned around and looked at the dozen laboring soldiers. "I can spare—"

"That chap there," interjected Frazer irritatedly. "He was swinging the lead when I rolled in here. What's his name?" He pointed toward the baobob tree.

"Nangle, sir?" queried Smith.

"The other one," said Frazer.

"Devlin, sir."

"Give me Devlin."

Smith hesitated. "Well, sir, like I was saying this morning, he's got a touch of the piles. Can't move around much and—"

"You're too damn soft with 'em," snapped Frazer. "Give me Devlin. I'll shake him up a little."

Smith surrendered. "Very good, sir." He stuck two fingers in his mouth and whistled.

The soldiers paused and looked up.

Smith pointed toward the baobob tree, catching the attention of Nangle and Devlin.

Nangle looked at Smith and pointed a finger to his own chest.

Smith shook his head and pointed toward Devlin. "Yes, you!" shouted Smith.

Devlin got slowly off his haunches and sauntered forward.

"On the double, man!" roared Frazer, fuming slightly as the gangly ex-factory worker grudgingly picked up his heels and loped over to them.

"Got some work for you, Devlin," snapped Smith. "Commander Frazer needs a hand with drawin' off *Mimi.*" He emphasized *Mimi.*

Devlin's heavy eyelids flapped.

Smith pointed toward the deck plate of the tractor. "All right," he said, in a clipped, official way, "hop to it."

As the tractor wheezed away with Frazer and Devlin, Smith stood looking after them. He removed his topee and scratched his balding skull deliberately. He replaced his topee and spent some time in an examination of the scalp pickings under his fingernails.

When the tractor was out of sight, Smith walked off to where the sailors toiled. He sought out CPO Stokes. The two huddled in

169

earnest conversation. "You tell your chaps, Charlie. Some of ours know already. I'll clue in the rest. And not a word to the officers, mind."

Stokes shook his head unhappily. "S'lot t'ask, mate—choppin' down on the water to save that bastard Devlin's skin. Liable to kick 'is bleedin' teeth in, they is. An' wot's it gonna gain us? They'll find out anyways, sooner or later. Then wot?"

"They're not going to find out till the bloody last moment, Charlie. And maybe by that time the doctor'll be back and—"

"Come off it! You think 'im an' Crann an' that kid Perkins's abaht to lug a bathtub o' H-two-bloody-O behind 'em?" Stokes rubbed his hand heavily down his face. "Christ, I'd like to kick 'im where 'is old lady never kissed 'im. Right 'ard, I would."

"Move over, chum. There's two ahead of you—me and Nangle," exclaimed Smith fervently.

"But I ask you: wot for?" persisted Stokes. "Why try to 'ide it? I know right well Tarzan's gonna pee on us from a dizzy 'ight when 'e finds out, but the sooner 'e knows abaht it, the sooner 'e can take some sort o' action. Wot kind, I 'aven't a clue. Maybe we can all piss in the boiler," Stokes added lugubriously.

Smith snapped, "I'll tell you what kind of action—sixteen hours a day of action, that's what, and without enough water to wet your whistle and him breathing down our bloody necks every step of the way. . . . No, Charlie, if that's what we're in for, then let's not start it till he finds out himself."

" 'E'll be like a bulldog with a toothache," concurred Stokes, "but Frazer's in command. 'E won't let big nasty shite on us too 'eavy." Stokes's tone rang more of hope than conviction.

Smith's eyes narrowed. "Have you seen him lately?"

Stokes wearily rubbed his face again. "Know wot you mean, chum. 'E looks like a proper animal trainer."

"Still think *he* can make 'im toe the line, Charlie?"

Stokes looked glum. "All right, mate." He groaned. "I'll tell my chaps."

"Good," said Smith, taking his leave.

Stokes shouted after him, "An', Andy!"

Smith turned.

"Keep the bastard out of me way, or they'll be more than his arse bleedin'."

Smith rejoined his squad. "Knock off for half a mo," he told them. "Over here! I want a word with you."

The soldiers did not have to be told twice to down tools. They grunted their relief and eased back on their haunches.

Smith hollered angrily, "This is no bloody siesta!" He beckoned emphatically. "Over here, I said!"

The men trudged over to him and clumped around him moodily.

"Now listen. I don't have much time, so shut your mouths and keep your ears open."

The men shuffled in the dust submissively.

"Devlin's queered the whole bloody works," he began. "The stupid sod got a pint of something from God knows where and got all lit up. Then he thought he'd have some fun, so he took a bleedin' bath—using most of *Toutou*'s tank . . ."

When he had told them the whole story, they stood in belligerent silence. There was no doubt about how they felt.

"So what would you like us to do?" drawled the North-Country soldier sarcastically. He was one of the two sentries who had helped clean up Devlin's mess.

Smith's jaw tensed. "Told you to shut up till I was finished," he rapped. "We've got to keep you-know-who from finding out about this. The moment he does, there'll be skin and hair flying—and most of it'll be yours, not mine. No, we keep this thing under our hats, and the M.O.'ll be back shortly. It's my bet if there's water out there, the M.O.'ll get it back, come hell or—"

"High water?" queried Nangle superciliously. "Being a bit optimistic, aren't we, Sergeant—the idea of three men bringing back water enough for twenty-five men and a machine?"

Smith glowered at him.

"We're big boys now. You can tell us the whole story—"

"Shut up!" roared Smith. He glared at Nangle and the others incredulously. "A few months outa Blighty and bloody discipline goes to the dogs," he said fiercely. "Listen, you," he snapped, pointing at Nangle. "You hold your bleedin' tongue till I say so. What you think this is—the bloody Girl Guides?" He breathed

171

noisily. "It's still the Army. Don't bloody well forget it. Just keep your mouths shut. That's all. If he finds out, he finds out. But if he does, it's not 'cos one of us here pulled the plug." He rubbed his dry, dusty lips with the back of his hand. "Come to think of it, that isn't all." He watched them closely. "We gotta cut down on that water. It's gotta last longer. Now, what's it gonna be—the morning or the evening pint?"

"Frig him," rasped one soldier. "I wouldn't give up a tear for him. Why should I?" He was the sentry who had led Devlin back to his tent that night, the medical orderly who had fired at Humphreys.

" 'Cos I say so," snapped Smith. "Is that how the rest of you feel?"

The Welshman said offhandedly, "Nangle's right, Sarge. That's a sweet bunch of nonsense about the doctor getting back with water for the lot of us. Besides, what the hell difference is a few pints going to make—maybe a couple o' miles one way or another?"

"And you two?" he demanded of the two closest soldiers.

"I was mad to sign up for this lot in the first place," grunted one of them.

Smith kneaded his right fist into the palm of his left hand. He was angry; it was the righteous anger of the veteran NCO finding his men flirting with insubordination. But as he fumed, he realized that this insubordination, which had crept up on him, had been of his own doing. For weeks he had looked into the eyes of the men before him and seen the eyes of the lost youth of Neuve Chapelle and Loos. He'd be the kind of sergeant to them that he hadn't had the chance to be to the others, he'd promised himself; but somehow something had got out of balance. They were trespassing on the rank, dignity and tradition of the British Army NCO. It wasn't that he gave a rap about Andy Smith. But these young conscript upstarts had forgotten where they were and what they were about. They were going to tell the British Army what it should and what it shouldn't do? God, they defiled the uniform they stood up in, 'cos it was the same one that A Company fell in; and A Company had carried out orders to the letter. He read in the soldiers' indifferent expressions the questionable results of his oversolicitude.

172

They'd lost the bearing of British soldiers, and the spirit. They'd become nothing more than a motley bunch of civilians sulking after a long day's outing. With a gang like that, they'd never get to the lake—even if they'd three Humphreys cracking the whip—unless they were all swiftly booted in the arse. "Well, that settles it," he announced.

"We thought you'd see it our way, Sergeant," said Nangle condescendingly.

"Good," replied Smith evenly. "If slashing the noon pint's your way, Private Nangle, then I see it your way."

Nangle looked confused.

"What?" said the dour North-Countryman. "Us pay for that bastard's mistakes?"

"It's no longer Devlin's affair," snapped Smith. "It's a question of doing what you're bloody well told to do—like soldiers are supposed to. You tailor's dummies've been getting away with murder. You don't like this; you don't like that. You'd rather do this; and you'd rather do that. Consider all that come to a screeching halt. From now on, not a one talks back unless he's spoken to. Get it? Moan if you want to, but not where I can hear it. I've heard too damn much moaning, do you hear?"

"We hear, Sarge," droned the North-Country soldier moodily, "but we also know you're as new to all this as we are." He inhaled deeply, forcing out his barrel chest and hitching the belt on his pants in another notch. He stood nonchalantly, his thumbs hooked in his belt. "You can't expect us to 'do an' die' when you're playin' it off the cuff yourself."

The others murmured their approval.

Smith took two paces forward. He stood but a hand's width from the man. "Go on," he said dangerously.

"We're all for turnin' Devlin in 'an gettin' this bloody water business to a head right away. The sooner we do it, the sooner we know where we stand." The soldier's face wore a look of defiance.

Smith stepped back. "Anyone else here who'd like to say his piece?"

None stirred.

Smith removed his topee and handed it to Nangle. "Here," he

snapped, "keep this till I get back." He reached up, removed the burly soldier's topee and handed it also to Nangle. "This, too."

The soldier frowned.

Smith curled and uncurled his forefinger in his face. "C'mon with me." He nodded his head in the direction of a large clump of bush fifty yards away and promptly walked off.

The soldier waited until the sergeant was off some distance before he extended his palms and shrugged his shoulders in the "search me" gesture toward the rest of the platoon.

"Go on, Geordie," they coaxed, "your dad has oranges for you."

"Frig you bastards," he shot over his shoulder as he took off in pursuit of the sergeant.

The two disappeared into the clump of thicket.

Five minutes later they reappeared.

The soldier took his topee from Nangle and rejoined the rest of the platoon. He looked rumpled. His breathing was heavy and there was a livid welt under one of his eyes.

Smith accepted his topee from Nangle and arranged it carefully on his head. He pulled the brim down to regulation level. "Now. Where were we?" he demanded of the burly soldier.

"Down to two pints a day instead of three, and not a word about Devlin's caper," he recited mechanically, rubbing his welt.

"You all heard that, I'm sure," observed Smith. He paused to observe any reaction. "All right, back to work."

About four o'clock, as Stokes's sailors were wetting their parched lips and throats with the afternoon water ration, Smith's thirsty squad sat disconsolately in the shade of the stacks of lumber and brush.

The Welshman lay on his side propped up on one elbow. "Did he beat you or bribe you?" he said to the North-Country private.

The others guffawed.

The North-Countryman had been sitting with his back to the Welshman. He pivoted on his buttocks and punched him squarely in the face. The Welshman's features squelched with a sound reminiscent of a heavy footstep in deep mud. He yelped—and flailed into his attacker. Before the burly one could organize his bulk, the Welshman hammered his bunched knuckles several times into his face. They writhed on the ground together, grappling.

The others tried to pull them apart.

"Give us a bloody hand, Nangle," shouted one.

Nangle, sitting with his back to the others and aloof from what was going on, replied conversationally, "As you people might say, frig 'em."

The sound of the tractor approaching came up out of nowhere.

Smith and Stokes raced onto the scene. They waded into the knot of writhing forms and yanked the grapplers apart—but not before the North-Countryman had unloosed a powerful uppercut that caught the Welshman below the navel.

The Welshman curled up like a snail plucked from its shell. He crumpled to the ground. The punch had choked off his air. His eyes were round with agony and his cheeks bulged blue.

Frazer and Devlin stepped down off the tractor platform and approached. They were on the sunlit side of the stack of logs, and had not seen the melee on the shady side.

Smith crouched on the shady side of the stack. "To the other side! Everybody!" he snapped. While the others drifted casually around into the sun, Smith crammed the Welshman's heaving form close against the base of the pile, then ambled around to the other side. Frazer and Devlin approached from a dozen yards off.

"Would have thought they had enough of the sun," Frazer commented dryly, looking at the soldiers sprawled around the log pile in sundry attitudes of studied casualness.

"So would I, sir," agreed Smith, standing with his hands on his hips and taking an occasional step away from the log pile, hoping Frazer would follow. Frazer seemed satisfied to stay put—a few yards away.

They deployed their small talk for a while, but suddenly a loud gasp interrupted them.

"What's that?" snapped Frazer.

"What, sir?" temporized Smith, cocking his head. "I don't hear anything."

Frazer listened intently for a moment, then dismissed the subject. "This is a good worker, here," he remarked, pointing to Devlin, who was standing guiltily in the background.

"Glad you like him, sir," said Smith.

Frazer unhooked his water bottle and looked at his watch. "About that time again, eh?" he observed.

"Yes, sir," said Smith. "We've . . . eh . . . already accounted for ours."

Frazer and Devlin stood within sight of the squad, drinking their afternoon ration of water.

Smith excused himself. "Half a mo, sir." He walked across toward the disorder of the resting soldiers.

"Right, Sergeant," said Frazer.

When Smith got to them, he stood over them as if in routine explanation of some workaday problem. "Sing, you buggers. Do some bloody thing to drown out that gasper on the other side," he whispered. Then in his normal stentorian tones he rasped, "All right, you men. You've three more minutes. Make the most of it."

Nangle sat up in anger at seeing Devlin. "Look at that pig swell his entrails," he breathed through clenched teeth.

"The dirty bastard," swore the North-Countryman.

"Three minutes," Smith rasped again, then *sotto voce,* "Sing, you . . . you." With that he walked back and rejoined Smith and Devlin.

Across the short distance separating them from the log pile came the hoarse rattle of a man desperately swelling his lungs to capacity.

Frazer jerked his head. "There it is again, Sergeant!" But as he concentrated, head bent to one side, the spiritless voices of the thirsty squad clashed in a dissonant parody of "It's a Long Way to Tipperary."

Frazer smiled in astonishment. "Good God, they've more spunk than I gave 'em credit for," he declared enthusiastically. He turned to Devlin. "Here, may as well finish it," he said, emptying the last few drops from his canteen into Devlin's mug. He flashed a private, knowing smile at Smith. "With that sort of spirit, man, we'll have no trouble getting there," he declared with deep conviction.

> It's a long way to tickle Mary,
> It's a long way to go.

"Dammit," continued Frazer, "I have to hand it to you . . . good NCOs! The backbone of the British services!"

> It's a long way to tickle Mary,
> To the sweetest girl I know.
> Goodbye, Piccadilly,
> Farewell, Leicester Square,
> It's a long long way to tickle Mary,
> That I've got to go . . .

14

A twenty-five-yard-wide section of crevasse had been stuffed with tree trunks, brush, loose earth and rock to form a causeway roughly level with the edges on both sides. The night before, Frazer had walked back and forth across it a half-dozen times, minutely inspecting every detail, calling for a hole plugged here, a log trimmed there, a doubtful spot shored up somewhere else. But in the damp of dawn its substance seemed to shrink. Better able to tell when the sun comes up, Frazer consoled himself, as he stood in the center of the makeshift bridge, occasionally stamping his steel-shod heel and feeling the vibration shiver through the timber and earthwork beneath him.

It would work, he told himself. It would work. It had to work . . . but how could he be sure? He had never done this sort of thing before. This wasn't his line, not by a long shot. How could he be sure? He had to admit that his credentials were singularly unimpressive—sand-castle building on summer holidays by the sea as a young boy and supplemented in later years by Tactics and Fortifications at Greenwich. But it looked solid enough to him as he viewed it in the first few fingers of sunlight tentatively touching the strange excrescence on the familiar landscape. . . . If it didn't work? He stamped hard again. If he could only be sure . . .

He could be sure—if he asked Humphreys. Humphreys would know. He knew this—Humphreys knew it, too, wherever he was. Where was Humphreys? He hadn't seen him in twenty-four hours. All day yesterday he'd been rehearsing what he would say when Humphreys charged onto the scene and demanded to know what the blazes was going on. . . . Yes, he could be sure. He could call in Humphreys to make the thing work—but at the cost of surrendering whatever he had gained since taking the helm. . . . He stamped again and again. Solid as a rock. If it wasn't, there'd be a tractor and two boats at the bottom of the ravine. The Belgians would have to twiddle their thumbs for the duration. Zimmer would hear about it sooner or later. It would be the butt of German mess-hall amusement for months. . . . "If preparation is three-quarters, what is the remaining quarter?" He could hear his unequivocal reply: "Analysis of the men's talents, m'lord, then the utilization of those talents in the place where they will do the most good." Was it just book talk, as the Third Sea Lord had said it was? He had no doubt where Humphreys' talents lay—or where his own lay. He could not permit his pride to endanger the success of the expedition. He would seek out Humphreys.

He returned to the headquarters tent and called for the orderly.

It was still not time to be up and about. The orderly finally appeared, having obviously just completed dressing in haste. "Didn't expect you this early, sir," he said softly, sniffing. His thick eyebrows raised a fraction at seeing Frazer fully dressed.

"You may as well get used to it," said Frazer evenly.

"Yes, sir," said the orderly.

"Tell Captain Humphreys I'd like to see him soon as he can manage it."

"Very good, sir," said the orderly. He made to leave. "Will that be all, sir?"

Frazer nodded curtly.

The orderly, a sailor, turned and left the tent.

Frazer stood in the middle of the tent, thoughtfully fingering his chin. Quickly he pivoted toward the tent entrance. "Orderly!" he called out.

"Sir!" acknowledged the sailor from ten paces.

Frazer beckoned. When the sailor came up to him, he whispered, "Make sure you bring two cups of tea. In fifteen minutes or so. Make it strong."

"Right, sir," said the sailor.

Ten minutes later Humphreys' bulk filled the entrance to Frazer's tent. "You wanted to see me!" he announced stolidly. It was a statement—not a question.

Frazer pulled the cold pipe from his mouth. "Ah, Captain, yes. Yes indeed." He waved him inside with his pipe hand. "Do come in."

Humphreys walked stiffly in. He comported himself as if on the parade ground. His topee rested close to his side in the crook of his left arm.

"Haven't seen much of you lately," bantered Frazer.

Humphreys looked down at him coldly. "Had you been looking for me?"

"Well, no, not really," replied Frazer. "It's just that, well, I suppose we've both been quite busy, eh?"

"I can only speak for myself," said Humphreys curtly.

"You usually do, Oswald," observed Frazer evenly. He turned away and began stoking his pipe. He crossed to his cot and sat down. He picked up some underclothing from the camp stool. "C'mon, Oswald, sit down, won't you?"

"I've had an adequate night's rest," stated Humphreys.

Frazer regarded him momentarily. "Dammit, don't you think you're carrying the Aldershot pose just a little too far, old man?" His tone was playful. "After all, we are in the backside of Katanga."

Humphreys looked down at him, running his glance over the jodhpurs and leggings.

Frazer felt the color flood to his cheeks. He fussed with his pipe to mask his embarrassment.

The orderly appeared. "Thought you'd like some tea, sir, I did," he said tactfully, placing two large steaming delph mugs on the map table.

Frazer thanked the orderly, reached for a mug and handed it to Humphreys.

Humphreys declined.

Frazer shrugged. "As you wish," he said. He took his place on the side of the cot. For a few seconds he sat staring into the vapors from the steaming brew. "Oswald," he began softly, looking up, "I do wish you'd sit down."

Humphreys continued to stand in the center of the tent. "And I wish," he said stiffly, "you would tell me why I'm here."

"Does there have to be a reason? After all, you are my Number One."

"I *was* your Number One."

Frazer jerked to his feet. "What are you talking about?" he demanded.

Humphreys eased himself up and down on his toes. The movement seemed to lend him importance. "I gather I may no longer act in that capacity."

Frazer gazed at him, then smiled a not altogether convincing smile. "Surely, old man, you don't think that because of yesterday morning . . ." His voice trailed off. He held out his hands deprecatingly.

"May I remind you of the arrangement decided upon in Capetown? It gave me full command of the mechanical side of the operation. I accepted that—*literally*. Yesterday morning you saw fit to renege on that agreement." He tossed his topee on the map table defiantly. "Just so the credit and discredit for this operation fall on the right shoulders." He turned to a wooden filing cabinet and slid open the top drawer. What he withdrew was a thick ledger labeled "Naval Africa Expedition—Daily Log." As he turned the pages, he produced a fountain pen. With a flourish he ran his thumb down the gutter and proffered Frazer the pen.

Frazer rubbed his face heavily. "No need for that," he said in slight annoyance, rising to his feet again. "Good Heavens, we're six thousand miles from that way of settling things. I like to think we've more of the 'village eleven' spirit here."

Humphreys' upper lip curled in an obvious sneer.

Frazer ignored it. "No intention to displace you, Oswald. You'd had a difficult night and I was merely going to—"

"—cash in on my efforts to date," interrupted the engineering officer sarcastically.

The Scotsman's pulse raced and his jaw muscles rippled as he bit down on his anger. He leaned on the map table and looked up at Humphreys. "Look here," he said slowly and deliberately, "what is it you want? Exactly what are you after? If the whole damn idea of being along bores you so frightfully, why in blazes are you here? The rest of us volunteered." He began to pace, his hands behind his back. "You despise every one of us, don't you? Nobody's as bloody colossal, as strong, as ingenious, as enterprising . . . nobody's the soldier you are. Isn't that it? We're all in your way. Everybody's a damned nincompoop but Captain Oswald Bloody Humphreys, Royal Engineers." He pivoted sharply to bring a baleful glare to bear on his adversary, whose face wore the bleak strain of boredom. "Who do you think you are, you . . . you crushing snob?"

Humphreys again proffered the fountain pen without comment.

Frazer scythed his right hand down in a sweeping arc, knocking the pen from Humphreys' hand. The pen slapped against the stiff paper of the log, spattering Frazer's neatly penned entries of the past two days with ink.

Humphreys sniffed disdainfully at the mess.

"Don't you know standing orders?" blared Frazer. He had noticed the topee on the table. "You wrote 'em yourself. Get your damn headpiece on, sir!"

Humphreys hesitated—then slowly reached for the topee. He picked it up and held it with his fingers inside the sweatband, spinning it around. Finally he put it on.

The yellow light of the lantern glinted off the Royal Engineers' badge on the topee. Frazer stared at the inscription, that of the Knights of the Garter, the highest order of knighthood in the Empire: "*Honi soit qui mal y pense.*" The evil of pride before duty, he thought. Frazer fixed his questioning gaze squarely on the bland,

182

indifferent visage of Humphreys. "What's the matter with you?" he asked sincerely. "What's gnawing at your bowels, man?"

"You are a fraud."

The conversational tone of the claim shook Frazer rigid. He swallowed. "I ought to clap you in irons," he said quietly.

"That," continued Humphreys, "is an example of what I mean. You've never clapped anyone in irons in your whole life. You may fool the others with your Captain Bligh manner and your bizarre taste in uniform—nonregulation, incidentally, as is most everything else about you—but I happen to know that assistants to Assistant Directors of Naval Personnel don't normally throw their weight about by clapping delinquent subordinates in irons."

"You insubordinate swine," grated Frazer. "Take that sneer off your face . . . or I'll—"

"Not the irons again," pleaded Humphreys. "That would be tiresome. Perhaps relieving me of duty would ease your frustration, but that would be shortsighted, might I point out. You'd like me to pass on that rubbish heap of a bridge. Can't very well do that if I get the sack. Can I, now?"

Humphreys' arrow slammed into the bull's-eye.

"You're supremely confident," said Frazer, forcing anger to submit to logic.

"You could say I'm standing on firm ground," Humphreys allowed expansively. "Substantially firmer than that maladroit attempt at bridge building."

Frazer's eyebrows raised. "Maladroit, eh? You've looked at it?"

Humphreys smiled enigmatically.

"If you have, it's your duty to give me your appraisal," snapped Frazer.

Humphreys continued to smile. "Duty? My duty, for your information, is to get us to the lake. Those are *my* orders."

Frazer bristled. "Rubbish. *You* haven't been given such an order!"

"Director of Plans Division has, though," said Humphreys offhandedly. "I'm to see you don't"—he paused momentarily, smiling —"fall into a crevasse, shall we say?"

183

The nausea of doubt pulled Frazer's stomach in spasm. He faked a contemptuous smile. "I expected more from you than lies."

Humphreys unbuttoned his shirt pocket and extracted a thick, leather wallet. He fished inside it dexterously, then handed the naval officer a neatly folded sheet of paper. "It's all supposed to be quite unofficial," he added smugly as Frazer read from the Admiralty letterhead.

Frazer slowly refolded the piece of paper, its import in his craw.

Humphreys interrupted his train of thought. "We'll carry on, then, as before," he declared as he carefully replaced the letter in the wallet and buttoned up his pocket. His tone indicated that the encounter was at an end. "No reason why this can't be kept to ourselves," he murmured, tapping his pocket, "unless extenuating circumstances develop, of course."

Frazer nodded tiredly. He looked around the floor of the tent.

Humphreys followed his glance. "By the cot," he said, pointing.

Frazer bent down and picked up Humphreys' fountain pen. He examined the nib. It was bent beyond repair. "Here," he said in a weak voice, offering Humphreys his own pen.

Humphreys took it without comment.

"You'll have no contact with Plans Division till we arrive at the wireless station in Albertville, then?" asked Frazer neutrally.

"Correct," snapped Humphreys. He stepped back two paces and raised his hand to his topee in salute.

Frazer returned his salute in the loose fashion of superior officers.

Humphreys did an about-turn and headed for the entrance of the tent. He paused at the tent flap and turned around. "The bridge will take it," he declared with authority. He glanced at his watch and said, "We can be under way within the hour."

"Oh?" exclaimed Frazer. He contemplated the blots on the log. He snapped it shut, put it under his arm, and walked toward Humphreys. "Since you won't hear from Plans till then, you'll go along with my nominal charge of things in the interim, I suppose."

"Naturally," grunted Humphreys, eyeing his superior curiously.

"That being the case," said Frazer offhandedly, thrusting the log

184

into the other's hands, "I'd like you to redo the blotted part. You have my pen—and you should have ample time."

Humphreys' face showed the first emotion of the whole morning. It was one of confusion.

"Lots of time, in fact," continued Frazer. "You're relieved from further duty and confined to your quarters."

The colorless eyes of the big Army officer bulged with stupefaction.

Frazer gave him no time to regain his composure. "That'll be all," he snapped.

Humphreys' mouth moved as the words slowly came.

But Frazer ground out his dismissal: *"That will be all!"*

Frazer stood by an improvised ramp up to the earthwork, his hands locked behind his back. Officers and men stood in silent clumps behind him, waiting for the order to move forward. Frazer could feel the dank air of their uncertainty seep through him despite the crisp, blue freshness of the dawn, in whose uncompromising reality the compost of sticks and stones looked painfully inadequate; more like the forgotten sweepings of some giant broom than a military structure. Yet he remembered Humphreys' words. He clung to them. But it was up to him, and him alone. If this was the loneliness of command, the sooner he got used to it, the better. . . . Even though Tommy didn't know a damn thing about things mechanical, he'd have been a comfort to have around. Tommy! Where in the blazes was Tommy? What day was it? The little man's words came back to him: "Give me eight days, then, about another eight days." How many days had he been gone? He could not remember. It was in the log. But the log was packed tight below the gunwales somewhere. It was the same day he had buried Martin and Peterson— or was it Martin and Porter? God, he ought to remember that.

Directly ahead the table of the plateau gleamed a new color—not purple, as it had been for the past weeks, seen from hundreds of miles off, but a grainy gray-brown not thirty miles away, almost as unreal to Frazer as some lunar promontory in a photographic close-up, unreal because it meant the end of the grueling uphill drag. What date was it? He didn't know. Smith would know. He didn't want to turn around and ask him. They had all read the uncertainty in his eyes. He stared at the tableland ahead and inwardly cursed, his mind gone blank. If he couldn't remember a simple thing like that, how in God's name could he—

"Chaps all ready to go, sir."

Good old Smith, thought Frazer. He turned around and faced the sergeant. "Have 'em start the tractor." Under the palpable impact of the men's appraising eyes he knew his voice wavered.

Smith shouted an order and the tractor huffed into action.

"What day is it, Smith?"

"Tuesday, sir."

"The date, man," Frazer snapped testily.

"The eighth, sir."

Frazer contemplated the plateau.

"Almost ten days to the hour, sir," murmured Smith.

Frazer's insides churned. *Two* days *overdue*. Two days ago he should have been on that plateau thirty miles away and shaking Tommy's hand. Humphreys must be gloating; he had sworn that Tommy would botch it. Frazer whipped up his binoculars and trained them carefully on the edge of the plateau. Not a sign of Tommy. He must have botched it. So they were both two days overdue. Both of us have botched it. And Humphreys would be gloating his ugly head off. . . . What's become of Tommy? Supposing he doesn't show up at all? What then? A search party? Not a chance, being two days behind the timetable already and not knowing when the rains'll turn the terrain into a complete shambles. If Tommy doesn't roll up with animal power of some sort, we'll never recoup the time already lost because of the tractor explosion. We'll have to scrap one boat, strip it of spares and hope to manage the show on the lake with one craft. One—against six Jerries! The prospect of his own certain failure and Humphreys' equally certain elation at it goaded him. He turned to the sergeant. "Smith, we'll move forward. Only one item crossing at one time. Heaviest stuff

186

first, lightest last. Get the tractor over to the far side. We'll use cabling. Once the tractor's over, we'll hitch up the heaviest trailer—that'll be *Toutou,* with a full tank—and cable her across. Then *Mimi* last. Move at my signal. Any questions?"

Smith looked at him with an expression of reluctant resignation. "No questions, sir," he said, saluting and adding in a low voice, "good luck, sir."

Frazer paced across the 25-yard-long causeway deliberately, making a final scrutiny of the makeshift structure. He halted at the end of the ramp on the other side and turned around. He raised his right arm and brought it down sharply.

The tractor belched smoke and steam. Slowly and trustingly it clanked forward, the men following guardedly at a safe distance. The vehicle's spindly front wheels eased up to the thick ramp planks. Against these the wheels came to a halt, circumference lightly kissing width, unanxious to force the acquaintance at an immodest pace. But under the profane coaxing of its master, the beast reluctantly ventured along the length of the ramp while the steel treads of the massive drive wheels cut cruelly into the planking. Inexorably it inched toward the edge of the crevasse. Thus far the structure had borne the affront with silence, passively indifferent to the improper advance. At the edge the tractor hesitated. Its master swore. It belched protest in cones of skyward steam, but the forced embrace stomached no frustration. The bridge lay prostrate under its metal substance. The timber and earthwork vibrated with the pulses of its iron heart. As it lumbered toward the center, its great treaded iron wheels furrowed the bridge's flesh. The bridge shrieked. The packed-in soil exploded in powdery puffs. Chunks of epidermal sod flew off the skidding drive wheels. A thick tree trunk arced high in the air, falling back on the bridge again to stand poised a moment on end like some pathetic arm raised in defense. The huge wheels, unquestioning the engine's order, fed ravenously on each log rolling into the place of the one before it tossed so contemptuously into the air. The bridge was foundering under the assault. The engine throttled back to catch its wind. The tractor's wheels stopped spinning.

187

Frazer clambered across to the center of the causeway where the others clumped around in dismal conference. Humphreys sat on a large rock a hundred yards away, eating a sandwich.

"Rotten luck, sir," said Lieutenant Magarity, shaking his head and surveying the mess.

"What now, sir?" queried Dodkins anxiously.

Bannister grunted morosely. "Means going around, the long way, that's all."

"Clearly impossible," groaned Leeds, the gunnery officer. "It would take us a week or more." He looked up at Frazer self-consciously.

"Go on, Mr. Leeds," Frazer said grimly.

"Well, sir," continued Leeds, "according to my computations, losing the tractor's put us seven days off our timetable. Even if the M.O. were to arrive back with help this very day, if we spend a week going around this thing, we'll be *a hundred miles* from the lake when the rain starts."

Dodkins exclaimed, "We'll just have to get cracking on a better bridge."

Bannister snapped, "We've done the best we can. What the hell else can we do?"

"I wouldn't know," said Lieutenant Magarity pointedly, "but I dare say there are some who do."

As a parade-ground movement all heads swiveled to the man on a distant rock consuming a sandwich, then back again to Frazer.

Frazer smarted under the unasked question on every face. "Smith!" he shouted.

The sergeant stepped forward.

"Replace those," he snapped, pointing toward the gaps in the log-lined surface of the bridge. "Wedge 'em in somehow. They were too loose the first time. Nail 'em, rope 'em, get 'em in there tight."

"Sir," protested Magarity, the marine engineer, "it's not going to do a damn bit of good. Starting torque on the tractor's too high. The slightest head of steam and those wheels'll knock 'em flying again."

Frazer rubbed his face.

188

Smith said, "All out of nails, sir."

Frazer persisted. "How about wedges, then? Taper down a few logs and drive 'em in between. That ought to tighten things up all along the way."

Smith contemplated his boots.

Magarity said tiredly, "That'd be like driving a wedge into a sponge, sir. The whole structure is too damn flexible. If you wouldn't mind, I'd like Captain Humphreys' opinion on this, sir."

"Get it, then!" retorted Frazer acidly. "Smith, do as I say. And fetch some cable. 'Starting torque' never worried me at Greenwich," he said with a forced grin. "And it won't here."

"That's the ticket, sir," murmured Smith encouragingly, "but what's up your sleeve?"

"Cabling in reverse. Secure one end of the cable to the biggest tree you can lay your hands on. The other end goes on the flywheel. Slap the drive lever in neutral. Start up. The flywheel turns—"

"It winds up the cable," interjected Smith enthusiastically, "and we freewheel the tractor across and Bob's your flippin' uncle and we're over."

Frazer raised his hand. "Not so fast, Smith. It takes care of starting torque, I think," he said, looking at Lieutenant Magarity, "but we've the boats to deal with yet."

"So much for starting torque, sir," conceded Magarity amiably. "You could cable the trailers across, too, in much the same way."

"Don't steal my thunder," said Frazer, trying to match the other's amiability, but not quite succeeding.

By noon the crevasse was seven miles behind them. The terrain had suddenly fallen away bald and threadbare, and the tractor with its two charges in tow moved forward unimpeded. Officers and men alike panted to keep up. They straggled in a line for a hundred yards behind, each man forcing his legs to move faster and farther apart. Calves bulged with pain. Skulls endured the hammer of the sun. Shoulders numbed under ammunition and loaded rifles, for the unknown lay on the other side of the ridge to which the eyes of

189

all were raised. Frazer marched directly behind the tractor, oblivious of the physical challenge, strangely exhilarated.

The officers clumped along together a dozen paces behind him. Humphreys marched tirelessly, effortlessly and in absolute silence.

Dodkins groaned, "Who's a bit peckish besides me?" He looked at his watch. "Ten past one," he muttered.

"Ten past lunchtime," puffed Bannister.

Lieutenants Magarity and Leeds exchanged eloquent glances but made no comment.

Fifteen minutes later Dodkins drew alongside Magarity. "Sir, I do believe the commander's forgotten the noon bite." He looked behind at the straggle of thirsty, wearied soldiers and sailors. "For the men, sir," added Dodkins.

Magarity looked over his shoulder. "There's nothing I can do about it." He looked at Leeds again, then looked ahead at Frazer. "I used to know what was going on once."

Farther back Smith and Stokes had the same thoughts on their minds.

"I can't last much longer, mate," grumbled Smith to the chief petty officer.

Stokes said nothing.

The recipe for the cake on Devlin's face was sweat and dust. He coughed noisily and wiped a layer of it onto his shirt-sleeve.

"Maybe he'd like a little water," panted the North-Country soldier.

The others laughed the only way they could—dryly.

"Eh, why not ask your lord and master to let you ride on the tractor again?" shouted the Welshman. He cracked a hoarse laugh. "A sip of hot stuff from the boiler'd clean you out."

"Frig you!" snapped Devlin, bursting into a paroxysm of coughing.

The North-Countryman slapped him heavily on the back. "Cough it up, you bastard," he rasped.

Devlin stumbled to his knees. Vengeful hands grabbed him and pulled him to his feet.

"Water," crackled Devlin. "Gotta have a drop of water."

"Suffer, you frigger," grated the North-Countryman. "Got more'n

190

your friggin' share riding with the gaffer, you did—a damn sight more'n us. Should've stored it like a camel, you should've, you humpy bastard."

One of the sailors unfastened his canteen. "He looks like he's all in." He moved to Devlin's side and uncapped the canteen.

The North-Countryman snatched the canteen from the sailor's hand. "Not on your bloody life, sailor," he threatened. "There's more deservin' causes than him."

"You, maybe?" countered the sailor. He stuck out his hand, "C'mon, hand it over or I'll kick your friggin' teeth in."

The big soldier clutched the canteen more tightly, scowling. "No damn swab's gonna open his yap to me like that."

Smith had let it go as far as it ought to. He shouted back to the soldier, "Like us to have another little chat, you?" He nudged Stokes.

Stokes responded. "Pipe down, back there! Keep your water. You may need it yourself before long."

The ragged column, hobbled by thirst, fatigue and stomachs empty since breakfast, began to string its length still farther along the line of march.

"To hell with it," shot Smith finally. "Let's break out the rations, chum." He looked ahead at the officers. "Can't wait for them."

"S'right, mate," agreed Stokes. He was about to pass the order along when Smith nudged him again.

"What about the water?" Smith asked quietly. "Can't keep my chaps on half with yours gulping down a full cup apiece."

"Wot?" grunted Stokes. "All down to three pints per, ain't we?"

Smith nudged Stokes ahead of the men's earshot. He explained how the soldiers' whole attitude had earned them a pint less per day than the sailors, and how he couldn't very well go back on his word without losing face. He warned Stokes that unless he cut the sailors' ration, there was liable to be a small civil war between the Army and the Navy when they both got the word to drink up.

"You just lose your bleedin' kisser, then." Stokes shrugged. The pace was beginning to etch its demands on his thin face.

"Fat lot of help you are, chum," snapped Smith irritably.

For five wordless minutes they panted along to the scuffle of

191

dried-up leather on loose earth and the metallic click of jangling equipment. Behind them they heard Devlin burst out again in a spasm of coughing, but they paid no attention until the corporal jogtrotted to their side.

"He's bringin' up blood, Sarge," warned the corporal. "Another half hour of this and he'll keel over."

Smith motioned the corporal to rejoin the others. "This is friggin' daft, Chief. I'm going up to see him."

"See oo?" quizzed Stokes. " 'Umphreys?"

"Why not?" said Smith. "Far as I'm supposed to know, he's still Number One."

Stokes shook his head. "Nark it, Andy. You 'eard the scuttle-butt."

"Sure I did," insisted Smith, "but there's that protocol nonsense. Wouldn't like to hurt anybody's feelings."

Stokes jerked his head back. "Wot about Devlin's feelings?"

Smith frowned beneath the grime. "Don't like them bloody britches, I don't." He stared ahead. "I don't like 'em; he hasn't been the same since."

Stokes made no comment.

"He's your lad, Chief. What do you make of him?" persisted Smith.

Stokes stared straight ahead. "Wot do you mean, wot do I make of 'im?"

"Come off it, chum," chided Smith. "What I mean is where's he hiding his swagger stick?"

Stokes faced him squarely with a long, thoughtful look, then jogged off ahead toward Frazer. . . .

"What's up?" panted Frazer.

Stokes's quick Cockney sense of humor came to the fore. "The odds, sir."

"Odds?" queried Frazer.

"The odds you've scrubbed the lunch bit, sir, and'll push on like this till dark."

"What the devil gave them that idea?"

"The time, sir. It's five past three."

"Good God!" he exclaimed, swinging his wrist before his eyes.

"It *is*." He held the square dial between his forefinger and thumb. The reflection of the sun did not blind him. He pointed ahead at the purple ridge marking the edge of the plateau. "How far, would you say?"

"Fifteen . . . twenty miles at the most, sir," responded Stokes.

"We're already two days behind, Stokes. A man can march four miles an hour. If we keep it up, we can make up for *half* a day at least. We can reach our objective by nightfall. Can't have Dr. Cavanaugh sitting on his bum waiting for us. The chaps can eat and drink on the march."

"Aye, aye, sir." Stokes nodded. "But I doubt if that Devlin could wot with 'is coughin' up like 'e 'ad t.b."

Frazer marched farther in silence. "The odds are up, you say, eh? Where's *your* money, Stokes?"

"On you, sir, like always, sir."

"That settles it. The sooner Devlin gets to the M.O. the better. Do what you can for him. Break out a stretcher. Pass the word down we eat on the march. Watch the water—a pint per meal. And no straggling."

" 'E's not as bad as all that, sir."

"Coughing blood, you said. That could be dangerous."

"Sir, that's why I suggest we make camp right away and 'ave somebody go for'd and fetch back the M.O., sir."

"Can't manage it. Can't afford the time."

"But we can afford Devlin, sir?"

Frazer related the advance of the column to his new role. Having overcome the massive inertia of his own lack of confidence, he was now rolling toward his true potential. If the column were to crumble to a halt, so might his command. "We arranged to meet Dr. Cavanaugh and his party at the ridge," he said. "That's what we'll do. Carry on, Stokes."

The chief petty officer's shoulders slumped. "Aye, aye, sir." He turned about and rejoined the main party. There he told Smith what had taken place.

Smith's face set in a grim cast. "Looks like we're going to be the cat after all, chum."

"Wot?" muttered Stokes.

"That lot about more'n one way to skin a cat."

Stokes nodded lugubriously. "We'd better get crackin', Andy . . . An' I'd say forget the bloody water business. With Devlin to lug along, they're goin' to be right narked as it is."

Smith spat out a batter of sand and saliva. "Frig 'em all," he snarled. "I hope to hell they've learned their friggin' lesson."

It was an hour from sundown. It was cold. Fatigue weighed leadenly, abrading movement to a stumbling plod. Bodies shivered, touched by cold sweat patches. Equipment clicked and shoes scuffled in the sullen silence.

The tractor coughed—then wheezed into one long, frightful expiration. It inhaled deeply, then burst into convulsion. Tractor and trailers ground to a halt.

As the tail end of the column shuffled up around them, Frazer stood looking up into the apprehensive face of the operator, Private Peterson, browbeating him for letting the boiler run low.

"Get cracking, man," shouted Frazer in exasperation, pointing to *Mimi,* the boat directly behind.

"S'empty, sir," croaked Peterson, wiping the dust from his face.

"Then draw from *Toutou,* blast you!" Frazer said impatiently.

Peterson clumsily swung himself down from the platform and stood spanking the dust from his clothes.

"Never mind that now!" snapped Frazer.

Peterson grabbed an empty jerrican from the tractor and sprinted over toward the rear tractor. All eyes held him as he bent double and crawled under *Toutou's* belly. He did not seem to be comfortable. He moved back, swept away some debris and gingerly knelt down again. He looked up bleakly into the faces of the onlookers.

"We're all waiting on *you,* Peterson," nagged Frazer.

Peterson slid the jerrican under *Toutou's* spigot and unscrewed the cap.

Frazer rapped out an order. The men hurried to form a human chain of jerricans linking the tractor to *Toutou.*

194

Frazer kneaded his knuckles. "Move along!" he rasped.

All awaited the familiar tympany of a water jet on the bottom of an empty can.

The men shuffled, examining the toes of their boots.

Devlin pushed himself up on one elbow on the stretcher and swallowed nervously. The officers relaxed and caught their wind. Humphreys turned his back and unconcernedly drummed a tattoo on his leather leggings.

Frazer motioned to Stokes. "See what's holding him up, dammit."

The chief petty officer shuffled toward his commander. "Sir," he began gravely, "I'm afraid there's—"

"Later, Stokes!" said Frazer angrily, striding toward *Toutou*. He bent double and crawled under the trailer beside Peterson. "What the blazes is—"

"S'empty, sir," Peterson interjected mournfully.

Frazer glowered. "Nonsense! She's full to the brim. Can't you even turn a bloody cock?" He worked the lever on the spigot.

Peterson moved back.

Frazer fiddled furiously with the lever. He stared at it incredulously. He hammered it with the heel of his fist. "It's empty!" he shouted. He hammered it again. "It's empty!" he roared. He unfolded himself from beneath the trailer, stood up and gazed at the spigot. "The damn thing's dry as a bone!" he yelled murderously.

Peterson scrambled over to join the other men.

Frazer continued to stare at *Toutou*. "*Smith!*" he roared.

The sergeant moved quickly to his side.

"It's empty!" Frazer cried in a tone blending pain with anger.

"I . . . eh, I know, sir," said Smith quietly.

"You know?"

"Yes, sir." Smith cleared his throat, trying to sound official. "You see, sir," he began, launching into a fictional but entirely plausible account of how a rubber gasket on *Toutou's* spigot had perished and the one he'd replaced it with obviously hadn't done the job.

"You awkward clod," stormed Frazer. "You knew all the time and didn't inform me?"

The sergeant nodded.

One of the officers swore violently as their predicament impacted fully. Slowly they rallied around their commander as if threatened with a mutiny.

Frazer kneaded his knuckles incessantly. "Who else knew about this?" His eyes searched the ranks of men. "Step forward one pace, every man who knew about this!"

Stokes stepped forward, embarrassed.

"Stokes?" breathed Frazer incredulously. "Anyone else?"

The corporal stepped forward. He was followed by the three soldiers who had stood sentry that night, then the two medical aides, then the cook, until the entire company had stepped forward —except for Devlin in the stretcher.

Frazer stared moodily at them. Finally he said, "Thanks for the vote of confidence. Someday I may be able to return it."

"Your orders, sir?" asked Lieutenant Magarity coldly.

"Without water we're scuttled," said Frazer bitterly. Frustration rankled within him. Suddenly he was his former ignorant, dependent, unsure self. He thought he detected amusement on Humphreys' face. The swine was enjoying it! "What in blazes is so damn amusing, Captain Humphreys?" He crossed to the engineering officer.

The other officers edged away discreetly.

"Your predicament," said Humphreys.

"*Our* predicament," corrected Frazer.

Humphreys shrugged. "*The* predicament."

Frazer noticed the other officers shuffling off. "Magarity, Leeds, Dodkins, Bannister!" he called. "Come over here!"

They turned around sheepishly and walked toward him and Humphreys.

"See anything amusing about all this?" demanded Frazer.

They were awkwardly noncommittal.

"Magarity?" challenged Frazer.

"I suggest, sir, we fall out the other ranks before we get into anything like this," replied Magarity softly.

"The men'll stay," snapped Frazer. He searched their faces. "Dodkins, you're a talkative sort. What do you have to say?"

The young subaltern said spontaneously, "Since you've asked

196

me, sir, I'd suggest we all put our heads together rather than lop 'em off."

Frazer smarted. The youth was absolutely right, and he knew it. He had allowed himself to fly off the handle completely. He tried to remind himself precisely why he was in Africa: to get two boats on the lake—not to get the better of some brute of an Army officer whom he had never seen before and would never see again. But he'd botched it just as Humphreys had expected him to; and—what was the final slap in the face—the men hadn't thought enough of him to trust him with the bad news about the water. Now, after his latest display, they would trust him even less. He gritted his teeth. "Water, Dodkins. Put your heads together on that one."

Humphreys suddenly came to life. "No need to," he declared, unless we also need a good speaker's platform."

Frazer strained to keep civil. "All right, Captain," he said. "What did you have in mind?"

"Water, naturally," said Humphreys smugly.

"Where?" snapped Frazer.

Humphreys squinted slyly. He tapped the pocket of his shirt.

Frazer caught on immediately. The price for water was a return to the status quo. In God's name, he wondered, was the smell of being first of the pack so irresistible that Humphreys would prostitute the uniform he wore? . . . But he must be bluffing. To the south there wasn't water for a hundred miles. . . . Up ahead? Humphreys was as new to Katanga as he was. He couldn't know about any water. He had to be bluffing. It was all a big show to impress the company. Well, he'd fix him. He'd call his bluff. "Agreed," he snapped, "but only if and when it's in the boiler."

Humphreys nodded curtly. He shouted an order to the two medical orderlies. They unstrapped a large galvanized pail from one of the trailers and carried it toward Frazer. Humphreys pulled off the lid. The water inside smelled offensive and resembled very weak soup. Frazer demanded to know where it had come from. The two aides told him.

"You were going to *drink* this?" Frazer asked disbelievingly.

One of the aides shrugged defensively. "We thought somebody might want it for something, sir."

"Good thinking," said Humphreys expansively. "Now toss it in the boiler." He swaggered across toward the tractor and mounted the platform. He stood by as the medical aides filled the jerricans and handed them up to Peterson, who, like a lifer reprieved, gratefully upended them into the insatiable void of the boiler.

A rifle shot shattered the twilight stillness. All heads swiveled to the north. Another shot rang out.

"Take cover!" roared Smith.

Officers and men threw themselves flat. Greased bolts snapped metallically.

Frazer kneeled behind the tractor, Webley in hand.

Smith crawled across to his side and looked at the pistol. "You might load it, sir," he said deferentially.

Frazer mumbled something and abruptly changed the subject. "What do you make of it?"

"I'll take a couple of the chaps and have a look-see, sir," volunteered Smith.

"Righto," said Frazer.

Smith took Nangle and the corporal with him. They quickly moved forward and were swallowed up in the approaching darkness. . . .

Ten minutes later a fusillade of shots ripped the night air—then silence.

In another ten minutes they could hear the heavy tread of an approaching column. Random voices carried on the cool mountain breeze.

The Britons tensed by their weapons.

"Pass the word," whispered Frazer. "Nobody fires till I fire."

A wild, heathen cry rent the night. "Frazer, ye Highland devil, ye! *Cead mile failte! Fag a balac!*"

Frazer's fatigue and frustration vaporized. "It's Tommy!" he shouted elatedly. "It's the M.O., lads!" A flashlight beam probed the dark, searching for the doctor. It found him astride an ox at the head of a span of oxen. Crann and Perkins rode behind him. A long double file of native bearers followed.

Smith, Nangle and the corporal clustered around the returned trio, jabbering excitedly.

"God, am I glad to see you!" shouted Frazer, pumping the little doctor's hand.

"Call me Tommy, lad," Cavanaugh bantered. "That other's a little rich for me blood."

"Damn glad," repeated Frazer.

The men surged around Crann and Perkins, backslapping and joshing, forgetting their weariness.

Spontaneously Dodkins and Bannister dashed into the spirit of the welcome, abandoning the formality of rank and station.

Cavanaugh raised his hand amid the clamor. "Wait a moment," he shouted, dismounting from the ox. "I thought you'd all sleep a mite better if you knew what we brought you." He pointed to the span of oxen. "Fourteen of the best," he shouted theatrically. "What am I offered? They're your new tractor."

The men cheered.

"No firewood and water for them, you'll be glad to know," he continued.

Again they cheered.

"And there's fresh meat for supper, too. Venison and pork appeal to you?"

The men cheered, mightily.

"You can thank the stout Basanga that carried it—aye, it and the 150 gallons of water too."

They cheered again.

Stokes stepped forward self-consciously. "Sir," he began, "you've done us real proud—you and young Perkins 'ere an' Crann, sir." He turned to the men: " 'Ip-'ip."

"*Hooray!*"

" 'Ip-'ip."

"*Hooray!*"

" 'Ip-'ip."

"*Hooray!*"

Cavanaugh smiled mysteriously. "That's generous of you all, I'm sure," he said, scratching his head, "but in all honesty I ought to say I did bring something that . . . well . . . I'm not just sure how. . . . What I'm trying to say is have any of you looked at our

199

Basanga friends? I thought not. Well, gentlemen, you're goin' to have to keep your blinds down at night. Half them are women!"

There was an explosion of cheers and whistles; then the men set to work making camp.

"Magarity, take over," snapped Frazer. "Leeds, tether the animals. Dodkins, secure the tractor and trailers for the night. Bannister, post a sentry on the water."

The officers quickly dispersed.

"You'll see the natives are settled, Tommy, won't you, before we turn in?"

"Aye," muttered Cavanaugh absent-mindedly, suddenly noticing the commander's nonregulation attire. "Tell me," he said, "would I be right in detectin' somethin' slightly rotten in the state of Denmark?"

"Nonsense," retorted Frazer.

"Not even a hair?"

"It's just my . . . new approach."

"Or your new britches, maybe," needled Cavanaugh. He sensed he had hit a sensitive spot. "Tell me," he said casually, "where is he?"

"Round about, I imagine," said Frazer. "I've relieved him from further duties."

"Have you gone daft? He's a swine all right, but it'll take a swine to get us down off this bloody plateau. It'll be murder."

"I can manage it," declared Frazer confidently. "I think I did rather well on the crevasse."

"It won't be crevasses you'll be botherin' about," the doctor warned. "Do you know what you're in for? It's as steep as a barn roof, I tell you."

Frazer regarded him seriously. "You don't really believe *he's* the only one who can see us through this lot?"

"Look, Ian," retorted Cavanaugh, "he's brainy, brawny and a hundred per cent ruthless."

"I'll give him the brawn all right," grated Frazer, "but I'll be damned if . . ." He waved his hand to dismiss the subject and pointed to the officers' mess tent. "Let's have supper." He brightened his manner studiously and engaged his arm in the doctor's. "C'mon, you can regale us with your exploits."

Around the mess table, they listened raptly to the doctor.

"What happened next?" asked Dodkins anxiously. "No weapons, out of salt and the wogs on your heels."

"That's where Perkins came in," said Cavanaugh mysteriously.

"How, sir?" queried Bannister.

"He's a powerful lad, is Perkins," emphasized Cavanaugh.

"That skinny little chap?" asked Leeds unbelievingly.

"I'll have you know that skinny little chap, as you call him," began Cavanaugh, "happens to—" He rose from the table and called out through the tent flap, "Private Perkins!"

Perkins detached himself from a campfire circle and doubletimed over to the mess tent.

Cavanaugh noticed he was still chewing. "I'm sorry, Billy. I didn't know you were still eating."

"That's all right, sir," said the boy, swallowing quickly. "I'd just finished."

"Come on in," said the doctor, putting a fatherly hand on the youth's shoulder.

Perkins was visibly ill at ease.

"I ask you, gentlemen," said Cavanaugh theatrically, "what would you say was Billy's most outstanding characteristic?"

Magarity said, "I seem to remember he's the only chap with ginger hair."

"Who *had* ginger hair, Magarity," corrected Cavanaugh. He turned to the youth. "Show 'em, Billy."

Perkins reluctantly removed his topee.

"What happened to you?" exclaimed Bannister.

Perkins' hair stood up in short irregular tufts.

"Who's your barber, Perkins?" joked Dodkins.

"I am," laughed Cavanaugh. "Perkins here is our *mathanjuki*. At least he is when we're in Wendi Macosi again. The Basanga've never seen red hair before, so when I starts chuckin' out the salt and they're comin' after us in droves, the credit's the young buck's here. He's the big juju, not me."

201

"They weren't after your *blood,* then?" quizzed Dodkins.

"Not in the least," announced Cavanaugh with a flourish, pointing to what remained of Perkins' hair. "They were after a hank o' this—for a charm."

The officers laughed freely. The Bushmills had percolated down into the reserve they usually adopted in the presence of other ranks.

Dodkins rose to his feet slowly, glass in hand. "Jolly good effort, Perkins," he said, slurring his words.

"Hear, hear," seconded the others.

"It's not every day one can give his hair for his King and country," observed Bannister. "I say," he continued, rising unsteadily to his feet. "I propose a toast. Gentlemen!" he intoned ceremoniously. "To Perkins' hair!"

"Splendid idea," declared Cavanaugh boisterously, reaching for his glass and rising.

Frazer shrugged and stood up, glass in hand.

Leeds and Magarity followed his lead.

The six officers stood waiting for the seventh.

"C'mon, Oswald," coaxed the doctor.

Humphreys glowered. His knuckles blanched white under the pressure of his grip on his untouched drink. Finally he rose with glass in hand.

"To Perkins' hair!" toasted Bannister, in the exaggerated seriousness of the drunk.

They raised their glasses.

"Wait a sec!" shouted Dodkins. He leaned over and whispered to Bannister.

The two overstimulated young subalterns nodded to each other. "To *Herr* Perkins!" they toasted in unison.

The canvas billowed with raucous, deep-souled guffawing that slumped the six officers over the table in wonderful exhaustion.

Humphreys stood contemptuously immune. He tossed his untouched drink on the ground and stiffly took his leave.

202

15

The sound of a lantern incandescing into life hissed into Cavanaugh's slumber. He rubbed his eyes and turned over on his side.

Frazer sat on a spindly camp stool fully dressed. He hunched over the map table, scrutinizing a large map of Katanga Province. "Ten past five," he murmured. "Time you were up and about. I want to be on the move before half past six—at the latest." He pointed to the map with his cold pipe. "Come see. The Maniku Plateau. Miles upon miles of flat, even going for us."

Cavanaugh dragged himself out of his sleeping bag and lumbered unsteadily across to the map table. He squinted in the yellow-white light and tugged at his crotch.

"Know what this means, Tommy?"

"I bloody well ought to. I came across it."

"Think we could squeeze fifteen miles a day out of it?"

"Twenty, if the lads are up to it. How've they been?"

Frazer resumed his scrutiny of the map. "Managing," he said casually, "managing." He traced the route for the next week on the map.

To the Irishman he seemed hungrily interested in making up

for lost time. "Well," he announced, "I'll leave you to it, boy. I'll browse around a bit."

"As you wish," murmured Frazer.

A half an hour later hobnailed boots scuffled on the hard plain. Mess gear clanked. Brusque orders cracked in early-morning voices amid a cold breeze scented with cheap soap.

Frazer paced nervously at the head of the assembling column. He kept glancing repeatedly at his watch and nagged the men for faster efforts.

He had not noticed the doctor approach until the little man was almost upon him. His brow wrinkled at the doctor's scowl.

"Manage!" snapped Cavanaugh. "Manage, you said!"

"What's bothering you?" asked Frazer.

"You seen Devlin?"

Frazer shrugged apologetically. "No, should I? He had a coughing spell yesterday."

"Coughing spell be damned. It might even be typhus. Typhus fever. What do you think of that?"

"What do you want me to think of it?"

"You've the nerve to talk of twenty miles a day and him with his intestines festered like a . . ."

"Sorry to hear it."

Cavanaugh stared at him disbelievingly. "I heard about it *five minutes ago!*"

A commotion between Smith and the Basanga pulled Frazer's attention away. Frazer looked toward the column. "Look, Tommy," he said, "you have a way with the wog lingo. Help Smith hitch the oxen to *Mimi,* will you?"

Cavanaugh caught him by the shoulder. "Typhus, I said, Ian. Typhus, man! You can't move a typhus case. His insides'll split like an overcooked sausage." His manner was deadly sober.

Frazer seemed to be concerned solely with Smith and the Basanga. "You don't *know* it's typhus."

"No, I don't *know,* but—"

"We'll move ahead according to plan."

"And Devlin?"

204

"He's a good man. If he can hang on for a few days, we'll leave him at Macosi."

"Hang on? For twenty miles a day?"

"You said twenty, old man. I said fifteen, but since you said twenty, it'll be twenty."

Cavanaugh stared at him as if not believing what he was hearing.

"And would you see to Smith and the wogs?" urged Frazer.

The doctor turned abruptly and left.

For days Devlin rode on a stretcher carried by four Masangas. His lower abdomen had swollen grotesquely; his labored breath was redolent of pus, and the corner of his mouth was never without a trickle of blood.

At night, by the light of a flashlight, Cavanaugh bathed Devlin's head and labored to make him comfortable. In delirium, his patient relived the incident with the water. Poetic justice, thought Cavanaugh, that he should be enduring this hell when the rest had taken so much on account of him. The dull skid of stockinged feet on the ground outside diverted his attention.

Sergeant Smith stood at the tent flap peering in. "How is he, sir?" he inquired.

"Poorly, I'm afraid," said Cavanaugh, renewing the cold compress and gazing at Devlin's thin face beaded with perspiration. "But I should think after what happened with *Mimi,* you wouldn't be too worried about him."

"*Mimi,* sir?" asked Smith.

"A man talks a lot of blather in delirium," he mused, nodding toward Devlin, "but he gets in a little sense too."

"Sir?" said Smith, affecting ignorance.

"Sergeant, I know all about the water business."

Smith's shoulders slouched. "We sorta thought we might just keep it in the family, long as Captain Humphreys was Number One —if you twig, sir."

Cavanaugh nodded. "No need to elaborate." He adjusted Devlin's compress. "Tell me, Sergeant. Things are different now, aren't they?"

"They are and they aren't, sir," said Smith, fidgeting. He told

Cavanaugh the chaps knew which side their bread was buttered on: the commander was more likely than not to run the show along bankers' hours. So when he'd taken over back at the crevasse, the younger lads expected easier going—which they hadn't exactly got. And the older heads: well, the whole bloody expedition might've been the commander's to start with, but the way everything the captain touched turned to gold, so to speak; well, the older lads couldn't take that away from him—and maybe the commander shouldn't have.

Cavanaugh understood perfectly. He had his doubts himself.

"Fire! Fire!"

Cavanaugh kicked over the stool, scrambling outside.

A sailor, his Lee-Enfield at the port, stood in the center of the campsite, shouting the warning in a voice pitched with nervousness.

"Where?" shouted Cavanaugh.

"Over by the ammo dump, sir!"

Men in various stages of dress and slumber cursed and shuffled out into the cool air of the high veldt. Frazer appeared in long underwear, thumbing the sleep from his eyes. He froze in a yawn. "The magazine!" he shouted hoarsely, loping across to where a half-acre carpet of savanna flamed solid yellow. Under a temporary lean-to near the inferno were stacked all the small arms, Maxim and three-pounder ammunition. Fanned by a stiff breeze, the danger crept toward the stack.

Frazer stood by the lean-to, the glare lighting up the indecision on his face.

The men clumped around him chattering—poised for his command.

Smith hobbled through them, one boot on, the other off, to Frazer's side. He, too, waited for the command.

"We don't have a lot of time, sir!" shouted Smith above the crackle of incineration.

"I know damn well we don't," retorted Frazer angrily.

206

Sparks carried by the breeze began dropping on the tents.

"If I was you, sir, I'd—"

"You'd what?"

"Half a dozen men on the ammo . . . the rest grab jerricans for a water chain from the boats."

The carpet of flame advanced.

"Let's get the wogs out with their blankets!" shouted Dodkins.

"Maybe hack down a width of grass 'tween it and us, too!" shouted Magarity.

"Or dig a trench!" bellowed Bannister.

"What'll it be, sir?" prodded Smith.

"Your way, Smith," said Frazer, hesitating.

Instantly Smith thundered, "Corporal Henry! Take your sentries! Move the ammo! Everybody else grab jerricans! A chain from the water!"

"Move!" urged Frazer, adopting Smith's decisiveness.

Bare feet hammered as Smith's command ramrodded action into officers and men.

"*Wait!*" bellowed a stentorian voice.

"Humphreys!" admonished Frazer.

Humphreys ignored him. He turned his authority to his subordinates. "We've fifteen minutes before it's on us. Strike camp and move around the damn thing. We can do it in fifteen. Don't bother with the bloody fire. It can burn from here to the Atlantic, for all we care—long as we're behind it."

The men turned their backs to the fire and faced what seemed to be a greater danger.

"How dare you?" grated Frazer.

"How dare *you?*" retorted Humphreys. "Spend time and water on a damn bush fire that can't singe a hair if we aren't too lazy to move out of its way!" He turned to the men. "Corporal! Your squad'll handle the ammo. The rest—every officer and man's responsible for his own gear and tent. Dr. Cavanaugh! Get the wogs in on this—and their oxen! No time to fire up the tractor. Hook the oxen to both boats!"

The men stood silhouetted in indecision.

"What are you waiting for?" bawled Humphreys. "*Move!*"

"*As you were!*" ordered Frazer. Sparks sprayed his legs. He flinched.

"Ian, for God's sake," appealed Cavanaugh.

"*As you were!*" quavered Frazer.

"What do *you* want us to do, sir?" pleaded Smith.

Frazer rubbed imaginary smoke out of his eyes. His mouth twitched.

"Sir!" demanded Smith.

Stokes moved from the edge of the sprinkled group of confused sailors and soldiers. "Sir," breathed Stokes in Magarity's ear, "you'd better talk to 'im."

"Captain Frazer," shouted the naval engineer, "we can't hold off much longer. I do believe the captain has it, though."

Frazer stared blankly at him.

The doctor grabbed him by both arms. "Ian, if *you* don't, *I* will!"

"Lean-to's afire!" yelled a youthful sailor.

Random sparks showered on the tarpaulin, igniting the canvas fibers wisping from its weather-burst seams.

The thought of exploding ammunition tightened them with fear.

"Doctor!" shouted Humphreys. "You're second senior naval officer."

"You're out of order, sir," declared Frazer. His statement had about it the comic propriety of a captain going down with his ship.

The doctor released his grip on Frazer and looked helplessly at Humphreys—then he nodded.

Humphreys exploded with orders.

All hands responded greedily in a barrage of action.

Frazer was abandoned as he stood, a gangling, disheveled figure in baggy underwear, whispering protests of insubordination. They were lost on the ears of all but Cavanaugh.

"I had to," said the little doctor sadly. "It was my duty.

"What do you know of duty?"

"I learned from you. From the time—"

"The wogs, Cavanaugh!" bellowed Humphreys from afar.

208

The stocky little man ran off. . . .

Later in the controlled stampede of men and equipment, he caught sight of Frazer standing exactly where he had left him, shivering despite the heat of the mushrooming fire, staring as though mesmerized by the leaping, consuming flames. "For God's sake, Ian, why the devil—" He stopped, grasped the Scotsman limp arm and monitored his pulse. A group of Basangas scurried by. He called to one in a low voice, a youth wearing the thin scars of a chief on his cheeks and forehead. "Take *Bwana* Frazer back to your camp. Have the women look after him. Give him water—boiled, mind you—when he asks for it, and tell them to keep him warm. If anything happens to him, there'll be no more salt, no more tobacco."

The youth padded south, leading Frazer by the hand.

"I won't waste your time with pleasantries," said Cavanaugh summarily to the five officers. "At least we're out of the frying pan for the time being, but we've another problem." He searched their faces. "Commander Frazer's on the sick list, I'm afraid."

There was no comment.

"That leaves me in an odd sort of a spot, something of a senior naval officer not afloat, you might say. At the same time I'm not an executive officer. As I can recall those RNVR lectures, I'm a specialist officer—not entitled to command one of His Majesty's men o' war."

Lack of sleep had sabotaged their interest.

"But, then, we're not at sea, and I don't recall any lecture covering that contingency. In other words, gentlemen, I'm in command for the time being; and I delegate executive power to Captain Humphreys until Commander Frazer is up and about again. Any questions?"

There were none spoken.

"I'm better with tonsils than tractors." He laughed gently and turned to Humphreys. "Oswald?"

209

The engineering officer stepped forward stiffly. "Dr. Cavanaugh, Sergeant Smith asked me to tell you he 'thinks we've lost Devlin'— if that means anything to you."

"Mother of God," ejaculated the doctor, hurrying through the tent flap.

Humphreys studied his watch. "I suggest you all get back to your tents," he said. "We move at six sharp. That gives you about three hours' sleep. That's all."

The officers were trudging out of the tent when Humphreys called Dodkins.

"Yes, sir," responded the subaltern.

"If Smith's right, we'll need a work party at four to take care of him."

"Yes, sir," said Dodkins glumly. "How will I know, sir?"

"Stay with him till you *do* know."

Frazer opened his eyes. They saw circles of blue through the brass eyelets of a canopy over the stretcher borne by four Masangas. His hand shot to his face to shield his weakened eyes. He felt the coarse stubble of days spring under the touch. Shadow dimmed the pain of his eyes—but not that of his humiliation.

He tried to call Cavanaugh. Only a croak issued forth.

He saw the bony, black face of a native peering in solicitously at him.

"Tommy!" he croaked again.

Cavanaugh's cherubic face beamed by his side. "Well, that's a lot better, now," he said approvingly.

"What is?" croaked Frazer. Blunt shafts of pain jabbed his brain every time his jaw moved.

"You being back with the conscious," said Cavanaugh. His deft fingers explored for a pulse, and he mentally noted the deeply sunken eyes, the hollow cheeks and the pallor. "How do you feel, old man?"

"What am I doing here?" Frazer whispered painfully.

"You passed out four days ago."

210

"Malaria?"

"Something like that."

Frazer closed his eyes and moaned. "C'mon, Tommy," he pleaded. "Out with it, what is it?"

"I quite frankly don't know." The doctor rearranged the pillow of rolled-up jodhpurs and tunic to make Frazer more comfortable and told him he had talked enough for a while. "Try to get some more rest, old man," he said as he started to take his leave.

"I could use some water," breathed Frazer.

"Sorry," said the doctor apologetically. "It's not the best thing for you right now."

Frazer's eyes opened to mere slits. "You do know, then."

"Could be a number of things," said the doctor evasively. "No sense taking any chances."

"No sense taking a chance telling me what I've got?"

"Oh, don't talk rot, Ian. I tell you I just don't know."

Frazer closed his eyes again. "Dengue? Kuku bug? Bilharzia? Encephalitis? Dysentery? What?"

The Irishman affected humorous surprise. "You're quite a diagnostician yourself. So it's you's been gettin' into me medical journals. Dammit all, nothin's safe any more. . . . Reminds me of a chap I was in digs with at Trinity. Never bought a textbook in his bloody life. Used mine, he did, an' I never could find 'em when I wanted 'em. How I used to envy the scoundrel. He never struck a bat nor turned a wheel. Too fond o' the ladies. But God, how he'd sail through exams. And me? When I *could* get me books from him, I'd sit up half the night for months with me head stuck in 'em and even then barely scraped through." He walked alongside Frazer's stretcher, reminiscing.

"How's that soldier—Devlin?" whispered Frazer.

"Left him at Macosi, just as you suggested," said the doctor casually. "Aye," he continued, picking up the thread of reminiscence, "the bucko's name was . . . now, what was it? Well, damned if it'll come to me, but I'll never forget his ructions. . . . There was the time in anatomy. We had one girl in the class. A big horse of a woman, she was. Didn't get on at all with us, nor us with her. There must be something cracked about a woman who wants to go

211

into medicine. . . . Anyway, she wasn't so bad the bucko wasn't always hangin' around her table—her dissectin' table. He was up to no good, an' she told him straight to his big face. He was as red as a beet. She took him down a peg right in front of the whole class. . . . Well, he was as sore as a boil. He was out to get his own back, so do ya know what the omadhaun did? His cadaver was an old lad. An' so he excises and plants it—well, I'm gettin' ahead of myself, but she was workin' on some old lady. So he lets all us lads in on it. An' the very next day we're all in there bright and early, real busy uncoverin' our day's work. So she whips back the sheet, an' she sees what she sees. We're all ready to burst when all of a sudden she says as quiet as you please, 'Well,' she says, 'all I know is some of you left in a great hurry last night.' You know, Ian, I never saw hide nor hair of the bucko since." He peered guardedly at the recumbent figure. The breathing was more regular. The eyes were shut, perhaps in sleep. He was about to slip away when Frazer said, "Why?"

"Why what?"

"Why'd you leave him?"

"He just got too ill to travel." explained the doctor guardedly.

"Why didn't you leave me behind?" Frazer's whole body quivered in spasm. A groan escaped his parched lips.

"Because you're on the mend, old man. . . . Now you've talked your fill for now. Get some more sleep. You're as weak as a kitten. You have to build up your strength."

The commander groaned again. He gripped the side of the stretcher and tried to pull himself up. The effort forced a whimper through his clenched teeth.

"What do you think you're doing?"

"Things can't run by themselves," said Frazer huskily.

"Oh, don't be so bloody heroic, Ian," rebuked Cavanaugh, placing his hands on the Scotsman's shoulders and pushing firmly. "They *have* for four days."

Frazer stubbornly refused to lie down. "Four days?" he asked. "Four days?" He seemed unable to understand.

"Be a good lad, now," coaxed the doctor, "and lie down."

Frazer refused. "You don't understand, Tommy," he persisted.

"Ian, boy," pleaded the doctor, still pushing gently on his patient's shoulders.

"Don't," Frazer said tenaciously. "I'm telling you, don't."

Cavanaugh laid hold of his wrists to ease away his support.

Frazer screamed wretchedly. "For Christ's sake, take your hands off me, you damned double-dealer. You've done enough as it is. Off me, do you hear?"

The doctor recoiled.

Frazer kicked off his blanket and dropped his legs over the side of the moving stretcher.

The doctor shouted.

The four natives halted and abruptly lowered the stretcher to the ground.

The ground hit the soles of Frazer's feet and knocked him off the stretcher. His big, loose frame slapped against the hard earth.

Cavanaugh shouted to the natives and jumped to Frazer's side. They lifted him back onto the stretcher.

"You dirty Irish bastard," ranted Frazer weakly. "You're all the same! Rebels! *I'm* commander of this expedition! What *I* say goes!" His skinny jaw slacked in abject disbelief as the natives knotted a rope around his feet, knees and chest. "Get those heathens off me," he cried feebly. Tears toppled the remnants of his composure. They ran freely down his face. "These ropes," he coughed. "Get them off me! *I'm* CO. Do you hear, Tommy? *I'm* the CO. Honestly, I am, Tommy!"

The appeal hammered the doctor's heart, but he stood silent as the natives went about their work.

"Tommy, Tommy!" came the croaked ravings. "Tell them . . . for God's sake, tell them . . . I'll do it, Tommy. I swear. I'll get there . . . just give me a chance! A chance!"

Cavanaugh waited until the last knot was secure, then moved to the commander's side.

Frazer grabbed his shirt with the frenetic, despairing strength of a drowning man. "A chance," he sobbed. "Another chance, Tommy."

"There, now. There, now," soothed Cavanaugh. "We'll give you all the chance in the world, we will."

213

16

Late autumn blew down Whitehall from Trafalgar Square. The gray of impending winter threatened the evening. Hundreds of Admiralty employees, their throats muffled and coat collars up, scurried home before the gloom of night caught them outdoors. Footpaths earlier clogged with clattering, dripnosed civil servants racing for the sanctuary of glowing coal fires now echoed to the shuffle of late home goers. A thousand omnibuses had tired of bellowing.

The quadrangular pile of the New Admiralty Building tried to resist the encroaching dark. From the footpath below, the corner towers above on the Italian Palladian structure were still visible, but the bell tower would be lost until morning.

On the windows of a room high above hung heavy curtains cloaking the glare of great incandescent ceiling lights reflecting off shiny wall maps. They looked like huge sheets hung out to dry, but black blobs and flags blemished their whiteness. The room was the innermost chamber of the British Naval War Staff, the nerve center of the Navy.

Anchored by the door was the heaviest, solidest, flat-top desk in all of London, manned by the First Sea Lord. The seventy-three-year-old Lord Fisher of Kilverstone, Admiral of the Fleet, suffered hard the circumlocution of the modern Navy—orders in the form of a naval cipher handed to a naval clerk, then transmitted via the wireless station in the bell tower above to the ends of the earth. He reveled in a passion for the personal and direct.

A door handle rattled. A rectangular hole jerked open in the wall; through it a snatch of clicking typewriters, a glimpse of clerks fussing with baskets heaped with correspondence, then a solid, square-rigged man gold-braided up to his elbows. He was heavyset, bulldogged of jaw, gray and wrinkled with experience. He slammed the door shut. A growl escaped his granite jaws. It was intolerable to preside over the first British naval defeat in one hundred years! Rear Admiral Cradock's South Pacific Squadron had been wiped out some hours ago off the coast of Chile.

Across the room Vice-Admiral Sir F. C. Doveton Sturdee, the tall, spare chief of the Naval War Staff, consulted quietly with his fellow juniors around a long table laden with maps and plans. His hair was gray, his manner grave. He gestured with his parallel ruler and dividers.

"Sturdee," snarled Fisher with a trip-hammer salvo of sarcasm, "you made all those nice plans for Cradock. Why didn't *you* carry them out yourself?"

The others stood awkwardly by. They knew Fisher's cry by heart: "War is violence, and moderation is imbecility." They could read the urge for vengeance in his every move.

Sturdee, the discredited strategist, smarting under Cradock's defeat, for which he was partly responsible, faced Fisher, but he did not speak. He was used to the First Sea Lord's tirades. Like storms at sea, they had to be waited out.

Fisher began pacing the room, hands behind his back, jaw thrust forward dangerously. "I've just come from the King and First Lord," he declared. The demeanor of his audience was that of errant boys scolded by their father.

"This is a dark day for England, gentlemen," continued Fisher. "A dark, dark day, I repeat. . . . First Lord wants some action, Sturdee. I want some action! The King wants some action! Britain wants some action, do you hear?"

215

Sturdee spoke quietly but firmly: "Sir, I'm convinced that's what the Germans want us to do—rush prematurely into some action purely for the sake of vengeance. They have us off balance now. Some ill-planned, ill-considered attack now—merely for the sake of attacking—would push us further off balance. I say wait until they attack us again—"

Fisher waved his hand disparagingly. "Offense, Sturdee—do I have to remind you?—is the best method of defense. We can't sit around waiting for them to come to us. You're right. We're off balance. 'Twould be downright foolhardy to hammer them now. They know that's how we're thinking. They know we won't attack. That's why we will attack! And hard. We have the element of surprise, man."

Sturdee listened patiently. "But what do we attack them with?"

Fisher wheeled to face him. "At Simonstown—battle cruisers *Inflexible* and *Invincible;* cruisers *Calliope, Royalist* and *Phaeton.*"

"That will leave us naked in the South Atlantic," protested Sturdee.

"We've been naked before," Fisher retorted. "Make a signal to Forbes immediately. Tell him Cape Squadron has twelve hours to put to sea. Time enough for provisions and coaling—and for you to dream up some more 'nice plans.' I want Von Spee's carcass on a spit!"

"Very good, sir," said Sturdee woodenly. He conversed urgently with his staff for several minutes. They finally left the War Room, burdened with their paraphernalia. Only a duty officer and a signal-man clerk remained in the room with the irascible old admiral. He plumped down into the leather chair behind the huge mahogany desk and stared across the room at the situation maps. His eyes were on the young signaler who held a sheaf of naval signals in one hand and a handful of colored pins and flags in the other. As the boy read from each signal, he would consult one of the wall maps and adjust the positions of the colored pins and flags. Fisher tired of looking. He pushed back his chair noisily and rose to his feet.

"Was there something, sir?" asked the captain dutifully, hastily rising from his desk.

"Sit!" ordered Fisher. He crossed the room toward the signaler. "Give me some of those, boy!"

The youth nervously surrendered a share of the signals.

"Pins, boy!" demanded Fisher gruffly.

Fifteen minutes later the two had emptied three baskets of signals. The situation maps were current, and Lord Fisher of Kilverstone was again without diversion. He turned his attention to the duty officer. "Let's have a look at new business."

The duty officer, a gangling captain with a weather-beaten face and a chestful of decorations, swiveled hard to port and withdrew a bulging, cardboard-bound ring file from a shelf groaning under similar records. "April, May, June, sir," he said, flipping open the cover and sliding the file across Fisher's desk.

The old man plunged into the thick wedge of carbon copies. They detonated a cannonade: Had Dorman Long fabricated the new gauge steel reinforcing for Scapa Flow's submarine net? What word from the Director of Naval Construction on the extensions to the dry dock at Valetta? Had intelligence any more reports of help given to U-boats off the southwest Irish coast by the natives?

The captain stood his deck, deflecting the barrage with the armor of quick, to-the-point answers.

The old admiral's heart was still with Cradock's ships on the bottom of the Pacific at Coronel. "Why don't you file monthly instead of quarterly?" he blustered. "Then I wouldn't have to go through this blasted nonsense with you."

"We've always done it this way, sir."

"Not any more, you don't," snapped the admiral. He glowered at the captain. "And what about that Lake Tanganyika business?"

"Lake what, sir?"

"Tan-gan-yika, Captain! Ever heard of it?" asked Fisher dryly.

The captain took a moment to focus his memory. "Well, sir. The last report was from Fungurume, Belgian Congo. They'd got the boats as far north as the railway—and telegraph lines—run. Nothing since then, I'm afraid."

The admiral cupped his chin in his hand. "Nothing since then," he repeated. "Nothing since then." He rose quickly and walked over to the map, the captain following.

217

Like some grotesque, misshapen shoe Africa was suspended before him, its heel bathed in the warm waters of the Mediterranean, its toe dipped in the frigid ocean of the Antarctic. He stared at the lake.

The captain looked over his shoulder. "We've heard from Commandant Fèvreaux at Albertville. Apparently Zimmer's being quite active. Bombardments of lake stations, isolated coast landings here and there, that sort of thing. Constant harassment. Zimmer's been ferrying Von Lettow-Vorbeck's troops up and down the lake by dhow—a mobility General Smuts is having a devil of a time matching."

"Uh-huh," said the admiral, continuing to study the map intently. "What was Fèvreaux's last cipher?"

The captain flipped through a stack of papers on a spike, removing two of them. He paraphrased the first: *"Hedwig von Wissman and Kingani cooperated with a company of Jerry infantry last week to make short work of a Belgian detachment in the south."* He pointed to a town where the southern tip of the lake washed the shore of northern Rhodesia. "Near Sumbu, sir. Fèvreaux lost ninety miles of telegraph wire and four machine guns."

The admiral pulled on his iron-gray beard. "Frazer, isn't it?" he said.

"Ah—" the captain hesitated—"not sure on that. I'll check on it, sir."

"Never mind," said the admiral. "It's Frazer."

The captain produced the second signal. "This one's a little more serious. We've no confirmation of this from Fèvreaux, but military intelligence reports they've been busy dismantling *Königsberg*."

The admiral's finger went immediately to the mouth of the Rufiji River, on the Indian Ocean. "Uh-huh," he said, "And?"

"And our people in Dar es Salaam saw them load two of her 4.1-inchers on a goods train."

Fisher's finger traced the railway running west from Dar es Salaam some 800 miles to Kigoma, the German base on the lake. "No need to wonder what they're up to," he said seriously. "One of them here on the fort . . . and the other . . ." He hesitated, pulling

218

on his beard. "Didn't they have something on the slips over a thousand tons?"

"One moment, sir." The captain examined the spines of scores of binders on the file-laden shelves. He plucked one out, blew the dust from it and fanned through the pages. "Here we are, sir." But as he read, a note of confusion crept into his voice. "Something wrong here, sir. Frazer's original intelligence estimate—you're right, sir, it was Frazer—his estimate showed *two* 4.1s on *Graf von Gotson,* 800 tons. It's dated November last."

"And those?" asked the admiral, indicating the two latest signals.

"Last month, sir."

"Little enough chance against *two,*" observed the old man moodily, "not to speak of *four.*"

"Of course, sir," the captain pointed out, "we've no guarantee that if these represent *two* new guns, they're intended for the lake, have we?"

"Keep your confounded optimism to yourself," growled the admiral. "We have to be realistic and plan for the worst."

"Of course, sir."

"When can we expect to hear from him?"

"Not until they reach Albertville, sir. Then we should get a wireless report."

"I'm to know immediately you get word."

"Yes, sir." The captain stood around, wondering if he were still needed.

"Carry on," said the admiral.

The officer returned to his desk, leaving Admiral Fisher contemplating the map. His hand slid inside his naval jacket and withdrew a letter already opened. The return address read: Vice-Admiral I. H. G. Frazer, RN (Retd.), Ardristan, Ardrossan, Scotland. He tapped the edge of the letter thoughtfully on the palm of his hand. "Captain, what's on the calendar for"—he opened the letter—"lunch on the thirtieth?"

The captain paged through a heavy black appointments book. "Hales, from the Ministry of Supply, sir. Cordite supplies."

The admiral sniffed impatiently. "Tell Sturdee to see him."

"Righto, sir." said the captain. "Then you'll be—" He looked up at his superior expectantly.

The admiral did not answer.

The captain persisted. "You'll be lunching where, then, Admiral Fisher?"

"Dammit!" snorted the admiral belligerently. "Do you *have* to know my whereabouts *every* blasted minute?"

"I'm sorry," replied the captain calmly, "but you did dictate the minute on it yourself, sir."

Fisher shuffled off, muttering. "All right, all right. The Army-Navy—if you must know. Anybody else—tell 'em I'm in the lavatory."

§

Among the splendor of rank, title and braid that patronized the Army-Navy Club, near St. James's Park, an admiral of the fleet was simply another naval person—even if he was Lord Fisher of Kilverstone, First Sea Lord of the Admiralty. He stood in the lobby shaking the raindrops from his heavily braided cap, then laboriously thumbing his way down and out of his greatcoat. He grunted thanks to a butler who magically appeared to take his things and sneezed violently into an acre of handkerchief. He braced his sea legs and scanned the expanse of dining room, flecked with the blue and khaki of every Allied power.

The serious table discussions concerted to a swell which washed the room, occasionally interrupted by the clink of cutlery and the rattle of crockery. Bent old men shuffled with discipline under a harassment of overladen trays and luncheon orders interrogated from a clientele too jingoist to eat.

Across the heavy maroon carpeting and through the sonorous roll and pitch of debate Admiral Fisher steered a course. His destination was the massively magnificent fireplace and the invitation glowing from the cherry-red logs. He left a wake of whispered awe and swiveled heads. He negotiated the straits of prattle and platitude without mishap and now ensconced himself in one of the two red leather armchairs by the hearth. "Damn good to see you again, Frazer," he said to the occupant of the other armchair, extending his hand. "Looking first-class, you are."

The aged Scotsman leaned heavily on the crook of his walking stick and slowly stretched out a white, blue-veined hand that trembled slightly. "And you're still a bloody liar, John," came the fast rejoinder, heavy with a Lowland burr.

Their old hands clasped firmly.

"Nonsense," scoffed Fisher. "Good Lord, I only hope I'm able to be gadding around London when I'm seventy-nine—and single, too."

"Seventy-eight," corrected Frazer, straightening in his chair.

"Ah, what's a year?" rumbled Fisher. He slapped his friend good-naturedly on the knee. "What's a year among friends?"

Frazer gazed at the uniform of his friend, his braid, his ribbons, his air of ocean and authority. His eyes dimmed. "A year," he said slowly. "A year between friends. It's such a fleeting thing at our age, a year." He rubbed his hands together and held them toward the blazing fire. "I'm famished," he shot briskly. "It's a dirty day. It's been a dirty week." He shivered. "How's the war going on up there without me?"

"I'm drowning under paper," groused Fisher. "You can't make ships out of paper promises, nor sail 'em with cardboard commanders who exist only on manpower drafts. It's a damnably dangerous situation, Ian." The admiral aimed his forefinger admonishingly at the elder Frazer. "You saw what happened to Cradock, by God!"

"Shocking," said Frazer sadly. "Absolutely shocking . . . poor Cradock . . . poor Cradock." Under his halo of gray wispy hair his face darkened. "The ships we can replace . . . Cradock, never. But didn't be go down grandly, man?" His voice rose. "Fighting to the bitter end. He knew it was useless. So did every man jack of 'em." He grasped the crook of his cane with both hands and raised his eyes above the mantelpiece to the huge portrait of King George V in the full regalia of an admiral of the fleet. The glow that began to suffuse his waxen countenance came from a source other than the logs crackling in the fireplace. "Out in the blue water . . . the bridge

221

rail between your fingers . . . the stunning detonations of the cannonade . . . the acrid smell of cordite . . . or back in the hush of the War Room . . . only the clocks tick . . . quiet men enter with quick steps laying slips of penciled paper before you . . . you draw lines, chart courses, scribble calculations . . . signal replaces signal, often in the wrong sequence, frequently of dubious import. . . . And out of these a picture always flickering and changing rises in the mind. . . . Imagination strikes out around it . . . at every stage twinges of hope and fear. . . . And across the mind flash memorial services in Westminster Abbey . . . the crowd and the uniforms . . . the coffin with the Union Jack . . . the searching music . . ." He turned abruptly to Fisher. "Let me come back, John. I must be back." He touched the admiral's sleeve with a trembling hand.

Fisher caught his hand and squeezed it. "You've done your share, and the good Lord knows it," he said quietly. "You and I, Ian. We must keep after these young fellows. Keep the spirit going. Keep the attack going. No lying back on your laurels—or defeats. D'you know what Sturdee wants to do? You know Sturdee. Master of the planned battle. All England demands vengeance and he wants to wait three weeks to prepare for it. Humbug! Von Spee's so damn bloated with success we can creep up on him and—" He brought his fist down heavily on his hand.

"They asked *you* back," persisted Frazer, "and *you* did your share. More than it." He searched his friend's face anxiously. "Isn't there something you can do? Even a desk, John. The Navy needs me. To keep the young lads at it. I can prod 'em." He stiffened in his chair and looked harshly into the face of the Admiral of the Fleet. "By God, and how I'd prod 'em."

Fisher leaned over and slapped him heartily on the knee. "I know." He laughed. "And how I know. Now, c'mon. Let's have a bite, eh?"

Over hot minced pie and English ale Fisher critiqued the naval war for his lifelong friend. "But that's not why you're here," he commented. "You want to know about the boy, eh?"

"Aye," said the Scotsman. "What've you heard?"

"They say no news is good news; and that's exactly what we've had—no news."

"Ye don't mean to tell me ye brought me all the way down from Scotland to tell me ye had no news, did ye?"

"Eat up. Your lunch is getting cold."

"Never mind my lunch. I'm asking, did ye?"

"Don't be silly. You know very well you come up to London every three months and there's not a damn thing could keep you away."

"Aye. But surely you must have heard something."

Fisher brought him up to date on German activity on the lake and casually mentioned *Königsberg's* 4.1-inch guns. "But this much we do know: They haven't reached Albertville yet, or we'd have a cipher from Fèvreaux. Since we haven't heard anything, we must assume all is going according to plan. By now they'll be on the down side of the plateau and on the way into the swampland."

"How many?"

"How many what?"

"Four-point-ones."

"We haven't quite decided that yet," said Fisher, going on to explain the possible duplication in the two reports.

"I told him he was off on the biggest thing in his life when he told me what he was up to. I knew he wanted to have a crack at it more than anything in this world. And I wanted it too—and maybe just as badly. But he'd never hear a whisper of it from me. Ye see, it has to be his decision entirely."

Fisher nodded.

"And I told him he hadn't had a command in twenty years—a real command, I mean—and that he didn't know the very first thing about Africa. He still wanted to go. I asked him if he'd ever handled explosives, or if he knew the first thing about fording a stream in the back of beyond with heavy equipment. I certainly didn't, I told him, and I've been in the Navy nearly sixty years."

"But like all the Frazers," interjected Fisher, "he's pigheaded and didn't pay the slightest attention to you."

"Not the slightest."

"And you quivering in your sea boots lest he might, eh?"

"Quaking for fear of it," exclaimed the elder Frazer excitedly, "for the Lord knows I'd have given fifteen years of my life for the chance myself." His brittle old body vibrated. "But I told him he didn't stand a chance of getting it, and he'd see that when he went before the Board."

"That was *before* you came to see me, though," reminded Fisher.

The older man scratched his head thoughtfully. "Aye, I believe it was."

Fisher suppressed a smile. "And to show you how much sway you have with me, Admiral Frazer, the minutes will show I was against the thing from the very start."

"I didn't have the slightest intention of swaying you. I considered it my duty to advise the Navy why he was about this in the first place."

"And don't you think *I* was aware of why? After all, it was *my* barge he rammed—and *me* and *my* staff he fished out of the firth." The admiral paused. His voice was tinged with regret. "And it was I who saw to it he'd never skipper anything faster than a desk."

Frazer's knobby hand patted his friend's sleeve. "Nonsense, man. Didn't he turn out to be the best young staff man we have? Twenty years ago that was, John," he mused. "Water under the bridge."

Fisher produced two large cigars and offered one to Frazer. "Here," he said. "With the compliments of First Lord."

Frazer passed the cigar along his nostrils. "I haven't had anything like this since the war started."

Fisher struck a match and offered a light. "Enjoy it! It may be your last."

"You're right," agreed Frazer, exhaling luxuriously. "We won't see another till it's all over."

"Didn't mean it that way," said Fisher. "Bloody lethal things, these. First Lord smokes up the whole damn War Room every time we run into a minor naval problem. Worse than chlorine, I tell you."

"And what else will you tell me?" asked Frazer, leaning back in his chair.

"Huh?"

"Can he bring it off? The lad, I mean."

Fisher took a long pull on his cigar. "You tell me," he said grimly. "Five hundred miles of virgin country, *virgin,* mind you . . . never been in the bush before . . . never had a command before . . . not knowing when the weather'll close in . . ." He puffed angrily on his cigar. "And if he does, it's over twenty years since he set foot in an MTB. Even so, Zimmer outnumbers him in weapon size and weight of metal."

"That's what I always said: the lad needed a challenge."

"A challenge, by God!"

"Aye, a challenge. Did ye not know it was an Andrew Frazer who caught Nelson as he was shot on *Victory's* quarterdeck? What greater challenge—to have to fill Nelson's shoes in the heat of battle, eh? And I don't have to remind you who won at Trafalgar, do I?"

"Be realistic, Ian. If you were chief of staff and Plans tossed those facts in your lap, what would your estimate be?"

"Exactly the same as yours, exactly—unless I knew things that would never show up on an intelligence report."

"Such as?"

"Such as spirit. I brought the lad up. He has a determination. You know, I took him up to Glasgow for his first sailor's suit. Well I remember it. The clerk said, 'Now, Master Frazer, should we be measuring you for a commander's rig, like your grandfather? Or are you interested in the seaman's rig?' John, do you know what the bairn said? He turns to the old fellow and says, as serious as can be, 'If I'm ever to give orders like my grandfather, I think I'd better start at the bottom and learn how to take them. The seaman's suit, sir, if you please.' "

Fisher looked at him stonily.

"You think I'm a sentimental old goat, don't you?"

"It's a nice little yarn, but it's shot and shell—not sentimentality —that's going to win this war."

"You never had a son, John. . . . I suppose you're right . . . absolutely right." The old voice diminished to a whisper. "It's just that I wanted this so very badly for him."

"Don't you think I want it too—after what I sentenced him to?"

"How were you to know the terrified young subaltern on the end of that bosun's hook was my grandson?" said Frazer kindly.

"Frazer or no Frazer," gruffed Fisher, "any fool who rams me in the beam's going to remember it."

"Absolutely," agreed Frazer. "It's only proper that he should— at least for a while."

"Just a while," explained Fisher, "that's all I intended. Wasn't there ever an application for sea duty?"

Frazer shook his head. "Several times I had him on the brink of it, but it was his duty to stay in the Secretariat, he used to say, for that was where he could serve best."

"Sounds like you," laughed Fisher wryly, stubbing his dead cigar in an ashtray. "But you're wrong on one thing: You don't have to have a son of your own to . . . how long ago is it we were together at Rosyth—the first time?"

"It must be over forty years. Why? . . . Wait! I can tell you exactly. The year they launched *Dreadnought*—in '75."

"He'd be forty then."

"Who'd be forty?"

"Remember Freddie Snow?"

"Uh-huh. He was lost when all hands went down with *Crécy* that winter. A week before his wedding."

"Remember the little lass he left behind?"

"Aye."

"Remember what he left her with?"

"Well, we took up a collection to send her home. I imagine she had the baby there. Didn't you handle all the arrangements?"

"She didn't go home. She tried to go it alone for three years in London. Then she met somebody—to give the child a name. I heard from her a year ago."

"Go on," said the Scotsman, his interest growing.

"She wrote to me. The little fellow went into the Army. He never knew a thing until his father—foster father—died. He'd been an exceptional officer. She said he was going through his father's papers and came across the birth certificate. He promptly went off on a binge. It's lasted three years. He's despised her ever since.

226

Career was going to the dogs. Drunk and disorderly most of the time. She came to see me in desperation. There was to be a court-martial. He was sure to be cashiered. I went down to see Kitchener. I promised to accept full responsibility if the War Office didn't press charges."

"Good for you, John," exclaimed Frazer. "But I don't see what—"

"He's in Africa—with the expedition.

"Oh?"

"He's a captain in the Royal Engineers—an expert at handling heavy equipment over rough terrain."

Frazer smiled in relief. "Then they should work well together."

"Yes, they should—especially across country. I knew your lad was new to that type of thing, so I suggested Humphreys—that's his name—I suggested he have the say-so in that department."

Frazer craned closer to his friend. "Wait," he ejaculated. "This Humphreys—is it?—he's actually in command?"

Fisher nodded.

"An officer who was almost cashiered?"

"He's second to none in the heavy-equipment area."

"Drunk and disorderly most of the time? Yet you put him over—"

"Protocol be damned, Ian. We needed someone. He happened to be there right when we needed him. If anyone can get them to the lake, he can. After that things'll revert to Commander Frazer."

The old Scotsman gripped the edges of the table and looked the admiral straight in the eyes. He spoke in a voice burdened with disappointment. "So this is how you made it up to him?"

"Don't make a bloody mountain out of a molehill, man," snorted Fisher. "This is war—not a personality contest. Humphreys is personally charged with getting them to the lake. It's that—or the court-martial. His head's on the block."

"And you'd swing the ax?"

"And why not? War is violence, moderation is imbecility. Don't ever forget it. Victory absolves us of all sin."

"All but the sin of playing God." Frazer sulked. "Ian stepped forward where no others stepped forward. It was his chance to redeem himself for twenty long years of frustration which you—"

"I know, I know," rasped Fisher. "I'm a swine, but it's over and done with. I'm responsible. I can't help it if you don't like it." His voice softened. "I know what the boy means to you . . . I'm sorry, Ian."

The aged Scotsman stared at him. "You're sorry, eh? Sorry? 'What in blazes good is it to be sorry?' you used to tell 'em when they botched something. Well, what good is your sorrow?"

Fisher gripped his table napkin. "Look, man. It's over and done with, I tell you. Now, whether I'm sorry or not won't change a bloody thing; so why don't you eat up? I've my hands full fighting First Lord. That's enough for ten men."

The elder Frazer's eyes moistened. "You know, don't you," he said softly, "he's the last of the line?"

"Line?" queried Fisher testily. "What line?"

"The line of Frazers, John."

"Oh, that line," Fisher sniffed.

"And every one a credit to King and country—ever since 1588."

"Sentimental nonsense."

"And because of your high-handedness the last of 'em has to end like this."

"Ian, man," pleaded Fisher, "can't you understand why it had to—"

"It's the tradition of the thing, John," declared Frazer trenchantly.

"Tradition be hanged!" growled Fisher, thumping the table. "There's only one kind of tradition—and it's not that hot-water-bottle brand of pious sentimentality." His face had turned florid. "That's the kind of bilge that gets in the way of progress. When it gets in the way of progress, it's bilge; when it draws you together and moves you forward, that's tradition, that is. Don't tell *me* about tradition."

Frazer's old jaw quivered as he stared at his companion. Slowly his head sank, and he picked absent-mindedly at his food for a moment. Finally he wiped the crumbs from his chin with his napkin and made to rise from the table.

Fisher lowered his cutlery. "I'm not very hungry either," he grunted, also rising.

Without another word they walked side by side across the dining room and donned their things in the vestibule.

The only sound came when the sergeant at arms latched the huge door of English oak behind them.

17

Under the unrelenting demands of Captain Humphreys, Naval Africa Expedition moved across the plateau.

Grit as fine as diamond dust infiltrated the men's bodies. It was a cruel abrasive against their eyeballs. The straps of their rifles had polished narrow strips of reflection on their shoulders. Underneath, the flesh had worn raw.

The pace was as fast as the two span of oxen could move: no challenge to the tractor, but murder on the men.

Their hearts thumped on the thin fuel of the 6,000-foot altitude, and the blood surging through their bodies suffused them with that rankling which nags every soldier toward the eventual completion of his duty.

Behind them the Basanga stretched out in a lazy winding line.

The doctor slowed down until the four Basanga stretcher-bearers caught up with him. He looked down at the occupant and laid a hand on his brow.

Frazer opened his eyes.

"Well, now, that's an improvement," panted Cavanaugh.

Frazer looked up at him.

"Fever's gone. Hungry?"

Frazer shook his head.

"We'll try a wee taste o' soup tonight to start with, and we'll have you back on your feet in a jiffy." He removed the jodhpurs from under the commander's head and punched some softness into them. "I think we can find you somethin' a hair more suitable than this," he remarked, grinning wryly at his friend. He dug into his knapsack and pulled out a thick, gray Arran Islands cardigan and rolled it compactly. "Elizabeth again," he explained self-consciously, placing the improvised pillow under Frazer's head. "How're you feeling, old man?" He sensed the commander's despondent mood. He had to get him to talk—about anything.

But several minutes of conversational tactics elicited from his patient the statement: "I don't feel a damn bit like talking, Tommy, please."

At least I managed to get that out of him, thought the doctor. "C'mon, now. Don't tell me you're going to have *another* nap. Want to sleep your bloomin' life away?"

Frazer tried to push himself up on his elbows. The rope cut into his chest. He let himself fall slackly back upon the stretcher.

"Just so you won't fall out," explained the doctor.

"That's a bloody chuckle," sighed Frazer despondently. "The one on my feet, too?"

"You were thrashing around like a chicken with its head cut off," said the doctor with a forced laugh as he untied both ropes. "We're doing very well, you'll be pleased to know, Ian. Close to a hundred miles in the last five days. No problems with the gear. Everyone doing his job." He waited for some response from Frazer but none came. "We'll be on the way down in a day or two. That's goin' to be the very devil, though. Got to get you back on your feet, eh?"

There was still no response from Frazer.

"I'd like to give you a goin'-over soon as we camp," continued the doctor. He pointed a finger at Frazer. "It's lucky you are, if you only knew it. *Plasmodium falciparum,* no less: the most dangerous malaria there is. And you're a damnably hard patient to have."

"I've been more of a liability than an asset," said Frazer bitterly.

"No more, no less than the rest," replied the doctor, panting heavily. "How do you feel, lad?"

231

"Weak as a kitten."

"Ah, you'll be the man you were in no time."

Frazer closed his eyes. "That's something I'll never be again, Tommy, and you know it."

That night, as for the past five nights, the expedition slept under the stars. Humphreys had dispensed with tents; they consumed valuable time which could be used to greater advantage on the march, he insisted, and none had opposed him.

Frazer could not sleep. He lay on his back and stared at the star-studded canopy of black. The sight magnified his insignificance; it seemed to proclaim his uselessness. He ruminated on vengeance. He knew how it must be done.

He unbuttoned his sleeping bag and elbowed himself up into a sitting position. It was almost more than his emaciated frame could endure. The simple effort rippled his body with weakness. His body rolled with sweat. He rested in a sitting position, then gingerly eased himself to his feet. The cool night air chilled his moist body. His teeth chattered. It was the first time he had been on his feet in a week. His legs had turned to rubber. He clenched his teeth but could not control the chattering. He picked up the sleeping bag and pulled its warmth gratefully around his huddled shoulders. He turned his head. His week-old stubble rasped deafeningly against the canvas covering of his sleeping bag, fluttering his heart in fear. . . .

He looked around for Humphreys. He knew he had been off alone somewhere, away from the others. Where were the riding boots? There by the tractor. He made his way stealthily across the ground, carefully sidestepping the other recumbent figures. Was that Humphreys? It was, lying on his side, snoring. He stood for an age looking down at the man who had changed his life.

And there was the Webley: in its holster on top of the knapsack . . . four inches from Humphreys' right hand. The flap was open. He could see the solid butt in the glow of the dying campfire.

Slowly he knelt down. His knees cracked like dry twigs, and he was seized by a brief panic that Humphreys might awaken and drill him through the forehead. But Humphreys snored on oblivious. The commander's hand trembled closer to the weapon. As his fingers curled around the butt, one of the oxen bellowed. His rigid bowels loosened in spasm. He tried again. His right hand wrapped greedily around the butt while his left hand steadied the holster. Metal scuffed on leather as he withdrew the pistol. Its great inertia firmed his hand and mind for what lay before him.

He squatted, facing the back of the sleeping form. He sweated. He stretched out his arm and shook Humphreys.

The slumbering giant did not respond.

Frazer shook him again; there was no response.

Pistol in hand, he moved around to face Humphreys. He crouched down and tugged at the sleeping bag. There was no response. He moved closer.

Suddenly the bulk exploded. The Webley was snatched from Frazer's hand, and he found himself peering into the diminutive bore of a Smith & Wesson two-two.

"Humphreys!" pleaded Frazer in an urgent whisper.

Humphreys squinted. "What in Christ's name's this?" he growled, the pistol never wavering.

"Oswald," whispered Frazer. "Easy, easy. I must talk to you."

"You almost had a hole between your damned eyes," snapped Humphreys, uncocking the Smith & Wesson.

Frazer squatted in embarrassment. "I thought when I had the Webley—" he said apologetically.

"You thought." Humphreys waved the Smith & Wesson. "What do you want?"

Frazer shivered in the early morning chill. He retrieved the sleeping bag, knocked off his shoulders in the scuffle, and huddled under it. "I must talk to you."

"You said that," Humphreys reminded him heavily, rubbing the sleep from his round, vacant face.

"Yes . . . I did," said Frazer. Enshrouded in the bulky sleeping bag, he presented a picture more of a human skull atop a Baluba dwelling than of a British naval officer commanding an expedition. His cheeks sucked in like the hollow side of a billowing sail; his

233

chin, leaned by illness, gleamed bone-sharp in the darkness. "Look," he began timorously, "I've been thinking what we might . . . what you and I might . . ." He glanced at the Smith & Wesson. "You can put that away."

"You've been thinking what?" demanded Humphreys, lowering the pistol.

Frazer peered ferretlike at the litter of sleeping forms. "I'd like this to be confidential," he whispered, shivering again.

"What?" demanded Humphreys.

With an effort Frazer composed himself. He said simply, "I give up, Oswald."

Humphreys stared at him smugly. "I always knew you would. It was just a matter of time."

"I suppose it was," whispered Frazer vacantly.

"I know a fraud when I see one."

"Yes, I'm a fraud all right."

"You've been getting in the bloody way from the start."

"I know."

"You belong back at the desk."

"Yes."

"And your delusions of grandeur?" Humphreys inquired smugly.

"I'm stepping down . . . out of your way."

"That's damned noble of you."

"The boats—that's all that matters."

"That's also bloody noble."

"I'm past caring what it is."

"You know what this means? You're finished."

"I know."

"I'm glad you know. I'm glad you're finished. I'm glad. I don't like you or your sort, Frazer. Officer and gentleman. Bred high . . . of noble ancestry."

Frazer shook his head. "You can't insult me, Oswald. I'm past all that. Let's just get the boats up."

"Good," snapped Humphreys victoriously.

Frazer took it all without emotion. "I'll get out of your way. Use me in any capacity you wish. Only let's get the job done."

Humphreys was skeptical. "No more kissing bruised knees?"

Frazer shook his head. "You're in full command. I've been a fool to think I could manage it." His brow glistened with sweat and the labor of confession. "You're the most able officer I've come across in twenty years, Oswald."

Humphreys smiled. "I know," he said. "Yet you had the gall to think you could compete with me."

"Not any more."

Humphreys paused. "Full control?" he queried.

Frazer nodded.

"I want it in writing," snapped Humphreys exultantly, "so there'll be no mistake."

"You have my word."

"Effective when?"

"Right away."

"Good," said Humphreys. An idea formed in his mind.

Frazer rose shakily to his feet and coughed. His body trembled despite the heavy sleeping bag.

"Tell you what," said Humphreys. "You won't be stepping down. I've decided you'll stay as you are. It wouldn't look very good. No, you stay put." He smiled slyly. "Better you carry on as is—only I draft the orders. You give 'em."

Frazer nodded, then hobbled off into the darkness.

18

Their heads tried to retreat into their bodies and behind the heavy woolen mufflers they wore to protect them from the sandblast of a stiff, hot, searing wind. From head to heavy boots they labored along, caked in a fine, floury topsoil which had discovered every crevice in their aching bodies.

In the rear Perkins tripped and fell. His Lee-Enfield smashed against the back of his head. His topee rolled in the dust. Chief Petty Officer Stokes scrambled to his side and attempted to help him to his feet, but the old sailor's years had taken their toll. He croaked for help. Crann shuffled back to help. He grabbed the lad by the arm and yanked him to his feet.

Perkins sobbed, "I can't go on, sir . . . I can't really . . . I can't go on."

"There, lad," soothed Stokes. "There, now. S'not more than a few miles more. Is it, Crann?"

"Chief's right, Billy boy. Just a few more miles'll do it," said Crann, breathing hard.

" 'Ow's your 'ead?" asked Stokes.

Perkins was dazed. He looked at Stokes as if he did not understand.

"Your 'ead," repeated Stokes. "You got a clout from this," he said, helping the youth to reshoulder the Lee-Enfield.

The boy felt his head gingerly. His fingers explored a lump rising quickly on the side of his head.

Stokes looked at the bruise. "Oh, you're as right as rain, chum," he said. "C'mon, now. Got to catch up with the others."

Crann and Stokes released Perkins, who stood still with a blank look.

"C'mon, now, get a move on," said Stokes cheerfully, panting hard.

"I can't, sir," mumbled Perkins, coughing.

Crann picked up Perkin's topee and put it on the youth's head.

"What age are you, boy?" demanded Stokes with an affected fierceness.

"Going on eighteen, sir," said Perkins, close to tears.

"Would you let an old bugger of fifty-eight show you up?" Stokes demanded. "Gimme that." He took the youth's rifle and added it to his own burden. "We'll move along, now."

"Yes, sir," mumbled the youth, trudging off between Crann and Stokes.

They had not gone more than fifty yards when Perkins' legs gave under him and his bony knees impacted audibly on harsh, abrasive ground. Crann and Stokes grabbed him by the shoulders and tried to pull him to his feet, but they too were tortured with fatigue, and the effort sent them wheezing.

Perkins knelt on the ground, his back arched forward and his head hung down between his thighs.

"C'mon, Billy boy," pleaded Stokes. "Once you get comfy-like down there, you'll never wanna get up." He tugged at the youth's tunic.

Crann looked ahead into the swirling dust and saw the rest of the column fast disappearing. "Get up off your arse, Perkins!" he ordered harshly.

The boy's head rose slowly so that he was looking up at the two older men. His was the manner of a supplicant. Tears had cleansed two rivulets through the chalky dust on his young face. "Sir," he sobbed, "I wanna go home."

"Oh, lad," soothed Stokes, dropping to one knee and putting a fatherly arm across his shoulders, "there's not a bloke 'ere that don't want to get back to Blighty—"

"We'll lose 'em, Chief, if we don't get a move on," warned Crann.

"We got a job to do 'ere," Stokes explained to the boy. "You wouldn't want it to get back to your dear old mother you was swingin' the lead on us, now, would you?"

Crann and Stokes slipped their hands under Perkins' armpits and eased him to his feet. Stokes went to his water bottle. It tinkled with the few drops of water in it. " 'Ere," he said, offering it to Perkins. "Wet your whistle."

The boy hungrily sucked on the canteen. Hardly had his Adam's apple begun to bob up and down with the swallowing when he pulled the neck from his mouth. His expression was fearful and apologetic. "I've gone and taken your last drop, sir." Automatically his hand went to his own canteen. His knuckles struck it, and the metallic ring it gave off said it, too, was empty.

"When are you gonna learn," gruffed Stokes, "you don't call a noncom 'sir'?" He jerked his thumb in the direction of the disappearing column. " 'Oppit, now, chum."

The trio set off again into the biting, dust-laden wind. Stokes tried to keep up a thread of conversation for the benefit of Perkins. He could sense what might happen. The boy was exhausted, and when the instinct to rest challenged the reason to go on, the first would always win in the end—given enough time. Time, he told himself, they'd be bound to have lots of that ahead of them; and if Perkins was down to his last few threads of resistance, he wondered just how many of the others would be all in. He knew that he himself was damn close to it—but they'd muddle through somehow.

He, Crann and Perkins got a move on, and soon they could make out the shadowy forms of the stragglers at the end of the column.

One of the forms turned and shouted through the swirling dust, "Another half a mo' and I was going to fetch you." It was Sergeant Smith.

Alongside the sergeant trudged the dust-laden figure of Private

238

Nangle. "What ever for?" he asked in a voice loud with sarcasm, angry with fatigue.

"Go and pedal your bloody bicycle," grunted Smith. It was obvious from his tone that he and Nangle had been having some kind of running discourse.

Nangle bore on, his head bent forward and his aristocratic chin set in upper-class determination. "We're all a bunch of damn fools!" he shouted above the whine of the wind.

Nobody paid any attention to him.

"We're all a bunch of damn fools, I said!" he shouted again.

"Nark it, mate!" shouted Stokes.

"Don't take any bloody notice of him!" shouted Smith. "He's been going on like that for the past hour. He's just blowing off steam."

"A bunch of damn fools," shouted Nangle again, "to ever think for one bloody moment we can get that mess to the lake—never mind write off Jerry."

Crann shouted, "What makes *you* so sure, Nangle?"

"We're victims of his bloody conceit!" he shouted, nodding toward the head of the column where Frazer marched. "Why go on deluding ourselves? We all know his record, don't we, Chief Petty Officer Stokes? And knowing that, we damn well know our chances. Christ Almighty! Two frigging punts against six Jerries."

Young Perkins came alive. "*Six* Jerries, sir?" he asked unbelievingly of the aged petty officer.

Before Stokes could reply, Nangle snapped, "*Six,* Perkins. *Six.* What do you think of that?"

Stokes threw his arms around the lad again comfortingly. "We'll manage, lad. We'll manage."

"Don't you believe it!" shouted Nangle into the wind. His face was a dust-laden mask of hatred. "We haven't a hope in hell, and we all know it. Those two glory hunters up there'll see to that. They'll never miss us at home. Don't you see? We're all part of the 'calculated risk.' Things so ghastly in France they need something to pep them up back in Blighty, so they send us out here to do the bloody impossible."

"Stow it!" ordered Stokes ominously.

Nangle ignored him. "But don't worry. We'll all come out of it heroes—one way or another." He reveled in his ability to deplete their already diminishing optimism.

"You're supposed to be a soldier," shouted Stokes, "and the first thing a soldier's supposed to do is take orders!"

Nangle turned theatrical. "Ours is not to question why; ours is but to do and die. Is that it?"

"You're bloody right it is," Smith chimed in. "And when you've been taking 'em for a while, then maybe you can start giving them."

"As long as you clods cling slavishly to slogans like that, you're never going to elevate yourselves. People are going to lead you around by the noses all your lives and bleed you white. Do-and-die be buggered. Yours *is* to question, and question *every* step of the way. Why do you think we're in this war anyway?"

"The rights of small nations, that's what," contributed Crann.

"Don't make me laugh," exploded Nangle. "The rights of a small bunch of corpulent little capitalists to make a quid on munitions. The right of these damned blockheads in Whitehall to get the Empire off the dole by plunging us into a war. The right of—"

"Wot the frig do you know about it?" shouted Stokes. "You're just a Poor Bloody Infantry like the rest of us. Just because you went to wherever the hell you went's no reason for big-cheesin' it over the rest of us. And that munitions talk. You're ravin' like a bloody Bolshie. You 'aven't a shred o' proof."

Nangle glanced sideways at the sergeant. His expression was one of contempt leavened with pity. "Harrow, old boy," he corrected. "As for proof: My esteemed pater is at this moment making more money hand over grubby little fist—him and his 'old school tie' chums—than he ever made in his life."

The four shuffled along with the wind whining through their thoughts.

Sergeant Smith had let Nangle ramble on. It helped to keep their minds off their aches and pains and sagging spirits. Normally he'd have told Nangle to shut up. The long-faced baronet's son had enough of an air about him; he knew about things the rank-and-filers never bothered their barmies about to force them to look up to him.

If none of them gave a frig any more about the whole damn business, he couldn't blame them. They'd all seen the maneuvering for prestige. Sure, the commander worried around them—like a bloody mother hen; and it was a bit of a novelty for the lads after the way the drill sergeants had kicked their arses, but when it got to a ruddy running fight over who was Cock Robin . . . well, all that was nonsense.

Could Nangle be right? This was all a big fat gamble from the start? Just to buck up the people at home? Did the brass hats really write them all off as soon as they'd cleared Southampton harbor? It'd be just like 'em. Who would miss 'em? The twenty-eight of 'em? God, what was twenty-eight when there was tens of thousands of 'em helping the French maggots grow fat and lazy?

But he couldn't forget Neuve Chapelle or the scared faces of the pale lads that weren't any more . . . cannon fodder. The word stuck in his throat like a lump of cloth. Out of the frying pan into, he thought.

It was a nasty lot—war, but being a soldier was the only thing he knew, and he reckoned if he found peacetime soldiering a good life, the price was someday having to spill some poor bugger's puddin's all over the place—or the other way around. Yet them that collected the VCs showed the bit of God in all of us—the bit that nothing but the fear of the filthy business could bring out. That was the bloody contradiction of it all—that most men had to become friggin' animals just to prove the bit of God in a handful of them: to reassure them that if God was in some, then He was in all, and that was why man was worth fighting for. But wasn't Jerry man too? He didn't have it worked out that far.

Meantime Nangle's harangue continued unabated: They were all the hapless victims of an incompetent War Staff of an obsolete Navy of a muddling Government of an Empire on its last legs.

"You're forgettin' one thing, mate," growled Stokes. "We're English. We built that bleedin' empire you're so ruddy quick to write off, and don't forget it. We did it once. We'll do it again."

241

Nangle smirked underneath the thick layer of dust. "English!" he shouted contemptuously. "The damned nationality myth. You believe all that bilge, don't you? Stiff upper lip . . . courage in the face of adversity . . . the salt of the earth . . . England expects every man to do his duty. Christ Almighty! They've been feeding us that stuff all our lives. A frigging confidence game it is, a way of getting their bidding done and no questions asked. The bloody nonsense preached in the name of nationality! English—strong, dependable, slow but thorough; always get the job done. Germans—thick-necked and stupid beasts. The French—just a bunch of froggies. Hell, we're as much Jerry, frog and God knows what as they are, all mixed up together in one bloody little island. Look at that old bugger Edward VII—the blooming Kaiser's uncle."

"We'll 'ave a little respect for the dead 'ere," warned Stokes, "an' for King and country."

Nangle shot back, "I will when he and it start having a little respect for us—and for the countries we've raped and the people we've rooked."

"Crikey," retorted Stokes, trying to make light of Nangle's obvious vindictiveness, "no wonder 'e didn't get a commission."

"We've raped and rooked, old sport," barracked Nangle, "and now, in our declining years, we're retired robbers turned pious and self-righteous."

"Speak for your own kind, Nangle!" shouted Stokes.

"I am!" Nangle shouted back. "And as for a commission, I turned it down. They said I had the right school, accent and breeding. Another myth—the aristocracy's 'divine right' to rule. Hogwash! What the hell do I know about it?"

"Lucky for us," Crann piped up.

"You'll never know just how lucky," said Nangle, scowling. "You might've had *me* up ahead instead of him."

Crann said, "I don't know which would've been the worst."

"Put your money on the commander, lads. I've never known 'im to come a cropper yet," exhorted the old petty officer, "an' I been with 'im when 'e wasn't much bigger than young Perkins, 'ere." He gripped Perkins' shoulders reassuringly. "Will you take a coupla quid on 'im, Nangle?"

"Gladly," agreed Nangle, fumbling for his wallet. "I'll cover your two," he announced condescendingly, thrusting a five-pound note in Stokes's direction.

"Two quid, I said," said Stokes frowning, looking at the five-pound note. "I'm not—"

"Five-to-two odds," challenged Nangle. "What more do you want? We're both going to lose anyway."

"That's what you bloody well think," growled the old sailor, grabbing Nangle's fiver and slapping it on his own two singles. He rolled the money into a tight cylinder. " 'Ere, young Perkins'll hold the stakes." He thrust the money into the youth's breast pocket and carefully rebuttoned it.

Perkins declined. "I'd rather not, sir," he pleaded.

" 'Y not, mate?" demanded Stokes, whose spirits were higher because of the bet. "Wot's the matter? I'll split me winnin's with you."

"S'not that, sir," said the lad, shaking his head.

"Your old lady don't like you gambling," joked Crann. "That it?"

"No, sir," said the youth.

"Now he's sirring *me*," quipped Crann.

"Cough it up, chum," shouted Stokes. "It's not so bad that two pound ten won't make it better."

Perkins looked up into the dusty, wrinkled face of the old Cockney sailor. There were tears in the youth's eyes. "I'm afraid we won't win the bet, sir," he sobbed.

Stokes patted him on the shoulders in fatherly fashion. "Wot's this, now?" he said chidingly. "Mutiny?"

"Oh, no, sir," Perkins assured him.

Stokes discerned something serious troubling Perkins. "All right, lad. Tell your old Uncle Charlie."

Perkins blurted out the scene he had witnessed from his sleeping bag the previous night when Frazer had talked with Humphreys.

Stokes's gravelly voice became brittle as china. "Bloody well dreamin', you was!" he shouted.

"No, sir," insisted Perkins.

"Dreamin', I say!" shouted Stokes.

"No, sir," maintained Perkins weakly.

They hobbled along in silence.

Sergeant Smith said, "Friggin' hell!"

"In that case," volunteered Nangle smugly, "we'll cancel the bet, Stokes." He reached forward to recover the money from Perkins' pocket.

Stokes brought his bunched knuckles down heavily on the back of Nangle's hand.

Nangle screamed with the sudden, stabbing pain.

"Leave it be," grated Stokes viciously, "or I'll smash your bloody face."

Sergeant Smith's stocky frame bowed under the march and the wind, and so did his spirit. If old Charlie was ready to smash somebody's face, then morale had gone to hell. Every damn one of them needed a day's rest and a good feed. That would tide their bodies over; but what about their minds? Even if the four of them swore to keep their mouths shut about what Perkins had seen, the word would get around somehow; and there had to be someone else who had seen. He coaxed his aching calves to a faster pace and moved up through the stragglers toward the front, where Humphreys bore along in the lead. Frazer suffered along behind him, leaning intermittently on Cavanaugh's shoulder.

Smith was shocked.

Even with the cosmetically concealing effect of sand and dust, Frazer's face was that of a hermit chained in some dark cellar to a lifetime of privation and suffering. The whites of his eyes glowed yellow. The eyes appeared widened and sunk still farther in his bony skull, giving him an expression of unrelieved surprise. The matted growth of beard failed to conceal the fleshlessness of his face. His gummy look reminded Smith of some ancient grandmother caught before breakfast without her dentures.

Smith called to him twice before he became aware of the sergeant's presence.

Frazer turned.

The fetid breath fell warmly on Smith's face, rolling his stomach queasily. Smith blinked. "I'd strongly recommend we slow down, sir."

"Slow . . . down," Frazer repeated mechanically.

"Maybe even a break, sir," urged Smith. He noticed Humphreys turn his head and glance over his shoulder at the two of them.

Cavanaugh coughed wretchedly. "It's no use, Sergeant," he gasped, spitting a bolus of floured saliva. "I can't get it through their thick heads we're finished if we don't."

Behind stumbled the four junior officers. At Cavanaugh's angry reference they exchanged glances which indicated that while they themselves were suffering just as miserably as the rest, they had somehow hoarded a propriety that took umbrage at one officer's berating another in the presence of an "other rank."

"It's senseless," muttered Cavanaugh.

"There's a lot of ill feeling brewing back there, sir," said Smith apologetically to Frazer.

Frazer leaned more heavily on the doctor's shoulder but plodded on oblivious of the sergeant.

"You're wasting your time, Sergeant," snapped the doctor. "I've been tryin' for hours. Adherence to the timetable, he says. What if we all dry up and blow away? Then where's your sacred timetable?"

"Perkins is badly, sir," continued Smith.

"What is it?" shot the doctor.

"I don't rightly know, sir," replied Smith loudly so that all could hear him. "He can't quite get his breath. Gets dizzy. Can't stand on his feet too long."

Cavanaugh turned and shouted back to the junior officers. "What do you think?"

None of the four was anxious to be drawn into the argument.

"Well," demanded Cavanaugh, "Leeds? Magarity? What's wrong with you?"

"We're damned tired," puffed Leeds. "That's what's wrong . . . and like the rest, we're here to take orders." The gunnery officer's generous lips were pulled into thin lines. He inhaled to continue. "If I were you, Dr. Cavanaugh, I'd leave—" His face puckered in profound confusion. His words came haltingly. "I'd leave . . . I'd leave . . . the running of . . . *aaaaaaaahhhhhhhh*." His legs buckled under him and he pitched forward.

The disheveled Britons shuffled to a halt around the gangly gunnery officer lying spread-eagled on the ground.

By the time Cavanaugh had finished his hasty examination, the entire unit had circled around him and the gunnery officer. They watched in the detached attitude of onlookers to an accident.

Cavanaugh rose to his feet. He said to no one in particular, "He's dead." He looked around. His eyes fixed upon Frazer. He walked toward him and asked very deliberately, "Satisfied? His ticker," he snapped, his once-round face gaunt with fatigue and anger. "The Lord forgive you!"

Frazer opened his mouth to say something. His lower lip pulled the dried-up skin off his upper lip. His swollen tongue inspected the raw flesh and recoiled at the salt taste of his own blood.

Cavanaugh stumped off.

"Sergeant Smith!" shouted Humphreys, his huge girth still heaving.

"Sir," responded Smith.

"You know what to do. Hurry up."

"Yes, sir." Smith turned and found the men crumpled in weariness on the ground, their heads shielded from the swirling dust with hands, arms, and collars high and topees low. He knew he would have to pick four men. He bellowed four names.

There was no response.

Again he bellowed.

There was still no response.

Smith's eyes roamed over the heaps of huddled figures in dusty khaki. He could not tell one from another. Their faces were buried in their misery.

He called the names again. "On your feet, I tell you!" he shouted in a cracked voice. "Did you four hear me? On your bloody feet, I said!"

The harsh wind swallowed his command.

Still there was no move. The wind howled and the swirling dust built up around the exhausted men, blanketing them in anonymity. Like spent men in the Arctic snow, for them to lie down was delicious but deadly.

Smith shuffled toward the human heap closest to him. He

knocked one topee flying. The man never budged. Smith howled in his ear. Fatigue had cast the man beyond the recall of discipline. Smith uncovered another head . . . and another . . . and another.

"What's holding you up, Smith?" It was Humphreys.

Smith turned to him wearily. "S'no use, sir. They're all in."

Humphreys' voice betrayed the fatigue that had nibbled away his strength like a school of piranha. "What's no use?" he shouted hoarsely. "They're still in the King's service, aren't they? I'll show you how to rouse 'em." He pulled his Webley from its holster and cocked it, then walked toward the nearest exhausted man, knocking off his topee with a contemptuous tap of his swagger stick. He jammed the pistol barrel into the back of the man's neck and shouted, "On your feet, or I'll put a hole in you!"

From a nearby heap of exhaustion a figure stirred. One soldier struggled to his feet drunkenly and approached Humphreys. It was Perkins.

"Please, sir," he croaked. "I'll take his place, sir." He could barely stand.

Humphreys recoiled angrily. "Who's talking to you? Get out of the way!" He turned his attention to the slumbering man. "You have one more chance. Get on your feet!"

Several men roused themselves, realized the danger and slithered off out of harm's way. But the slumbering man had disconnected from the world.

Humphreys cocked the Webley.

Those who could still marshal some reserve of consciousness watched in mute fascination as the pistol barrel wobbled beside the man's head.

"I'll count to five!" screeched Humphreys, barely able to keep his balance.

"Don't be mad!" screamed the doctor, bent over Leeds's body.

"One! Two!" counted Humphreys.

"Humphreys!" cried Frazer, crawling across the hard, baked soil on his hands and knees.

"Three! Four!"

Perkins had reached Humphreys' side. "Please, sir," he beseeched in a tiny voice, laying a hand on the officer's gun hand.

"Five!" screeched Humphreys, striking the youth across the face with the swagger stick. The sickening crack of hard wood on harder bone—then the click of the Webley's hammer on soft brass. Humphreys spun the chamber. This time it wouldn't misfire.

Dull metal impacting on a tough hemisphere of bone. Humphreys lurched forward from the blow and fell flat on his face.

Cavanaugh awoke trembling in the sharp night cold, his forehead and neck wet with sweat. There was tugging at his sleeping bag.

"*Bwana,* how are you?" asked the figure squatting by his side. It was Matubele, the young Basanga prince in charge of the natives.

Cavanaugh ached all over. His tongue, dry as biltong, filled his mouth; but his mind was clear, and he felt a strange peace with the world. "I'm well," he said furrily. "What do you want?"

Matubele told him how the Basanga had seen the whites fight among themselves but had not interfered. They waited until they had fallen in sleep; then they had covered them with their cowskins so that they might not all go to a noble death in the cold of night. They had buried the dead white man in the manner of the whites; that is, lying on his back, not sitting up as was the Kisanga custom; but unlike the custom he had learned at the mission, he had not marked the burial site because he knew some of his own tribe to be of the Bakasandji.

The doctor knew of the Bakasandji. They were a sinister secret fraternity into which none was initiated who had not eaten human flesh. Their principle: "I am now a superman, for I am myself and the other man as well."

He noticed that Matubele was dressed for traveling. "Where are you going?" he asked.

The boy told him that the edge of the plateau was less than an hour's journey away. They had journeyed with the white men as far as they had promised. Now they must return to Wendi Macosi before the rains turned land to lake.

The doctor had expected it—but not so soon. Because only he spoke Kisanga, it had been left to *him* at Wendi Macosi to make the agreement with them. The Basanga had abided by their end of the bargain as if it were a sacred covenant. They would expect the white men to do no less. His spirits sank at the thought of the steep descent without native help, without the strength of the two span of oxen. Could not Matubele leave the oxen?

He could not. It would be against his father's wishes; but he and his brothers had filled the stomach of the iron *kifaru* with water and dead branches, and now they would have to go. They would leave them in the hands of the large man, who was the greatest they had ever seen, and who seemed to have some of the strength of the Great God, Nzambi.

Cavanaugh knew that if Humphreys knew what was going on, he would force the Basanga to stay at gunpoint, maybe even shoot a few of them out of hand to put the fear of the devil into them.

Matubele rose and saluted him with open hand outstretched at shoulder level. He said in a steady voice, "Whether the cock crows or not, it will dawn. Goodby, *Bwana*."

The doctor raised his hand. "The Lord look after you, lad."

The youth turned and padded off into the darkness.

The doctor watched him until he disappeared. He listened sharply. There was nothing but the random night calls and complaints of the African animal kingdom crisp on the cold night air. He smiled. Matubele had his head screwed on. He had marshaled the oxen and his people out of earshot *before* he had come to bid farewell.

19

The descent was dangerously steep. It was relieved by a succession of "steps." Humphreys had evolved a standard technique: The tractor would descend to the step. He would run a cable from the flywheel uphill, under the trailer, around a convenient tree or stump, then back again to the rear axle of the trailer. This allowed "cabling" in reverse. The technique had become routine. Peterson looked out of the canopy of the tractor late that day and up the mountainside at the trailer he was "reeling in." He steadied the steam lever which controlled the flywheel revolutions. The tractor, commandeered by the Navy from the London County Council, was long overdue for an overhaul. The lever, like so many other controls, did not always stay put. When *Mimi* had trundled downhill to within 100 feet of the tractor, Peterson slowly eased the steam lever toward "off." He looked down to make sure it was ratcheted in position. He heard shouts. He snatched his attention away from the controls. "What the bloody hell?" he swore. *Mimi* was slowly— but unquestionably—moving *back* up the mountainside! He thought the heat had got him. He heard the shouts turn to laughter.

"The lake's that way, chum!" shouted Crann, pointing down the slope. "Shut her off, you silly basket!"

Peterson slid the well-greased control all the way forward and grinned with embarrassment. The cable had completely unwound from the flywheel and had rewound a couple of revolutions, thus reversing the direction of the trailer's movement. Now the flywheel turned the other way.

Mimi was still a hundred feet from the "step." There was no cable left to be unwinched.

"We'll have to manhandle her the rest of the way," suggested Frazer to Humphreys.

Smith said, "About fifty feet of spare cable stowed away in *Toutou,* sir."

Humphreys surveyed the situation. "Fifty feet's not worth a damn," he spat. "Back to your stations!"

The men stood around confused.

Frazer stepped forward and pulled the empty pipe from his mouth. "Well . . . you heard the captain," he said officiously, but it was obvious that he was in the dark too.

Peterson shrugged and climbed onto the footplate of the tractor. Stokes and Smith herded the soldiers and sailors back to their positions around *Mimi's* trailer.

Humphreys hopped onto the tractor beside Peterson and clipped out commands.

The tractor engine revved up. Humphreys' arm shafted forward. Gears clashed. The tractor lumbered forward. *Mimi* now slipped downhill toward the tractor. Humphreys' tactic was obvious. But would it work? For every yard *Mimi* moved down, the tractor moved forward a yard. Eventually they would meet at some point along the cable joining them. If they met on the level, that would be exactly what Humphreys had reckoned on. But if they met up the slope somewhere? It would be Humphreys' first boner. Mathematically they would meet exactly halfway between their positions at any given time. It would be a definite spot on the terrain, one difficult to predict because of the problem of judging distance along a slope. As *Mimi* and the tractor moved closer, there was not a man who failed to predict that halfway point to be well off the "step" and up the slope.

Sergeant Smith nudged Stokes. "This one he's called too close."

251

"Looks like it, don't it?" murmured Stokes. "I ain't so sure, though."

They watched the distance between tractor and trailer diminish.

"You still got that extra tin o' Gold Flake, Andy?"

"Uh-huh."

"You always did 'ave your weather eye on that bottle o' rum I got 'id away. Tell you wot. My rum agin your tobacco, eh?"

"Should've been a bleedin' bookie, Stokes. Nothing doing."

"Where's your sportin' blood?"

"This isn't sport."

"You were the bloke wot said 'e wouldn't make it."

"Wishful thinking."

Stokes rubbed his nose. "Know wot you mean. Too friggin' good, 'e is. Useful bastard, though."

Smith kept his eyes on Humphreys, standing with head bent beneath the tractor canopy. "You know," he said deliberately, "I hope to God he gets his."

Stokes's bantering manner tautened. "S'not like you, Andy."

Smith faced the old petty officer squarely. "It mightn't have been, but by Jesus, it is now."

"Nark it, chum," scoffed Stokes. "We're over the 'ump, ain't we?"

"But not the Humphreys," said Smith evenly.

"The lads's workin' like I never did see 'em since we started off on this lot. Right spirited they are," protested Stokes.

Smith sniffed disgustedly. "A wooden bone to a blind dog, chum. That's old Tommy Atkins for you. Give him an inch and he'll give you back a mile. Reel the poor sod in like a fish, that's how." He nodded toward the tractor. "And well he knows it."

"Oh, I dunno," temporized Stokes.

"Well, I do," grated Smith. "I saw it in Flanders. Poor dumb bloody sheep. Don't know when they're being exploited—their bodies and their souls."

"Lost me, you did, mate," Stokes chimed in.

"A day and a half off," sneered Smith, "and then all's forgotten and everybody's lovey-dovey. Shit. If he hadn't got rapped over that big head of his, we'd all be six feet under. Poor bloody Tommy

252

Atkins—he'd walk himself into the bleedin' ground and die knowing he was obeying orders. Nangle's right about these friggers. Mark my words, Charlie. If it's the last thing I bloody well do, I'm going to see he gets his. The likes of him gives the Army a bad name. He'll stand court-martial one day, or my name isn't Smith."

Stokes toed the loose soil in contemplation. "Aye," he said, "but 'e gets the job done. Beggars can't be choosers."

"That's supposed to make up for everything, is it?"

"'Y did we come along on this lot, if it don't? We got a job to do. I don't like the bugger any more'n you do, but 'e's gettin' her done, ain't 'e?"

"What about Martin and Leeds, and Porter and Devlin?"

Stokes glanced up and saw that *Mimi* was just a few feet from the level. "Cor," he exclaimed. "'Ow about that, Andy?" And as the trailer's rear wheels rolled off the slope and onto the level, the front end of the tractor bumped gently against the nose of the trailer.

Spontaneously the men crowded around in silent, grudging admiration at Humphreys' astute judgment.

Humphreys jumped off the deck plate. "Move!" he shouted. It was his way of telling them to get on with the next stage of the descent.

Humphreys stationed himself behind the drove of oscillating arses. He brooded about the lack of progress. Because of the lesser gradient they should have covered more ground, and he would not accept the growing impenetrability of the brush as reason why they had not.

The tractor stood impatiently wheezing steam, waiting for the panga swingers to finish, using up the meager reserves of wood and water. Peterson sucked greedily on a Woodbine butt, watching the drudgery from the shade of the canopy.

"You!" shouted Humphreys.

"Who? Me, sir?" stuttered Peterson. The butt stuck to his slack lower lip.

"Spit that damn thing out and climb in there," ordered Humphreys, pointing toward the panga wielders.

Peterson responded sullenly. He unsheathed his panga and set to work in slovenly fashion.

Humphreys walked up and down tapping his leggings with his swagger stick. Suddenly he rapped his right leg extra hard, as if underscoring a decision. He prodded the first backside with the brass-tipped swagger stick. "Move!" he commanded. He prodded the next behind. "Move!" And so on down the line: "Move! . . . Move! . . . Move! . . . Move! . . . Move! . . ."

The men ignored his prodding.

When he came to Nangle, he poked nothing but air. Nangle had moved forward, stood up and turned around with an enraged expression on his haughty countenance.

"Well?" glowered Humphreys.

"I gather, sir," Nangle said stiffly, "you're attempting to get my attention."

Humphreys eyed him speculatively. "I've seen your record, Nangle. You refused a commission. You don't like officers."

"You are right, sir," declared Nangle.

Humphreys' eyes glinted. His swagger stick touched the bandage on his head. "It was you. . . it had to be you."

Nangle smiled mysteriously while Humphreys tried to intimidate him with a stony stare.

"Back to the job," said Humphreys finally, tapping his swagger stick lightly against Nangle's forehead. "Back—on—the—job," he repeated slowly, tapping with each word.

Nangle snatched at the swagger stick.

Humphreys pulled it back smartly and tapped Nangle on the temple.

Nangle yelped and clapped a hand to his head.

Sergeant Smith appeared. "*Nangle!*"

"Get out of the way, Smith," shot Humphreys.

Work slithered to a halt.

Humphreys' withering dismissal turned Sergeant Smith's face livid.

By this time Frazer, Cavanaugh and the other officers were walking onto the scene.

"Not again," groaned Frazer. "Doesn't he know we're—" He shrugged helplessly.

Blood trickled from the nick on Nangle's temple. His profound surprise had ebbed. He now confronted Humphreys with an expression of glowering contempt. Slowly and distinctly he said, "You're a pompous bastard . . . sir."

Humphreys' bland features condescended to the register of pained sufferance. He moved a step closer. "I was hoping you'd say something like that. For it, Nangle, you'll be sorry."

"And I'm a witness, sir," interrupted Smith thickly.

Humphreys smirked. "For me . . . or against me?"

Nangle stiffened indignantly. "Thanks, Smith," he said acidly.

"*As you were, Nangle!*" roared Smith. "An 'other rank' speaks only when he's spoken to!"

Humphreys smiled. It had never happened before. He turned to survey the sergeant's face, then Nangle's. He seemed to be enjoying some private joke. "Good for you, Smith," he said sarcastically. His tone changed, and it became evident that he was addressing all assembled. "Insubordination at any time," he declared, "is intolerable. In time of war it is deadly—for all parties concerned." He turned about and aimed his swagger stick up at *Mimi's* sharp bow. "Take him up there, Smith, and chain him!"

Cavanaugh nudged Frazer.

"I think he's learned his lesson, Captain," suggested Frazer weakly. "He'll be punished when we get to Albertville, I can assure you."

Humphreys ignored him and continued with his order to Smith. "Make sure he's far enough forward—"

"Captain!" protested Frazer.

"Commander Frazer, discipline's the beginning and end of the Establishment!"

Most of the men had stepped back from the center of the dispute and lay stretched out full length on the slope.

"Look!" snapped Humphreys exultantly, jabbing with his swagger stick at the recumbent figures.

255

One reclining sailor muttered to his comrade, "Who the bloody hell's runnin' this friggin' mess, mate?"

Humphreys' head swiveled like a sound detector zeroing in on target. He strode into the group of men, grabbed the sailor by the scruff of the neck and dragged him to his feet. "I'll show you who's running it," he grated. "On your damned feet . . . all of you!"

The men slowly rose, rubbing their faces wearily and shuffling despondently.

"Get Nangle up there, Smith!"

The doctor could stand it no longer. He elbowed Frazer angrily. Frazer shrugged.

"You're just goin' to stand there?" whispered the doctor incredulously.

Smith grasped Nangle by the arm. His temper simmered. "One of these days . . . so help me," he muttered fervently as he led Nangle away.

"Ian!" demanded the doctor.

"I can't, Tommy," he muttered hopelessly.

"For God's sake, *you're* the CO!"

"You don't understand, Tommy," said Frazer weakly. "For all practical purposes—"

"For all practical purposes you're givin' up! You're abandonin' your ship! Now, are you goin' to march right over there an' tell him where he gets off?"

"I can't, Tommy," insisted Frazer, "I can't. I gave him my word—"

"You gave your old grandfather your word once, too!"

"Stop it!"

"You'll do nothin', then, is that it?"

Frazer turned ashamedly and walked away. Inside his emotions churned.

At the first tinge of dawn, the camp was alive.

Humphreys straddled the topmost limb of a huge baobab tree which was rooted at a point where the terrain fell off sheer into a deep valley. He scanned the terrain ahead, making copious entries in a small notebook.

The tractor stood puffing on a slight incline, with *Mimi* and *Toutou* loaded and in tow. Peterson jammed a final armful of brushwood into the firebox. He slammed shut the heavy iron firebox door and stepped down for a quick fag. They would be under way in five minutes, and it would take that long to work up a full head of steam.

As his foot left the deck-plate steps, the tractor moved forward. Peterson sucked on a short butt, watching the others scurry around with last-minute details.

Someone screamed a warning.

Peterson swore and scrambled after the train. He just managed to leap aboard, for it was already lumbering speedily downhill. He slapped the steam lever into reverse, but there was not enough boiler pressure. He swore again and desperately threw his weight onto the brake lever. Brake lining burned uselessly to arrest the momentum of the tractor and trailers' fifteen tons.

The shouts pulled Humphreys' attention from his survey. He swore. His mind slid into gear. "The tree!" he shouted powerfully. "The tree! Steer for the tree!"

"He's mad!" exclaimed Dodkins. "The bloody tree'll be bowled over, and he'll fly clear over the side and Peterson with him!"

"It's an eighty-foot drop!" cried Bannister.

"Jump for it, Peterson!" yelled Frazer.

"Mother of God," prayed the doctor.

"The tree!" shouted Humphreys again. "The tree! The tree!"

Peterson furiously cranked the steering wheel.

The plunging train arced toward the tree.

Peterson jumped from the deck plate.

Humphreys jumped from the tree.

The tractor impacted with a sickening crash. *Mimi's* trailer whipped around and overturned, spewing cargo. The tree had burst its roots and poked out over the cliff with the awkwardness of a dislocated arm. The tractor's smokestack had collapsed forward. Peterson had wrenched his ankle, and Humphreys had impaled himself on his swagger stick.

257

20

Four hundred and fifty miles northeast, as the crow flies, stood Lieutenant Commander Zimmer of the Imperial German Navy. From the lookout tower 30 feet above Kigoma he peered through binoculars westward across Lake Tanganyika. He fiddled with the adjusting screw as he sought to bring Kalemie into better focus.

They're up to something, he thought. His native spies had reported on the enemy's defenses, but the 40-mile distance was beyond the resolution of his field glasses. He could only imagine them.

The defense of the colony, however, could not rest secure on imagination alone, Zimmer had been reminded by General von Lettow-Vorbeck, the German East African Commander in Chief. A week had passed since the general had visited Kigoma to inspect his left flank. He told Zimmer that he was worried about intelligence reports of unusual Allied operations in the offing. He warned him to be constantly on the alert. He reemphasized the importance of continuing German naval supremacy on the lake.

Zimmer did not have to be reminded. For months those English invading the colony from Uganda in the north and those driving up from the Rhodesias in the south had tried desperately to link up along the narrow coastal plain. Such a link was the key to their strategy for the conquest of the Kaiser's largest foreign possession. Once linked, they would advance eastward with their numerically superior forces and sweep the German askaris and their few European officers into the Indian Ocean. Scores of times Zimmer's gunboats and converted passenger ships had stood offshore shelling attempted enemy linkups.

Indeed it was precisely that point which had brought the resourceful German general so far west. The English had failed to take Kigoma from the landward side; now they might be up to something else, he suggested to Zimmer, maybe even an amphibious landing mounted from Kalemie. He cautioned Zimmer to be ready for anything and suggested that his native spies on the other shore redouble their efforts, for they did not know exactly what the Allies were up to, even with their elaborate network of native spies throughout the whole Baluba nation. Kigoma was the hinge of their left flank. Without it, the German Naval Squadron would be birds without a nest; and there would be nothing to avert the execution of the enemy's grand plan.

Zimmer and the general at the time had laughed at this hypothetical possibility. The general had remarked that it was almost as rich as the gratuitous speculation of the native bush telegraphers who, at the time they had transmitted the news of the English being in southern Katanga, predicted that the English were preparing to build a bridge across the lake! They both had laughed again, and the general had commented that one had always to bear in mind that every native spy added to otherwise objective intelligence reports his own highly subjective embellishments. For example, the general had said, his present worry stemmed from a report from two informants of the Sanga tribe at Wendi Macosi; a report which had been relayed successively via the Yeke, the Bemba, the Kunda, the Shila, the Bwile and finally the Tabwa. Seven tribes, seven embellishments, Zimmer had commented. Possibly, the general had mused, but the *verdammte* English hauling two boats through the brush was a report he could not dismiss, fantastic though it might be. But if it did turn out to be true, then thank God for the Basanga. And the general's pride over Teutonic thoroughness knew no bounds when Zimmer had casually mentioned

259

the actual names of his agents among the Basanga. "Thank God for Kongolo and Mukulu," he had said.

The general had left a week ago, and once again he was on his own as the commanding officer of 200 officers and men of the German Navy, plus two 53-ton gunboats, two armed passenger steamers, several steam pinnaces and small motorboats. As far as any naval threat was concerned, Zimmer felt quite secure. The Belgians across the lake had little to cause them worry—a 90-ton unarmed steamer, *Alexandre Delcommune,* and four unarmed motorboats. In any all-out contest Zimmer and his men were sure to be victorious—even if they were not members of the regular German Navy. He had heard the English during his prewar days as an officer with the German East Africa Line use the term "a mixed bag," and that was exactly how he would have described his command.

Eight hundred miles to the east lay the African coast and the estuary of the Rufiji River, up which two marauding German battle cruisers had already fled when pursued by the vengeful British Navy. Not only had they fled; they had been bottled up on the mud flats and been useless to the point where their crews cannibalized them, blew them up and railed the salvage west to Kigoma. The two cruisers had been *Möwe,* and then some months later, *Königsberg.* Zimmer's command was officially known as the Möwe Detachment, since its nucleus was 106 men from the *Möwe.* It had swelled with 55 officers and men from *Königsberg;* then to its present strength with 44 reserve officers and men from German East Africa liners caught in Dar es Salaam at the outbreak of hostilities.

Zimmer had confidence in his sailors, but he had more confidence in his ships, especially the very latest addition to his squadron—*Graf von Gotson,* 800 tons, 200 feet long and a speed of 8 knots. Hardly three months ago she had slid down the greased slipways of the Kigoma dockyard. She was equipped to play a dual role—troop carrier and long-range artillery. Von Lettow-Vorbeck relied heavily on Zimmer to rapidly transport his infantry to any point on the lake's 400-mile-long coastline. And when the landlocked British infantry sought to counter these guerilla sallies in their rear, it took them five times as long to get there. The enemy's handicap was not only lake-versus-land mobility but *Graf von Gotson's* armament: two 4.1-inch long-range naval-artillery pieces salvaged from *Königsberg*. For closer ranges she mounted a 22-pounder cannon and a 37-mm. Hotchkiss pom-pom. For landing operations, she should carry 900 fully armed infantry. By lake standards she was a superdreadnought.

Zimmer lowered his binoculars. Born in Hamburg of a seafaring family forty-four years ago, with twenty-five years' service in the German merchant marine, he was a confident but not a complacent man. What were they up to? He was also a man with sporting blood running in his veins. He had never relished standing offshore in *Gotson,* pounding the hapless British troops caught undefended in the open. Like every real soldier or sailor, he craved the acid test for his mettle. His time had come: He would find out what the enemy was up to by paying them a visit.

He chose the next moonless night. His plan: to steal the 90-ton *Alexandre Delcommune* from right under the noses of the Belgians. His reasoning: Whatever the Belgians might have up their sleeves, it would surely involve the *Delcommune.* But there was the formidable problem of the Belgian defenses. He knew of the pits, earthworks and barbed-wire entanglements; and the 12-pounders. *Gotson's* 4.1-inchers could handle them, but *Gotson* he would not use. She was his ace in the hole.

Hedwig von Wissman, a light passenger vessel armed with a pom-pom, was in the van of the raiding party which glided out of Kigoma harbor that dark October night. Two platoons of infantry squatted on her decks. She towed a raft. Precariously balanced on it were Zimmer, four gunners, ammunition and two 22-pounders. A small armed steam pinnace cruised alongside like a sheep dog with a stray lamb.

As the raft lapped gently along in *Wissman's* wake, a luminescent blemish on the water's mirror surface, Zimmer expected the element of surprise. The shock of not getting it reinforced his conviction that the enemy had to be up to something; otherwise they would not have been on the alert on that random night at the purely arbitrary hour of four in the morning. Four thousand yards from the shore the Belgian 12-pounders belched; 3-pounders barked amid a fusillade of rifle fire. Zimmer fired several flares. When they exploded, the 22-pounder belched back, *Wissman's* pom-pom chattered and rifle fire spat spasmodically from her deck.

At 2,000 yards Zimmer spotted *Delcommune,* moored well inshore. At 90 tons she would have been a valuable asset. That was why he had planned for the steam pinnace to steal inshore, land a skeleton crew and abscond with her. Now that was impossible. They would have to destroy her, he feared; but even with the element of surprise gone he would try it once. He ordered the pinnace in at 1,800 yards. She ran aground on a sand bar 150 yards from her quarry and was sprayed with machine-gun fire. The Belgians had caught on. Zimmer could not wait. He swiveled the two 22-pounders off the enemy fortifications and over onto the classic lines of *Delcommune.* The raft bucked dangerously. Each recoil set the surface awash, but a dozen rounds crashed into *Delcommune,* listing her heavily to starboard. The enemy fire lifted from the stranded steam pinnace onto the raft. The pinnace crew climbed out and pushed the craft, damaged in the rudder and holed below the waterline, off the sand bar to limp back home. . . .

They were back in Kigoma before the sun, no wiser than before.

Several days after the raid Zimmer was handed an intercepted Belgian wireless message. They were starting construction of a 1,500-ton armed steamer which they would christen *Baron Dhanis.* Where were they going to build it? Did this mean they knew of his ace in the hole, *Gotson?*

He held a staff conference. His officers—still flushed with the recent action—were unanimous: Find her and sink her! But another raid was no longer feasible. The enemy would be doubly on the alert. It would have to be a reconnaissance in stealth by one or two men.

Zimmer knew just the two who could pull it off.

21

It was a new world of half-light, breeding huge trees that grew up bald and branchless, then exploded in foliage. They clustered close as corn stubble. Their topmost foliage matted in a web of impenetrability, cutting off the light. The steam heat of 118 degrees incubated claustrophobia.

Even though the dry season was almost at an end, low-lying patches of terrain stagnated with swamp and smell; and everywhere the immaculate symmetry of the tall huge-girthed trees with their coal-black bark suffered a litter of dead tree limbs and insidious creeper vine. A strange, echoey emptiness haunted the imagination with a fear of slithering things lurking beneath primeval slime.

"The ropes!" bellowed Sergeant Smith.

The wearied men listlessly took hold of the ropes dangling from the trailers.

"Take the strain!" bellowed Smith.

They leaned forward, supported by the ropes, which they had wrapped around their bodies.

On the tractor Peterson notched the steam lever forward. The drive wheels spun uselessly in the furrow they had already gouged into the steep face of the rise.

"Heave!" shouted Smith.

Instantly the steel teeth bit in. Slowly the train creaked upward. . . .

The doctor made his way up toward the tractor.

Frazer stepped down off the deck plate. He was as wasted as if he had been laboring with the others. He caught sight of Cavanaugh. "How is he?"

"I haven't seen him yet," said the doctor. "I thought we both might . . ."

"Of course," agreed Frazer.

Together they climbed up *Toutou's* stern and crawled over the bulging, tarpaulin-covered cargo between her gunwales.

Humphreys lay in a depression in the cargo, in shirt and trousers. Layers of bandage bulky as a tire encircled his chest. Shirt, trousers and bandages were soaked with sweat and tinged red with blood. His left eye was almost closed where a colony of tsetse flies had feasted on his blood.

They knelt by his side.

"How are you feeling, Oswald?" inquired the doctor.

Humphreys tried to say something but exploded in a paroxysm of coughing. Each time his massive chest contracted, the red on the bandage dyed deeper. The coughing spell subsided. "Did you . . . do as . . . I said?" he whispered. The effort caused him great pain.

The doctor beckoned to Frazer to come closer. "I think he wants a word with you."

Frazer moved forward and bent down toward the captain. "We're getting closer and closer, Oswald. Any time, now."

Humphreys' swollen lips parted. "Did you follow the route?"

"Yes, old man, to the letter." He put his hand to his shirt pocket and touched the black notebook. He turned to the doctor. "Tommy, can't you stop the bleeding? His bandage's soaking."

The doctor shook his head. "I've packed it with everything I've got. If it doesn't stop soon, nothing'll stop it."

Humphreys stirred again. "How . . . far?"

"We're about a dozen miles from Gule . . . but we can manage.

Why don't you leave the rest to us? You've lost a lot of blood and—"

"Not as long as there's breath in me, Frazer," coughed Humphreys. "Remember your agreement."

Frazer knew it was useless to argue. To do so would only weaken Humphreys further. If Humphreys went . . . "I'll let you know when we reach Gule."

Frazer and the doctor withdrew to the stern.

"What do you think, Tommy?"

"He's damned lucky he's paralyzed from the waist down, otherwise the twistin' and turnin' would make him scream. But did you see his eye? An' I haven't heard a whimper from him all the time—and I've been listenin' for one."

"Will he make it, I mean?"

"God only knows. I've a mind to leave him with the Gule natives—"

"You can't do that!" exclaimed Frazer.

"Why not? He's not much good lyin' on his back."

A ready answer formed on Frazer's lips, but he canceled it and shrugged. "We need him, Tommy."

"Once I'd've cut me tongue out for sayin' it, but you're right. But, Ian, the hole through him's not goin' to get much of a chance healin' with all that pitchin' and rollin'."

"There'll be a lot less of that when we reach Gule," declared Frazer with unusual conviction.

"Well, that's your department. . . . Look, when you go down, send an orderly up with some fresh bandages and water." He surveyed the huge body of the engineering officer. "It's hard to imagine him so useless."

His work over, Cavanaugh climbed down out of the boat and made for a tree where Perkins rested. He sat down and sucked judiciously from his canteen, exploring each drop with his tongue, commending the experience to memory. "A Navy man at heart, you say, Billy?"

Perkins shifted uncomfortably. "Yes, sir," he confessed shyly.

"Why the Navy? Are you from the seaside?"

"Oh, no, sir. I never saw the sea till Southampton."

"Why, then? I'm curious, Billy."

"Oh, I don't quite know, sir. I read about it a lot. Maybe that's it, sir."

Cavanaugh leaned back against the tree and closed his eyes. "Why does anyone do anything, Billy?"

"I dunno, sir."

The doctor opened one eye. "Lie down, Billy. You don't have to sit at attention 'cos I'm here, you know."

"Thank you, sir," said Perkins, leaning back. He was uneasy about sharing an officer's informality and would not close his eyes.

They rested in silence. Gradually Perkins' thin frame lost its rigidity.

"Probably saw the poster, eh? 'Join the Navy and See the World,' " mused Cavanaugh.

Perkins sat up stiffly.

"For the love of Mike, lie down," snapped the doctor. "I never saw such a jack-in-the-box. Besides, Billy, I'm only RNVR. A doctor at that. Not a real officer."

Perkins toyed with his canteen uncomfortably.

"Drink a sip, Billy. We'll be movin' on in a jiffy."

"I never touch it at noon, sir!"

The doctor opened his eyes in surprise. "You don't! Why don't you? Against your religion or something?"

"Oh no, sir. I'm Catholic . . . too, sir."

"Sorry, Billy. I was just tryin' to be humorous. But why not? Aren't you thirsty, lad?"

He grinned shyly under the sweat and dirt. "I am, sir . . . but I just don't give in to myself."

The doctor shook his head. "Billy Perkins, you're a strange customer."

"I'm sorry, sir."

"No. No. No. I don't want you to apologize for bein' what you are, lad."

266

"No, sir. Thank you, sir," stammered Perkins.

The whistle burbled. They struggled to their feet, arching their backs, resenting their recall.

Perkins turned to the doctor and inquired, "RNVR, sir? The volunteer reserve?"

"The 'wavy navy,' they call it, Billy," laughed the doctor. "Sunday sailors."

"Is that what the commander is, sir," asked Perkins cautiously.

"Why, Billy?"

"Oh, nothing, sir," he replied evasively. "I was just asking."

"Why?"

"Wasn't important, sir, really," said Perkins deferentially, sidling toward his station on the trailer.

Cavanaugh caught his arm. "What's botherin' you?"

It was hard for the young soldier to talk. "They're saying things, sir," he said, shifting uncomfortably.

"Such as?"

Perkins' lips tightened. "I won't repeat it, sir."

The doctor looked at him seriously. "All right, Billy. All right."

Up ahead Frazer consulted with CPO Stokes. The water supply was running low. They had crossed two streams marked on the map as flowing year around, but they had turned out to be dried up.

"Doesn't make sense, does it, sir?" observed Stokes. "Bloomin' rivers gone but all them bloody bogs still."

"No," replied the commander absent-mindedly, his mind on something else. "What's the water situation?"

"About twenty gallon in *Toutou* for us, sir. An' about thirty-five in *Mimi* for the tractor—about one good boilerful between the both of 'em."

Frazer studied the map intently. "It shows two more streams between us and the next village," he mused.

"But they might be dry too, sir," Stokes pointed out.

"I know it," said Frazer with irritation. "Let me think."

Stokes pinched the end of his nose thoughtfully. "If you don't mind, sir, I 'ave an idea."

"Well?"

Stokes suggested that the men spread out over a wide area and use their topees to carry water back from the swamps. His face corrugated with the effort of computing how many topeesful it would take and how long it might require. "Say two pints to a topee, maybe. An' with a 75-gallon boiler. Let's see, now. Six hundred pints, sir. Right? An' let's say twenty topees." Stokes computed laboriously. "That's about thirty times."

"Thirty journeys back and forth between here and *one* water hole'd be time-consuming as it is. We'd have to search for hours for one big enough for our purposes. Won't work, Stokes."

" 'Ow about a lot of little ones, then, sir?" submitted Stokes patiently.

"No time for that, man," said Frazer decisively. He pointed to the trailers. "Dump the lot in the boiler."

"The 'ole lot, sir? 'Ow about drinkin' water?"

"Tell each man to fill his canteen. Tell 'em to be damned thirsty before they touch a drop of it, for everything else goes into the tractor."

"Aye, aye, sir," said Stokes, leaving to pass the word down.

Smith and Stokes lined the men up in front of *Toutou*. Smith operated the spigot as the men held out their canteens. The men drained their canteens of the last drop before refilling. Perkins was the exception.

The sound of the jet hitting his canteen told Smith the youth's canteen was already half full. He turned off the spigot. "Get rid of that lot, chum, before I top you up."

Perkins declined. "That's all right, sergeant. I don't mind."

"Suit yourself. But if I was you I'd grab it while I'd the chance. Your tongue'll be hanging out for it pretty soon."

Perkins reconsidered. He peered into his canteen. "What'll I do with it?"

One sailor nearby said, "I'll tell you what, mate. Right in here." He opened his mouth and pointed inside.

"Want it?" asked Perkins.

"Do I what?" shot the sailor eagerly, grasping for the canteen.

"Me, too!" shouted another sailor, stumbling over.

Soon a line of men waited for a free swallow.

Smith grew indignant. He knew that the pace had frazzled their military bearing, but the exhibition of greed sickened him. Yet there was nothing he could do. Perkins had volunteered it. "A swallow apiece as long as she lasts," he snapped.

The canteen passed down the line. Each drinker closely watched his neighbor to see that he got only one swallow. There were half a dozen still waiting when one sailor tipped his head back all the way. The North-Country private was next in line. He screamed an obscenity and clawed at his neighbor's face. "You dirty sod, you swiped the bloody lot!"

The sailor wiped his bearded face with the back of his hand. "Frig you!" he grunted fatly. "S'empty."

The angry private punched him viciously on the side of the head, knocking the canteen flying.

The sailor was stunned. He lashed out with his hobnails and caught his attacker on the shins.

The soldier screamed.

Smith strode deliberately into the melee. He reached down and pulled the whining soldier up by the scruff of the neck. "I saw that, you bleeder," he said venomously.

The man's face was contorted with agony.

"Serves you right, you scum," said Smith. "Another move like that and I'll kick you myself. Hear?" He left the limping soldier and returned to make sure the spigot was properly turned off. He observed Perkins' look of amazement. "Fat lot of good that did," he muttered.

"Sorry, Sergeant Smith," he apologized. "Honestly, I never wanted to cause no trouble, sir."

"I'm not 'sir,' Perkins. Can't you remember that? What the hell are you trying to do? Be some sort of bloomin' hero?"

The lad fumbled with his words. "I had half a canteen I didn't —"

"Forget it," Smith said roughly. "Just look after yourself from now on."

Perkins looked defeated. "What'd I do wrong, Sergeant?"

"Not a friggin' thing—if you like being called an arse creeper."

Perkins' blue eyes dimmed. He did not understand, but the words made him sick.

The whistle trilled. The men and machines moved forward.

"Take the strain!" shouted Sergeant Smith hoarsely.

They leaned on their ropes.

"Heave!"

Gobs of mud prevented them from digging into the face of the steep hill. Their bony legs pistoned furiously and they slid to their knees.

"Heave!"

They thrashed in the slime.

"Heave! Dig in!"

The tractor wheels spun wildly, gouging deeper.

"Stop!"

They sagged, their breath rattling.

Smith climbed the hill to join Frazer, whom he discovered just climbing down off *Toutou*.

"Looks bad, sir. My idea would be to—"

"Never mind, Smith," interjected Frazer. "Put two men apiece to each wheel!"

"If we do that, sir, we'll—"

"Move!"

Smith slithered down to the bottom of the slope where the wheel of *Mimi's* trailer stood hub-deep in the ooze and *Mimi's* fragile bronze twin screws dripped slime and wiggling worms of vine. He waded across to where Stokes and the others hung on the craft's gunwales. He pointed to the screws.

"I know," puffed Stokes. "One kink an' we're scuttled proper."

"He wants two blokes on the wheels, Charlie."

"That won't do it."

"Tell *him* that."

Perkins jumped forward to volunteer.

Someone sighed: "Arse creeper!"

270

"Nark it, you bleeder!" roared Smith.

Perkins joined Crann on one of *Mimi's* front wheels. They stuck their hands in the slime and felt around for a horizontal spoke, grabbed it and waited for the command.

"Aaaaaaeeeeeh!" screamed Perkins, shaking his right hand above his head with epileptic intensity. A fat black leech had anchored its sucker on the inside of his wrist. Perkins trembled with revulsion, his eyes rolling in his head. Crann grabbed him, pinning his arms to his waist while Stokes plucked the parasite from its nestling place. Perkins trembled.

Panic worked its peristaltic way through the men's insides. Leeches! The fat, black thought sucked at their imaginations. They waited in the slime.

"Take the strain!" shouted Smith.

They braced themselves.

"*Heave!*"

The train budged out of the quagmire and up the slope. *Mimi* began to cant at an ever-increasing angle as her trailer's front wheels hit the slope. Her stern was soon submerged in the slime.

"The screws!" screamed Stokes. He groped deep to shield them. *Mimi* jerked forward and pulled him under, leaving only the tenacious knots of his gnarled hands showing. His grip broke, and he fell full length on the side of the hill, his body buttered with black slime.

The tractor ground to a halt again, almost at the crest of the hillock.

"On the wheels again!" shouted Smith.

The men stumbled toward their stations.

"Take the strain! *Heave!* Don't lose her! Don't lose her!" raged Smith.

Perkins wedged his half-naked body against the wheel and dug in.

"Don't lose her!" bellowed Smith.

"She's slippin'!" shouted someone.

"Hold her!" shouted Smith. "Don't lose her!"

"She's goin'!" sobbed another.

"*Look out, Billy!*" screamed Crann.

Perkins screeched for his mother as the wheel crunched over his leg.

🝤

The campfire flickered vapidly in the night. Shadowed ghosts on stilts flitted through the trees. Bullfrogs croaked. There were the oblong sounds of a flatulent swamp.

The hoarse whispers of Frazer and Cavanaugh punctuated the musty silence.

Someone moaned. It was a short, disciplined release—then silence.

"Poor little beggar," whispered Cavanaugh prayerfully. "You can't. You just can't, I tell you."

"You tell me nothing, Tommy," said Frazer stiffly. "He stays."

"God forgive you."

"Leave God out of it."

"God's all that can save him if you leave him."

"And if we try? Then what? A compound fracture. Your diagnosis. All right. So we do put him in with Humphreys. Every bump'll be hell. How long can he last? And how long can they last knowing it stops when they stop—and starts all over again when they start? No, I say. No! No! No!"

The doctor regarded him curiously. "No need to get hysterical."

"Don't talk rot, Tommy."

"You can just leave the lad—to die?"

"Nonsense. We'll send natives from the next village to take care of him. We'll fetch him back from Albertville—when we get there."

"How do you know the Gule natives'll want to accommodate us?"

"We'll have to take that chance."

"Perkins'll have to take that chance, you mean."

"We'll all have to take that chance."

"What'll they do if gangrene sets in? It's sure to."

"You're the expert. You've been among them before."

The doctor knew that when it came to gangrene, the Baluba and

272

British therapies differed only in the keenness and cleanliness of the saw blade. "Have you ever thought what it'd be like?"

"What?"

"Going through life with one leg?"

"No. And I don't intend to."

"Because it might influence you?"

"My mind's made up."

"Your mind's been made up for you ever since you were five, man," the doctor said with a scowl. "Just once why don't you try to make up your own mind on things?"

"It won't work, Tommy. You're wasting your time."

"You don't mind if I keep on trying?"

"Go right ahead. You can curse me . . . damn me . . . hate me. I expect you already do. But it won't work."

"I don't hate you, Ian," said the doctor softly. "I pity you."

"Save your pity for Perkins. He'll need it—one way or another."

"I pity you 'cause you're leavin' him behind. It'll feed on your dreams the rest of your life."

"If I don't get *Mimi* and *Toutou* to the lake, I'll have to live with that."

"Nuts 'n' bolts mean more to you than flesh 'n' blood, eh?"

"Oh, shut up. You know what I have to do."

"I do," mused the doctor. "I do. . . . But I never dreamed you were up to it." He laughed dryly. "Funny how wrong you can be about someone you've known twenty-five years."

They lapsed into silence.

"Funny how wrong you can be about yourself," brooded Frazer. "I can't leave Perkins behind."

The doctor jerked. His tenseness visibly melted. He put a hand on Frazer's sleeve. "In the name o' God, Ian, don't ever put the fear o' hell into me like—"

"That's why I *have* to leave him."

Cavanaugh snatched back. "What kind o' sense is that?" he ejaculated.

"If the rains catch us here, we're finished. Every hour's precious. It could start anytime, and you know it. Tonight, tomorrow. He'd slow us down. His presence would jeopardize the success of our mission." It sounded like a defense before some formal board of inquiry. He faced his small friend. "And I'd have to leave you, Tommy, if it were you."

"I believe you would at that." The doctor cocked his head and asked archly, "Tell me, now. Would you've left the old man?"

"I would," declared Frazer without emotion. "He'd have left me. He would have to."

"Then why don't you leave him too?" The doctor nodded toward the dark bulk of *Toutou*. "Most o' the time he's unconscious—not carryin' his weight. Answer me that."

"But some of the time he *is*."

"Well, I'll save you the trouble o' leavin' me."

"What?"

"Me and Perkins'll stay together. How's that suit you?"

"You are going with us."

"And supposin' I don't?"

"You know your duty."

"Aye. That's why I'm stayin' with the youngster."

"Your duty as a naval officer comes first."

"And who says so?"

"You took an oath, Tommy."

"There was an oath I took before I took that one."

"There are twenty-two of us who may need medical attention."

"Mosquito bites. There'll be the two aides for that."

"If statistics appeal to you, it's twenty-two of us to one."

"Not a bit. Perkins' need's as clear as a pikestaff. Yours and the rest of them's a probability."

Frazer said flatly, "You'll be ready first thing in the morning, Tommy."

Cavanaugh bristled. "My, but it's the big, strong commander you've turned into," he said sarcastically. "Where was all that when Nangle was gittin' his face caned, eh? Seems to me you were a little backward in comin' forward."

"I'm not going to argue with you, Tommy."

"You know, Ian, you really ought to take a mornin' off an' have

274

a batman wash out them jodhpurs. Very becomin', they were—for what you're becomin'."

"That'll be all, Tommy."

"Oh, no, it won't," said Cavanaugh contemptuously. "You can't order me around like a bloody subordinate. If you want to be official, all right. My rank happens to be Surgeon *Commander*. So don't bother your head talkin' down to me. Don't forget you *asked* me to come along. I didn't volunteer. I wasn't ordered. I promised you I'd do everything humanly possible to get you what you wanted. But leavin' a boy in this Godforsaken swamp with a compound fracture of the tibia?"

"I've no wish to discuss it further."

Cavanaugh writhed like a ferret unable to coax a rabbit from its warren. "You don't wish to discuss it further," he sneered. "What about Mr. and Mrs. Perkins? Do you think they might like you to discuss it a little further?"

"Shut up!"

"Admit the only reason you won't go back on your decision's 'cause good commanders don't do that sort of thing!"

"I'm warning you, Tommy!"

"And I'm warnin' you, Ian. His little face'll keep you awake the rest o' your life. Admit you're gropin' in the dark. Admit you slipped for a jiffy an' got duty and stubbornness mixed up! Admit you're a fraud, an' I'll respect you for it."

The word kicked Frazer in the throat.

Too late, the doctor bit down on his tongue.

In the void Frazer's breath betrayed his angry hurt. He turned to walk away.

"Ian," beseeched the doctor softly, "he admires you so."

Frazer's lips tightened.

"He thinks the world of you. You should've heard how he stuck up for you with the others. If it hadn't been for him, we'd never've got out of Macosi alive."

Frazer was beyond recall.

"All right, then," said the doctor bitterly, "will you be the one to tell him, by God?"

275

Frazer nodded.

"How?"

Frazer shook his head. "I'm open to suggestion," he said quietly.

"You have your nerve," said the doctor, turning away. "I'm goin' to bed."

"I don't," declared Frazer heavily, "but I will by morning."

The doctor squelched his way across the swamp and through the trees.

Frazer brooded alone. . . . His hand explored the pocket containing Humphreys' notebook. He extracted it. His silent fingers found the folded letter. He repocketed the notebook and fidgeted with the letter.

Much later he tore the letter in many pieces and dropped them where he stood.

22

" 'Ow is 'e, sir?" asked Stokes.

"Full of morphine," said the doctor. "But God help him when it wears off." He passed his hands over the bulky, leg-long splint.

"A hell of a way to wake up," muttered Smith darkly. "To be told you're excess baggage."

"Wot's 'is chances, sir?" asked Stokes.

The doctor shook his head seriously. "If the natives can get him back to Gule in a few days, if he can keep 'em from tryin' out their cow-manure compresses, good, I'd say."

"And if not?" asked Smith.

"Infection," murmured the doctor. "Gangrene . . . swamp fever . . . malaria . . . heatstroke. If one doesn't get him, the other will. It's a dirty shame that—"

Perkins stirred. He moved his legs. He groaned and opened his eyes. The pupils of his blue eyes were wide with the wonder of the morphine. He looked up into the faces of the three men, confused. His hand crept to his flaming red hair and tugged at it for inspiration. His pale, freckled face shone with incomprehension. Suddenly he reacted as if caught in his palliasse after First Call. He tried to rise. The pain felled him. He moaned.

277

"Easy, Billy," soothed the doctor.

" 'Ow abaht the lazy little blighter?" said Stokes in an attempt at lightness.

"Some blokes have all the luck," quipped Smith. "I'd swap places with him any day of the week."

Perkins stared up at them. "My leg's broke, sir," he quavered. "Isn't it?"

"Aye, Billy," said the doctor. "How do you feel?"

Perkins bit on his lip to kill the tremble of his jaw. "Woozy, sir." He looked down at the splinted limb. "It doesn't hurt badly, though."

"Good," said the doctor. "Sleep well last night?"

"I had a horrible nightmare, sir," he said with a morphine giggle.

"At least 'e dreams," commented Stokes. "I 'aven't 'ad a dream since I was a nipper."

"How's Mr. Crann—I mean Crann, sir?" asked Perkins.

"Right as rain," said Stokes. " 'E rolled outa 'arm's way. 'Fraid you're the only one wot gets to spend the rest of our little African campaign in bed."

Perkins heard the noise of the camp breaking up and men getting ready for the march. He eased off his sleeping bag and looked around. He ran a trembling hand through his hair and eased back onto the sleeping bag. "I'm going to be a terrible bother to you," he quavered abruptly.

"Now, Billy," preambled Cavanaugh, getting down on his knees beside the lad. "What we—"

"I'll not be pulling my weight, sir. A stretcher'll make us short two more men."

The doctor removed his topee and scratched his head. "Billy," he began, "there isn't goin' to be any stretcher."

Perkins smiled nervously. "There's really no need for one, sir. Prop me up like Captain Humphreys. That'll be champion, sir."

Cavanaugh looked up at Stokes and Smith with a look of pleading on his face.

Stokes knelt down beside the doctor and put his hand on Perkins' arm. "You've been a jolly good soldier on this lot, mate. I've been with you when the goin' was 'ard an' tempers short." He rumpled

Perkins' hair good-naturedly. "S'truth, if it 'adn't been for that ginger 'ead of yours, we might never've got this far." The old sailor licked his lips and looked at the doctor. "Wot Dr. Cavanaugh's tryin' to say, lad, is this."

"He's thinking the bumping around'll be too much for me," declared the boy. "But honest, I can take it. It really isn't hurting like it was. Honest."

"No, son," said Stokes dejectedly. "It's not that either. Wot the doctor's tryin' to say is this." He breathed heavily. "Well, lad. Sometimes a man's far more use—"

The whistle shrilled.

Perkins laughed nervously. "I'd better get aboard, hadn't I?" He tried to push himself up into a sitting position. He groaned with pain.

The doctor stood up abruptly. "Come with me, Stokes. Sergeant, keep him company till we get back." They picked their way warily through the mire toward the tractor where Frazer stood.

"What's up, Sergeant?" Perkins asked, his tone taut with suspicion.

Smith looked at the young soldier and thought of Flanders. Nineteen per cent casualties for A Company once. He could see in the lessening gloom of sunrise the doctor, Stokes and Frazer in earnest conversation.

The trio suddenly headed toward him.

"Morning, Perkins," said Frazer evenly. "How's the leg?"

The youngster tried to get up.

"Never mind that," Frazer said.

"Thank you, sir," said Perkins in a voice calculated to conceal his growing pain.

"How's the leg?"

"Fine, sir. Fine."

"Good." Frazer glanced at the doctor. "Good, Perkins." He hesitated. "Perkins?"

"Yes, sir?"

"We're going to leave you here for a few days," Frazer said casually.

"Alone, sir?" quavered Perkins.

279

"Not exactly," explained Frazer offhandedly. "You'll have enough provisions to last a week to ten days—"

"Please, sir," stammered Perkins. "My leg's fine, sir, and—"

"Hear me out, Private Perkins. Provisions for seven to ten days. Three canteens of water. The sergeant here'll see to it you have a Webley and ammo. We should reach Gule not later than the day after tomorrow. We'll send some natives back for you. You may have to spend the next few weeks at Gule. But we'll send a party back for you when we get to Albertville. . . . Any questions?"

Perkins' Adam's apple bobbed. "The day after tomorrow, sir?"

"Approximately. . . . Any further questions, Perkins?"

The lad's mind reeled. "No, sir."

"Very well," announced Frazer. He looked at Cavanaugh, Smith and Stokes. "I'm ready when you are." He looked down at Perkins. "All right, Perkins," he said jauntily. "Keep a grip on yourself, eh?"

"Yes, sir," said Perkins, his skin-deep smile flaking.

Frazer left.

"Good luck, sir!" Perkins called after him.

Cavanaugh knelt down beside him again. "Billy. See these?" He held up a small bottle of tiny white pills. "If the pain gets too bad, take one of these. I wouldn't take more than two a day. Three at the most."

"The lads wanted you to have some more water," said Stokes. "They all tossed in a drop or two." He pushed three canteens toward the lad.

Smith removed his pistol belt and unholstered the Webley. He broke it down expertly and spun the chamber. "She's loaded," he said professionally. He shoved the weapon into the holster. "And here's some extra—just in case." He stacked three small boxes on the holster and slid the lot into the folds of the sleeping bag. "Thirty-six all told, Perkins. Twelve to a box." He held a single round between his thumb and forefinger. "See this one?" He unbuttoned Perkins' pocket and dropped the single round into it.

"What's that for?" Perkins asked innocently.

Smith caught the doctor's disapproving glance. "Eh, well . . . your baker's dozen."

The doctor pulled the old Aran Islands cardigan from his pack and thrust it under Perkins' head.

The whistle blurted imperiously.

The soldiers and sailors fidgeted through their goodbys.

"Eh?" chortled Crann. "I hear you're takin' it easy from now on, mate."

Perkins tried to smile.

"Good luck, Billy boy," said Crann, rushing off.

Stokes rose. "We'll be back in two shakes, Billy."

"Wait . . . wait," stuttered Perkins. He fumbled to unbutton his shirt pocket. He withdrew a small, cylindrical roll of colored paper—the stakes he had been holding. "This belongs to you, sir, and Private Nangle." He looked around anxiously. "Where's Nangle?"

"You 'old 'em," insisted Stokes. "Then you *know* we'll be back." He laughed dryly.

Smith beckoned to Nangle.

Nangle came reluctantly. Smith whispered in his ear.

Once he was by Perkins' side, Nangle's demeanor changed. "You lose those stakes, Perkins, and I'll be back for a strip of your hide," he chaffed.

The group withdrew as one man.

Perkins raised a thin hand.

Propped up on one elbow, Perkins watched until the men disappeared. When he was sure they had gone, he lay down on his side. He vomited . . . and sobbed. His nightmare had become a reality.

They arrived two days later at Gule and were greeted by frolicking vermin, stale ashes, lopsided huts and the flat smell of death. Sleeping sickness had put Gule to bed—forever.

A week later along the worn trail from Bukama came the hammer of children's horny feet, the persistent barking of mangy whelps,

the garbled cluck of scrabbling hens, the hollow sound of a warning bass drum on the humid evening, and the exploratory shyness
of the stick-thin villagers. . . . But they noticed none of this.
Nothing could match the shimmering before them—the tepid,
brown tributary of the Congo River.

That night Sublieutenant Dodkins hurried into the headquarters
tent. "Sir," he declared breathlessly.

"What is it?" snapped Frazer irritatedly. The trek had abraded
his tolerance.

"*Mimi* and *Toutou,* sir," Dodkins said excitedly. "The heat
must've done it."

"Done what?"

"Timbers are all warped, sir. Sprung as wide as my finger."

"*What?*"

Stokes approached, carrying a lantern. "Bad luck, I'm afraid,
sir," he said dismally.

"Luck, my bloody backside," grated Frazer. "You damn fool,
you. *You* were supposed to keep the tarps taut every foot of the
way. *You* were supposed to check them stem to stern each and
every night, weren't you?"

"Yes, sir," said Stokes.

Dodkins said softly, "The tarps *were* on tight as a drum, sir."

"How long to fix 'em up, Stokes?"

The old man shuffled around in thought. "Take the engines out
. . . sink the 'ulls for three or four hours . . . whip 'em out an' dry
'em . . . caulk 'em up again . . . an' bung 'em in again—the engines
. . . we start first thing'n the mornin', sir—under three days, I'd
say."

"Three days!" stormed Frazer, berating the silent men for their
incompetence. He cursed them for their stupidity. The boats had
possession of him; for him theirs was a feminine fragility. All he
cared for was the boats. . . the boats . . . the boats. The word
pounded inside his head as if he were inside a huge iron pail and
someone was pounding on it with a hammer. He held his aching
head. "*Three* days!" he shouted sarcastically. "*Two* days if we
start right here and now."

"But the blokes are sleepin'," protested Stokes incredulously.

"We've reached the water, sir. The rain's a problem no more. We oughta stand down for a bit, sir."

"Get 'em out, the lazy bastards," croaked Frazer. "Get 'em out, I tell you. Get 'em out. Do you hear? Get 'em out, I say."

Mimi and *Toutou* slid down the muddy bank of the Lualaba River and eagerly cleaved the scummy water with their sharp bows. They rode high in the water with the empty water cans lashed to their sides to lessen the chance of holing in the strange, poorly charted waters—at their lowest in years. They floated jauntily, as if proud to be independent again, eager to cut loose under their own power.

Frazer rode in the lead raft with the officers and NCOs. In the rear raft rode the men and equipment. Between them floated the gunboats, pulled by ropes leading from their prows to two dugout canoes rhythmically paddled by natives.

As they pulled away, the villagers lined both banks.

"Looks like you're out of a job, chum," quipped the Welshman to Peterson, the tractor driver.

The two stared at the silent hulk of iron that had served them so faithfully.

"Old Bessie," murmured Peterson nostalgically.

"Eh," said the Welshman. "Can you imagine thirty years from now? Some big white explorer finds that lot. 'How the frig did that get here?' he's going to say. What a waste. I'd get a hundred quid for the scrap that's in her in Swansea, man."

"S'funny how you can get stuck on a bloody piece of machinery."

"Or on a body."

"Perkins?"

"Aye."

"Poor little bugger."

23

A small German steam pinnace rocked gently by the jetty in Kigoma harbor. The easy evening swell rolled across the harbor boom and lapped against its hull. The crew busied themselves with last-minute preparations while three officers conversed earnestly on the dockside. The night lay heavy with a damp heat. The heavyset, bearded man was Lieutenant Commander Zimmer. He spoke precisely, for he knew precisely what he wished Lieutenants Rosenthal and Odebrecht to do. "First: Make no move until dark. The moon's on our side tonight—there is none." He faced the tall fair-haired boy in bush jacket and shorts. "Odebrecht. Do you have everything?"

"*Ja,* Herr Commander," he replied confidently.

"Rosenthal. Wait not more than four hours for him."

"*Ja,* Herr Commander," replied the short officer, also in bush jacket and shorts.

"And remember: If they take you, not a word about our suspicions."

"They will not take us, Herr Commander," said Odebrecht confidently.

They exchanged salutes. The two younger men climbed aboard.

The crew cast off the bow and stern loops, and the pinnace steamed off.

Zimmer watched until the gathering night had engulfed them.

By midnight the pinnace had cut her steam and bobbed on a swell off the Belgian-held coast. The crew lowered a dinghy. By the binnacle light, the two officers synchronized watches. Clad only in swimming trunks, his shoes tied around his neck, the fair-haired Odebrecht nimbly climbed over the side and lowered himself into the waiting dinghy.

"Good luck," Rosenthal called down.

Odebrecht waved and rowed into the night.

The oars, wrapped in heavy sacking, were noiseless and enabled him to get within 300 yards of the shore. He shipped the oars and waited, listening. There were neither sounds nor lights. Undoubtedly Commandant Fèvreaux's Belgian Marines and askaris were sleeping; but there would be sentries on the mouth of the Lukuga River guarding the slipways where *Baron Dhanis* was under construction—and more patrolling the beach for a mile north and south of it.

He slipped the oars into the rowlocks; then he dipped the blades deeply and glided south for two miles. . . . He shipped the oars again, lowered an anchor and climbed over the stern.

For a marker he hastily piled some driftwood in a heap by the water's edge. He had but three hours. He quickly put on his shoes and stole into the brush and small trees encroaching almost to the water's edge.

It cost him a half hour to make his way north to the Belgian compound at Albertville. Belgian sentries were all around—the result of the recent German raid.

Odebrecht stood in the bushes at the edge of the Lukuga River. He was on a height and looked down on the three askaris patrolling the river's bank below. By the opposite bank stood the skeleton of a large ship—*Baron Dhanis*. He could just make out the keel and ribs. Was the deck in place? The engine? How long was she? He would have to get closer.

He waited until two of the three native guards passed each other; then he stole down to the river's edge. He dislodged some loose gravel. A sentry shouted a challenge. There was no turning back. Odebrecht bore on down the slope and dropped into the river. Three sentries assembled above him. Odebrecht swam underwater until his lungs burst. He surfaced one-third of the way across. He saw flashlight beams stab the brush where he had been hiding.

Ten minutes later he panted on the other side of the river, upstream from the ship. Here more sentries padded around on the alert. He crouched, undecided about what to do. He knew Zimmer had not thought he could get this close to *Dhanis*. The mission was to have been only a reconnaissance to estimate her size, weight and speed, to determine if *Dhanis* might pose a threat to *Graf von Gotson*.

From where he lay, Odebrecht could see that the ship on the slipway was—or would be—much larger than *Gotson*. She would be all of 1,500 tons and a good 15 or 20 meters longer. His eager mind sifted the possibilities. Why leave content with this information? Why not destroy her? He had brought matches along with a pistol in the waterproof bag. If the Belgians built their ships like the Germans, the place would be knee-deep in wood shavings. . . . But the jittery guards would not calm down for another hour. He had an hour and fifteen minutes to get back to the beach, swim out to the dinghy and rendezvous with Rosenthal. Not enough time for what he had in mind . . . but he grinned as he visualized the look on Rosenthal's face if he were able to bring it off.

He crept along the bank through the thick ferns. In a few minutes he was in the water and clinging to the mossy uprights under the jetty. He looked up at the huge "wishbone" forming *Dhanis'* rearmost rib. Yes, the deck had been begun, and the planking for the sides lay stacked on either side of the slipway. Not fifteen feet from him was a mound of wood chips and tools. Odebrecht thanked the Belgian shipwrights for their neatness. A sentry's shuffle on the bank high above froze him. He timed the beat of the sentry—twice in five minutes. About two minutes was all he would have, he told himself.

He scurried back and forth scooping up armfuls of chips and stuffing them loosely under the keel.

The strong smell of oil and pitch stung his nostrils. Of course, he told himself. Why not? But where? The neat Belgian shipwrights would not leave expensive—and dangerous—materials like those carelessly around. He searched the darkness. Two huts—halfway up the bank! Two minutes! The *verdammte* sentries. Could he make it? He would never know if he didn't try.

The sentries pass. He scrambles uphill through the brush and ferns. The first hut. A wooden latch on the door. He slides it back and enters. He can see nothing at all in the inkiness of the windowless structure. The pitch and oil smell stronger. He feels his way around. He trips and crashes to the floor. He lies where he has fallen, trembling, bracing himself for the hoarse discovery of the guards. . . . He steals to his feet and resumes his blind inspection of the hut. Five minutes later he knows that the hut is nothing more than a tool shed.

The next hut. Another wooden latch. The fumes sting his nostrils. His foot strikes something. The sound of a drum. He bends. His moist palms touch the neck of a metal container. He feels around. More containers. He uncorks and sniffs . . . shellac . . . paint . . . turpentine . . . linseed oil . . . pitch . . . more paint . . . *paraffin oil!*

He opens the door slowly and squints out. He can hear the sentries patrolling along the top of the bank. He waits until they meet and pass directly above; then he hugs the paraffin drum to his chest and slithers down the bank toward the slipway.

Good. The shavings still in place. He plucks the cork eagerly and soaks them in oil. Still no alarm. He fumbles in the waterproof bag pinned to his swimming trunks for the box of matches. The match head mushes on the emery. He tosses it away and fumbles for another. The phosphorous head sloughs away from the matchstick. He curses and gropes angrily for another match . . . and another . . . and another.

He curses fervently. He considers emptying his pistol into it. No, ignition point of paraffin too low. Besides, if the matches are ruined, the pistol's probably useless.

He loathes his carelessness. So close. He hates to leave. He is heavy with failure as he slips back into the Lukuga and floats downstream toward the lake.

A quarter of an hour later Odebrecht was there. He flipped over onto his chest and swam strongly south. Five hundred yards south of the Lukuga estuary he arched toward the beach and crawled out onto the still-warm sand. His watch showed little time left. Rosenthal was his friend, but he would wait not a minute longer than four hours. Rosenthal always carried out orders to the letter. Had Rosenthal been entrusted with the job, he would have been content with the dimensions of *Dhanis*. He would not have tried to destroy her. The enemy would discover the paraffin-soaked shavings in the morning. That meant that the next time they went on a recce, there would be double the guards and defenses to penetrate. Rosenthal wouldn't like that. *He* would have to make that penetration. . . .

The dinghy was where he had anchored it. He swam around to the stern and pulled himself aboard wearily. . . .

Eager hands from the pinnace reached down and pulled him over the gunwale.

"*Was war mit dir?*" asked Rosenthal solicitously.

"I'm tired," sighed Odebrecht. He was shivering uncontrollably. One of the crew threw a blanket over his shoulders.

The pinnace slipped away at low speed.

Rosenthal asked with a grin, "Is it dangerous to swim here?"

Odebrecht pulled the blanket close to his shoulders. "Next week, my friend, *you* will find out."

With more than a hundred miles of the Lualaba River behind them, Naval Africa Expedition soured with inactivity. On the shadeless rafts the sun bleached them by day; by night, camped on the bank, clouds of insects fed on the rancid fatness of their indolence. Dormant irritations ripened in the moist heat. Tempers splintered like costly china.

For too brief a span the splendor of the Congo held their interest—luxuriant trees, pendulous with fruit, leaning out from the riverbanks; stately palm trees poking up as imperious overseers of river traffic; a verdant carpet of undulating grass and ferns guiding the river's meandering course to the horizon; and through occasional gaps in the jungled river confines, rolling prairie thronging with exotic buck and buffalo. But to stare at the bovinely indifferent elephants and rhinos on the riverbank was not diversion enough.

Smith had just squeezed off half a dozen pistol rounds to break up a colony of stubborn crocodiles ahead of the lead raft.

A Lee-Enfield barked in the rear.

"Crikey, you got 'im!" shouted an exultant voice.

Smith glimpsed a huge bull elephant shy spastically and vanish into the foliage, trumpeting madly. Shooting at a defenseless big elephant doing nobody any harm! "Bloody well cut that out!" he bellowed. "There's no call for that damn nonsense." He felt dirty inside, too. It was them, the lot of 'em. Nobody'd told him to fire his weapon, whoever he was. A round of ammo? A sixpenny bit of brass maybe and tuppence worth of powder. But that wasn't it. Somebody'd just upped and fired at a bloody old elephant. 'Cos he was bored? Fed up? Wanted to show his mates how good a shot he was? Good reasons—for ruddy civilians. For soldiers? British soldiers? This lot weren't soldiers; not like the lads at Ladysmith and Mafeking and Majuba Hill, like the poor buggers he'd left in Flanders.

He felt dirty inside 'cos he'd given them an inch and they'd snatched a mile. Rabble in the King's uniform. Just rabble. Didn't have the faintest notion about Army, about *giving* to a group only to *get* something greater, grander than the sum total. By the left! Quick! March! . . . By the Cenotaph at 120 a minute . . . every arm swinging stiff and straight from the shoulder, back as far as she'll go till the biceps hurt, then forward and up as high as the shoulder in front of you . . . and a whole battalion's worth of steel heels hammering rhythmically into the tarmacadam with a powerful crunch that pumps your ego and rattles your hip joints . . . a crunch and a cadence that's a metronome for your whole life, so that long after the group's gone on, they'll point at you as you walk down the street and know you were one of them; because you gave yourself when you joined up, and you got that—and more—back when you left. The more: putting the next chap before yourself, and putting them all before anything or anyone.

But these young buggers? Putting the Army to shame, disfiguring it, making a bloody mockery of what others had fought for, won and stood for; thumbing their snotty little noses and daring him to do something about it. He'd given them an inch. Just like passing the hat around and not even getting the hat back. . . .

Frazer selected a clearing and ordered Smith to make camp.

The sharp corner of the raft dug into the bank and oozed to rest. The men, stiff with inactivity, jumped off clumsily into it, the mud sucking on their boots; then came Humphreys on a stretcher.

Stokes, with the doctor as interpreter, supervised the tying up of *Mimi* and *Toutou* by the Baluba. The men of the lead raft started campfires and cleared the area of snakes. Those on the second raft formed a human chain and unloaded stores and equipment.

Winged pests that crawled into their food made supper the usual hasty misery. The urgent need for solitude after twelve solid hours of cramped togetherness drove them to early beds.

Smith sank his stocky frame into the softness of the sleeping bag. He gazed up at the moon, golden as a sovereign, close enough to touch. The bass humming of the Baluba around their distant fire soothed his thoughts—being away from civilization three months.

A looming figure shadowed out the moonshine. It was Stokes. He squatted silently by the sleeping bag ten feet from Smith and kneaded the stuffing into a softness acceptable to his old bones. He eased himself cautiously back and sighed heavily.

"All tucked in?" whispered Smith.

"Thought you was asleep," replied Stokes.

"Too nice a night for that."

"Not for an' old bloke like this'n."

"Could make a chap homesick," Smith observed, noticing Stokes also entranced with the moon's beauty.

"Not me, mate," gruffed Stokes. " 'Ome's where the Navy 'angs me 'at for me." He stretched and yawned.

"Wonder how the war's coming, Charlie."

"*This* is the war, ain't it?"

"I mean the real war."

"Huh, this'n's real nuff for me."

"You know what I mean, Charlie."

"Wouldn't bother me barmy 'bout it tonight. You'll know soon enough. 'E says we'll reach some bloody place called 'Catcher' day after tomorrow."

"Hm, that soon, eh? He didn't tell *me* that. . . . You mean Kadja, don't you?"

"Don't let it worry you, Andy. I 'ad to find out from Crann. Catcher. S'wot I said. K-A-D-J-A. Catcher."

"Bit of civilization, then, eh?"

"Some froggy post. You'll find out all about the war then."

"*I'll* find out? Aren't *you* a little curious too?"

Stokes harrumphed. "What for? Only a matter o' time, that's all."

Smith smiled inwardly. "I suppose so. . . . But what if we lost?"

"Wot if the moon's made o' green bloody cheese?"

"What if they were all Nangles? Then what, Charlie?"

"They're not, thank Christ, but they all need a good boot'n th' arse—that's wot. That'll straighten 'em out."

"That's the point, Charlie. We're the ones who have to boot 'em. Somebody should've booted 'em years ago. Long before the Army ever got 'em. . . . Anybody have to boot you ever?"

"Me ole man. All the bloody time. Never did me no 'arm, though."

"Me too," said Smith, scratching his head. "Are we odd or something, Charlie? Take our generation. Never ones to wave the Jack much. And 'Land of Hope and Glory.' A bit sticky for me."

" 'Land o' Soap an' Borax' you mean, chum," laughed Stokes.

Smith laughed too. "But when it comes right down to it," he added as if thinking aloud, "there always *will* be an England."

"S'pose so." Stokes yawned. "That reminds me. I'm 'avin' my

lads spruce up a bit for Catcher. Can't do much in the way of shaves 'n' 'aircuts, but I told 'em to scrounge some soap an' a bit o' Cherry Blossom from somewhere. They'll 'ave clean K.D.s an' boots to match when we see those froggies."

"*Belgians,* Andy," Smith corrected good-naturedly.

"All the same, mate." Stokes yawned again, flopping over onto his face.

Smith closed his eyes. There was an amused grin on his face. " 'Land of Soap and Borax,' " he muttered.

The Belgian fort was but a half hour's journey downriver. The Lualaba had taken eleven days to grow from a shallow ribbon of dirty-brown stagnancy to a broad gray expanse glittering in the pink evening sunlight, its ripples corrugating the expeditioners' shadows beyond recognition.

On the rear raft Smith sat almost lulled by the sonorous chant of the Baluba canoemen; fascinated by the harmonious rippling of the sealskin bodies with each powerful paddle pull. The effort bulged the ebony sheen of their powerful, vase-shaped trunks and rapidly dissipated down and beneath the garish Manchester cottons swaddling their loins.

Above the chant and the churn came the voice of Stokes on the lead raft. "All right, Sergeant Smith!"

Smith turned to his ten subordinates. "All right, you men," he told them. "Let's get into our gear."

The men turned to their packs with grunts and groans. "Can't let a bloke be," grumbled the North-Countryman.

"Nark it and get cracking!" commanded Smith, glaring.

Frazer, sitting up forward on crossed legs, stared out at the river. His mind dwelt on the mute figure on the stretcher directly behind him.

Since the accident, he had noticed Cavanaugh lavish attention on Humphreys, but strictly professional attention. The little doctor had changed his bandages regularly, bathed his brow daily, but volunteered little conversation during the big engineering officer's bouts of consciousness. These were becoming more frequent now that the hole was healing over and fever no longer racked his body, but the little Irishman adamantly remained his noncommittal self— to everyone.

Frazer knew why. He understood. Once he would have felt exactly the same. But now? Something had changed. What? It had eluded him ever since that morning on the slope, for that was when it had happened. All during the rest of the trek it had gnawed away at him. The long days of river travel had crystallized it; and because of it he could no longer in justice harbor his hate for Humphreys. Hate had been diluted to dislike . . . to grudge . . . to apathy . . . to indifference . . . to neutrality. He found his conclusion unavoidable: Humphreys had deliberately ordered Peterson to steer the runaway tractor into the tree, cold-bloodedly risked his life—for an expedition he didn't give a damn about. An expedition he was hell-bent on physically driving into the ground. Why? Frazer told himself he would probably never know; but this he did know: *Humphreys had almost killed himself to save the boats.*

He stole a fleeting glance at the sleeping object of his reverie, then turned around to stare again into the water. He could not believe it, but there it was—his neutrality was crumbling.

Abruptly the commotion broke into his thoughts. He looked up in irritation. "For God's sake, Stokes, this is no time for swimming," he snapped. He jabbed his finger downstream. "Don't you realize the Belgians are down there?"

"That's wot I 'eard, sir," replied the old petty officer cheerfully. He shook his head. "Not swimmin', sir. Me and Sergeant Smith thought we oughta 'ave a nice turnout for 'em. B'sides, sir, 'slikely they been out 'ere so bloomin' long they'll take us for Jerry if we don't look halfway decent."

The five officers watched as the men unrolled crudely pressed but reasonably clean uniforms and took turns dressing in the center of the raft.

Sublieutenant Dodkins surveyed the appearance of the other officers. He grimaced.

Stokes and Crann, both transfigured by stiff, clean shirts and shorts, poked with scraggly shaving brushes for the hard grain of polish in a battered Cherry Blossom tin.

While the officers looked on uncomfortably, the rest disrobed and changed in businesslike fashion, amid a flurry of waving underwear and cannonades of profanity.

"If you don't mind me sayin' so, gentlemen," said Stokes to the officers, "you'd best be gittin' a move on." He pointed to the bulging barracks bag before them.

Dodkins grabbed it and began digging out rolled-up clothing.

Bannister snapped up a pair of shorts.

Frazer stared at him disgustedly. "Who's at the bottom of this damn nonsense?"

"Me, sir," confessed Stokes conversationally. "Me an' the sergeant. An' if you don't look slippy, sir, we'll be all out o' your size."

With that the doctor carefully extinguished a pathetically short cigarette butt in the water, pocketed it briskly and elbowed his way into the pile of clean laundry. He withdrew a pair of shorts and inspected them gingerly. He stood up shakily and held them to his waist. The legs hit him well below the knees. He raised them until the length was right, but the waistband caught him in the neighborhood of his armpits. He snorted and tossed them back into the commander's lap. "Not my size," he muttered, reaching for another pair.

Lieutenant Magarity joined the doctor and the two sublieutenants in their activity.

Frazer sniffed and looked critically at the shorts in his lap. He got up off his haunches reluctantly, removed his own shorts and climbed into the clean ones.

Dodkins and Bannister stood up, freshly outfitted.

"A lick of your Cherry Blossom, Chief?" asked Dodkins.

" 'Bout a lick left, sir," said Stokes, handing over the tin.

"On it next!" shouted Bannister.

"These aren't my bloody size," Frazer complained, knobby, hairy knees poking down from stained and baggy drawers.

"Sorry, sir," apologized Stokes, sizing him up clinically. "You'd be a 'large,' sir, wouldn't you?"

"How the hell would I know?"

"You're a 'large,' sir," declared Stokes professionally. " 'Aven't forgotten when you was in charge o' stores on Scapa, sir, 'ave you?" He relieved his irritable superior of the offending garment and held it aloft. "A 'medium' for a 'large,' anybody?" he announced with the solicitous earnestness of an auctioneer. "C'mon, somebody. A 'medium' for a 'large.' "

From the rapidly disappearing pile of clean uniforms a bundle flew against Stokes's chest. He caught the shirt and examined the neckband. "A 'large' in a shirt, sir," he said enthusiastically, handing it to Frazer.

Still intolerant, Frazer nevertheless removed his shirt and donned the clean one.

The complements of both rafts looked their most military in months.

Five hundred yards downstream the Belgian fort roosted high on the western bank.

Frazer was still without a clean pair of bush shorts.

"A 'medium' for a 'large,' anyone?" pleaded Stokes, still waving the oversize shorts hopefully. "Going . . . going . . . gone." He turned to Frazer apologetically. "I am sorry, sir. 'Fraid we'll 'ave to make do with these." He handed them to Frazer again. "We don't 'ave much time, sir," he reminded him discreetly.

The men could see the Belgian sentries in the wooden parapets silhouetted against the evening sun; but they also beheld the spectacle of their half-dressed commander, who had lost his balance while removing his dirty shorts and fallen flat on his backside.

Dodkins reached out spontaneously to help.

"I can put on my own pants, thanks," said Frazer acidly, rubbing his buttocks tenderly.

" 'E's worried 'bout you gettin' those'ns off, sir," commented Stokes. "All right," he said to the others, "fill in around 'ere."

Quickly they formed a protective ring around their seminude commander.

As Frazer dressed, willing hands buttoned his shirt and buckled his pistol belt. Somebody was on hands and knees with the old shaving brush, attempting in three minutes to remove the dirt of three months.

A bugle blew.

"They've seen us!" shouted Crann excitedly. "They're wavin'!" He waved back.

"Enough o' that," snapped Stokes. "We'll 'ave a proper military bearin' at all times."

A wooden jetty jutted out from the base of the fort into the river. They poled the rafts toward it. As they tied up, a large stockade-like door in the base of the fort swung open and several smiling Belgians advanced down the jetty.

Frazer was first to set foot on the jetty. He stood at attention as the Belgians approached. At three paces his hand whipped to his topee in salute. "Commander Frazer, Royal Navy," he said simply.

"Lieutenant Paul André, Belgian Marines," replied the leading Belgian rapturously, pumping Frazer's hand, embracing him and planting an audible kiss on each cheek.

"Ah, Commander, Commander," enthused the Belgian officer. "Commander Frazer!" He extended both arms theatrically in extravagant surprise. "But long ago we had given you up for lost. Over three weeks ago, they said, you were to be here. *Mon Dieu!* How did you manage it?" Pride and admiration shone from his face. "And look at you. Months in the Congo and . . . *mon Dieu* . . . the uniforms! If I did not know better, I would say you had stepped off the boat from Aldershot—is it not?"

Suddenly André apologized. "Please forgive me, Commander. I forget in my excitement. You and your men—you must be tired, hungry." He rattled off some orders in French to a subordinate, who scurried off. "Come! You are our guests." He put his arm in Frazer's and they walked toward the door, followed by the other welcoming Belgians. Just before he left the jetty, Frazer said, "Take over, Number One."

"Very good, sir," responded Magarity, the engineering lieutenant, who promptly delegated that responsibility to Stokes.

The old petty officer assumed the crustiness and swagger of his breed. "Fall in!" he bellowed.

"The eighteen soldiers' and sailors' boots thundered on the jetty as they fell into a column of threes.

"Atten—*shun!* Heads up! Chins in! Shoulders back!" Stokes's voice sounded like coal sliding down a chute. "You're rusty, the lot of you." He walked up and down before them. He looked around the jetty. There were half a dozen askaris and several Belgian other ranks. He faced the men again. "All right. Wot you all say to a little bit o' square bashin'?"

The men groaned.

"I thought so," said Stokes with a straight face. "Well . . . if you insist. Sergeant Smith!"

Smith smartly took one pace forward and snapped his heels sharply.

Stokes said, "Find a little flat space somewhere an' let's show these Belgian blokes 'ow it's done." He stepped aside.

Smith marched forward, pivoted right, marched stiffly to the center of the squad, then pivoted right again. "Stand at . . . *ease!*"

The men's rifles leaned forward—on their butts. Their right hands wandered to the small of their backs.

"Stand . . . *easy!*"

They relaxed in place.

"Stand at . . . *ease!*"

They braced themselves.

"Atten—*shun!*"

The ragged line of slanted rifles swung back sloppily into the vertical. Heels scuffed together arbitrarily in a travesty of parade-ground precision.

"Bloody awful! Stand at . . . *ease!*"

Again rifles canted forward, right hands to their backs.

"Atten—*shun!* . . . That was better. Not much, though. Let's have another go. Slope *arms!* Order . . . *arms!* Present . . . *arms!* Order . . . *arms!* Shoulder . . . *arms!* Present . . . *arms!* Order . . . *arms!* Stand at . . . *ease! Stand . . . easy!*"

Stokes strode over to the sergeant. "Maybe it wasn't such a good idea after all," he said confidentially, but loud enough for the men to hear.

"P'haps you're right, Charlie," muttered Smith, catching on. "They're liable to show *us* how."

"Give it another bash," advised Stokes lugubriously, retiring to the flank.

"Atten—*shun!*" barked Smith. For over five minutes he ran them sweating through the manual of arms.

"That'll do, I'd say, sir," said Stokes to Lieutenant Magarity.

Magarity nodded deferentially. As an engineering officer, he was more at home with spanners than with close-order drill.

"As you were, Sergeant," Stokes called to Smith. He strolled over to the squad again, hands clasped behind his back. "I don't need to tell you the commander expects nothin' less'n a proper military bearin'. Hear? . . . All right. Now let's get up on deck 'n' see if we can do it twice as good. Sergeant!"

Smith took over again. He had the men follow Magarity and Stokes through the stockade door and up a winding staircase. A hatch cover opened above their heads. They climbed through it and found themselves inside a large rectangular open area. It consisted of living quarters at one end and an open courtyard at the other, sealed off from the outside jungle by a high stockade. High up on the corners were parapets connected with one another by a narrow catwalk. From one post a flagstaff poked up into the approaching night. The Belgian tricolor fluttered down its length, guided by a Belgian NCO and a squad of askaris formally mounting retreat at its base.

The Belgian commander stood in the middle of the courtyard, proudly showing off the fort's defensive appointments to Frazer.

"Are you in wireless communication with Albertville, Commander?" asked Frazer.

The Belgian pointed toward the aerial mounted on one of the parapets.

"Then you're not as out of touch with things as I'd thought!" exclaimed Frazer exultantly. "How's the war going? What's the Hun up to these days? What about France? The Dardanelles operation?"

The Belgian held up his hands as if to stave off further questions. "Tell me," he said guardedly, "how long have you been—how you say—out of touch?"

"Since August," said Frazer.

"Ah," began the Belgian. "I have long been an admirer of the great English. We Belgian Marines—our model is your wonderful Royal Marines."

"Indeed that is very gracious, Commander, but—"

"And as for the great British Navy, in peace and in war, the world can depend—"

"Lieutenant André. What about the war?"

The Belgian's tone deadened. "It is not so good, Commander Frazer."

"Why?"

"Why?" repeated the Belgian. "You have not heard, then?"

"I told you we've been gone since—"

"You did, my commander. I apologize. The news is not good. The Dardanelles—this was a failure."

"Failure?" said Frazer incredulously. "I don't understand. When we left . . . my God, what a fleet! We could've forced the Narrows *without* the Army and—"

"Your brave British troops perished by the thousands under the guns of the Turks. Your splendid Navy lost heavily."

"But it doesn't make a damn bit of sense," insisted Frazer, as if somehow the Belgian might be able to undo history. "Everything was to hinge on the element of surprise. And we *had* that. What ships?"

The Belgian shrugged. "I do not remember very well, my commander. You English have such majestic names for your ships." He rubbed his brow. "There was the—eh . . . a name of great irony. The—eh—*Triumph*—"

"My God," groaned Frazer dismally. "The son of one of my men was on her."

"I am very sorry, my commander," said the Belgian softly. All hands lost. And there was *Irresistible*—a heroic name for heroic men. But the others? My memory fails me."

"It doesn't matter," said Frazer sadly. "Two battleships! Incredible." He shook his head. "Admiralty must've been in a chaos."

299

"More than your Admiralty, my commander. Did you not know? Your whole Government. There has been a great change."

"Change?"

"A coalition government of both your major parties."

Frazer swore. "After that Dardanelles bungling I'm not surprised."

"It was *before,*" the Belgian pointed out. "A scandal in your munitions industry. Shortages of shells in France . . . insufficient weapons of all sorts . . . obsolete weapons . . . faulty ammunition —"

"What? It could not happen in England," he said intensely.

"I am deeply sorry. I should not go on."

"Go on," grated Frazer. "It's just that . . . that after what we've come through . . ."

"A—what you say—bitter pill?" The Belgian nodded understandingly. "Serbia has been destroyed. Bulgaria has joined the enemy . . ."

"Things couldn't be much worse."

"And there have been changes in your Admiralty."

"Who?" asked Frazer cautiously.

"A new First Sea Lord."

"Lord Fisher gone?" Frazer shouted.

The Belgian nodded. "Resigned."

Frazer's lean frame went limp. He stared unseeing at his feet. "Damn!" he said roundly.

The grind of boots in unison on the courtyard jerked Frazer's head up. A few yards away Naval Africa Expedition marched, shiny weapons glittering in the evening sun, backs straight as ramrods.

At the base of the flagstaff, two Belgians had just finished formally folding the flag.

"*Sacrebleu!*" exclaimed the Belgian commander.

Frazer was speechless. His feelings harked back over the years to his grandfather's analysis of the men he would one day command—nine-tenths ache and complaint, but built into them that irrational tenth, the dimension that tied them all together when the outsiders were looking on.

300

They marched . . . and wheeled . . . and turned. Horny hands hammered dusty rifle stocks as they sloped . . . presented . . . and ordered arms.

And there was old Stokes swinging along six paces behind, his frail old body coaxing his stick-thin legs to the measured cadence, his only son Harry lying fathoms under the Dardanelles. It wasn't right that such should be an old sailor's reward for long and faithful service, thought Frazer. "Now take my boy 'Arry," he could hear him say down the long years of their association. Now what would he say? What would an old man do now without his Harry?

Obsolete weapons, duff shells, the Dardanelles down the drain. He smoldered. How dare they? How dare they betray the flesh and blood marching out there? Simple soldiers, sailors and their non-coms, he thought: armed with their cause—inscrutable though it might be—they with their virtues would in the end retrieve the blunders of staffs and cabinets, admirals, generals and politicians—including his own.

C-A-R-O-O-O-O-O-O-O-O-M-M-M-M-M-M-M.

A hundred thousand doors slammed in the empty cathedral of the sky. Heavy layers of black cloud licked and curled in from the east.

Frazer and the Belgians stared at the sky.

But not the marchers. Left-right, left-right, left-right, left-right . . .

Again the heavens exploded. The clouds ruptured and emptied their deluge on the earth, gratefully like a woman after birth.

"Left . . . *wheel!*" bellowed Smith through the slanted streaks of rain.

The rain soaked Frazer to the skin. It seeped through his sodden topee and trickled down his forehead.

"Unbelievable," said the Belgian commander.

Frazer could not reply.

"Left-right, left-right," Stokes sang out.

The rain washed all over Frazer. England's hope . . . the world's hope. Little men just . . . little nobodies. Pigeon-toed privates . . . knock-kneed seamen . . . groaning, griping, lead-swinging, awkward

301

little misfits . . . the damned, blasted irrational tenth that had built a bloody empire.

Under the rain he stood cast adrift, weeping.

They had feasted on roast venison, fresh white bread and more Belgian beer than they had ever drunk in their lives. They sat around the table reveling in a pleasant, bloated feeling and exchanging experiences.

With typical Continental abandon the Belgian commander had fallen sentimental. "*Mon Dieu!*" he was saying. "You mad English." He smote his forehead theatrically with the palm of his hand. "What is it about you? A nation of shopkeepers, no? Yet you do this thing. When Commandant Fèvreaux at Albertville sent me *le message,* I said, '*Impossible.* To bring two ships through *la jongle. Sacrebleu!* They are mad,' I said. 'Not even the Belgians could do it. It is *impossible.*' " He laughed whimsically and smote his forehead again. "And you do *l'impossible.*"

"You're much too kind, Commander André," said Frazer soberly. "No, not just the English." He turned toward the doctor. "Dr. Cavanaugh, here. He's from Ireland."

"Ah, do tell me, *monsieur le docteur,*" insisted the Belgian amiably.

Cavanaugh held up his empty glass.

"Forgive me," said the Belgian, leaning over the table to refill the doctor's glass.

"Ah, sure'n you're a gentleman an' a scholar," slurred Cavanaugh in maudlin tones, "an' an officer 'n' gentleman." He coddled his brandy glass. "So you like to hear the Irish side, eh?" He emphasized Irish. "But now, Commander dear, you're a man of charm an' education, an' surely you must've heard there's really no Irish side to it any more. I mean, all that foolish shootin' and brawlin's all water o'er the bridge. We're friends now." He scratched his head contemplatively. "Aye, the Irish've grown up, didn't they tell you? Sure'n it must be ages since the English had to give us a good canin'. You see, Commander dear, the trouble is we wanna think

302

with our hearts—an' the English'd like us to think with our heads. Then we could all drive the pigs outa the kitchen an' become big gentlemen farmers and business tycoons and that sorta balderdash."

The Belgian smiled in embarrassment. "Did you have much trouble, *mon ami,* on the way?" he asked cordially, changing the subject.

"That all depends on what you mean by trouble," said Cavanaugh thickly.

"The man on the stretcher?" queried the Belgian solicitously.

Frazer interjected, "That was my Number One, Captain Humphreys. He injured himself trying to . . . in the line of duty. He's going to be all right."

Cavanaugh glared up from his drink at Frazer. "So now you're diagnosin' for me," he snapped.

Frazer shifted uncomfortably and leaned toward the Belgian. "A bad chest wound. Dr. Cavanaugh did a splendid job on it." He glanced around at Magarity and the two sublieutenants. They were enjoying it no more than he. "Commander, you've been very gracious to us, and I'm sure you've other duties to attend to. My men and I'll turn in—"

"Wait, wait, wait, wait," slurred the doctor, rising. "Our Belgian host here'd like to know the score, wouldn't ye, Commander André? After all, it's not polite to drink his booze an' run. Tut, tut, Ian. Where's your nice manners?"

Frazer approached the doctor to steer him out of the room. "Thanks for your kind hospitality, Commander. We shall all feel much better after a good night's—"

"Hold your horses," said the doctor belligerently, twisting out of Frazer's grip. "Commander, you'd like to know why he's so bloody modest, surely, now."

"C'mon, Tommy," urged Frazer. He turned to the other officers. "Let's get him to bed."

"Modesty covers a multitude of sins, don't ye know," declared Cavanaugh.

André took the Irishman's hand warmly. "You all are brave men, *mon ami.* I shall look forward to breakfast. I wish to hear all about it. Every detail that—"

303

"Sins, I said," insisted the doctor drunkenly.

"Every detail that occurred," repeated André, helping the others to steer the doctor toward the door. "I must have something to tell my grandchildren when the war is over. *Sacrebleu!* All I have done is grow fat here at Kadja."

The doctor stuck his face almost against the Belgian's. "Ask him to tell ye how he left wee Perkins behind in the swamp."

"One of my men," explained Frazer cursorily. "A fractured leg. He'd have been in too much pain if we had taken him along. We left him behind. Arranged for the natives to pick him up."

"That was unfortunate," said André sympathetically.

Frazer turned to Dodkins and Bannister. "Get him to his quarters. See that he goes to bed."

The two young sublieutenants hustled the protesting little physician through the door and into the howling rain.

Magarity excused himself for the night, leaving André and Frazer standing alone in embarrassed silence.

"Your glass, Commander," said André, raising the brandy bottle.

"No, thanks," declined Frazer. "I'm a bit woozy myself."

"As you please," said André, refilling his own glass.

The rain drumming on the compound's corrugated-iron roofs was background to the ensuing silence.

Suddenly Frazer quickened.

André frowned. "What is it?"

"Shush," admonished Frazer, putting his fingers to his lips. "Listen!"

Through the din came the strains of "Tipperary."

They both smiled—and listened.

"You English," said André, shaking his head in admiration. "You'll win this war yet."

Frazer was more relaxed. He affected umbrage. "And why shouldn't we?"

André turned serious. "You asked me about the war, *mon ami.*"

"Yes. There's more bad news?"

André looked into his drink. "Commander, what would it mean to you—to us—if your Royal Navy should—well, should change its mind? The lake, I mean."

Frazer pulled himself upright in his chair. His face hardened. "Impossible. Even if Fisher's gone. He was First *Sea* Lord, Commander. It's Churchill who's First Lord. First Lord of the entire Admiralty. He's behind us one hundred per cent!"

"Yes," ruminated André, "that is how I thought it was."

"You thought *what* was?"

"*Mon ami,*" said André gently, "I told you of changes in your Government."

"So?"

"*Monsieur* Churchill himself was dismissed several months ago."

"Tipperary's" strains again obtruded upon their mood.

André laid a hand on his guest's sleeve. "Today should have been a day of glory for you and your valiant men. I shall wireless Albertville in the morning. They will know if London has canceled the operation."

"No," Frazer said. "No, I don't wish you to do that."

"Be practical, Commander Frazer," urged André. "You and your men will have to know sooner or later."

"I prefer later—for their sakes."

"And for your own?"

Frazer leaned forward. "Commander, as one sailor to another, I want you to do me a favor. I don't want you to report our arrival at Kadja to Albertville."

"But, Commander," remonstrated the Belgian, "Kadja is an important lookout. I am supposed to see everything that goes up or down the Lualaba River. If you arrive at Albertville and I have not reported your presence to Commandant Fèvreaux in advance, I could be court-martialed for not doing my duty."

"Please, André. I will take full responsibility."

André searched his guest's face seriously; then he smiled. "I think I understand. You would rather not know at this moment what London has decided. You prefer to wait until you reach Albertville."

Frazer nodded.

André nodded.

Frazer slumped in his chair with relief.

André rose. "Forgive my ungraciousness, Commander Frazer. You are extremely tired. I will show you to your quarters."

"I'm all in," sighed Frazer.

André hesitated. "One other thing."

"Huh?"

"The man you left behind in the swamp."

"Perkins? What about him?"

"Exactly where?"

Frazer rubbed his face. "Let me see . . . near Gule. Ten or twelve miles south of Gule."

"Is he dead?"

"I hope not," blurted Frazer. "Why? We had some of the Bukama natives go back for him."

"Commander, there is something about the swamp you do not know."

"That's impossible," yawned Frazer wearily. "I remember every damn inch of it."

"You don't understand."

"Understand what?"

"The Bakasandji."

"The what?"

André explained.

"My God," ejaculated Frazer. "We must fetch him right away." His face was stamped with horror and revulsion. "Oh, my good Christ! What've I done?" He grabbed André by the arms and shook him. "You must help us, André. If anything happens, Tommy'll never . . . When can you—listen, I'll leave the doctor and a couple of men. Can you have a party take 'em back?"

"Not tonight—or in the morning. It is impossible in the rain. Maybe in a few days. The rains start intermittently, but in two weeks it will rain constantly day and night."

"All right, André. A few days. Can I tell Tommy—Dr. Cavanaugh—you'll take him?"

André nodded understandingly.

Frazer hurried out of the building and squelched across the compound to the doctor's quarters.

24

When Odebrecht returned to Kigoma, he reported to Commander Zimmer. The stolid, pedestrian commanding officer of the Möwe Detachment did not hide his displeasure at his young subordinate's failure to adhere precisely to his orders. Now, he told him, the enemy would be alert to the object of their curiosity and would probably mount a double guard during daylight and a treble watch by night, and his maladroit attempt at heroics might conceivably cost them control of the lake.

"Wasn't the idea eventually to destroy *Dhanis?*" asked Odebrecht stiffly.

"*Natürlich,*" Zimmer had conceded, but only when the odds were better than they had been for him—and even then, he reminded Odebrecht heavily, only when ordered. He paced the plank floor of the detachment headquarters, hands clasped behind his back.

Odebrecht stood squarely erect, facing his superior's desk, his eyes dutifully straight ahead.

Zimmer halted by the young officer's side. "When do you think we should try again?" he asked.

"In a fortnight," said Odebrecht.

Zimmer looked at him questioningly. "A fortnight?" he said. He growled and continued his pacing. "Perhaps out of the frying pan into the fire," he muttered. He halted by Odebrecht again. "All right. A fortnight. That is all. Send for Rosenthal."

Odebrecht's military bearing masked his disappointment. "*Jawohl,* Herr Commander," he said, saluting and stiffly taking his leave.

Under cover of heavy rains and howling winds, Rosenthal crawled out of the rolling surf a hundred yards south of the Lukuga estuary, dripping in his shirt and pants, his normally hard, lean girth broadened by a waterproof waist belt bulging with six potato-masher hand grenades—one for each of the six massive stanchions driven into the riverbed on which the building slip and the skeleton of *Dhanis* rested.

He jogtrotted along in the loose sand, safe in the knowledge that the roar of the elements would mask his approach. Suddenly he remembered the stoveblack in his waist belt. He stripped to the pelt and smeared himself. He shivered distastefully.

He didn't like it—nor Zimmer's idea to blow up the *Dhanis* on the slip. He and Odebrecht and the other young officers yearned for a good sea battle to kill the boredom. How *verdammte* one-sided the war had been ever since the British had chased them up the Rufiji River. He dwelt on that action and tingled. And it had taken them over nine months before the grand old *Königsberg's* guns had stopped spouting cordite and lead, he proudly remembered. Even then, it wasn't the Engländers' shells that had done it. Zimmer had given the order to dismantle and scuttle. Ever since then the war had been as easy as skiing down one of the slopes of his native Zugspitze. Lake Tanganyika had been as safe for German trade, navigation and commerce as the Rhine. Let them build their *verdammte Baron Dhanis.* Let them launch it—even make a few sorties on our coast—then go after them with *Gotson* and *Kingani!*

But Zimmer was too old, too cautious.

The plan was simplicity itself: Lash the grenades to the stanchions. Tie a length of twine to each of the grenade pins, then swim away from the slip, paying out the twine as you go. At a safe distance jerk the twine—and take your chances with a flotilla of predatory Belgian patrol boats, with the odd crocodiles that always go mad in heavy weather and search for something to gnaw off their ill humor on, and with the pinnace crew, nervous with waiting and ready to weigh anchor at the slightest provocation.

He had memorized Odebrecht's map. He had no trouble finding the slip; and there was *Dhanis,* her white ribs glowing like the skeleton of some huge prehistoric mammal. And there were the sentries—at least a dozen of them patrolling the south bank.

Rosenthal watched for an hour.

The Belgians patrolled vigilantly. NCOs with storm lanterns checked on the sentries every fifteen minutes. Arc lights floodlit the slip and the surrounding water; but underneath was bathed in shadow.

The more he assayed the risks, the less he liked them. He studied the stanchions. His heart plummeted. Above the level of the lapping water he could see barbed wire strung between the stanchions.

No, he couldn't pull it off. The risks for one man were too great. Zimmer had ordered him to return in that event. His knees cracked noisily as he stood up. He looked at his watch, then stole back to the beach.

He walked along the beach unhurriedly. He had plenty of time. Overhead the sky was rent by a vicious crack of lightning. Before the thunder had rolled away, the clouds burst and rain spattered on sand. Again the sky erupted. Lightning illuminated the broad white ribbon of beach. Rosenthal frowned. Something up ahead. He crouched, waiting for the next lightning flash. When it came, he could not believe what he saw: two boats, fifty yards away. Medium-sized craft . . . not lake craft . . . their aft quarters covered with black tarpaulins . . . very high freeboard . . . ominous tarpaulined outlines on the foredecks.

"*Mein Gott!*" What had he stumbled upon? He stole closer and saw why the freeboard had looked so high. Both boats—torpedo-boat class, he estimated—were mounted on trolleys. The trolleys ran on rails. The rails ran into the water. "*Donnerwetter!*" Quickly boyish wonder succumbed to military training. Zimmer will want to know everything, he reminded himself. He coolly began studying details and dimensions. The gun! He had to know the size. Where were the guards? There had to be guards, but he didn't have the time to worry about them. The pinnace would be along promptly. He grabbed hold of the foredeck rail and pulled himself up onto the bow of the first boat. The knots on the tarp were big and loose. The guns were the type the English called three-pounders.

"Eh, what the bloody hell are you doin' up there, wog?"

The voice from nowhere froze him solid. He heard a rifle bolt click. He leaped onto the sand and raced madly for the water.

A rifle cracked—and again—and again. Suddenly there were other voices.

Rosenthal felt the useless sand melt away under him as his nervous legs thrashed for traction. He stumbled and fell.

"Don't let the bastard get away!" roared an authoritative voice.

Four shadowy figures with rifles at the high port skidded across the sand.

Rosenthal's stomach quivered. He wanted to retch. He forced himself to his feet. He prayed as the water buffeted his shins. He belly-flopped into the surf.

"In after him!" shouted the authoritative voice.

Rosenthal felt angry hands grab his flailing arms and churning feet.

Sublieutenant Dodkins was the orderly officer that night. The corporal of the guard roused him. He came to the tent flap, rubbing his eyes and yawning. "What is it?" he mumbled.

"Caught a wog mucking about with the boats, sir," explained the corporal.

"Good Lord," said Dodkins. "Where is he?"

"This way, sir," said the corporal.

He followed the corporal through Naval Africa Expedition's encampment to the edge of the lightly wooded area where three sentries stood with their weapons trained on Rosenthal.

"What have we here?" bantered Dodkins, playing the beam of his torch on the black figure.

"Want me to get the doctor, sir?" asked the corporal.

Dodkins peered suspiciously at their captive. He rubbed a finger down Rosenthal's chest, leaving a white track. "Thought so," said Dodkins. "No more wog than I am." He said to Rosenthal, "Who are you? Where do you come from?"

Rosenthal stood mute.

Dodkins pointed to the waist belt. "What's in that?"

The corporal unbuckled the belt and examined its contents. "From the other side, I'd say he was, sir. Six potato mashers . . . a ball of string."

"Up to no good," concluded Dodkins seriously. "He's Jerry, I'm sure." He played the beam on Rosenthal's face again and demanded to know who he was and where he had come from.

Rosenthal turned his head to avoid the intense light. His eyes caught a pinpoint of light out in the water. On and off it flashed. It was the "O" Morse signal—O for Odebrecht. Surely Odebrecht must have heard the shots. Why didn't he leave? Why didn't he obey orders to the letter? But that was Odebrecht. The fool would flash for another hour—if the English didn't take him, too.

He had to get them away from the lakeside. "My name is Rosenthal," he announced in perfect English. "Hans. *Leutnant . . . Deutsche Marine.* . . . I am cold, hungry and tired."

"That's better," said Dodkins. "Speaks it like a native, too. See what you can do for him, corporal. Then put a man on him for the rest of the night. I'll have the commander see him in the morning."

"Very good, sir," said the corporal.

"Good night," yawned Dodkins.

"Night, sir," chorused the men, leading their prisoner away from the edge of the lake toward the mess tent.

311

25

"Get much out of the Jerry, sir?" queried Stokes.

"Sweet Fanny Adams," said Frazer. "We'd better take no chances, Stokes. Have the tender push *Mimi* and *Toutou* back into the woods. If my guess is right, Jerry'll be snooping around here a lot more'n he has these past weeks."

"Wot about the breakwater, sir?"

"Same as usual, Stokes. Can't haul *it* back among the trees."

"Aye, aye, sir."

The "same as usual" meant working on a breakwater behind which *Mimi* and *Toutou* could be launched without fear of the potentially dangerous surf. Daily hundreds of local natives carried rock out into the water and dropped it in the shape of a wide semi-circle having its center on the beach between the two boats.

Frazer's constant worry was that the enemy's random patrols might happen upon them before they had completed the work. They were defenseless at this point, and half a dozen well-placed enemy shells could abort everything. Thus, the lookout post at Mtoa, 20 miles up the coast, had to be especially vigilant. Mtoa was connected by telegraph wire with the Belgian wireless station at Albertville. When Mtoa sighted an enemy ship, Albertville blew three long whistle blasts, which carried the 500 yards down to Kalemie, the lagoon where Humphreys' ideas were shaping up.

Abruptly the whistle shrilled.

"Scramble!" roared Frazer.

The natives dropped their loads of stone and scurried for the woods. The soldiers and sailors ambled off the beach and flopped down in the shade.

Dodkins and Bannister stood with Frazer among the trees.

"Your turn, isn't it?" he asked Bannister.

"Yes, sir," said the young sublieutenant enthusiastically. He left the shade and hobbled across the hot sand toward the breakwater. He walked out along the neat rock causeway until he reached the deep end—the spot where the spur of railway track would gradually sink below the water level, enabling *Mimi* and *Toutou* to roll off easily and float freely in deep water. He held his hand to his forehead and gazed at the northern horizon—a gauze of dirty smoke. He whipped up his binoculars and brought *Kingani* into focus.

Fifteen minutes later Bannister lay flat on his stomach on the breakwater. The big German warship, squat because she carried twelve times the weight of *Mimi* or *Toutou* on the same length of beam, cruised defiantly up and down about 1,500 yards away. Fine, thought Bannister, as he inspected her from stem to stern and made notes and sketches on a small pad by his face.

A crisp *cr-u-u-u-m-mp* shattered the noon peace. Bannister heard a stiff, whooshing sound above his head and a shell exploded back in the sand, close to the trees. Two more shells exploded in rapid succession, this time churning up the water close to the breakwater.

Bannister studied the gun closely. It was *Kingani's* forward armament, a heavy six-pounder—but of *British* design, thought Bannister. He sketched rapidly.

The shells tore in a round a minute, accurately straddling the breakwater. "Bastards!" swore Bannister as one blew a gaping hole in it. "They must really believe it!" he exclaimed incredulously, as he recalled the rumor Frazer had circulated among the natives to explain the breakwater—the start of a bridge across the lake—

313

knowing word would ultimately reach Zimmer. Bannister could make out the faces of the German crew. They were smiling as if on an afternoon's target practice, but not so casual as to wander into range of the Belgian coastal 12-pounders.

Bannister noticed that the enemy gunners fired only when *Kingani* turned around at each end of the figure-eight course she was patrolling. He wondered why. Then it hit him—the position of her funnel and deck hamper. They masked the gun, limiting its traverse. This meant that the dangerous-looking 6-pounder was effective only against targets dead-ahead, but not from astern or abeam; but the fully traversible 1½-inch Hotchkiss pom-pom in the stern chattered intermittently during the quarter of an hour of target practice on the breakwater. . . . Eventually Bannister saw the 6-pounder crew elevate their weapon and loose off half a dozen shells that whistled well into the woods. It was the final flourish. *Kingani* heeled to the northeast and soon sank below the horizon.

By lantern light Frazer sat around in the headquarters tent with the two sublieutenants. "Damn good," he said, congratulating Bannister. "We hadn't known about the six-pounder." He extended his hand. "The sketch . . . and they've moved the pom-pom off the bow into the stern."

Bannister eagerly handed him the rude drawing.

"Obviously one of ours," concluded Frazer. "Probably captured. Yes, a six, all right. A standard six—3,000 yards."

"Three thousand five hundred, sir," said Bannister deferentially.

Dodkins asked eagerly, "Sir, why don't we have a bang at them next time?"

Frazer regarded his subordinate reprovingly. "We're not fully organized yet," he answered testily. "That's why. Ninety per cent of the success of any undertaking is organization, Bannister; the other ten per cent's luck. And we certainly haven't had much luck so far, so this thing's going to be organized before we make our move. . . . Dodkins! You've been keeping score. How many visitors have we had to date?"

The young subaltern fished for a notebook. "Today was the second time for *Kingani*. We don't really care if she never shows up again. We have her down to a T." He pointed to the sketch. "And *Hedwig von Wissman* snooped around long enough last week so that Bannister got all we need on her; and the week before *Pangani* lobbed a round or two at us, and he got her, too."

Bannister produced his own notebook. "So I've been able to bring your original intelligence estimate up to date, sir." He proffered Frazer the notebook. "Now we know exactly what we're up against."

Frazer studied the notebook in silence. "Not quite." He snapped the notebook shut. "We haven't seen *Gotson*."

"Well, sir," commented Dodkins, "if we want to be completely accurate, we haven't seen *Wami* yet either."

"*Wami's* a tug, Dodkins," said Frazer heavily. "I'm not worried about her. I'm worried about the four 4.1-inchers Zimmer salvaged from *Königsberg*. Where are they? *Gotson's* 800 tons. They could be on her."

"Four of 'em?" questioned Bannister.

Frazer shrugged. "Well, two certainly . . . then where'd they have the other two? Part of the Kigoma harbor defenses?"

"I suppose it'd be nice to know if they did have two at Kigoma, sir," observed Bannister, "but does it really matter what they have there? I mean, sir, *Mimi* and *Toutou* are hardly going to attack Kigoma."

"But they *are* going to attack *Gotson*," spat Frazer. "One round of a 4.1 within ten yards'd blow them both to kingdom come—and all that's in 'em. That's what we're up against." He handed back Bannister's notebook. "That's all, gentlemen. Good night."

It was Christmas Eve, 1915. Except for a few sentries, most of the officers and men had gone up the beach to Albertville for the season's festivities.

Inside the headquarters tent Frazer had just closed a small, dog-eared volume and put it under his pillow. He got up off his cot and stood in the middle of the tent, deep in thought. He pulled on his peaked naval cap, left the tent and entered the next tent.

It was completely dark inside. "Anyone at home?" he inquired casually. He knew that there was. He wondered if he should strike a match—or wait for him to say something. . . . He struck a match and lit a lantern.

The large figure on the cot stirred.

"Ah, Oswald," apologized Frazer. "Hope I didn't waken you." Humphreys had been facing the tent wall; he turned to his visitor.

Frazer said, "I though you'd like to know: We finished her."

"The entire causeway?" asked Humphreys cautiously.

"The lot," said Frazer casually.

"The railway spur, too?"

"Everything."

Humphreys was panting with the exertion of movement. He lay flat on his back again. The lantern's yellow light gave his pallid face a sulphur color. Droplets of sweat glistened on his brow. "Everything the way I told you?"

"To the letter."

Humphreys closed his eyes. "My part's done," he muttered. He lay there, not saying a word.

Frazer sensed that his presence was unwanted. He picked up the lantern's glass globe and blew out the flame. He walked outside. The evening's overcast had cleared. The moon flooded the night. The lake mirrored its splendor. He could hear his men in Albertville singing carols. He hurt inside. No one had stopped by and asked him to come along. He wondered where Tommy would be and what he'd be doing. Had he, Nangle and Crann found Perkins alive? If he weren't, Tommy would be cursing the day they ever met. And why shouldn't he? Frazer idly wondered how he would write to Perkins' parents explaining that their only son had been eaten by the Bakasandji. He shuddered. Why in God's name had he ever left his desk at the Admiralty? He hated himself.

He walked back into Humphreys' tent and relit the lantern. "Oswald," he said evenly, "I want you to see it."

The engineering captain was lying as Frazer had left him. He opened his eyes.

Frazer crossed to the cot and looked down at him. "C'mon. I'll give you a hand."

Humphreys stared at him blankly. The chest would be completely healed soon, but the tip of the swagger stick had dug into his spinal column, damaging the nerves to his legs. One leg had recovered; the other dragged flaccidly. Humphreys had adamantly refused to limp about on a crutch as he might have. He was not about to parade his incapacity before their vindictive eyes. That was a shame he could never bear. To him the lesser shame was complete surrender to a sickbed.

"I said I'll give you a hand," repeated Frazer.

"Go away and don't bother me," breathed Humphreys.

"You conceived it. You planned it. You told me what to do, and I did it. It's done. I want you to see it." He grabbed Humphreys by both shoulders and pulled him into a sitting position.

Humphreys swore violently.

Frazer paid no attention. He had to exert himself hugely to force the big captain to his feet, then to pull his reluctant arm around his neck.

Humphreys continued his profane protest as they shuffled out of the tent and through the trees. It was not until they reached the beach that the magic of the night worked its spell. Humphreys shut up. His eyes explored the construction's shadowy details while he struggled to calm his labored breathing.

"Well," said Frazer.

The surf crackled.

Humphreys' breathing was silent. His nostrils flared. "My part's done," he mumbled. He removed his arm from around Frazer's neck.

Frazer faced him. "What is it, Oswald? I mean, honestly. What makes you tick? I'd like to know, really. I know what you think of me. I'd known it before you told me. But . . . I mean, can't you let bygones be bygones? Sure, I'm a fraud . . . a fake. But I've learned something . . . a lot of things about myself. I should never have taken this lot on. You think I'm not good enough? Or maybe too good? Maybe you resent—"

317

"It's none of your business," growled Humphreys.

Frazer paused. "I know this'll bowl you over, but . . . well, I'd like . . . to be your friend."

Humphreys peered at him with beetle-browed incredulity.

"Every man has to have a friend," continued Frazer. "Especially the likes of you and me. It's a toss-up, did you know, between you and me?"

"What are you talking about?"

"As to whom they dislike the most—maybe hate."

Humphreys' eyes glinted. "Hate can bring out the most in a man!" he blurted—then suddenly became silent.

Frazer looked long out onto the lake. "Somebody must have done you a frightful wrong once, Oswald."

"Oh, shut up, for Christ's sake."

Frazer persisted. "I wonder if it's hate . . . or self-pity, Oswald?"

"By God, Frazer, you wouldn't talk that way to me if—" He looked down at his bandaged chest and dangling leg.

"Course not," admitted Frazer freely. "You'd knock my block off. Yes, now that I give it a little thought, it's probably self-pity . . . the same sort of thing you're wallowing in now. I suppose you blame me for your accident, too. I mean, if I hadn't thought this whole thing up, you'd never've been in Africa in the first place. Sounds very logical, doesn't it? But why stop there? You wouldn't be in this mess if you'd never been born in the first place."

Humphreys swung feebly at Frazer's face. The effort pulled on his wound. He moaned with sudden pain.

Frazer stepped back easily. "Ah, so we're touching the nerve, eh? Self-pity. The hate that comes from self-pity." His tone erased its sarcasm. "Do you want to talk about it, Oswald?"

Humphreys bore his pain in silence with bent head.

"All right, man. It's your own business," said Frazer. "And as you said, your part's done." He looked out at the construction. "Beautifully done. . . . You know what night it is? Christmas Eve." He glanced at his watch. "Correction. It's Christmas Day. I've a present for you."

Humphreys raised his head.

"I think you've spunk enough to make it back to the tent under your own steam, Oswald. Good night."

On Christmas morning Frazer stopped by the Belgian compound at Albertville to talk to Commandant Fèvreaux.

"Merry Christmas, Commander Frazer," welcomed Fèvreaux warmly. "This is a pleasant surprise. I don't think I have had this honor since you arrived."

"I'm afraid we've been quite busy," apologized Frazer.

"Ah, yes." The Belgian nodded. "Your precious boats." He wondered why the visit. "More natives, perhaps, my commander?"

"No, not natives. The job's about done."

Fèvreaux frowned. "You mean—"

"Yes, we're ready," declared Frazer positively. He had purposely avoided Fèvreaux not only because he had had neither the mood nor the time for socializing, but because he had sensed the other's resentment at their first meeting. After the platitudes and pleasantries of their first meeting, Fèvreaux's manner had been one of "so the English are going to show us lazy Belgians how it's done," but he had too much sophistication to say it directly.

The Belgian produced a bottle and two glasses. "First we shall drink to your success, *mon ami*." He popped the cork. "And then we shall send the good news to your Admiralty."

"No!"

Fèvreaux put down the bottle. "Commander," he admonished. "It is high time *I* communicated with *my* superiors. I cannot go on keeping them in ignorance of your presence here."

"Commandant, I have—"

"I must remind you, Frazer, I am in command here. Antwerp expects my weekly messages to keep them fully informed of *everything* under my jurisdiction. . . . And André will be taken care of for his omissions."

"Listen, Fèvreaux, I have already explained that to you. Zimmer monitors many of your transmissions. You told me so yourself.

319

Probably André's too. I told him not to signal you. I haven't come this far to hand to Zimmer on a plate what he'd give a battleship to find out. André understood that. Can't you?"

"We Belgians are not idiots," commented Fèvreaux. "We do use code."

"And even Belgian codes can be broken," interjected Frazer.

Fèvreaux shook his head in puzzlement. "I cannot understand," he muttered.

"What can't you understand, Commandant?"

"You English—so correct about rules and regulations." He laughed dryly and shook his head again. "I mean, isn't it simply good manners to let them know where you are . . . how you are doing?"

"My superiors will be in touch with me when they wish to, Commandant," said Frazer curtly. "In the meantime I expect the co-operation promised to us by the Belgian ambassador in London. Isn't it simply good manners to honor the promises of a superior?"

Fèvreaux poured two brandies. "Come, Commander Frazer," he said placatingly, "we are supposed to be fighting Germany—not each other." He slid a drink across his desktop.

"Not on duty, thanks," said Frazer stiffly.

Fèvreaux shrugged and downed his drink. "What is it you wish?"

"To talk to the prisoner."

Fèvreaux downed the other glass, carefully corked the bottle and stowed it away in a bottom desk drawer. "At your service, Commander," he said resignedly. "Follow me."

He followed Fèvreaux down a set of winding stone steps into the fort's musty cellar. The daylight seeped in through tiny barred windows, revealing a row of cells. Two Belgian askaris stood guard outside one cell.

"It depresses me to come down here," complained Fèvreaux sensitively. "You wish me to—"

"I'll manage," interrupted Frazer.

Fèvreaux turned hastily and climbed the steps. "If there's anything, Commander—" he called from the landing; then he ordered the guards to open Rosenthal's cell.

Rosenthal was lying stretched out on a cot. When Frazer entered, he sprang to his feet and snapped to attention.

"As you were," said Frazer.

Rosenthal relaxed.

Frazer sat down on the edge of the cot. He invited the young German to sit down.

"I prefer to stand, sir," said Rosenthal correctly.

"As you wish," assented Frazer. He looked at his young captive. "You being treated all right?"

"I have no complaints, sir."

"Good. Where are you from, Rosenthal?"

"You must know, sir, all I can give you is my name—"

"Not that. In Germany, I mean."

"München, sir."

"That's the south, isn't it?"

"Yes, sir."

"I hear it's very beautiful. This time of year especially."

"It is, sir."

"Fine skiing, too."

"Yes, sir."

"It may be some time before you see it all again."

"That will make it all the more beautiful when I do see it, sir."

"True, true," said Frazer, pausing. Then he asked casually, "You know what we're up to, of course?"

Rosenthal said nothing.

Frazer began to relate some of Naval Africa Expedition's exploits in the bush.

The young German listened. He seemed to grow more at ease. "You are courageous and daring men," he said simply.

"No more so than your Commander Zimmer—and young Odebrecht."

"It's a pleasure to serve with them," said Rosenthal warmly.

"Then you *are* from Kigoma," said Frazer positively.

Rosenthal remained silent.

"You speak excellent English," observed Frazer. "Whereabouts in England did you go to school?"

"The commander is observant. Harrow, sir."

321

"Ummm," said Frazer, acting suitably impressed. "Isn't it a little . . . eh, difficult for you? Harrow and all that? Knowing us so well, I mean?"

"The English I admire and respect, sir," admitted Rosenthal. "That is why victory shall be so sweet—to defeat an enemy admired and respected is the measure of true success."

Frazer stood up and began pacing the small cell. "Rosenthal, you've seen what we have—two fast gunboats. You're a sailor. You know the value of speed and surprise. Even with *Kingani, Pangani, Gotson, Wissman* and the rest, we have speed and surprise." He stopped pacing and faced the German. "I know what you're thinking: What good are speed and surprise against the help from *Königsberg*? Right?"

"*Königsberg*, Herr Commander?" repeated Rosenthal naïvely.

"Come, now, Rosenthal," said Frazer curtly. "Your serial number which you so readily gave me is that of an officer of the Regular Navy. That means originally you're either from *Möwe* or *Königsberg*. I say *Königsberg*. . . . Tell me, Rosenthal, what's Commander Zimmer done with those 4.1-inch pieces? *Kingani* isn't mounting one. Probably not *Pangani*. *Wissman*? Hardly. She's too frail. That leaves *Gotson*. . . ." He sought to impress Rosenthal with how much he already knew, hoping the young officer would feel further resistance to interrogation was pointless; but Rosenthal remained adamant. He tried a new tack. "*Kingani*'s been by two or three times, making a damned nuisance of himself—Odebrecht, I mean." He didn't know; he was guessing. "How much does he know?"

"All he needs to know," said Rosenthal smugly. "Now your advantage is speed, only."

"If that's the case, why did you have to bother to pay us a visit?"

Rosenthal thought for a moment. "You saw the grenades. I was going to destroy your two boats."

"That sounds logical," conceded Frazer. "So we just have speed . . . and *Gotson* has her 4.1-incher."

"I didn't say that," shot Rosenthal.

"You being treated all right here?" inquired Frazer, suddenly changing the subject.

"I didn't say that!" repeated Rosenthal angrily.

Frazer smiled at him. "No, Rosenthal, you didn't." With the young German's emphatic denial, he was sure that the 4.1-inch gun *was* on *Gotson*. His original intelligence estimate had always indicated this, but it had been made almost a year previously. And he had to know where the other 4.1-incher was. Or was it other*s?* Was it—were they—part of the Kigoma harbor defenses? The 4.1s were the key. He had to know. He couldn't afford to guess. "Well," he said finally, "I won't bother you any more." He rose and motioned for the guard to open the cell door. He clanged it behind him and turned to Rosenthal. "Anything I can get you? Maybe a few books or something?"

Rosenthal shook his head.

Frazer turned away and began to climb the steps.

"Herr Commander!" called Rosenthal.

Frazer looked over his shoulder.

"Would it be possible to have some writing materials?"

"Letters, Rosenthal? War'll probably be over before they reach their destinations."

"A prisoner of war has that right," said Rosenthal stiffly.

"Righto," agreed Frazer. "I'll see what I can do. . . . Merry Christmas."

Several days later Frazer visited Rosenthal again. They chatted for an hour. The tone of interrogation had gone. They had been discussing the general naval war situation. The tenor was that of two who, even though they were enemies, shared a naval tradition which transcended their enmity. For Frazer the association with Rosenthal had been profitable, but he was still in ignorance of the dispositions of the 4.1s.

As Frazer rose to leave, Rosenthal jumped to his feet quickly and saluted. Frazer returned the salute. "Well," he said, "I'll be quite busy for the next week or so. I shan't be stopping in for a while. A happy New Year."

"A happy New Year to you, sir," said Rosenthal. As the cell door clanged shut, he remembered something. "Sir, these letters." He extended four envelopes. The flaps had been sealed, but Rosenthal had slit them along the edge to reopen them. "I forgot," he apologized. "You'll probably want to look these over."

Frazer took them and looked at the addresses. "Frau Rosenthal . . . Fräulein Haas . . . Commander Zimmer . . . Leutnant Odebrecht." He held up the letters addressed to the two officers. "These," he said, "will take the longest. To Rhodesia, I suppose, then via Portuguese East Africa. Too bad," he added whimsically. "Otherwise we could just row 'em across ourselves. Cheerio, Rosenthal." He bounded up the stone steps.

Rosenthal called from below. "Sir!"

Frazer turned on the top step. "Yes?"

"I'm afraid I'm getting a little scruffy, as we used to say at Harrow, sir." He held up a bundle of dirty clothing.

"Toss it up!"

Rosenthal squeezed the roll between the cell-door bars to the sentry.

"*Njo hapa,*" Frazer called to the native.

The native quickly climbed the steps, and the bundle of laundry changed hands. "I'll get these off right away," called Frazer, holding up the letters.

"Thank you, sir," replied Rosenthal. He paused, then added, "And may the best man win."

"The best man always wins," said Frazer. And the cellar door boomed behind him.

That night after dinner Frazer told the orderly to steam open the sealed flaps on the four letters.

"Excuse me, sir," said the orderly, pointing to the ragged slits, "but they are open."

"I know," said Frazer. "Just do as I say."

"Right, sir," said the orderly as he walked toward the mess, shaking his head.

"What's up, sir?" inquired Dodkins.

Frazer told the three officers of his talks with Rosenthal.

The orderly returned and handed him the letters.

"Just as I expected," said Frazer. "I'd have been disappointed if he hadn't."

"Hadn't what, sir?" asked Bannister.

Frazer passed around the letters. On the envelopes where the flaps and the body of the envelope came together there was writing, now slightly smudged from the steam.

"Can you make it out, sir?" asked Dodkins.

Frazer shook his head. "You, Magarity?"

The marine engineer examined all four letters. He seemed to think the same message was written on each envelope.

"What he's done is send the same message to all four," explained Frazer, "assuming at least one'll get through."

"How's What's-her-name," asked Bannister, looking at one of the letters, "Fräulein Haas, to know she's to steam the flap? How are any of 'em?"

Dodkins said, "Maybe some code instructions in the letter."

Magarity asked, "What's the message, sir?"

Frazer withdrew his pipe thoughtfully. "It doesn't really matter. I know what he's trying to do. He knows what we're up to. I told him quite a few things about what we were up to, hoping to swap them for some info on the 4.1's."

"Wasn't that a bit risky, sir?" queried Magarity. "After all, he's still a Hun."

"No, Magarity. Why? It would've been if he had a way of getting it to Zimmer—which he hasn't any more." Frazer held up the letters, then minutely examined the fine writing on the gummed surfaces. He nodded. "A worthwhile risk. He's got the specs on *Mimi* and *Toutou* here . . . armament. Ah, he tells Zimmer we know about *Gotson's* 4.1."

"Wizard, sir," crowed Bannister. "At last we know what *Gotson's* mounting."

Before he dismissed them, Frazer ordered Bannister to put Rosenthal's letters in fresh envelopes and promptly dispatch them.

The following morning the orderly dropped Rosenthal's laundry off at the native laundry in Albertville. "Don't get it mixed up with the other stuff," he warned them. "It belongs to that Jerry we copped."

The headman of the laundry was a native who had been ed-

325

ucated in a German missionary school. Like everyone in Albertville, he had heard about the prisoner. Unlike everyone else, however, he had a special interest in the German. The headman was one link in an intelligence chain which began in Albertville and ran north to an isolated point on the lake coast, then by boat across the water to Kigoma—when the weather was good. He had been chosen for his intelligence, and because he spoke both German and French.

At least the dossier on him at Kigoma had indicated this, Rosenthal had recalled; and when he etched the complete disposition of the British forces on the inside of his dirty underwear, he had prayed that the dossier entry had been made in good faith.

Had he been able to see north through the fine night twenty-four hours later to an isolated coastal inlet, his rest in the damp cell would have been a less fretful one. There three natives strained as they slid an awkward dugout canoe across the soft sand onto the smooth lake glass. One hugged a small sack close to his chest as he stepped into the prow of the canoe. The others pushed strongly. The canoe broke loose from the clinging sand and floated free. Nimbly they climbed in and paddled eastward.

26

It was Sunday—again, the start of another dragging week of watch and wait.

Frazer stepped out of the tent, followed by the three officers. He saluted and nodded to the sergeant.

"Stand at . . . *ease!*" barked Smith.

A single crunch of shodded heels in the gravel.

"Stand . . . *easy!*"

Frazer fussed with the fluttering pages of his Church of England Book of Common Prayer. "You may sit."

"We are gathered here today," he told them, "to give thanks to God Almighty for his safe deliverance of us to this place, and to ask Him for his further protection in what lies ahead.

"Here we pray many thousands of miles from our homes and loved ones. We are but a handful compared to the millions who are locked in mortal combat in France and other parts of the world, but we are soldiers and sailors in the service of the King, and we do our duty. What that duty consists of is not our concern; merely that it is our duty. That should be our appetite; the food for our souls.

"We have come on a long and arduous journey together. The battle is about to be joined. Whatever has happened in the in-

327

terim should be wiped from the mind. It is immaterial and ir-
relevant. What is material, what is relevant, is that *Mimi* and
Toutou are ready to do battle."

Frazer paused to observe his flock. He caught sight of a Belgian
officer whispering excitedly in Dodkins' ear. "What is it, Dodkins?"

The young subaltern jumped to his feet and quickly crossed to
the commander. The two conversed earnestly for several seconds;
then Frazer told Dodkins to return to his place.

Dodkins looked confused.

"Men," said Frazer, "I've just been informed that the Mtoa
lookout reports *Kingani* on her way south into Tembwe Bay."

A raucous roar went up from the assembly. "Wot are we waitin'
for?" shouted one of the sailors.

"Let's nab the bastard!" roared another.

The men scuffled to their feet.

"As you were!" commanded Frazer. He glared. "I didn't give
the order to fall out!"

The men crumpled dutifully.

Frazer returned to his prayer book. "The first part of Psalm
Eleven."

> In the Lord put I my trust; how say ye then to my soul, that she
> should flee as a bird unto the hill?
>
> For lo, the ungodly bend their bow, and make ready their ar-
> rows within the quiver, that they may privily shoot at them which
> are true of heart.
>
> For the foundations will be cast down: and what hath the
> righteous done?

He looked up from the prayer book. "Stokes," he shouted in the
rising wind, "would you like to choose the first hymn?"

Stokes, bareheaded, on one knee in the front row, could hardly
contain his impatience. "'Ow about 'Now the Laborer's Work is
O'er,' sir?" he said meekly.

Above the whine of the wind the men's impatience rumbled.

When the hymn was over, they donned their topees.

"Psalm 108," Frazer continued resolutely, "the first part."

Furtively the men removed their topees.

328

O God, my heart is ready, my heart is ready; I will sing, and give praise with the best member that I have.

Awake, thou lute and harp; I myself will awake right early.

I will give thanks unto thee O Lord, among the people; I will sing praises unto thee among the nations.

For thy mercy is greater than the heavens, and thy truth reacheth unto the clouds.

Set up thyself, O God, above the heavens, and thy glory above all the earth;

That thy beloved may be delivered: let thy right hand save them, and hear thou me.

He glanced up at the men, dutifully devout with bare heads bent. "Psalm 140, verses four to seven."

Keep me, O Lord, from the hands of the ungodly; preserve me from wicked men, who are purposed to overthrow my goings.

The proud have laid a snare for me, and spread a net abroad with cords; yea, and set traps in my way.

I said unto the Lord, Thou art my God, hear the voice of my prayers, O Lord . . .

In a loud, clear voice he orated the concluding lines:

O Lord God, thou strength of my health; thou hast covered my head in the day of battle.

The men timorously raised their heads.

"Stand!" shouted Frazer.

They rose obediently.

They began the hymn with the deference accorded a choir master by his choirboys, but by the middle of the second verse the militancy of the theme had caught their anticipation of the impending action. Lustily they ended it and with defiance at the wind blowing the words back into their faces.

Frazer nodded to Stokes.

"*Action stations!*" roared the old sailor.

329

27

Fat with fuel, laden with ammunition, *Mimi* and *Toutou* jar on the troughs as they scud after their quarry.

Up forward in *Mimi* Frazer crouches. He steadies himself with one hand on the taffrail; the other grips a large megaphone. The whitecaps burst. The wind snatches the spray and flings it into his face.

Stokes crouches on hands and knees on the foredeck. His gnarled, practiced fingers pick at the knots of the 3-pounder's tarpaulin.

Dodkins' knuckles blanch on the helm. He stares ahead, honed to a keen excitement for his first action since Channel duty a life ago.

A naval rating nervously clicks the bolt on the .303 Maxim machine gun in the stern. Two others hug rounds of 3-pounder common and lyddite shell, poised for the order.

Mimi rushes eastward, her twin 100-horsepower Thornycroft Diesels thrumming richly.

All eyes search the north.

Mimi bucks viciously.

"Damn lucky if you can load in this muck, let alone fire, Stokes," megaphones Frazer.

Stokes, his khaki shirt and shorts sodden, flashes a grin. "I've 'ad worse, sir," he bellows back. "Get me within range, an' I'll nail 'er right proper, I will."

"Any sign of her, sir?" shouts Dodkins, searching the horizon.

Frazer points north-northeast. The south arm of Tembwe Bay bulges out into the lake several miles from them. "She ought to clear the headland any moment," he shouts. Frazer's plan is elementary. He has borrowed it from the slim but profound little volume stuck inside his shirt: *Elements of Naval Tactics*, by Vice-Admiral Ian H. G. Frazer, RN—the same volume which has grown thumb-marked and dog-eared over the months of the trek and been the object of his candlelight concentrations. The idea: Intercept the enemy "by crossing his T"; in other words, he will permit *Kingani* to proceed on her southerly course, then dart in from the west at her dead amidships. This tactic will exploit *Mimi*'s strength and *Kingani*'s weakness. *Mimi*'s 3-pounder can only be fired dead ahead: Fire to right or left can capsize her and splay her fragile deck timbers. *Kingani* can't bring her dangerous bow 6-pounder around to repel a beam attack: The weapon's traverse arc is limited to a few degrees by her funnels and deck hampers.

"Half speed," megaphones Frazer.

"Aye, aye, sir," responds Dodkins, guiding back the twin throttle levers.

Mimi's roar subsides. Without the stability lent by fast forward movement, she rocks wildly in the choppy swell.

"Don't want to overshoot," shouts Frazer, his hand shielding his eyes as he gazes to the north.

"There she blows, sir!" screams Dodkins above the howl of the wind.

Kingani has rounded the Tembwe Bay headland and cruises idly south on a course that will take her directly across *Mimi*'s bows.

"Quarter speed!"

"Aye, aye, sir."

Mimi pitches wildly. At times her prow is submerged in foam. The wind fills the gun tarpaulin like a sail and blows it over the side. The tightly packed-together 3-pounder shells can break loose and rip through the thin, three-eighths mahogany hull.

But apprehension loses to surprise: For ten bucking minutes they watch. *Kingani* steams by as serenely as if leading a naval review.

"The bloody idiots!" shouts Stokes. "They're actin' like they never seen us."

"Either that," shouts Dodkins, "or seeing us on their private little lake's thrown them into a blue funk."

Two miles away to the southeast *Toutou*, with Bannister at the helm and Crann on the 3-pounder, executes a prearranged maneuver. She now sweeps east across *Kingani's* course at full speed. In minutes she will arc north to cut in between *Kingani* and Kigoma. Her retreat will be cut off. *Mimi* will bore in on her amidships at full speed.

"Full speed ahead!"

"Bloody well aye, aye, sir," roars Dodkins exultantly, punching forward the twin levers.

The engine note whines upward, and *Mimi* surges forward. . . .

In seven minutes the range is down to 2,000 yards. Stokes feeds a round into the breech. The standard Hotchkiss mount has been sawed down to keep *Mimi* from being top-heavy. Stokes kneels to load. His leathery old face is shirred as he closes one eye to sight on target. "Sittin' bloody ducks," he whispers with incredulity.

Mimi bores onward. Her bow cleaves cleanly. Her engines hum a promise to the drenched crew. The engine's might is theirs. The stiff wind's rush inflates them full. Their bowels quiver.

Lieutenant Horn stands in *Kingani's* wheelhouse beside the helmsman. His legs brace against the bucking deck. His eyes peer through the spray-washed glass at the rolling, tufted wave tops; but his thoughts are with the Fatherland. When will it be over and done with? When can I go home again? Once his heart longed for adventure in Germany's wondrous African empire. Then he was a boy; now he is man, and Lake Tanganyika is no more romantic than his native Baltic—so vast, so temperamental and so German is it.

"Herr Commander!" shouts the lookout. "Craft to starboard!"

"*Ja!*" Horn shouts back, glancing eastward to his right. He sees the craft. Stupid Belgians. Don't they know enough to stay on dry land during foul weather? They must really be feeling the pinch to be out fishing today. But, then, the Belgians would rather fish than fight any day.

Kingani steams south and past the sheltering bulge of Tembwe Bay, into open water, which buffets her heavily. Horn grasps a stanchion pipe and forces his shoulders into the corner of the wheelhouse bulkhead; but his thoughts rescue him from the dull monotony of the wasteful patrol which Zimmer has sent him on. Ah, things were never dull on *Königsberg*. Yes, it was short while it lasted, but crammed with action and good-fellowship like that of Odebrecht and Rosenthal. He would never forget the night they sped up the Rufiji and eluded the angry English Navy. Odebrecht turned to him and—

"Herr Commander! Another craft! Ten degrees off the port bow!"

Horn starts—and stares. Crazy Belgians: fishing out in *open* water? He raises his binoculars. He focuses toward the southeast. He jerks around and focuses westward. "*Donnerwetter!*" His brow creases with incredulity. He freezes. "*Achtung!* Hard to port!" *Kingani* wheels over violently. He snatches at the voice pipe. "Action stations! Action stations! Full speed!" He bursts from the wheelhouse out onto the deck. "Action stations!" he shouts shrilly into the wind.

The befuddled crew scramble awkwardly along the heaving deck to their stations: the bow 6-pounder and the stern 1½-inch Hotchkiss pom-pom. Their faces are haggard with a sudden nausea; their out-of-practice fingers pick hard at the old tarpaulin knots.

Horn stumbles in on top of the 6-pounder crew, nervous with the delay. He points toward the southeast. "Fire!"

The azimuth and elevation screw wheels are red with the rust of months of complacence. The gun mount squeals and scrapes as if it is loath to kill. Off goes the first round. *Kingani* staggers, forgetting the proper reflex, then recovers as the cannonade splutters from the 6-pounder's big muzzle.

Horn's heart pounds—he sees the craft from the west bear into *Kingani's* beam. "Cease fire! New target!" he roars hoarsely, stabbing the acrid blue smoke in the direction of the Belgian shore.

The 6-pounder grinds agonizingly around the 135 degrees.

Horn is about to rap out the fire order when he quails. *"Gott im Himmel!"* If the gun goes off, it will send its fat, short projectile crashing into *Kingani's* deck hampers! *"Nein!"* he screams. "As you were! First target again!"

The frightened, sweating crew crank the rusty piece around to bear on the southeastern target again, and open up.

Horn crawls aft to the Hotchkiss in the stern. *Kingani* now holds a course so that the Hotchkiss pom-pom can bear on the craft churning in from the west. "Fire!" he shouts.

Both guns are now belching metal . . . but the two craft race in like hounds on a hare.

"Herr Commander! Ammunition running low!"

Frazer blows spray from his binoculars. He focuses on *Toutou,* fattening in the lenses. "Bannister's changed course! Coming north now!"

Kingani's straddled: *Mimi's* closing in from the west, *Toutou* from the southeast. No retreat for her to Kigoma!

"Blimey!" curses Stokes.

Kingani heels around in a tight turn, presenting her stern. The sudden spew of froth there means the German commander has clanged "full speed ahead" to his engine room.

"You may open fire, Stokes," megaphones Frazer calmly. "Common shell. One per minute for the time being."

The old petty officer's eye is bonded to the rubber-lined ring sight. He snaps the lanyard.

Mimi shudders under the compact thunder.

All eyes squint at the narrowed target.

Stokes's round smashes into *Kingani's* afterdeck. On her aft gun the shield shreds. Some of the men it failed writhe on the afterdeck. Others crawl to cover. Their bow 6-pounder belches a plume of dirty smoke—southeastward; they're firing at *Toutou,* now knifing in from the quarter.

The wind is behind *Toutou.* She is running with the sea. She stabs through the foamed eruptions of the German's near misses. But Bannister cannot open up until he is within range.

Frazer swings his binoculars to read the message semaphored by *Toutou's* signalman: "Save a bit of her for us." He swings them round onto *Kingani* again.

The target broadens as Kingani angles northeast.

"She's making a run for it, sir!" warns Dodkins.

"That's what she thinks," shoots Frazer.

"Sir!" shouts the signalman. "*Toutou* signals 'She's all yours.' "

Frazer thinks fast. It's now between the two of them. Because *Mimi* can fire only in the direction in which she's traveling, Stokes's rounds, hitting *Kingani* on her new northeasterly course, will glance off her. He must get into position to again "cross the T" so Stokes can pump shells square into her fat beam. He'll have to chase *Kingani* on a parallel course, draw ahead of her, then arc around. He must have more speed—or time—to do it. He glances at the engine levers. Is that it, Dodkins?"

" 'Fraid so, sir!"

Frazer must have more speed—somehow. "Stokes!"

"Sir?"

"How many cracks do you need to finish her off?"

"A dozen, sir."

"Dodkins, over the side with all but a dozen rounds!"

The young sublieutenant balks. "But, sir!"

"But nothing! An extra five knots are better right now than fifty rounds!"

Over goes the precious ammunition.

Mimi greases forward, her engine note whining upward. Gradually the angry, whitecapped distance narrows. *Mimi* draws ahead, less than 1,500 yards from her quarry.

"Now, Dodkins!"

The sublieutenant spins the helm. *Mimi* eases over in a wide arc toward *Kingani*.

"Fire at will!"

"Aye, aye, sir," acknowledges Stokes. Now the waves squarely buffet *Mimi's* starboard side. She rocks dangerously. Water swills over her meager freeboard. The crew stands shin-deep in it.

Stokes clings to the 3-pounder. He snaps the lanyard. *Mimi* shudders. The shell misses.

The 6-pounder in *Kingani's* bow swivels.

Stokes lies spread-eagled on the fo'c'sle. His big hands caress the azimuth and elevation wheels. Through the eyepiece he looks right up the 6-pounder's muzzle. He snaps the lanyard as a huge wave hits them broadside. A flat sheet of water slaps his shoulders.

Dodkins looks at his feet. They are under a foot of water. "We can't keep this lot up much longer, sir," he shouts above the din.

"Show a leg, Stokes!" exhorts Frazer.

Ahead the water explodes in a gigantic spout. *Kingani's* big 6-pounder has cut loose. Again *Mimi* is lashed by water.

"Hold 'er steady!" pleads Stokes. He squirms on his slippery perch. "Take my 'Arry, would you? You bastard." He yanks the lanyard.

His high-explosive shell bursts with an orange flame in *Kingani's* wheelhouse. . . . When the smoke clears, the upper-deck silhouette resembles bottom teeth with several missing.

Abruptly *Kingani* yaws.

"We got her!" yells Dodkins.

"Damn fine shooting," megaphones Frazer. "You got the helmsman."

Again the sea ahead of *Mimi* heaves in an enormous geyser of sound and spray.

"Get the bloody gun, Stokes!" megaphones Frazer. "The next'll be in our laps."

" 'Ere's another, 'Arry lad." Stokes jerks the cord. The shot misses. So does the next . . . and the next . . . and the one after that.

A yard from *Mimi's* starboard side another enemy shell ruptures the water. The fragile little craft heaves over on her port side.

Stokes dangles from the breech on his 3-pounder. The others are dashed against the inside port gunwale. The unguided helm spokes spin blurrily. Bilgewater settles aft in the port side. *Mimi's* prow cants skyward. Her flat keel slows her like a huge paddle. She shudders down to half knots.

Frazer clambers onto the fo'c'sle beside Stokes. The prow drops a few degrees. "Bail!" he roars. "For God's sake, bail!"

They bail frenetically.

Kingani is churning off to safety.

"We're going to lose her!" shrieks Dodkins. He secures the helm with a swing clamp. He grabs a bucket. Wildly he bails.

"Never mind that!" screams Frazer. The wind blows the words down his throat.

Dodkins doesn't hear.

"*Never mind that!*"

Still Dodkins bails.

Frazer slithers down off the fo'c'sle. He snatches back the swing clamp. He rams the twin levers forward.

Mimi staggers. The three bailers are kicked flat on their backs. The eager craft cleaves the spout of another enemy near miss. Solid panes of water fracture on their bodies.

Frazer embraces the helm. His body is rigid. His legs are spread apart. His purpose is unyielding.

Gulping fuel, *Mimi* lunges for the enemy's belly.

Through the eyepiece Stokes reads death's fear on the magnified faces of the enemy gun crew. He snaps the string. A second later the sight is jagged with stabs of orange color.

"They're hauling down the flag, sir!" shouts Dodkins.

Frazer turns to the youth at his side. "Take over. Half speed."

Aft on the wallowing *Kingani* the German tricolor flutters down the jackstaff. Figures amidships jump over the side. . . .

Frazer circled the battered German vessel, picking up survivors. It took the three escort craft five minutes to arrive. While *Netta* covered her with her two machine guns from a cable's length off,

Dix Tonnes tried to put her party of British ratings aboard. In the high water the two vessels hammered each other repeatedly: The ratings hopped from one heaving deck to the other. Aboard *Kingani* a line snaked out to *Mimi*. Stokes quickly roped it into the hawsehole and heaved, pulling *Mimi* snugly against the beam of the captured vessel.

Frazer almost lost his balance on *Mimi's* fo'c'sle. Several hands extended down from *Kingani* and pulled him aboard. As his foot cleared *Mimi's* fo'c'sle, her thin hull crunched.

"We're shipping water, sir!" shouted Dodkins.

"How bad?"

"Bad enough so's I can't tow you back, sir."

"Never mind, Dodkins. *Toutou's* coming alongside." He waved him away. "Take her back. Bannister can tow me in."

"Aye, aye, sir," Dodkins acknowledged glumly.

The boarding party stood guard over the German prisoners huddled on *Kingani's* shredded afterdeck. Frazer looked them over. He noticed the absence of officers. "Where is your commander?" he demanded in German of two whites, a chief engineer and a helmsman.

They shook their heads.

"Did you search her?" Frazer demanded of the boarding party NCO.

"Yes, sir," responded the seaman. "A warrant officer and a petty officer dead, sir. And one native. And one—a set of . . . a pair of . . ."

"Pair of what?"

The seaman gulped. "Legs, sir."

"Legs?"

"From here down, sir," said the seaman, pointing to his belly.

Frazer turned to the German warrant officer. "Where is your chief officer?"

"I don't know," said the German.

Frazer turned to the seaman. "Towline fast?"

"Yes, sir."

Frazer cupped his hands to his mouth. "Bannister! Prepare to tow as soon as your line's fast."

He stood astride the deck of the enemy vessel *he* had just captured. He was overcome with a magnificent sense of power, inflated with a sudden reality of accomplishment not experienced before. He thought of the mildewed years in musty Admiralty halls, of all the years he might have spent as he was spending that ineffable moment; of an existence at half-mast instead of one snapping briskly at the top of the jack staff, whipping in the breeze of challenge.

"Survivor off the starboard bow!"

All eyes followed the rating's pointing finger. A dark shape tossed on the churning lake several yards away.

Frazer crossed to the edge of the foredeck.

"Shall I come about and pick him up, sir?" shouted Bannister from *Toutou.*

"Stand fast," Frazer shouted back. "He's washing in on us."

The black shape bobbed closer and closer. Soon it thudded sickeningly against *Kingani's* wooden hull.

"He's had his," observed the rating, "otherwise he'd be shouting his ruddy head off for help." He leaned out over the side and peered down. "Looks like a Jerry officer."

"Proper waterlogged he is, too," said his companion. "Here's your gaff." He handed his friend a long boathook. "Hold on, chum. I'll get some help."

"Never mind," called the first rating. "We can manage."

"You out of your bloody mind?" queried the second rating. "Two of us gaff him out and him soaking wet? Don't make me—"

"Laugh? Not on your life, chum," interjected the first rating. He hooked his gaff into the survivor's uniform.

The second rating did likewise.

Together they carefully gaffed the survivor aboard.

Frazer's sense of magnificent and overpowering vindication evaporated. It was like a kick in the groin—the initial shock . . . the dread of pain impending.

From head to the end of his bloody torso the German was only two feet long.

Frazer vomited into the wind.

28

Twenty-four hours later, Lieutenant Commander Zimmer paced the bare floor of his headquarters. He was scowling as he addressed the junior officers of the Möwe Detachment. "*Wo ist* Kingani?" he demanded for the third time. "When will she return? What has happened?"

His subordinates shifted uneasily on their squeaky wooden benches.

One suggested that she might have foundered in the storm.

Zimmer retorted that it had been rough, but not that rough.

A fire at sea, perhaps, submitted another.

Zimmer scoffed.

Or maybe mechanical trouble, said someone else.

Again Zimmer scoffed. If there had been a fire or engine trouble, he asserted, the crew would have taken to the boats and, even with the storm, some of them would have reached shore.

Odebrecht respectfully took issue with the likelihood that *Kingani's* crew could have made landfall under storm conditions, especially since the wind had been a southwesterly, which would have driven survivors onto the enemy shore.

Zimmer harrumphed. It was the Belgian gunners, he declared,

340

pure and simple. In weeks of scouting along the Belgian coast without mishap *Kingani* had become careless and complacent. The enemy coastal artillery had been waiting for just the right moment. Sometime during the past twenty-four hours it had come. But *Kingani* might still be afloat and adrift, part of her crew aboard, the rest in lifeboats.

Thus they would search for her.

Odebrecht stood up. "When do you wish me to go?"

"Not you," said Zimmer.

Pangani slipped her moorings that night. Under the tense commands of her cautious young commander she steamed swiftly westward. . . .

The gale had blown itself out. The ferment of the lake survived only as a broad expanse of heaving water.

Dawn found *Pangani* north of Albertville, following the coastline south at reduced speed a mile off the Belgian shore, searching for possible survivors of her sister ship. They were poaching in the enemy's backyard, invading waters which they had never before navigated.

A sailor starboard forward took soundings every minute as the squat gunboat nosed uneasily into the shallow lagoons and inlets choked with weeds and coarse-leaved papyrus. The crew stood at action stations. The bow 6-pounder and the 1½-incher aft were loaded. Belowdecks, both stokers stood ready.

The German helmsman skillfully nosed her into the contour of the fifth inlet of the morning. As he eased her out along the headland and into the arc of a wide lagoon, the lookout shouted, "*Achtung!*" Dead ahead a slim, gray motorboat tugged restlessly on a bowline tied to an aged, weather-beaten jetty.

The commander shrilled a command.

The 6-pounder swiveled and coughed a tongue of flame at the motorboat.

The commander yelled down the voice pipe for full pressure. "*Gott im Himmel!*" he swore. "Gunboats!" His mind spun. If he stood and fought, he might lose. If he ran, Zimmer would have the answer to the riddle of *Kingani*. Only one small gunboat! But what if he lost? Zimmer must know. He fired an order at his helmsman. *Pangani* heeled about in a violent turn to seaward.

The deafening thunder of a hundred locomotives screeching to a halt ground through *Pangani's* hull. Every soul aboard slammed against the deck. She was foundering on an underwater sandbar, water already seeping through buckled seams into her ruptured hull.

At the Mtoa lookout station ashore, the crew of the tiny *Vedette* doubled up in laughter, so that they could barely make themselves understood when they telegraphed Albertville.

Toutou raced north with Frazer aboard, Bannister at the helm. *Dix Tonnes* putted along in her wake with a boarding party. As they approached *Pangani*, *Toutou* fired over her bow. Something white was run up to her yardarm. Bannister throttled back and slowly circled the enemy vessel.

Dix Tonnes tossed a line up to them. They tied it fast. One by one the disgruntled Germans shinnied down the line and sullenly surrendered to the British ratings.

With *Dix Tonnes* en route for Albertville, *Toutou* stood off at point-blank range and shelled *Pangani* to a battered, splintered hulk.

A pall of bewilderment hung over Kigoma. Two ships and thirty men lost without a trace in three days; half the Möwe Detachment's squadron gone. Incredibly the indolent, decadent fun-loving Belgians had taken on the stature of contestants. Germany had been injured and insulted. Morale had slumped. Rumors seized upon doubt.

Nothing less than the destruction of Albertville would satisfy Zimmer. Nothing would be spared. Two companies of German marines under a junior officer would stay at Kigoma. Every other available man would be pressed into service to crew *Wissman*,

Gotson, Wami, the steam pinnace, assorted unarmed motorboats towing native dhows, and an infantry landing party.

A week later the only blank in Zimmer's methodically detailed battle plan was an up-to-date survey of Albertville's defenses and fortifications. Odebrecht volunteered. Zimmer accepted.

It was midnight. The attack would be mounted in twenty-four hours. The German flotilla fretted at anchor.

Odebrecht stood by *Wissman's* gangplank receiving Zimmer's last-minute briefing: He was to make his observations as soon after dawn as possible, then swiftly steam back to a rendezvous point halfway across the lake to await the arrival of the invasion flotilla. They swapped salutes.

The night soon swallowed Wissman's black bulk.

Zimmer went back to work on the rafts and the 22-pounders they would be floating into battle.

Dawn flushed the sky pink. There was no wind. The water lay still. *Wissman* had the lake to herself. Odebrecht held his clumsy, 70-foot-long wooden vessel on a course due south along the enemy coastline three miles offshore.

Wissman was rigged for action; but Odebrecht was under orders to avoid action. That would come.

The Lukuga estuary and Albertville solidified through the waning haze. The crew tensed. Above the throb of *Wissman's* turbine the sharp bark of a dog ashore stabbed their vigilance. Across the lens of Odebrecht's telescope ambled the magnified images of a Belgian shore patrol. He focused on the ribs of *Dhanis,* still under construction on the building slip. His lens moved off the slip, across the river and up the steep bank to the cliff line where the gray, rectangular bulk of Fort Albertville stood partly obscured among the trees.

At the edge of the cliff the sun glinted off long, extended spirals of barbed wire. Behind the wire entanglement the green-carpeted earth bosomed into gun emplacements from which poked the gaping muzzles of 22-pounder field artillery pieces.

Binoculars to his eyes, Odebrecht dictated tensely to a signalman. A lookout yelled, "Vessel off the port bow."

Odebrecht jerked around. He shielded his eyes against the naked sun. He could see nothing.

The lookout chattered a more precise compass bearing.

In seconds Odebrecht had her on his lens. He called to a senior NCO. "Look." He handed the man his telescope.

The NCO carefully focused the instrument. "*Kingani, Herr Leutnant!*" he shouted exuberantly.

Kingani hadn't foundered at all! Hadn't been destroyed at all! The fever blazed through the crew like fire in tall, dry grass. The deck erupted in wild cheering.

Odebrecht's heart leaped. He shouted a command. *Wissman* veered around on a heading toward *Kingani*. He would have words of welcome for her young commander—and a few of reprimand. But what a blessed relief: *Kingani's* rapid-firing 6-pounder would be there to level the defenses for the landing on the enemy shore. Through the telescope he examined the gun. He frowned. Maybe it was the haze, but . . .

After the rigid confines of *Toutou, Kingani* feels like an ocean liner to Frazer, Stokes and the sailors who man her. Her wide expanse of deck gives room to think; but at a six-knot maximum, it is like riding an elephant after a horse. And the bow is down with the three-odd tons of iron and ammo that is the Belgian 22-pounder fieldpiece they talked Commander Fèvreaux out of. The big spoked wheels are gone, and the nubs of the axle niche into slots cut in Humphreys' improvised timbered supports bolted to the deck. Like the 3-pounders on *Mimi* and *Toutou,* the 22-pounder shoots only dead-ahead.

Stokes is down on his hunkers. He snaps back the breechblock and sights down the inside of the open barrel. "Left a hair!" he shouts to the rating on the azimuth wheel. "Down . . . just a bit!" he shouts to the elevation wheel operator. "Spot on!" he shouts. " 'Old 'er right there, mates!" He continues to stare at the toy form of

Wissman bobbing around in the circle of the barrel. "Loverly grub," he says, patting the breechblock fondly. "Do your stuff, you nice big bugger." He rises and turns to admonish the two ratings holding between them a large 22-pounder shell. "Look slippy, you two, when the time comes!"

Frazer stands behind the gun, close to the wheelhouse. He watches *Wissman* intently through his binoculars. "Steady as she goes, helmsman!" he shouts. He lowers the binoculars and looks dubiously at the gun. "Wish we'd been able to test-fire her just once, Stokes."

"That makes two of us, sir," agrees Stokes.

"Hope Captain Humphreys knew what he was up to. What if she tears loose the first go?"

Stokes laughs dryly. "She'll recoil an' proper mash the lot of us agin the bleedin' wheelhouse, that's wot, sir."

Frazer rubs his mouth with the back of his hand. "Can't we maybe lash her down somehow?"

"Six thousand yards!" shouts a rating.

Stokes shrugs. "No time, sir."

Frazer raises his binoculars and watches *Wissman*—gliding toward them on a collision course.

"Fifty-five hundred yards!" warns the rating.

The ammo handlers poise.

Stokes squats and squints down the barrel.

"Five-two-five-oh!" shouts the rating.

"Five-two-five-oh!" repeats Frazer. "Steady as she goes, helmsman!" He adjusts the thumbscrew on his binoculars. "Stand by, Stokes!"

♒

"Something's wrong!" shouts Odebrecht. He scans *Kingani's* upperworks. His mouth dries. His tongue cleaves to the roof of his mouth. The flag on *Kingani* is the white ensign of the British Navy!

Kingani's bow explodes in flame.

Wissman's crew cowers as a shell whistles over the smokestack. Odebrecht chills. Two long, lean, close-to-the-water craft angle out from behind the approaching *Kingani*. They have been following in line to stay hidden from view.

Like the ripping of a dozen canvases *Wissman's* six-barreled 1½-inch revolving one-pounder Hotchkiss in the bow spews angry flame.

Another enemy shell whooshes overhead.

Odebrecht thanks God they can't get the range. By the sound of them one of those shells will be enough. He crouches down behind the gun shield. He estimates the range at 5,000 yards. It's hard to be sure. The lake surface is polished glass undulating to a gentle swell. That makes two targets—one real, the other reflection. He can't distinguish one from the other. He swears. Ahead of the target the water froths—the 1½-incher's cannonade is falling short. Tactically he's in an untenable position: the enemy can hit him, but he can't hit them. If he waits till they come within range, he'll probably be blown to bits in the meantime by the huge weapon. Now he's close enough to recognize—*Gott im Himmel!*—one of the 22-pounder coastal artillery pieces. If that doesn't do it, the two gunboats will. Where'd *they* come from? He scrutinizes them from stem to stern. No doubt about their capabilities. He remembers the invasion flotilla poised at Kigoma.

Zimmer must be warned!

He cups has hands to his mouth and bellows an order. Hard over goes the helm. *Wissman's* big, ungainly tiller flaps. She lurches into a turn she was never designed for. Odebrecht orders oil on the fires. The coal burner's funnel exudes a thick, dirty-black smoke. She surges toward Kigoma, impelled by three extra knots from the turbine.

Their superior speed widens the water between them and *Kingani*. Her 22-pounder projectiles no longer breeze through the rigging.

They're not out of danger. The two gunboats are tearing up his wake at thirteen knots. He speculates on the cannons in their bows. The craft are too fragile for anything heavier than a one-pounder ... 2,500 yards probably—same range and caliber as his bow and stern mounts. But since his are six-barreled revolving models—a six-to-one advantage—he's forced to shoot it out. Better still, swing

Wissman around 90 degrees athwart them. That'll bring *both* fore and aft weapons to bear on the enemy—a twelve-to-one advantage. The stern gunners crouch behind their gun shield. They wait for the range to drop to 2,600 yards—their maximum; then *Wissman* will come around.

The enemy gunboats skim along low in the water 3,200 yards away.

For three minutes that range holds fast.

Why don't they close in? wonders Odebrecht. What are they up to?

He cuts his own speed three knots. They should close in rapidly. . . . They don't. Their bow splash has fallen away—they've reduced speed too. Now he knows what they're up to!

A small-bore weapon cracks across the 3,200 yards—the water plumes 30 yards off *Wissman's* port side.

"Verdammte Engländer!" rips Odebrecht. They've a bigger weapon than a one-pounder!

They can bombard him at will. He can't return the fire until they're within 2,600 yards.

Another sharp crack—a crunch of orange flame on *Wissman's* deck—the bridge port side demolished. Two near misses. . . . Another direct hit—a hole as big as a suitcase above the waterline.

Frantically Odebrecht checks his position. He's close to the rendezvous point with the rest of the German flotilla. If only *Gotson* and her 4.1 were here. He prayerfully scans the eastern horizon for her upperworks. Nothing. Not a wisp of smoke. He shouts to the helmsman. *Wissman* heels around 90 degrees. . . . "Fire!"

On scud the two gunboats. . . . 2,800 yards . . . another hit amidships. 2,700 . . . "Fire!" yells Odebrecht.

The shiny barrels vomit fire. They fuse blue with the effort of purging their magazines.

A roar of elation—one gunboat's skewering off, engine spluttering.

But the other bears on.

"Rifles!" yells Odebrecht.

Mauser muzzles through the rails splutter a hail of fire.

More 22-pounder shells whoosh through the rigging. Odebrecht's

347

empty stomach shrivels. He's floated in his 90-degree-athwart position too long. *Kingani's* closed in again!

"Full speed ahead! Oil on the fires!" shouts Odebrecht. Again he prays for *Gotson*.

Wissman's turbine is sluggish to the stokers' urgings. Six knots . . . seven knots . . . they're pulling away from the monstrous 22-pounder . . . a boiling geyser of foam to port . . . another to starboard . . . eight knots . . . *Wissman's* frame vibrates . . . nine knots . . . *Wissman* shudders ominously. *BAAAAAAAAAAMMMMM.* . . . In the hot engine-room crampedness the whine of rendered iron, the anguished howl of sharded blood and bone.

Wissman stills.

"*Fire!*"

Wissman is wreathing in flames.

"Abandon ship!"

Stout timbers crackling to carbon . . .

Survivors jumping overboard.

Odebrecht can't believe it. His uniform hangs in shreds. His face is streaked with oil. He inhales the smell of burned flesh. He vomits. "Damned treacherous English!" The tears scour rivulets of clean skin down his cheeks.

He looks back once more. . . . He jumps.

Only a captain and a signalman were present in the War Room when a clerk hurried in with a fistful of ciphers. The captain fanned casually through them, slotting them in their respective pigeonholes. Halfway through he frowned—a cipher without a pigeonhole! He pinched his lip reflectively. "Signalman!"

"Sir?" said the youth.

"Hunt this one down for me, will you?"

"Very good, sir," said the signalman. He accepted the piece of paper and examined the message momentarily. He crossed to a shelf of dust-laden, cardboard-bound ring files. He pulled one out and noisily blew the dust off it. He brought it over to the captain. "Belongs in here, it does, sir."

"Hm," commented the captain, frowning. He studied the file intently, then reread the cipher. "Signalman, take this lot down to the ADNO's people. Ask them what we ought to do about it."

When the ADNO saw it, he was confused and asked, "Frazer? Must've been something Fisher had on." He, in turn, took it into the DNO's office.

The DNO mulled it over for some time. He was quite upset. While it was profoundly stirring to learn of Naval Africa Expedition's success during a period of repeated Allied reverses, it was equally embarrassing to have been entirely ignorant of its existence.

He took it up with the new First Lord. "I'm afraid we somehow missed it in the transition," he apologized weakly, "but now that they've done it, I was wondering just exactly . . ."

"Give it here," commanded the First Lord. "It's *good* news for a change. . . . That's all. If you need me, I'll be at the Palace."

Albertville boiled over with revelry. A Christmas kind of camaraderie and Belgian brandy diluted long-nurtured chauvinisms: Belgians and British alike, they were all brothers under the skin. The Hun was dead, and they were dancing at his funeral.

The Belgian mess swelled to the tumult of victory.

A soldier Highland-reeled his heavy shoes into the top of a stout timber table circled by a drunken audience clapping in flagrant disregard of the beat.

Against a doorpost a stupefied trio hung to one another for support as they brayed a bawdy parody on "Mademoiselle from Armentières."

In a corner a brace of British and Belgian officers mutually eulogized each other's countries. Fèvreaux, regal in ceremonial tricorn hat and sword dangling from his ornate belt, toasted England and her sons, his glass raised high.

Bannister affected suitable humility, then embarked on a paean to his hosts.

As he ascended to embarrassing peaks of oratory, Dodkins descended to floor level with a pair of scissors. . . .

The doorlatch rattled. Frazer and Humphreys entered.

Someone shouted, "Atten-*shun!*"

The din dribbled off. The glassy-eyed revelers laboriously hauled themselves upright, many canted dangerously off plumb.

"Gentlemen," announced Frazer solemnly, "I have just had word from London." He searched their faces.

A boot sole on the bare floor scuffed the silence.

"Captain Humphreys!"

Humphreys adjusted his crutch and produced a piece of paper. He cleared his throat roughly. "His Majesty the King desires to express his appreciation of the wonderful work carried out by his most remote expedition." He folded the message meticulously and pocketed it.

"God save the King!" intoned Frazer.

"God save the King!" chorused the company.

"Carry on!" said Frazer.

Stokes shouted, "Three cheers for Commander Frazer! 'Ip-'ip!"

"*HOOR-AAAAYYYYEEEE!*"

" 'Ip-'ip!"

"*HOOR-AAAAYYYYEEEE!*"

" 'Ip-'ip!"

"*HOOR-AAAAYYYYEEEE!*"

Self-consciously the revelers sought to resurrect the ribaldry.

Stokes and Smith interrupted the silence and crossed the floor to the two officers.

" 'Ow abaht a drink, sir?" suggested Stokes to Frazer.

"A nip, maybe," said Frazer airily.

Smith skulked aside; through brandy-dimmed eyes he appraised Humphreys. The round, ugly face . . . the fish eyes. He'd like to kick his face in. He could always say the drink got the better of him. . . . Better to *hammer* it in, maybe. A sensuous hate bleared his vision as he vicariously enjoyed the feel of hammer mashing fat lips over splintering teeth. "Perhaps Captain Humphreys'd like a nip too, Chief," he said civilly.

Humphreys nodded stiffly.

The two NCOs led them to a table shared by Dodkins, Bannister,

Fèvreaux and several Belgian officers. The table company rose as they approached.

"As you were," said Frazer lightly, dismissing their gesture with a wave of his hand.

"Ah, my commander," declared Fèvreaux with alcoholic exuberance, "this is a day of days, is it not?" He snapped his fingers against the resuming din of celebration in the background. "Brandy! Brandy for the great English commander and his—" He peered stupidly at Humphreys. "This officer. He is new, Commander?"

"My bad manners, Fèvreaux," apologized Frazer. "This is Captain Humphreys, Royal Engineers, my Number One. We had an accident on the way. He's just been up and about a day or so."

The sudden starched, formal atmosphere was welcomely interrupted by the arrival of a native servant with the brandy. The burbling young subalterns had quickly become chastened in the presence of their commanding officer. Smith still felt the hammer in his hand. Only Stokes seemed oblivious of the tension.

"An accident?" questioned Fèvreaux after the glasses had been passed around. "Impossible! Accidents in other navies, yes. In the English Navy? Never!" His tone of feigned surprise had been honed to an edge of sarcasm. He swilled his brandy. "How did it happen, Commander?"

Frazer shifted. "It all took place so quickly," he temporized. "Captain Humphreys was in a better position to . . ."

Humphreys gripped his glass in obdurate silence.

"How clumsy of me," intoned Fèvreaux, affecting apology. "We Belgians are *so* clumsy. We can do nothing right. That is so, Commander?"

"Jolly fine shooting today, Stokes," observed Frazer.

"Just usin' the old fleet gunnery manual, I was, sir," grunted Stokes.

"Do not forget," cautioned Fèvreaux, "it was a *Belgian* gun! On a *German* ship!"

"An' a *British* gunner, don't forget," Smith retorted proudly. "An' the 'King' would never've got a smell of 'er without *Mimi* an' *Toutou*. Them bein' there's no accident!"

351

Fèvreaux smiled sleekly. "Accident!" he repeated thickly. "We seem to come back to the accident." He looked around with an exaggerated air of mystery, as if expecting someone to satisfy his curiosity.

"Ain't nothin' to it, sir," volunteered Stokes bluntly. "Just n'accident. Captain 'Umphreys 'ere came a cropper when the bloody tractor banged into the tree 'e was up. 'S'not the only one we 'ad, neither." Stokes launched into a long-winded account of the other misfortunes of the trek. "Our Navy's just as frigged up most o' the time as any other body's Navy." He laughed. "But some'ow we always manage." He took a drink. "Just n'other friggin' accident. Right, Andy?" He turned to the sergeant.

"Cap'n Humphreys don't think it was n'accident," observed Smith dryly.

"What's that supposed to mean, Sergeant Smith?" asked Frazer, frowning.

"Beggin' the commander's pardon," droned Smith, "but the cap'n'll tell you better'n I can."

"I asked you, Smith," persisted Frazer cautiously.

Smith turned in his chair.

The table company craned forward ferretlike.

"Well, sir," commenced Smith, rubbing his mouth, "like I said —"

"It was no accident," interjected Humphreys flatly.

All eyes locked on the huge engineering officer.

"Oswald! That's a damnably serious charge!"

Fèvreaux grinned anticipatingly.

"It was no accident," repeated Humphreys. His large eyes socketed as he panned his audience. The injury had diminished his once huge physical presence. His tone had surrendered its inherent belligerence. "I'd expected it much earlier."

The table was an enclave of awkwardness in the background rumble.

"Gentlemen," said Frazer officially, "this isn't the place and time—"

"But Commandant Fèvreaux would like to know," said Humphreys.

352

Fèvreaux shrugged. "*Messieurs,*" he said thickly, "this is the time for celebration. Soon you will be leaving us. Your work is done here, and Belgium is forever in the debt of England and her Royal Navy." He gulped down the dregs of his glass.

"Leave, sir?" shot Bannister, "What about *Gotson?*"

"We don't mean to leave until we get her too," Frazer briskly interjected, "unless you've grown tired of us, Commandant."

Fèvreaux gasped theatrically. "My commander, how could you think such a thing?"

"Enough of this nonsense, Fèvreaux," said Frazer wearily. "Don't you think I know? Don't you think we all know? I'm sorry, but we've our duty to do. I know you've been area commandant for twenty years. The lake's your responsibility. All your life you've longed to be able to do exactly what we're doing. But your hands were tied. The only fight you've had in your entire career was over my men fishing in Lake Tanganyika, the private fishing preserve of Prince Albert. You won, but a military man rots on that kind of fare, Fèvreaux. Believe me, I know. But neither you nor I have time for petty little grouses. That goes for every one of you here. Do you hear? I won't hear another bloody word from any of you. We're here to do a job, and if anybody gripes or swings the lead any more, I'll deal with him."

They all stared at him. He had never spoken to them like that before. He had to be drunk. But he wasn't.

"And we aren't finished here yet, by God. We're not finished till we do to *Gotson* what we did to the other two. Quit moping in your beer, Fèvreaux. There's a part in this for you. The world hasn't passed you by—not yet. You've a chance to grab on yet . . . a chance to do something you can tell your grandchildren without spinning 'em a pack of lies. . . . I'll need *Dhanis.* When'll she be ready?"

Fèvreaux looked up defeated. "I do not know," he muttered wearily. "I do not know."

"You'd better know when I call on you in the morning," announced Frazer. He looked at them contemplatively. "London is very pleased with the news. They want us to go after *Gotson,* and they've promised us the gear to do it. Humphreys! You'll work with

Magarity on the boats. The Admiralty's sending out the gear to refit *Mimi* and *Toutou* as torpedo boats. It should be here in six to eight weeks—via Leopoldville. They also told me something you neglected to tell me, Fèvreaux. That seaplane your people are transporting in. You can forget about the wireless transmission experiments. I may have plans for that seaplane."

"Wizard," crowed Bannister.

"That's the ticket, sir," shouted Stokes, pounding the table.

"First-class!" squealed Dodkins, grabbing Bannister excitedly.

Fèvreaux spat. "Seaplane! *Sacrebleu!* They have been 'transporting' it for three years. If it ever comes," he snorted disgustedly, "you can have it—with my compliments." Again he drained his glass.

Humphreys turned impassively to Frazer. "I don't know a bloody thing about torpedoes."

Frazer pointed to Magarity, the always taciturn naval engineering officer at the end of the table. "He does. You'll work under him. He'll teach you all he knows. Won't you, Magarity?"

Magarity nodded with great embarrassment.

"Fèvreaux!" challenged Frazer. "Are you with us?"

The Belgian shrugged. He seemed to be very tired—or very drunk. "I am at your service, *mon ami.*" He rose from the table.

It was the signal for the rest to rise.

"Stokes!" called Frazer.

The old petty officer knew what to do. "Time, gentlemen, please!" he bellowed to the other ranks around the mess.

Fèvreaux left the mess flanked by Frazer and Humphreys.

Behind them walked Dodkins and Bannister, their faces betraying their profound apprehension that the Belgian commandant might glance down and fail to appreciate the fact that his ceremonial dress pants had been scissored off at the knees in a spirit of good, clean fun.

29

It was the end of February, 1916.

Dhanis was ready.

Where was *Graf von Gotson?*

Around the clock they stood poised on the beach by *Mimi* and *Toutou,* drilled in the use of the torpedoes, waiting for the horizon to be broken by a superstructure drawn from meager fact and much fantasy, for *Gotson* had never actually been seen by Briton or Belgian.

A March dreary with inaction abraded tempers.

There *was* a *Gotson* . . . wasn't there?

It was late when Frazer and the doctor turned in.

"How'd you *really* manage, Tommy?"

"If you mean the walkin', then I don't have to tell you. You've done your share. If you mean the lad, the Balomotwa had him when we got there. Delirious, he was. A woeful infection all the way up his leg. That's why it took us so long. The bone got infected. But

355

he was a plucky little bugger. Never a whimper when he was conscious. But, you know, he knew we'd fetch him."

Frazer looked guilty. "I wonder how. I didn't know myself."

"You said you'd fetch him back, that's what, Ian. Your promise."

Frazer lay silent in his cot. "It must've been rather dreadful."

"It must've, but he won't say a word. All the weeks his leg was mendin' and all he could think of was hopin' there'd be no action till he got here. Been through a nightmare—lyin' alone in a swamp for a week. But God's my judge, you'd never know it."

"We need more like him, Tommy. A lot more. . . . How'd Nangle do?"

"*Wie, bitte?*"

"Where'd *you* learn German?"

"Nangle. We had to kill time somehow. When this damn war's over, Perkins and Nangle and me are goin' to take a holiday in Bavaria. Listen! *Herr Ober, die Rechnung, bitte.*"

"Waiter, the bill," translated Frazer.

"*Ich möchte einen Tisch für vier Personen haben.*"

"May I have a table for four persons."

"*Eine Flasche Rotwein, bitte.*"

"Give me a bottle of red wine."

"*Bitte, lassen Sie das Orchester 'Wiener Blut' spielen.*"

"Please ask the orchestra to play *Wiener Blut.*" Frazer grinned approvingly. "You have the essentials, old man."

The doctor laughed. "You've been boning up too, it seems."

"Absolutely had to, with the Jerry prisoners."

"And last, but not least: *Sie sind so schön. Ich habe Sie sehr gern. Wann kann ich Sie wiedersehen?*"

Frazer translated. "You are so beautiful. I like you very much. When can I see you again? . . . A little old for that, Tommy, aren't you?" he mused teasingly.

"Nonsense," gruffed the doctor. "Don Juan died of arteriosclerosis, they say—the octogenarian's disease—an' I've a long way to go yet."

"All right, all right," conceded Frazer. "Speaking of Don Juan, the lads've had little to do for weeks but twiddle their thumbs. I've a feeling—"

"They've been twiddlin' more'n their thumbs?" laughed the doctor.

"Yes," said Frazer. "Seems a bit incredible, though."

"An' why should it, now?"

"Natives, I mean."

Cavanaugh chuckled. "Ian, sometimes you're so bloody middleclass."

They lay in the dark and listened as the waves washed the shore. After a while Frazer asked softly, "What does it remind you of?"

"Rosstrevor?"

"Uh-huh. And a lot of water under the bridge, eh?"

"Lots."

There was a long patch of silence.

"He still limps a bit," said Frazer.

"Who?" Cavanaugh asked, and yawned. "Perkins?"

"Yes. Anything permanent?"

"I don't know. It'll take a while. Why?"

"The Navy mightn't take him."

"He's already in the Army."

"Of course. . . . How long do you mean—a while?"

"He had a woeful infection. It was touch and go for a week. I almost had to amputate."

"Christ Almighty!"

"Aye, that's who did it."

"Who did what?"

"Jesus Christ. Saved his leg. If he said his beads once, he said 'em a hundred times that week. I'd the scalpel in the candle flame four times that week. Each time I was ready, somethin' stayed my hand. Laugh all you want, but there you are."

"Losing a leg's no laugh."

"And look at him now. Right as rain."

"I was. Today. And I thought to myself: Supposing you hadn't gone back for him."

"Well, it's a black thought, it is." The doctor yawned. "An' another black one: What if I'd amputated?"

"You'd have been doing what you thought was best."

357

"But I'd have been wrong."

"My wrong would've been the greater, Tommy. I left him there."

"You did what you thought was best, didn't you?"

"Yes."

"And were *you* wrong, Ian?"

"I don't know yet."

"Even with three-quarters of the Jerry Navy at the bottom o' the lake, an' you don't know yet?"

"Perhaps I'll never know," mused Frazer, "but I'll always wonder."

The doctor yawned heavily. His cot squeaked as he rolled over on his side. He closed his eyes. The restless churning of the lake was washing him into sleep. . . . He stirred. "I was just thinkin'," he whispered.

"What?"

"Of Elizabeth." The doctor's fingers explored the resilient nubbiness of the pullover rolled up under his head. "I was wonderin' what she'd have thought. . . . It's a funny pair we are, you and I, Ian. Me an' my Elizabeth. You and the old man. . . . I was thinkin' it's two down an' one to go. I was thinkin' I'm not out o' debt yet."

"What do you mean?"

"I mean we—I mean I lost Martin an' Porter an' Leeds on us, an' I held on to wee Perkins . . . an' to . . . Oswald."

"Do you know, Tommy, I've never heard you call him 'Oswald' before."

"I never felt he deserved it before."

"You noticed it, then?"

"I did indeed. He's made an incredible recovery. Nine out of ten wouldn't have survived it. But more incredible's what happened on the inside. Of course I also noticed he's doin' his damnedest to hide it—but it's there all right." He smiled to himself in the dark of the tent. "Me an' Elizabeth . . . you an' the old man . . . Bannister and Dodkins . . . Stokes an' Smith . . . maybe that's how He meant it. No man's an island. No man has it all by himself. He has too much of one thing, not enough of another. So maybe he sort o' searches around for some other poor devil who's searchin' for him. . . . Maybe that's what it's all about. . . . An' I thought to myself when I

358

examined the big lad today, he's maybe found what he's been searchin' for . . . an' I wondered who he found."

"We've got to nail *Gotson,* Tommy. It's three down and one to go with me."

The doctor smiled again in the dark, and yawned. "Well, he said, "I hope we both get our 'one' before too damn long. You've a bunch o' fed-up lads on your hands as it is. They'll be up to all sorts o' ructions before long."

April labored by. During it there were drills, inspections, equipment cleanings—but no *Gotson;* and the rains lifted, and there were games of soccer and cricket, too many of which ended in blood and profanity, for still there was no *Gotson.*

It was a May morning in the headquarters tent. They dismally reviewed the situation.

"*Gotson, Gotson,*" declared Fèvreaux impatiently. "That is all I hear you say, Commander Frazer. How do we know there *is* a *Gotson?*"

"How do we know?" retorted Frazer. "Your own wireless monitored Kigoma's transmissions, for one thing. For another, there's the Admiralty intelligence report."

"The one *you* yourself prepared," pointed out Humphreys flatly. "Is that really evidence?"

Frazer glared at his staff. "Do you think I'd be wastin' my bloody time here if there wasn't a *Gotson?*"

No one replied.

"I do believe you do, by God," he said with soft incredulity. "All right, Fèvreaux. If *Gotson's* all in my head, you'll have no particular objection to taking *Vedette* and *Dix Tonnes* for a reconnaissance of Kigoma for her tomorrow morning."

"Why not *Mimi* and *Toutou,* sir?" questioned Bannister.

"Because, Bannister, I believe there is a *Gotson,* and she'll blow *Vedette* and *Dix Tonnes* out of the water with her 4.1. Commandant Fèvreaux doesn't."

"And if I fail to return?" asked Fèvreaux stiffly.

359

"You'll know you were wrong," said Frazer coldly.

Fèvreaux returned—but not without mishap: Kigoma's 4.1s had destroyed *Dix Tonnes* and her crew before they had got close enough to see if there was a *Gotson* behind the harbor boom.

At a staff meeting that evening, Frazer turned sour under his mounting frustration, for he sensed the mounting doubt of his officers. "There *is* a *Gotson*," he told them fiercely. "There *is* a *Gotson*. Do you all hear that?"

"Then where is she?" demanded Humphreys. "We've waited three months."

"And we'll wait three more if necessary," snapped Frazer. "We're going to raid 'em. We'll needle 'em into some kind of counteraction. Make 'em thick enough at us for 'em to come and get us. And when they do, we'll be ready 'n' waiting."

"Why just needle them, sir?" asked Dodkins. "Why not hammer *Gotson* while we're there and get it over and done with?"

"Because," said Frazer tiredly, "we're not going to raid Kigoma —not after what happened to *Dix Tonnes*."

"I am glad we were able to make some contribution," observed Fèvreaux, bowing with ill-concealed sarcasm.

Frazer gritted his teeth. "Here's the plot." He outlined a plan for *Mimi* and *Toutou* to drop off two loads of raiders commanded by himself and Humphreys to destroy an enemy outpost south of Kigoma. "That'll make Zimmer see red," he reasoned, "and he'll be after our blood with *Gotson*."

"And if there isn't a *Gotson*," Humphreys reminded him heavily, "we're wasting our time."

"It's not *our* time, Oswald. I thought I'd settled all that. It's the Navy's time—not yours or mine. The Navy's."

"Give me ten minutes with Rosenthal and Odebrecht and I'll be able to tell you if there's a *Gotson*."

"I'll have none of that!" shouted Frazer. He dismissed them summarily.

When they had gone, Cavanaugh said, "Ian, Zimmer may have given up, thrown in the towel. That *could* be the explanation. Oswald may be right about our—the Navy's time."

360

Frazer said doggedly, "We have to get our 'ones,' Tommy. Remember?"

May had almost ended when the German outpost was successfully destroyed. *Mimi* and *Toutou* raced back to Kalemie, swapped troops for ammunition and waited. . . . And during the rankling, waiting weeks that followed, Kalemie buckled under a regime as strict as any other Royal Navy shore station. And like any other shore station, there were those who nightly sneaked past the sentries through the barbed-wire perimeter to Albertville.

All NCOs and other ranks stood "to" one morning in June for roll call and their first medical examination in months.

By noon it was over.

Stokes stood before the doctor and tapped his chest. " 'Ow does she sound, doctor?" queried the grizzled old sailor.

"Like a bloody alarm clock."

"And the lads?"

Cavanaugh glanced at his journal. "One possible hernia. Three lung congestions. One systolic heart murmur, best heard on the left side. Everybody has bunions . . . and"—he ran his fingers down a list of names—"I'd like to see these privately."

"*Privately,* sir?"

"You know how it is, Stokes. Boys will be boys, eh?"

"I twig, sir. When would you like to see 'em, sir?"

"Perhaps after dark would be best?"

"Aye, aye, sir."

The medical tent had been divided into three sections. One was the examination room, where Cavanaugh sat behind a camp table under a hurricane lamp. The second was "medical records," where Stokes laboriously logged the results of the morning's examinations. The third was a waiting room.

A group of men waited there in their shorts.

"Very good, Stokes," called the doctor. "Send them in, will you?"

"Aye, aye, sir." Stokes pulled aside the tarpaulin. "All right. The M.O.'ll see you now."

Stokes returned to his work.

The four men emerged sheepishly.

"Fine," said the doctor, rising and coming around to the front of the camp table. "Line up!"

The men responded sluggishly.

"Now, drop 'em," said the doctor casually.

The doctor bent to peer at the first man. "Hmmm," he said, taking a glass slide and handing it to the sailor. "A little on the slide."

He moved to the next man, peering. "Splendid."

"Back a little more," he urged the next man. "Fine, fine. A little on the slide."

Finally he had worked his way to the end of the line. He sized up the last man, a sailor, questioningly. "Didn't you hear me? I said drop 'em."

The sailor's Adam's apple ratcheted.

"Well?"

"I heard you, sir," said the sailor weakly, slowly complying.

Abruptly the doctor recoiled. "Oh, for God's sake, man, I can't examine you that way," he stammered. "Go off somewhere till you're . . . till you're decent."

The other men grinned crudely.

The doctor snatched their slides. "Be off with you," he gruffed.

The tent cleared.

The sailor scurried for the privacy of the waiting section.

The doctor plumped down heavily behind the camp table and quickly immersed himself in official paper work. Occasionally he consulted his watch. "Let's have another look at him, Stokes," he called.

"Right, sir," responded the chief petty officer, appearing from behind his tarp and crossing to the waiting section. He stood outside and announced flatly, "All right, you. The M.O.'ll 'ave another

362

go." Quickly he nipped back behind the tarpaulin of "medical records."

"Fine," preambled Cavanaugh, not knowing if it really was. "How're you feeling?"

The sailor reddened violently.

"Let's have a look," suggested the doctor amiably. . . . "Damn!" said Cavanaugh squeamishly. "I can't possibly examinue you in . . . in that condition."

"I'm awfully sorry, sir," blurted the cringing seaman, loping back to the cover of the tarp.

Back at his desk once again, Cavanaugh slid toward him a stack of medical records. Slowly and deliberately he made notations on every one. Fifteen minutes later he scrutinized his watch thoughtfully. "Stokes!"

"Right, sir," responded Stokes, sliding back his tarp and crossing to the waiting section. "All right," he called. "M.O.'ll 'ave another bash." Again he promptly vanished.

"It's getting late," the doctor neutrally informed the agonized sailor. "Let's get it over with. . . . Oh, good heavens, man," he said impatiently, "come back when you're, eh . . . proper."

The sailor dressed with unusual haste. Seconds after he left, "medical records" tarp billowed with a gale of guffawing.

The doctor pulled back the tarp and surveyed the hastily straightened faces of Stokes and the two medical aides. "Any of you offer an explanation?" he asked seriously.

Stokes adopted a clinical demeanor. "Well, sir, if you don't really mind me sayin' so," he sniffed, "I think the bloke's taken a likin' to you."

30

The engine thrummed. The pusher airscrew on the Short Brothers double-winged seaplane was a disk of sheen in the brilliant June morning sunlight.

The Belgian pilot coaxed her beak into the wind. The rich, cavernous synchrony of twelve cylinders thinned to a hornet's ugly drone. Gradually the ungainly boxlike machine gathered speed. . . . Several minutes later the sound was swallowed in the distance.

To the anxious Britons and Belgians thronging the shoreline she was fast becoming a gnat in the eastern sky.

Aloft, Perkins succumbed to the wonder of human flight. Underneath his black leather flying jacket, leather helmet and goggles he lay limp and silent, transfixed by the shrinking world 1,500 feet below.

Never water so blue, nor earth ahead so richly green. Cripes! That must be the Jerry coast.

He shook the leather shoulder of the helmeted figure in the front cockpit.

The pilot flashed him a wide grin.

Perkins pointed to a cluster of buildings over the pilot's shoulder about three miles away.

The pilot nodded vigorously.

Perkins felt the wooden box on the floor between his legs. He had twenty Mills grenades. Frazer had sent him off with the words: "You've never flown before. Neither have any of the rest of us. You'll probably do as well as anyone."

Perkins prayed he would do well.

The left wingtip dropped as the seaplane arced in over the harbor. It has to be the harbor, Perkins thought. Yet it looked unreal, somehow like a picture out of Lilliput.

Right smack ahead she was—*Gotson!* It had to be *Gotson!* Frazer had told him she would be a big vessel—the biggest in the harbor—and she would have two masts and two funnels. "That's her!" he screamed. "That's *Gotson!*" And big? From 1,500 feet the harbor formed a huge horseshoe. The ship below was longer than the smithy's nail. The seaplane thundered in at low altitude. Tiny black shapes wiggled across her bleached deck and onto the bridge.

Perkins watched entranced. Red streaks stabbed at him from the bridge. He had never been fired at before. His excitement chilled.

The pilot looked back and with his teeth pulled the pin from an imaginary grenade. He eased the stick forward. The seaplane floated along on a cushion of air about 100 feet up. He held up his hand.

Perkins reached down for two grenades. He hooked his thumbs in the rings and held them over the side.

Down flagged the pilot's hand.

Perkins jerked the pins and opened his hands.

Both grenades missed.

They floated in lower the second time.

As the pilot banked away he kissed his hand theatrically. Both grenades had churned up splinters of lifeboat amidships.

For fifteen minutes they flew "pylon-eights" and bombed *Gotson* although continuously peppered in the wings and fuselage by the pom-pom and small-arms fusillade flung up from below.

The grenades had the effect on *Gotson's* 800 armored tons of a flea biting an elephant.

Perkins tapped the pilot on the shoulder, and the big biplane banked in a lazy turn and headed out to sea. . . .

"The old tub's there, all right, sir," Perkins told them excitedly after he landed. "Just a thread of steam up, and nothing but a deck watch that I could see. We gave 'em a jolly good peppering, sir," he bragged.

"Did it do any good?" demanded Frazer.

"I think we nabbed two of the deck watch for certain, sir, but the shrapnel bounced off like marbles."

"The 4.1?"

"I dunno if it was a 4.1, sir, but there was one whacking great piece in the front."

"In the *bow*, Perkins."

"In the bow, sir."

"That was the 4.1," said Frazer definitely. He paced the tent in thought. He halted by the two sublieutenants. "What's your state of readiness?"

"We've been practicing every day for the last fortnight, sir," said Dodkins confidently. "Averaging seven out of ten with the dummy warhead."

"Bannister?"

"Almost as good for *Toutou*, sir."

Frazer resumed his restless, predatory pacing. "You're sure of the two funnels."

"Quite sure," said Perkins. "As big as a house—each of 'em."

Frazer looked at him questioningly. "What'd you say?"

Perkins looked unsure. "I said she had *two* funnels, sir."

"Not that—the bit about the house."

"I meant they're so big you—you could drop a house down it, sir."

Frazer pivoted and jabbed the air with his finger. "That's it! That's it!" he shouted exultantly. "Humphreys! A packet of something down the funnel—into the boilers! Can you whip something up out of all that dynamite we've lying around?"

"Tape half a dozen sticks together with a long fuse," responded Humphreys. "But how long the fuse? And how high can he drop it from?"

"That's your problem—and Perkins'. Get cracking on it right away. We've no time to lose. They're probably stoking her up this

366

very minute. We've got to hit her at her most defenseless—while she's still in dock. If she gets out, she can hide in a hundred places."

"What if we miss, sir?" said Bannister, visibly deflated at the prospect of missing a sea battle.

"If Perkins misses, then it'll be up to you and Dodkins. Zimmer's no fool. After today's effort he must know it's only a matter of time before we drop heavier stuff. He knows we'll destroy *Gotson* at her moorings eventually, so he'll coal up and slip his cables as fast as he can. But we've got to act faster! I want you two to proceed to Kigoma immediately. Lie offshore far enough so the 4.1 can't get your range. And if *Gotson* shows her nose . . . well, you both know what to do."

"And if she won't come out, sir?" queried Dodkins.

"Perkins'll blow her boiler to bits at first light *tomorrow* morning!"

The excitement of impending battle vibrated through their bodies. This was the moment they had longed for—like a huge appetite worked up for a long-promised meal.

"Scramble!" shouted Frazer.

The tent cleared in seconds—but for the doctor.

"This is it, Tommy!" said Frazer passionately, raising his fist. "This is it!"

"So it is," concurred the doctor thoughtfully. "It's your 'one.' But—"

"But what?"

"What if she doesn't come out, an' Billy—Perkins—misses?"

"We just stay put till she *does* come out—or till Perkins *doesn't* miss."

The doctor shrugged. "Aye, that's logical, I suppose. . . . Did he tell you about the ground fire?"

"Well, naturally there'd *have* to be a bit of small arms stuff."

"*Pom-poms,* Ian! *Pom-poms!* Didn't you see the way they'd made a sieve out o' the wings?"

Frazer nodded. "Stokes is fixing that." He knew what was in his friend's mind. "He's a soldier, Tommy, like the rest of us." His brow crinkled. "Did *he* tell you he didn't want to go? He ask you to ask me?"

367

"Nonsense," snapped the doctor, nettled at the implication. "It's just that he's gone once already and—"

"That's why he's the only one who has the experience. That packet of dynamite has to go *smack down the funnel!*"

"Come off it, Ian. Any lad to ever stone a fish'd have a feel for it."

"Look, Tommy, I'm asking you to—"

"And I'm just asking you for a chance at my 'one.' "

Frazer pondered. "I suppose Oswald could do it," he said in acquiescence.

"Nangle wants a crack," pleaded the doctor. "He asked me to put in a good word for him."

Frazer turned to the camp table and stared down at the large map of the lake. "Oh, what's the use," he muttered resignedly. . . . "All right."

"Grand," chortled the doctor. "Just grand, Ian. An' now I'll get from underfoot and let you be." He hurried off to alert Nangle.

The engines of *Mimi* and *Toutou* purred powerfully as they glided at half speed through the night. No one spoke. There was no need for words.

Frazer stood braced by *Mimi*'s helm beside Dodkins, gripping the taffrail. His mind was on *Gotson*—her 800 tons . . . her 4.1 . . . her armor. He looked at the foredeck where the 3-pounder used to be and felt naked. Even the elongated bulk of the torpedo-tube mount failed to give him the comfort he sought. The thought that somehow . . . somewhere . . . something was going to come unstuck lodged like a cork in his gullet. He remembered the day when the personnel request had stared up from his desk. He thought about how it had all begun . . . and how it was about to end—the final downward step in a long flight of stairs. But it was a descent in the dark. He did not know just where the last step was. He worried that it would come so suddenly that he would fumble and trip. . . .

With the first gold shafts of morning sunlight through the east horizon's waning night came the angry rasp of the seaplane. The pilot lost altitude and zoomed in thirty feet above the flotilla, waggling his wings and circuiting.

Frazer could see Nangle waving from the rear cockpit. "Right on time," he said to Dodkins. "From here on," he added seriously, "nothing happens according to timetable."

"More watch and wait, sir," commented Dodkins, trying to suppress his excitement.

The seaplane made a final circuit and droned off toward the enemy shore. . . .

Mimi and *Toutou* continued to hold stations out of range of the enemy shore batteries. They patrolled up and down on parallel but opposite courses, waiting for the explosions which would mean Nangle had gone into action.

"He should be there," muttered Frazer, examining his watch. He felt the cork swell in his gullet. He relaxed his sternly braced legs. One knee trembled.

The crew crouched at their stations, stiff with tension.

"If she does make a run for it, what course'll she steer, sir? South-southwest?"

"That's the most logical—to stay close to her own shore. And if they fight—they'll come straight for us. One of us'll have to draw the fire while the other darts in abeam."

"Which'll we do sir?"

Frazer shook his head. "What in blazes is keeping him?" He knew something was up. . . .

A distant, hollow boom rolled across the water.

Frazer instantly glanced at his watch. "Three more to go!"

Another boom.

"Two minutes, thirty-five seconds!" shouted Frazer.

Five minutes later the third explosion had not sounded.

"Might've been a dud, sir," suggested Dodkins.

Ten minutes later it sounded.

"He mustn't be using the same approach each time," said Frazer, trying to explain the irregular intervals between explosions.

"He did say *four*," said Frazer.

Another boom thundered across the water.

"Four it is, sir," said Dodkins with a wide grin on his face.

369

"Make a signal to Bannister: Maximum alert. Maintain present patrolling stations," ordered Frazer.

The signalman semaphored *Toutou.*

Fifteen taut minutes later the seaplane's buzz pulled all eyes fifteen degrees above the eastern horizon.

The crew cheered wildly.

The aircraft billowed in on a wide turn. Its wing waggled.

Again the crew cheered.

Dodkins smiled at Frazer but shook his head ruefully. "I would like to've had just one crack at her, sir."

Frazer had Nangle in his binoculars. He was waving furiously. "Wait a moment! Nangle's pointing down . . . toward the water. He's something in his hand. Looks like . . . a bottle. He's going to throw—" He turned to the signalman. "Make a signal to *Toutou:* Stand by to pick up bottle from plane."

"What's up, sir?" Dodkins asked anxiously.

"Dunno," snapped Frazer.

The seaplane's circuits wound tighter. Its altitude dropped. A white object plummeted seaward. . . .

Frazer coaxed the damp paper out of the empty brandy bottle. It was a rolled-up page from an Army paybook. Scrawled on it was a message: "Wide Search. No trace *Gotson.* Obvious she made run for it during night. Dynamited suitable targets."

For the rest of June, Frazer corroded with his passion for finding *Gotson.* By the end of the month, *Mimi, Toutou, Kingani* and *Dhanis* had hunted in every major estuary, inlet and lagoon. Frazer, Humphreys, Bannister and Dodkins had laboriously interrogated hundreds of natives in a score of coastal villages. For weeks on end they were absent from Kalemie.

In early July, the crews of the four predatory vessels met again. They assembled in the stiff, white headquarters tent. Studied attempts at levity had fallen flat, and now they waited in desultory silence for the arrival of their commander.

Frazer curtly gave his report. As commander of *Kingani* he accounted for his activities, none of which included the sighting of *Gotson*.

Dodkins and Bannister followed with monotonously similar reports.

Even with his vast intelligence network of native spies Fèvreaux could throw no light on the mystery. Nor could the pilot of the seaplane. "It would seem, gentlemen," concluded Fèvreaux, "that our Zimmer has retired from the war and is content to await an Allied victory hidden safely up some unnavigable stream." He rose from his camp stool and approached Frazer, his right hand extended in congratulations. "You have done more than your duty, Commander," he declared generously. "You and your men can return to England with honor."

Frazer declined the handshake. "Hidden safely up some 'unnavigable' stream," he insisted obdurately, "waiting for us to fall into exactly that kind of complacency—ready to blow us to bits when we least expect it."

Fèvreaux stood awkwardly, his unshaken hand dangling. "*Mon Dieu!*" he exclaimed. "What is there left to do? Twenty-four hundred kilometers of shoreline you have searched! Every inlet you have explored! And what? Absolutely nothing. *Gotson* is gone, I tell you. . . . Believe me, my commander, I know well how you feel. You would like to have the evidence before your very eyes. Be reasonable. What more can we do?"

Frazer unfurled the map and brought it down so that his knuckles hammered the table.

Dodkins and Bannister exchanged weary glances.

"We can search where we haven't searched!" exploded Frazer lividly. "Here! . . . Here! . . . Here! . . . Here! . . . Here!" He jabbed at the map. "I'll get *Gotson* or I'll rot in hell!!"

The hunt wore on—relentless, futile, maddening. Frazer's stubborn anger had cowed his men. Nothing else mattered. They had all capitulated to the miles of desolate shore, scores of silent, papyrus-choked inlets and the blank stares of a thousand natives.

But Frazer had not.

§

The crews returned haggard and spiritless one July day, their anger divided between Germans too wily to do battle and a CO obsessed with total victory to the point of irrationality.

That night the atmosphere in the British mess was stiffly proper throughout the meal. Dishes clicked discreetly. The diners chewed earnestly as if hoping that no one would obtrude upon their pre-occupation with conversation. Brandy glasses clinked.

A brooding Frazer stared into his untouched goblet. "It will take us a week to refit," he announced. He looked up at his Belgian host. "This time, Fèvreaux, we'll be lucky. I know it." He pointed to his chest. "I can feel it in here." He glared across at the two sublieutenants. "Eh, Dodkins?"

"Yes, sir," responded the cowed young officers.

"Yes, sir, my foot!" exploded Cavanaugh. "Have an ounce of gumption, Ian. It's as plain as a pikestaff you'll look from now to kingdom come and never see hide nor hair of her."

"Carbuncles and backsides," scoffed Frazer.

"You're impossible," sighed the doctor, shaking his head and rising from the table.

"Where're you going?" asked Frazer.

"Where people's talking a little common sense."

"I'm not talking sense, am I?" muttered Frazer. He turned to Dodkins. "You! Fetch me Rosenthal!"

"Sir," protested Dodkins. "It's almost eleven o'clock, and they're sure—"

"*Quick!*"

Dodkins returned with the German officer, accompanied by two Belgian askaris. It was obvious from the German's appearance that he had been dragged out of bed and had dressed hurriedly.

Frazer introduced his captive and inquired about his health and conditions of captivity.

Rosenthal said that he had no complaints.

Frazer asked how much he knew about the conduct of the war on the lake.

Rosenthal pleaded ignorance.

"What would your reaction be," asked Frazer, "if I were to tell you that *Pangani* and *Wissman* had been destroyed, and that *Kingani* now flies the white ensign?"

"What could it be? We are imprisoned with survivors from all three. It is true. I grieve for the brave men who went down with them."

Frazer addressed his table company. "Rosenthal's a good officer. He tried to smuggle word out to Zimmer about the boats. Now, there's loyalty for you. . . . Sorry you lost, Rosenthal. Oh, the letters'll be delivered all right—in new envelopes."

Rosenthal's eyes were downcast.

"Rosenthal!"

"*Jawohl,* Herr Commander!"

Frazer rose and placed his hands on the back of a chair. He chose his words carefully. "Rosenthal. What if I told you *Gotson* had sailed from Kigoma?"

"I would wonder if it were true."

"It's true!" Frazer blurted out.

"Then I would expect the tide of fortune to change very soon, Herr Commander."

"You would, would you?"

"*Jawohl,* Herr Commander."

"And if I were to tell you she's not to be found—disappeared. Then what?"

Rosenthal pondered, then smiled enigmatically. "If you remember, Herr Commander, there was another famous vessel which was 'not to be found.' The battle cruiser *Königsberg.*"

Too well Frazer remembered.

"That's all, Rosenthal," he announced bluntly.

When the askaris had led the German from the room, Frazer declared trenchantly, "What did I tell you! She's up to *Königsberg's* tricks, I tell you. That's what he said."

"Ian, has it occurred to you he might possibly be lying?" asked the doctor wearily.

Frazer ignored the possibility. "You all know what that means. *Gotson's* out there! And we're going to get her." His face flushed with new excitement. "Somewhere we missed her. Someplace." He hammered the table. "But not for long. Not for long, gentlemen. I promise you." He surveyed his company's unenthusiastic faces. "At first light tomorrow, we'll refit and refuel."

"Commander Frazer," said Fèvreaux tiredly. "Since you bring up the matter of fuel, I must point out that our supplies of Diesel oil have almost run out. The weeks and weeks of—"

"Run out?"

"Regrettably I have barely sufficient to meet my own meager needs until supplies come in three months' time."

"Nonsense," grated Frazer. "Do you know what you are saying? That it's more important for your little punts to piddle around than—"

"I am merely pointing out, sir," said the Belgian patiently, "that we must have some fuel for emergencies and that—"

"You refuse to advance me any further requisition?"

Fèvreaux nodded.

Frazer stood erect. The veins on his temple pulsed with the anger of his heartbeat. "Is that all, Commandant Fèvreaux?"

"What more is there, *mon ami?*"

"I should like to use your transmitter first thing in the morning," Frazer announced in a clipped, official manner. "I will inform the Admiralty of your decision. Undoubtedly they shall inform your superiors of your ill-considered judgment. . . . Good night." He picked up his chair, placed it tightly against the table and walked stiffly toward the tent flap.

Fèvreaux swiveled in his chair to watch him go. "Commander," he called.

Frazer halted and looked over his shoulder disdainfully.

"You might also tell your Admiralty *Gotson* was reported at the bottom of the lake last week by one of my native spies. We . . . we thought it better if you didn't . . . after all, if the fuel was gone and . . ."

Frazer froze. . . . The stiffness finally thawed from his backbone. . . . Slowly his shoulders seemed to become too heavy to bear.

"Loaded with dry concrete," continued Fèvreaux painfully. "Then they raised enough steam to get her clear of Kigoma . . . then opened the scuppers . . . the night after the first seaplane raid."

A chair creaked in the stale silence.

"Damn shame," whispered Dodkins miserably. . . .

Frazer shuffled out of the tent into the night.

3 1

There was a war to be won, but busy London found time for pause.

In the summer sun Captain I. H. G. Frazer, RN, Major O. H. Humphreys and the members of Naval Africa Expedition joined the parade that left Buckingham Palace and wove its way through winding City streets to the Guildhall for a reception by the Lord Mayor.

The new medals jingled on their breasts. Their stride was long, lean and measured—the crisp crunch of accomplishment hammered into streets no strangers to heroes.

Flags snapped in the breeze. Faded bunting fluttered. Crowds cheered them on their way.

Ahead clopped the horses of the jangling Household Cavalry, whose burnished breastplates mirrored sheets of light. Next came a khaki-clad, back-from-France contingent of the Brigade of Guards, arrogant with their stiff necks, eyes masked under the severely slanting peaks of their forage caps, impeccably precise. Behind them marched a regimental band, its elderly members red-faced from 120 paces to the minute and the demands of "The

Grand Little Army." Bringing up the rear was a long, sinuous phalanx of bluejackets from the Royal Naval Division, their bleached puttees gleaming, their Lee-Enfields sloping like freshly scythed wheat stalks.

Frazer, tall, spare and deeply tanned, marched along in loose naval fashion. His eyes were dead ahead, his thoughts on the challenging new post he had been offered—Assistant Director of Naval Intelligence.

Humphreys stamped along directly behind him, rigid and precise in his movements, awkward without his swagger stick.

Behind him swung Dodkins and Bannister, proud and jaunty.

Chief Petty Officer Stokes strode easily as if it were just another parade, with Sergeant Smith by his side, seriously dedicated to a proper military bearing.

Up ahead the band came to the end of "The Grand Little Army." A solitary drum went *dit, dit, dit-diddle-dit. Dit, dit, dit-diddle-dit. Dit, dit, dit-diddle-dit. Dit, dit, dit-diddle-dit.*

Then *roooommmm . . . roooommmm . . . rrrrrrrroooommmm.* The imperative cadence of two bass drums, the side and snare drums. Subtly the unalterable, rolling chords of "Land of Hope and Glory" swelled the morning mood. Imperceptibly a thousand steel-shod heels lightened with the beat.

Smith swung more stiffly from the shoulders. His chest was out an extra inch. He copped a glance at Stokes, who winked back at him."

Understanding glimmered.

Smith smiled inwardly and softly sang "Land of Soap and Borax."

Some months later the leaves had changed color. Some of them made a scraping noise as the wind blew them along the street outside Admiralty House.

A thin figure in the uniform and greatcoat of a naval rating timorously approached the two burly Royal Marine guards at the entrance.

"Wotcher want?" demanded one.

"I'd like to see the Assistant Director of Naval Intelligence," said the rating respectfully.

"You would, would you?" temporized the other Marine.

"Yes, I would," declared the rating firmly.

"Wot's the nature of your business, chum?" demanded the first Marine.

"With the Assistant Director," replied the rating undaunted.

"Who are *you*?" asked the second Marine.

The rating fumbled inside his coat and produced his identification. "I was with the expedition—Lake Tanganyika," he added.

The face of the first Marine lit up. "Wot a lovely bloody show that was! W'y didn't yer say so?" He took the rating by the arm, gave him an admittance pass and directions. "Listen, chum. This'll get you upstairs far as 'is secretary. You're on yer own from there. All right?"

"Thanks," said the rating.

He climbed the stairs two at a time and found himself on a landing, overseen by an officious-looking sublieutenant behind a desk. "Well?" demanded the sublieutenant.

The rating came to attention and saluted. "Sir, the Assistant Director of Naval Intelligence. Which way, sir?"

The sublieutenant surveyed the rating curiously. "The Assistant Director of Naval Intelligence?"

"Yes, sir."

The officer finally shrugged and pointed down a hallway.

The rating walked down a long corridor past many impressive doors bearing more impressive gold-leafed titles. When he came to one marked SECRETARY, ADNI, he paused, knocked, heard a male voice bid him enter, and opened the door. . . .

He emerged five minutes later flustered and confused. He made his way back to the sublieutenant at the desk, who looked up from a newspaper. "Find him?" he queried haughtily.

" 'Fraid not, sir," replied the rating in embarrassment.

The officer looked at him suspiciously. "Let me see your pass."

The rating produced it.

378

"Looks all right," sniffed the sublieutenant. "Can't follow directions very well, can you?"

"It's not that, sir," explained the rating. "It's just Captain Frazer's not the Assistant Director of Naval Intelligence."

"I never said he was, did I?" queried the officer.

"Well, no, sir. But I thought Captain Frazer—"

"*Frazer?* If you want to see *him,* you're absolutely in the wrong wing. Personnel's what you want. Look. Take Corridor F to the end and turn left by the alcove. Go up the three little steps . . ."

Frazer had just dropped a stack of correspondence into his "out" basket when he looked up and saw the rating standing by the door, hat in his hand. "Perkins!"

The occupants of the other desks in the room jerked momentarily from their office stupor.

Frazer rose from his deal desk and beckoned to Perkins.

Perkins edged inside, self-consciously twisting his hat.

"Very thoughtful of you to drop by, Perkins," said Frazer casually.

"I'll only stay a jiffy, sir," apologized the youth. "I'm on my way to Portsmouth, sir, and I couldn't leave without thanking you." He smiled. "H.M.S. *Canopus,* sir. She's a battleship."

"Nonsense, man. It was the least I could do for one of my men. After all, that's what a personnel department's for—the right man in the right job. Dr. Cavanaugh always told me you wanted to be a sailor."

"That's very kind of you, sir. But you'll never guess, sir."

"I'll never guess what, Perkins?"

"You'll never guess, sir, who's CPO on H.M.S. *Canopus.*"

"I haven't the foggiest," lied Frazer.

"CPO Stokes, sir!" exclaimed Perkins.

Frazer suppressed a smile. "Well, I never!"

Perkins shook his head in wonder.

"How's the leg these days?"

379

"Right as rain, sir, believe me," Perkins assured him. "Dr. Cavanaugh's a fine gentleman—and a fine doctor, too."

"Indeed he is."

"Have you heard from him at all, sir?"

"Indeed I have. He's fine. Working hard—as usual."

"A fine gentleman," said Perkins fervently. "A good man. . . . And yourself, Captain Frazer," asked Perkins. He looked around warily at the other occupants and lowered his voice. "We all thought you'd—" He could not put his confusion into words.

"Ah, still in Personnel," said Frazer conversationally.

"I see, sir," said Perkins, but he really did not.

"It's actually what I do best," Frazer added, hoping that would suffice.

"But, sir," protested Perkins loyally, "you sank the lot!"

Frazer shook his head disparagingly. "All but one."

"She's at the bottom too, sir," insisted Perkins.

"So you're off again, you and Stokes, eh?" observed Frazer, changing the subject, slowly filling his pipe.

"Yes, indeed, sir. But, sir, we did win. I mean . . . we did what they asked us to, didn't we?" He fidgeted with his uniform.

Frazer continued filling his pipe.

"The new job, sir. All the lads—they thought it was grand, they did. And then to hear—"

"Nonsense," responded Frazer easily. "Got my stripe out of it." He held up his cuff, stiff with the four new, freshly sewn bands of gold braid.

Perkins stared at them.

Frazer puffed leisurely on his pipe and regarded the youth appraisingly.

"It's still not right, sir," insisted Perkins. "First they offer it, then they don't."

Frazer withdrew his pipe. "You don't understand, Perkins. They offered. I didn't accept. That's all."

"You're right, sir," said Perkins sincerely, "indeed I don't understand."

Frazer was aware of the baleful stares of the office's other occupants. He motioned to Perkins. "C'mon. Let's go outside."

There was little privacy in the corridor. A steady stream of naval officers and other ranks trafficked back and forth on a score of errands.

"You see, Billy," Frazer was saying, "it's nice to be doing what you want to . . . but if you don't do it very well . . . if you see what I mean."

"We beat 'em, sir," persisted Perkins. "We licked 'em proper. Everybody says so."

Frazer examined the bowl of his pipe. "It's not just beating 'em . . . winning. Perhaps part of it's *how* you win, I think . . . how efficiently you win—or inefficiently. . . . Yes, Billy, we won. I suppose you might even say *I* won. But does that mean I can do it again? The amateur does it once; the professional does it consistently. I pulled it off once. What qualification's that? You have to be true to yourself, and that means first of all finding out who you are . . . what you are . . . finding a role for yourself in a world that didn't stand still while you did." He surveyed the confused young face. "I'm afraid I'm rather bungling this." He rapped the pipe in the heel of his hand decisively. "Look, Billy. I think maybe . . . come inside. I've something to show you."

They left the busy corridor and returned to the office. Frazer slid open the center desk drawer a few inches and motioned for Perkins to look inside.

Perkins obediently looked. His freckled face clouded.

"And sometimes only another can show you what you are— or aren't," added Frazer quietly.

Perkins turned slowly from the desk. His eyes were his soul. The flat clangor of Big Ben obtruded on his reverie. "Three o'clock, sir." There was a certain catch in his voice. "I'm on the three-twenty from Paddington." He crossed to the chair and picked up his greatcoat.

Frazer walked him to the door. Outside in the corridor they shook hands. Perkins tried to say something, but Frazer raised his left hand, then lowered it and patted him on the arm. "Cheerio, Billy . . . Godspeed."

Perkins tried to say "Godspeed," but the words wedged in his throat. He pivoted abruptly and hurried down the corridor. Just

381

before he disappeared down the stairs he looked back. He saw Frazer standing there and he waved.

Frazer waved, and the lad was gone. He crossed to the window and looked out on the courtyard below and the street beyond, watching the young bluejacket with the kit bag standing at the bus stop.

"Oh, Captain Frazer."

Frazer wheeled around to behold an Army major with a sheaf of papers in his stand. "Yes?"

"About Second Lieutenant Nangle, sir," said the major. "We've finally run him to ground—Sixth Battalion, Royal Scots Fusiliers."

"*Scots,* major?"

"Yes, sir."

"I see. Whereabouts?"

"The Somme, sir."

"When should we expect anything definite?"

"Corps says not for about a week, sir."

"Casualties?"

"Quite heavy, I'm afraid, sir."

"You'll let me know if you hear anything, eh?"

"Of course, sir."

"Thank you, Major."

Frazer turned around and resumed his watch from the window.

The major hurried down the corridor. He bumped into another Army officer.

"I say," whispered the newcomer. "Isn't that Frazer up there?" The major nodded.

"What a waste, eh?" said the newcomer.

"Damn shame," said the major. "The bloody trouble is we never let the right hand know what the left's up to."

"Spending thousands of quid and buckets of sweat," continued the newcomer, "to mop up the lake . . . handing old Smuts a piece of cake for a thrust up the left flank . . . and then he changes his bloody mind and lays on the main effort 800 miles away—the Moschi-Taveta area, no less."

"Tricky blighters, those reformed Boers," laughed the major grimly. "Have to watch 'em all the time."

382

From the window Frazer saw the bus roll up to the stop and
Perkins hop aboard. The bus lumbered off.

Frazer walked slowly back into his office.

The center drawer was open just as he had left it. He slumped
into his swivel chair and pondered the past. . . . He leaned forward
to close the drawer and noticed Tommy's last letter:

Wendi Macosi
C/O White Fathers Mission House
Elizabethville
Belgian Congo
14.IX.1916

Dear Ian,

The next time you see King George, thank him for the D.S.O.
Seriously, though, it was thoughtful of you to put it in the post to
me. He may not like it, but it's hanging from the neck of the little
black nipper who brings me my letters. Maybe when he grows up
to be a big lad and I've really earned it, he might let me have it
back.

And thanks for fixing it up so that I could stay out here. I know
what you're thinking—back to backsides and carbuncles. But you
can't tease me, my lad; not since I found out they're what I should
have been treating for years. That's what is strange about it. The
answer was as plain as the nose on my face, but I couldn't see it,
or I wouldn't. What was it you said that day? Switch it off like a
light? Wring it out like a sponge? Thanks to you, "God's in His
heaven; all's right with the world."

And what of yourself, now that it's done with? Have you seen
much of the old man since you got back? Give him my best. (I
mean that.)

Listen. There's one thing that's been bothering the devil out of
me. Did anyone ever find out who clouted Oswald on the nut that
day? Did *he?* I don't suppose it matters much now, but it did that
day.

Anyway, I'm as busy as a hen on a hot griddle these days, and
enough of my blather, so I'll leave you be.

God knows when you'll hear from me again, but until you do,

may the road rise with you; and the wind be always at your back; and may the good Lord keep you in the palm of His hand.

Tommy

Frazer smiled wistfully. He carefully folded the letter and placed it back in the desk drawer.

Before he slid it shut, he took another long look at the swagger stick inside.